The Theatres of Boston

The Theatres of Boston

A Stage and Screen History

Donald C. King

McFarland & Company, Inc., Publishers
Jefferson, North Carolina, and London

Donald C. King died in 2004,
shortly after completing the manuscript for this book.

LIBRARY OF CONGRESS CATALOGUING-IN-PUBLICATION DATA

King, Donald C.
The theatres of Boston : a stage and screen history / Donald C. King.
p.   cm.
Includes bibliographical references and index.

ISBN 0-7864-1910-5 (illustrated case binding : 50# alkaline paper) ∞

1. Theaters—Massachusetts—Boston—History.
2. Motion picture theaters—Massachusetts—Boston—History.
3. Performing arts—Massachusetts—Boston—History.   I. Title.
PN2277.B6K56   2005   792'.09744'61—dc22   2005000886

British Library cataloguing data are available

Cover photograph: The Tremont Street entrance that led
to the Crystal Tunnel to B.F. Keith's Theatre, 1906 (Library of Congress)

Manufactured in the United States of America

McFarland & Company, Inc., Publishers
Box 611, Jefferson, North Carolina 28640
www.mcfarlandpub.com

Acknowledgments

The Boston Public Library: Laura V. Monti, Keeper of Rare Books and Manuscripts; reference librarians, Humanities; Aaron Schmidt, Print Department.

The Bostonian Society: Philip Bergen, librarian from 1986 through 1994; Douglas Southard, librarian in 1998; Nancy Richard, Director of Library, Special Collections 2001.

The Harvard College Theatre Collection, Houghton Library: Fredric Woodbridge Wilson, curator; Ann Fern, librarian.

Earl Stanley Stewart, professional scenic artist, theatre historian and collector.

Fred McLennan theatre historian.

Ron Salters, theatre historian.

Lee Fernandez, theatre historian.

Raymond O. Daugaweet, former manager of The Normandie (B.F. Keith's) and the Bijou.

Charles Otis King, Lillian A. King, and Elizabeth J. Bennett, my father, mother, and great-aunt, who shared their memories of these old theatres and took me to many of them.

Ernest E. Huyett, a dear friend who helped to get this work published.

Table of Contents

Acknowledgments   v

Preface   1

Chapter 1   5
God Bless the British
1750–1776

Chapter 2   10
Foiling the Bluenoses, Lecture Halls, Rooms and Museums
1791–1794

Chapter 3   15
The First Theatres
Battle of the Managers
The Lion and the Lamb
1794–1841

Chapter 4   28
Exit Tremont Theatre, Enter Tremont Temple
The Rise of the Boston Museum
1841–1843

Chapter 5   31
The End of the World
Enter the Howard Athenaeum
The Boston Museum Moves up Tremont Street
1843–1846

Chapter 6   37
Exit the First Boston Theatre
The Adelphi and New National Theatres
1847–1852

Chapter 7   43
Ancestors of the Movie Palaces
The Boston Music Hall and the Second Boston Theatre
1852–1857

Chapter 8   51
The Great Financial Panic of 1857
The Prince of Wales Comes to Boston
1857–1861

Chapter 9   55
Minstrels, Aquariums and a New Boston Museum
The Second Tremont Theatre and the Selwyn
1861–1873

Chapter 10   63
Abbey and Schoeffel Meet John Stetson Head-On
The Park Theatre Is Built in Fifty Days
1874–1879

Chapter 11   67
The First "Movies" and Summer Theatres
The Boston Bijou and Thomas Alva Edison
1879–1882

Chapter 12   86
Benjamin Franklin Keith Comes to Boston
Battle of the Museums
The Hollis Street Theatre
1883–1885

Chapter 13   92
The Year of the "Mikados" and the Grand Opera House
George E. Lothrop's Lady Natators
Colonel Austin and Alexander Graham Bell
1885–1889

Chapter 14   95
Improvements at the Boston Theatre
The Third Tremont Theatre
1889

Chapter 15 97
B.F. Keith Invents Vaudeville
Enter Edward Franklin Albee
1889–1891

Chapter 16 103
The Bowdoin Square Theatre
B.F. Keith Builds a Palace
1892–1894

Chapter 17 116
Cyclorama to Castle Square Theatre
The End of an Era
1894–1896

Chapter 18 127
The Motion Picture Comes to Boston
Keith Builds a Subway
Burlesque at the Palace and the Old Howard
1896–1897

Chapter 19 133
The Last Days of the Boston Museum
European Music Halls in Boston
1898–1899

Chapter 20 135
B.F. Keith and the Vaudeville Wars
The United Booking Office
William Morris and the Boston Music Hall
1900

Chapter 21 137
The Colonial, Majestic, and Globe Theatres
The Brothers Shubert Arrive
1900–1903

Chapter 22 144
The Music Hall Becomes Loew's Orpheum
A Sleeping Giant Wakes Up
The Poor Man's Amusement
1905–1908

Chapter 23   151
The Gaiety Theatre, the Boston Opera House
The Sam S. Shubert Theatre
1908–1910

Chapter 24   157
The National and the Plymouth Theatres
Tremont Temple Becomes a Movie Palace
Gordon's Olympia and Saint James
The First Feature Length Films
1911–1912

Chapter 25   164
Famous Players in Famous Films,
in Famous Theatres: Enter Adolph Zukor
1912–1915

Chapter 26   171
Boston's First Movie Palace
Loew's Braves Field
The Shuberts Build a Subway and the Copley Turns Around
1915–1924

Chapter 27   178
The Third Boston Theatre
The Mighty Metropolitan
The Mystery House
1925–1927

Chapter 28   188
"Auld Lang Syne" at B.F. Keith's Theatre
The Voice of the Screen
The B.F. Keith Memorial Theatre
1926–1929

Chapter 29   197
Albee Out, Kennedy In, RKO Is Born
The Shuberts in Receivership
The Great Depression and Proven Pictures
Memories of the Scollay Square Palace
1929–1937

Chapter 30 208
U.S. Sues Paramount Pictures over Monopoly
Walt Disney's *Fantasia* Saves the Majestic
The Coconut Grove Tragedy, Bye Bye Bijou
1938–1949

Chapter 31 214
U.S. Sues Shubert over Monopoly
3-D, CinemaScope, and Cinerama
Ben Sack Steps In and the Boston Opera House Steps Out
1950–1958

Chapter 32 221
The Old Howard's Swan Song
Ben Sack Takes Over the Met and
Keith's Pornography Comes to Washington Street
Sarah Caldwell Gets Her Opera House
1958–1979

Chapter 33 231
Lose Some, Save Some
Bringing Back Boston's Downtown
Memories of the Bijou
1979–2002

Appendix 1 237
Boston Theatres in Chronological Order

Appendix 2 248
How Patrons Got to Boston Theatres

Chapter Notes 255

Bibliography 259

Index 261

Preface

It has been a pleasure for me to write this history, having been in the theatre business a great part of my life, 42 years, eventually operating my own motion picture houses, even constructing two. I retired from show business in 1980, the owner of the last operating downtown motion picture theatre in Washington, D.C. However, I kept in touch with show business as a member of a theatre historical society, for which I wrote many articles for its quarterly journal. This history was originally written for the society, but it was too large for its resources. The present work is a greatly expanded version.

Although I continued to live in the District of Columbia, I visited Boston frequently, to dust off my tombstone and to visit my friends. One day, I suddenly realized that I was getting into my 70s and should finish this history of Boston's theatres. I had accumulated a large collection of theatrical history books and periodicals; my real estate office was practically next door to the Library of Congress, where I spent afternoons and evenings researching its newspapers, collections and fire insurance maps. The maps are amazingly accurate for theatre locations and floor plans.

When I was in Boston I spent much time at the Bostonian Society, the Boston Public Library, and the Harvard University Pusey Library Theatre Collection, dredging for information. I made the acquaintance of Earl Stanley Stewart, an elderly theatre historian and scenery painter, who sent ancient clippings to me frequently; a visit with him in his studio was a trip in itself. There was theatre information in huge piles; yet my friend Stanley knew where everything was. He was a fine white-bearded gentleman; I spent as much time as possible visiting him at his gallery, listening to his recollections and getting copies of them. Through him I met other theatre historians. Stewart filled my Washington mailbox with pages from aged newspapers almost daily.

There was little written information about the earliest Boston theatres. Even historians of the time left scant material about them. I have studied William W. Clapp, Jr., who was the best published source, being editor of the early *Boston Gazette*, and who in 1853 had put together a book *Record of the Boston Stage*. I found further information in Arthur Hornblow's *History of the Theatre in America*, published in 1919. He wrote that "outside of Clapp, Jr., until now, no attempt has been made to produce a work embracing the entire field of American theatre history, from the earliest beginning in Colonial days.... George O. Seilhamer began the publication of a history of

1

Gov. Bernard, the Commissioners, &c. to the British Ministry.

Capital of New-England; and of the Landing of ——— Troops in the Year 1768, in Consequence of Letters from

A Prospective View of the Town of BOSTON, the

P. REVERE.

1 Beaver. —— 2 Senegal. —— 3 Martin. —— 4 Glasgow. —— 5 Mermaid. —— 6 Romney. —— 7 Launceston. —— 8 Bonetta.

the American theatre, perhaps the best, because [it is] the most complete chronicle, up to the time of the Revolution, that we have. Unfortunately Mr. Seilhamer died when this history reached the year 1797."

I found Mary C. Crawford's *The Romance of the American Theatre*, from 1913, most enlightening. It described the early days of the British soldiers' theatricals at Faneuil Hall, Boston's first theatre. I believe that she and Hornblow, among others, leaned on Seilhamer's works.

I gleaned some humor from Otis Skinner's memoirs, *Footlights and Spotlights* (1923), and *Daniel Frohman Presents* (1935). A complete list of reference books, periodicals, and newspapers appears in the bibliography. Without further ado, let us begin a fascinating journey into two centuries of theatre.

Opposite: British ships in Boston Harbor, 1768 (Library of Congress).

Chapter 1

God Bless the British
1750–1776

Arthur Hornblow, in his *History of the Theatre in America*, reminds us that

> In view of the more than scant information regarding plays and players in the pre–Revolutionary newspapers and chronicles of the time, it would be an impossible task to attempt to ascertain when or where the first theatrical performance took place on the North American continent. It is likely that there were scattered dramatic performances of a sort in all the Colonies many years before we have any records of them, particularly in the South where the prejudice against the stage was less violent than in the North. But singularly enough it is in the Puritanical New England provinces that we find the first actual records of public theatricals, and in Quaker Philadelphia that the drama first found a permanent home. That so little should be known of the early beginnings of the acted drama in America is not surprising when one considers the intolerance of the age against the theatre and the player. In face of the almost general condemnation of the playhouse, the journals of the day were not encouraged to give much, if any, space in their slender columns to the doings of player-folk. It was also the custom at that time for the actors themselves to distribute handbills at the houses of prospective theatre goers, and thus stir up interest in the coming performance, instead of depending solely on newspaper advertising as is the modern practice. These reasons, perhaps, sufficiently explain the almost total absence of theatrical news in pre–Revolutionary newspapers, a fact which has rendered exceedingly difficult the researches of the historian.... In the South the Colonists had imported a taste for the drama together with their other English customs, but in the North the playhouse was still considered the highway to hell and was everywhere fiercely condemned if not actually forbidden under the severest penalties.

In 1750, the General Court of Massachusetts passed an act prohibiting stage plays and theatrical entertainments of any kind. On May 31, 1759, the Pennsylvania House of Representatives passed a law forbidding the showing and acting of plays under a penalty of 500 pounds. In 1761, Rhode Island passed an act "to Prevent Stage Plays and other Theatrical Entertainment." The following year the New Hampshire House of Representatives refused a troupe of actors admission to Portsmouth on the ground that plays had a "peculiar influence on the minds of young people and greatly endangered their morals by giving them a taste for intriguing, amusement and pleasure." President Dwight of Yale College, in his "Essay on the Stage," declared that to indulge a taste for play going means nothing more or less than the loss of that most valuable treasure—the immortal soul.

The theatre had a difficult time establishing itself in Massachusetts because the colonial authorities in Boston were very much opposed to theatrical amusements. About 1714 Justice Samuel Sewall wrote, "Let not Christian Boston goe beyond Heathen Rome in the practice of Shameful vanities." In 1745 theatricals were performed in private homes, causing a puritanical uproar.

The *Boston Gazette*'s William W. Clapp, Jr., noted "that these puritans in their ignorance deemed the theatre the abode of a species of devil, who, if allowed once to exist, would speedily make converts. The first public dramatic performance in Boston appears to have been 'The Orphan, or Unhappy Marriage,' which was produced at a coffeehouse on State Street by two English actors, and some local volunteers. The affair was such a novelty and the curiosity of the Boston public so keen that the doors of the coffeehouse were besieged and an incipient riot took place. This disturbance caused such a scandal that the authorities were compelled to take notice."

The event so provoked the puritanical element that their protests caused the General Court of Massachusetts to pass an act in March 1750. It read:

> For preventing and avoiding the many and great mischiefs which arise from public stage-plays, interludes, and other theatrical entertainments, which not only occasion great and unnecessary expense, and discourage industry and frugality, but likewise tend generally to increase immorality, impiety and contempt of religion. Be it enacted by the Lieut. Governor, Council and House of Representatives, that from and after the publication of this act, no person or persons whosoever shall or may for hire or gain, or for any valuable consideration, let or suffer to be used and improved any house, room or place whatsoever for acting or carrying on any stage plays, interludes or other theatrical entertainments, on pain of forfeiting and paying for each and every day or time such house, room or place shall be let, used or improved, contrary to this act, twenty pounds.
>
> Sect. II—And be it further enacted that if at any time or times whatsoever from and after publication of this act, any person or persons shall be present as an actor or spectator of any stage play, interlude or theatrical in any house, room or place where a greater number of persons than twenty shall be assembled together, every such person shall forfeit and pay for every time he or they shall be present as aforesaid, five pounds. The forfeiting and penalties aforesaid to be one half to His Majesty for the use of the government, and the other half to him or them that shall inform of use for the same, and the aforesaid forfeitures and penalties may likewise be recovered by presentment of the grand jury, in which case the whole of the forfeitures shall go to His Majesty for the use of the government.

Hornblow reminds us by way of Spencer's *History of the United States*: "Yet Boston, early in the Eighteenth Century, was not such a place of gloom or solemn visages as New England tradition would lead us to think. This, one can readily believe after the following description of one of the principal residences of the town. There was a great

View of Faneuil-Hall, in Boston, Massachusetts.

Faneuil Hall was used by British soldiers as a theatre from 1775 to 1783 (Library of Congress).

hall ornamented with pictures and a great lantern and a velvet cushion in the window seat that looked into the garden. In the hall was placed a large bowl of punch from which visitors might help themselves as they entered. On either side was a large parlor, a little parlor or study. These were furnished with mirrors, oriental rugs, window curtains and valance, pictures, a brass clock, red leather back chair, and a pair of huge brass irons. The bedrooms were well supplied with feather beds, warming pans and every other article that would be thought necessary for comfort or display. The pantry was well filled with substantial fare and delicacies. Silver tankards, wine cups and other articles were not uncommon. Very many families employed servants, and in one we see a Scotch boy valued among the property and invoiced at 14 pounds ten."

In 1774, relations between the Colonies and England were so strained that a Congress met in Philadelphia, where on October 24 members passed a resolution recommending suspension of all public amusements. In 1778, a more stringent decree was issued to prohibit play-acting in any form. Puritans, a majority in Boston's population of 20,000, welcomed this law.

Fortunately for Boston theatricals, invading British officers brought with them a love for the theatre. From 1775 until 1783, the year before the declaration of peace, the British military occupied all theatres in the areas that they controlled, producing their own plays in a professional manner. In 1775, General John Burgoyne, an actor and playwright, converted Faneuil Hall into a theatre. Among other productions was his second drama, *The Blockade of Boston*. Young subalterns, and sometimes officers' ladies, played the female roles. Military thespians performing on January 8, 1776, had to halt the show because American patriots were attacking them at Bunker Hill.

Mary Caroline Crawford, in her *Romance of the American Theatre*,[1] colors the story:

> Faneuil Hall was the theatre used for these exhibitions, and announcements of the plays to be performed were made by hand-bills. Mrs. Centlivre's comedy *The Busybody*, Rowe's *Tamerlane* and Aaron Hill's *Tragedy of Zara* were among the attractions offered, the drawing power for the latter being considerably increased by the fact that Burgoyne himself wrote a prologue for it. An interesting contemporary allusion to this entertainment is found in a letter sent by Burgoyne's brother-in-law, Thomas Stanley, the second son of Lord Derby, to Hugh Elliott: "We acted the *Tragedy of Zara* two nights before I left Boston for the benefit of the widows and children.
>
> "The prologue was spoken by Lord Rawdon, a very fine fellow and a good soldier, I wish you knew him. We took above 100 pounds at the door. I hear a great many people blame us for acting, and think we might have found something better to do, but General Howe follows the example of the King of Prussia, who, when Prince Ferdinand wrote him a long letter, mentioning all the difficulties and distresses of the army, sent back the following concise answer: 'De la gaiete, encore de la gaiete, et toujours de la gaiete.'"
>
> The performances at Faneuil Hall playhouse began at six o'clock, and the entrance fee was one dollar for the pit, and a quarter of a dollar for the gallery. For some reason, either because the play was immensely popular, or because the currency gave trouble, those in charge were obliged to announce after a few evenings: "The managers will have the house fully surveyed and give out tickets for the number it will contain. The most positive orders are given not to take money at the door, and it is hoped that gentlemen of the army will not use their influence over the sergeants who are door-keepers to induce them to disobey that order, as it is meant entirely to promote the ease and convenience of the public by now crowding the theatre."

The most notable piece presented at Faneuil Hall was the local farce *The Blockade of Boston*, generally credited to General Burgoyne. Whether the general wrote this piece, he was the ruling spirit in its presentation. He was an amateur actor of no mean ability and had already written his first play, *The Maid of the Oaks*, before coming to America. This play was originally acted in 1774 at the Burgoyne home, The Oaks, on the occasion of a marriage fete in honor of Burgoyne's brother-in-law, Lord Stanley. David Garrick was so taken with the piece when he read it that he brought it out at Drury Lane in 1775, with Mrs. Abingdon in the chief role. So if Burgoyne did not write *The Blockade of Boston* it was not because he lacked ability to write a good play.

Whether this was a good play we have no means of knowing. It has come down to us in history, not by reason of its dramatic eloquence, but because of certain "business" not planned. It was booked to be given, for the first time on any stage, at Faneuil Hall on the evening of January 8, 1776. The comedy of *The Busybody* had been acted, and the orchestra was playing an introduction for the farce, when the actors behind the scenes heard an exaggerated report of a raid made upon Charlestown by a small party of Americans. Washington, represented by an uncouth figure, awkward in gait, wearing a large wig and rusty sword, had no sooner come on to speak his opening lines than a British sergeant appeared on stage and exclaimed, "The Yankees are attacking our works on Bunker's Hill." At first this was thought part of the farce; but when General Howe, who was present, called out sharply, "Officers, to your alarm posts!," the audience quickly dispersed.

Timothy Newell, in his diary, says there was "much fainting, fright and confusion." And well there might have been, with the officers jumping over the orchestra at great expense to the fiddles, the actors rushing about to get rid of their makeup and costume, and the ladies alternately fainting and screaming. They had to revive themselves, however, and get home as best they could. For some time it was the chief delight of the patriot dames to relate how maids and matrons of the Faneuil Hall audience were obliged to pick their way home through the dark streets unattended by any of their usual escorts.

The Tory sheet published by Madam Draper all through the siege of Boston, after reporting the interruption of the premiere of the *Blockade*, adds: "As soon as those parts which are vacant by some gentlemen being ordered to Charlestown can be filled, that farce will be performed, with the tragedy of *Tamerlane*." The diary of John Rowe records that the play was staged on January 22.

It has been said that the desire to offend the prejudices of Puritan New England was a strong motive in the acting of the Boston thespians. That handbills of entertainment were sent regularly to Washington, Hancock, and other leading spirits, bears this out.

Chapter 2

Foiling the Bluenoses, Lecture Halls, Rooms and Museums

1791–1794

After the war, theatre lovers turned to the two nontheatrical amusement places available, the hall and the museum. In August 1792, an "entertainment" was given at the mid–18th century Concert Hall, on the southeast corner of Hanover and Court streets. Charles Stuart Powell, a young British actor direct from the Theatre Royal at Covent Garden in London, performed there, presenting selections from various plays, titled "The Evening Brush, for Rubbing Off the Rust of Care."

Other halls presented variety shows that were considered educational and athletic exhibitions featured tightrope walking, tumbling and juggling. Museums showed wax figures and art exhibits that were "informative." Who could object if the patron visited the museum's Lecture Hall to hear recitations! The first such operation opened at the American Coffee House on State Street in 1791.

Citizens to whom the anti-theatre law was anathema made many attempts to have it repealed, but there was too much opposition. Even liberal Samuel Adams was known to be bitterly opposed to the acted drama. Not until the 1790s were people sufficiently confident of public support to organize the building of a theatre to challenge that legislation.

Hornblow, quoting Seilhamer, wrote: "In 1792 a company of thespians headed by Mr. Watts, an English actor, appeared at Portsmouth, N.H., and performed 'The Absent Man' and 'Lethe.' From Portsmouth the players went to Salem, Mass., where 'The Beaux Stratagem' and 'Miss in Her Teens' were given. From Salem, Watts' players went to Dorchester and a few weeks later to Boston."[1]

But the players found themselves blocked. There was no getting around the law against acting. Finally, a group of theatre lovers formed an association, to subscribe funds for a building which was to be a theatre in everything but name. Ground was purchased on "Broad" (Board) Alley, near Hawley Street, and the New Exhibition Room was the first playhouse built in Boston.

There existed a large stable along Board Alley, a plank- and dirt-covered passage leading from Milk to Summer Street, which was merely a lane through which residents of the North End made a shortcut to old Trinity Church on Summer Street. Entre-

The Concert Hall, at Hanover and Court streets, was built in 1750, as seen in an 1869 drawing (Courtesy of Boston Public Library, Print Department).

preneurs acquired this structure and set about converting it into a theatre. One row of boxes ran around three walls, while nestled up against the eaves was a small gallery; a stage was erected against the fourth wall. At ground level, enclosed by all of these improvements, was the pit, or main floor. The New Exhibition Room—its sponsors were not yet ready to use the word "theatre"—opened August 13, 1792, and could hold 300 people. Its entranceway later became Bishop's Alley (present-day Hawley Street). Joseph Harper was manager, and a playbill of the time announced:

NEW EXHIBITION ROOM
BOARD ALLEY
Feats of Activity
This evening, the 10th of August, will be exhibited dancing on
The tight rope by Monsieurs Placide and Martin
Mons. Placide will dance a Hornpipe on a Tight
Rope, play a violin in various attitudes, and
Jump over a cane backward and forwards.

INTRODUCTORY ADDRESS
By Mr. Harper
SINGING
By Mr. Wools
Various feats of tumbling by Mons. Placide and Martin, who
Will make somersets backward over a table, chair, etc.
Mons. Martin will exhibit several feats on a Slack Rope.
In the course of the evenings Entertainment will be delivered
THE GALLERY OF PORTRAITS
OR
THE WORLD AS IT GOES
By Mr. Harper
The whole to conclude with a Dancing Ballet called The Bird Catcher
With the Minuet de la Cour and the Gavot

Mary Caroline Crawford continues: "The steps leading up to these 'feats of activity' in Board Alley are full of interest. On June 5, 1790, Hallam and Henry, who had already established playhouses in Philadelphia, New York and Providence, presented to the Massachusetts Legislature a petition praying for leave 'to open a theatre in Boston under proper regulations.' The petition was not considered."

Two years later, however, an important contribution toward the establishing of such a theatre was made by John Gardiner. In a speech delivered to the House of Representatives on the expediency of repealing the law against theatrical exhibitions, Gardiner gave evidence of deep learning as well as of a fine spirit of toleration. Since this speech, when printed, totals nearly 30,000 words, it must have consumed several hours in its delivery. The legislators could not have failed, as they listened, to learn a great deal about the history of the drama.

"I have lately dedicated a small portion of my early morning hours from other public business to investigate this subject," Gardiner confessed naively at the outset, "inasmuch as the drama and theatrical exhibitions have been hitherto unknown in this country, and their history, nature and tendency little understood." He proceeds to argue that "a theatre will be of very general and great emolumentary advantage to the town of Boston because working men must be employed to build it, and printers retained to get out its play-bills after it has been built." Moreover, he points out: "Strangers who visit us complain much of the want of public places of resort for innocent and rational amusement; as in the summer and fall months, our only public places of resort for amusement (the concert and Assemblies) are dead and unknown among us.... Did the town of Boston possess a well regulated theatre, these strangers would, most probably, spend double the periods of time they generally pass in this town, to the great advantage of stable-keepers, the keepers of lodging houses ... the hairdresser, the shoemaker, the milliner and many others." Gardiner had a wonderfully keen appreciation of the relation between plays and plumes.

That the ancient drama "took its rise in religion," that Saint Paul quoted liberally from Greek poets and Greek writers of poetry, and that "The Song of Moses" is a sacred dramatic performance were other arresting ideas set forth in the early part of this speech. Gardiner argued that the manners of Bostonians needed the improvement that must inevitably follow carefully regulated dramatic entertainments. For, of course, it was decent drama only that this good citizen wanted and to ensure such, he suggested the appointment of "five or more censors who should be annually chosen in town meeting from among the worthy fraternity of tradesmen, the respectable body of merchants, the learned sons of the law, and even from the venerable, enlightened, and truly respectable ministers of the gospel in this great town."

Gardiner's arguments were opposed by Samuel Adams and Harrison Gray Otis. Nonetheless, a theatre was soon possible, in thanks to Gardiner's speech, an effort that has been called "the most scholastic argument in defense of the stage ever written by an American." Not that the obnoxious law was repealed. With characteristic Puritan stubbornness, the Massachusetts legislators refused to remove the prohibition from the statutes. But Gardiner's speech had so influenced public opinion that during the summer of 1792, a few gentlemen determined to erect a theatre in Boston to prove that a playhouse need not be the highly objectionable resort its detractors doggedly declared it. John Gardiner had spent many of his impressionable years in England, which accounts for his liberal attitude toward the theatre.

Crawford continues: "For almost two months 'somersets backward' and their ilk continued to be the pabulum here offered. And then, by way of transition to actual theatrical performances, came the disguised drama, which we have met in other cities. 'Othello,' 'Romeo and Juliet' and 'Hamlet' were among the Shakespeare plays masked and mangled in Boston. Considerable ingenuity was exercised, also, in remodeling Garrick's farce 'Lethe' into a satirical lecture called 'Lethe, of Aesop in the Shades' pronounced by Mr. Watts and Mr. and Mrs. Solomon. Otway's 'Venice Preserved' was announced as a moral lecture in five parts, 'in which the dreadful effect of conspiracy will be exemplified.'"

Growing a bit more bold, the management advertised that on October 5 "the pernicious effect of libertinism exemplified in 'The Tragical History of George Barnwell, or the London Merchant' would be presented—still as a moral lecture, though delivered by Messrs. Harper, Morris, Watts, Murray, Solomon, Redfield, Miss Smith, Mrs. Solomon, and Mrs. Gray." Never before spoke a lecturer through so many mouths![2] Of course the enemies of the theatre were not so stupid as to miss the fact that a play with a good-size cast was being presented at Board Alley. The aid of the law would have to be invoked to suppress such an outrage. The first attempt to do this failed, and performances continued to be given at intervals of two or three days. On November 9, Garrick's version of *The Taming of the Shrew*, under the name of "Catherine and Petruchio" was presented; on November 30, *Hamlet* was staged, with Charles Stuart Powell as the title character; and on December 3, the same actor assumed the leading role in *Richard III*.

Then the blow fell. During a performance of *The Rivals* on December 5, Harper was arrested by Sheriff Allen, at the end of the first act, for violating the law against theatrical presentations. The audience, largely composed of young men, resented this treatment of their favorite and proceeded to tear down the seal of the United States from the proscenium arch and to cut in pieces the portrait of Governor John Hancock, whose hand was seen to be behind the arrest. Only when Harper was committed to bail would his overstrenuous friends desist from rioting and disperse to their homes. The following day they attended a hearing for the actor in Faneuil Hall. Perhaps it was their presence that secured for him a dismissal on the technical ground of illegality in the warrant of arrest. The fact that Otis, who had hitherto opposed the theatre but was not on the side of play-acting, doubtless had its effect, also. But Hancock's opposition did not slacken in the slightest, and in a subsequent session of the Legislature, he alluded to the theatrical row as "an open assault upon the laws and government of the Commonwealth."

That the people were determined to have theatrical performances could not have failed to make itself clear to him, however. And here again *The Contrast* came in to render its service of pacification. For that piece by a native Bostonian of irreproachable character was now presented in the New Exhibition Room—the last performance of any note to be offered there.

The experiment had been a success. The improvised theatre had served its purpose, and in the spring of 1793 it was demolished and a movement initiated for the promotion of a playhouse on a larger scale. Subscribers to the project were found among the best people without any difficulty—this in spite of the opposition of Samuel Adams, who in 1794 succeeded Hancock as governor and who, though he felt himself in ordinary matters to be simply an executive officer, stood out stubbornly as long as he lived against the popular desire for theatrical entertainments.

Chapter 3

The First Theatres
Battle of the Managers
The Lion and the Lamb
1794–1841

The new theatre was at Federal and Franklin streets, and with its opening on February 3, 1794, the dramatic history of Boston may be said properly to have begun. The playhouse was called the Boston Theatre (later the Federal Street Theatre). It had been erected from plans furnished by Charles Bullfinch, then a young man. It was 140 feet long, 62 feet wide, and 40 feet high, and was a lofty and spacious edifice built of brick, with stone facings, iron posts and pillars. The entrances to the different parts of the house were distinct. In the front a projecting arcade enabled carriages to pull up completely under cover. After alighting, a theatregoer passed through an elegant saloon to the staircases leading to the back of the boxes. Pit and gallery patrons had separate side entrances.

A contemporary[1] described the Boston Theatre:

> The interior was circular in form, the ceiling composed of elliptical arches resting on Corinthian pillars. There were two rows of boxes, the second suspended by invisible means. The stage opening was thirty-one feet wide, ornamented on either side by two columns between which was a stage door opening on a projected iron balcony. Above the columns a cornice and a balustrade were carried over the stage openings; above these was painted a flow of crimson drapery and the arms of the United States and the commonwealth blended with emblems tragic and comic. A ribbon depending from the arms bore the motto, "All the world's a stage."
>
> The boxes were hung with crimson silk, and their balustrade gilded; the walls were tinted azure, and the columns and fronts of its boxes straw and lilac. At the end of the building was a noble and elegant dancing pavilion richly ornamented with Corinthian columns and pilasters. There were also spacious card and tea rooms and kitchens with proper conveniences.
>
> Great state was observed in performances here. The "guests" were met by a bewigged and be-powdered master of ceremonies and escorted to their boxes.

The Boston Theatre, at Federal and Franklin streets, was built in 1794. Samuel S. Kilborn's wood engraving, circa 1883, shows the building in 1794 (courtesy of Boston Public Library, Print Department).

Thence, however, they could see the stage but dimly at best in the feeble light of candles or by means of the more objectionable, because smoky, illumination of whale-oil lamps. Moreover they might freeze in winter, for all the effective heating apparatus provided. Very likely it was to keep warm that the gallery gods threw things. At any rate the orchestra was obliged to insert a card in the newspaper requesting the audience to be more restrained in the matter of pelting musicians with apple cores and oranges. The music, by the way, was of high standard, Reinagh of Philadelphia being director. In short, though Boston had come on slowly, it was now conceded to possess the finest theatre in the country.

It would be several years before "pit" became "parquet" or "parquette," and eventually "orchestra" level. The name originated in early London theatres where it was considered the lowest of the low. First-class customers sat in the boxes, lesser attendees sat in the gallery atop the boxes, cheapest admissions were in the pit, which did not always have seats, maybe benches or standing room. Rowdies roamed the streets and were a concern for many years to come; the third tier was usually the gallery, often equipped with a bar; police were needed to keep order.

In 1894, *Bostonian Magazine*'s Albert Corbett, Jr., wrote about those early days: "The ancient and objectionable pit, with its name of sinister suggestiveness, the factional riots, in which partisans of rival actors or politicians took part, the notorious third tier with its bar, and often time objectionable habitues of both sexes."

Admission to first and second tiers cost $1, pit and third tier cost 50 cents, gallery 25 cents. Curtain was 6 P.M., and no cigars were permitted. Shaw's description of Boston (1817) commented, "The first building erected purposely for theatrical entertainments ... was opened ... with the tragedy 'Gustavus Vasa Erickson, the Deliverer of Sweden'; the selection of the play was judicious, as it suited the temper of the times." Actors were Messrs. Baker, Jones, Collins, Nelson, Bartlett, Powell, S. Powell, Miss Harrison, Mrs. Jones, Mrs. Baker, and the child by Miss Cordelia Powell, being her first appearance on any stage. The program also had an entertainment titled "Modern Antiques or the Merry Mourners," Mr. and Mrs. Cockletop played by Mr. Jones and Miss Baker assisted by Messrs. S. Powell, Collins, Nelson, Baker plus Mrs. Jones, Mrs. Baker and Mrs. Collins. An overture (or rather several musical pieces) consisted of a Grand Symphony by Signor Charles Stametz, Grand Overture by Signor Vanhall, Grand Symphony by Signor Hayden. Also were played "Yankee Doodle," the Grand Battle Overture in *Henry IV*, and General Washington's March.

Doors opened at 5, the curtain drawn up precisely at 6 o'clock. Clapp Jr. tells us:

> Among the actors above enumerated the name of Snelling Powell occurs. He was born in Camarthen, Wales, and commenced his theatrical career at an early age. His father was a manager of a theatre, and had a respectable company and circuit. Mr. Powell, at an early period of his life devoted his attention to printing, and when he came to America, in 1793, with his brother Charles Stuart Powell, he brought with him considerable printing apparatus, which he used, in printing the programmes of the theatre. In 1794, Mr. Snelling Powell married Miss Elizabeth Harrison, who also came out under the auspices of Mr. C.S. Powell. This lady was born in Maraison, the county of Cornwall, in the year 1774.... Miss Harrison previous to her visit to this country, appeared before George the Third, by command; and she also had frequent opportunities of performing the second characters to the queen of tragedy, Mrs. Siddons, who was much pleased with her acting, that she obtained permission for Miss Harrison to accompany her through a circuit of the provincial theatres.

Charles Stuart Powell, late of London's Theatre Royal and of the Concert Hall's "Rust of Care," became the first manager of the Boston Theatre. It was also known as the Federal Street, New, or simply Theatre, and in later years it was affectionately known as "Old Drury."

Hornblow relates an amusing incident regarding Joseph Jefferson, the second of the well-known family. "At the Boston Theatre he at once found favor in old men roles.... A kind hearted lady had watched him one evening bent over and tottering about on the stage, and she determined to help remove such an old person from the boards by raising a subscription so that his last days might be spent in comparative comfort. She went to the theatre the next morning to consult with the management about her plan, being thoroughly convinced that the actor was infirm and she prompted by a charitable impulse to do good. She carried with her a list of well known names, which she had procured as probable subscribers with her own at the head. But Jefferson himself, lively and full of the buoyancy of youth happened to pass at that moment. He was stopped and introduced to his would-be benefactress, who, astounded and confused, beat a hasty retreat. His grandson, Joseph Jefferson, III, was later famous for such caricatures as in 'Rip Van Winkle.'"

Clapp said that because of a misunderstanding in the second year, Powell was dismissed. Crawford writes that "Nonetheless the new venture was a constantly losing one at first, and at the end of the second season Powell retired in disgust and bankruptcy. He chose to consider himself a much injured person, too, from the fact that the managers of the Boston Theatre, who were Federalists, were, as he believed, using their playhouse to offend their political opponents, the Jacobins."

Undaunted, Powell gave several appearances at Concert Hall. His grievance seemed so real to him that he was able to make it real to his friends, and they promptly set about erecting a new playhouse. This British actor was clever as well as popular, and using his charm and appeal and taking advantage of politics, Powell proposed the building of a competing theatre, financed by a stock subscription. He would lease the new playhouse for $1,200 a year. At a meeting in Concert Hall, all shares of the project were promptly sold and a site was chosen on Common (later Tremont) Street, between Sheaf's Lane and present-day Boylston Street.

In record time, a tall, almost top-heavy, wooden structure was erected. The Haymarket Theatre opened December 26, 1796, bragging of three tiers of boxes curving around three sides of the pit, with a gallery above. The house had a good-size stage with ample dressing rooms, and its audiences enjoyed a fine saloon, or drawing room. The opening production was *The Belle's Stratagem* with the ballet pantomime *Mirza and Lindor*. Admission was $1 for boxes, 50 cents for third-row boxes, 50 cents for pit and 25 cents for gallery. A tavern and hall adjoined the theatre, offering medley entertainment from time to time.

Despite the wording "saloons and drawing rooms," there were no hints of toilet facilities in theatres of this time. Most likely men went to an adjacent or nearby tavern, using its outhouses; ladies had learned to control their needs.

Powell had put together a good company, and the Haymarket was successfully launched. Unfortunately, there was not enough business to support two theatres. An intense rivalry developed between stockholders, managers, and actors of both houses, who competed in every possible way. Prices were cut and dirty tricks played, but the Boston was the finer theatre and had that advantage.

However, before any serious actions could be taken, the older house caught fire. Its thick brick walls confined the conflagration, yet the interior was in ruins. A porter had lit the house's stoves in the afternoon, so that the auditorium would be warm for the evening performance, and left some green logs under the stoves to dry out. Unfortunately the extra wood ignited, setting the house ablaze. When one of the players, a Mr. Barrett, rushed into the flaming playhouse to rescue his wardrobe, a burning door fell on him, causing serious injury. Boston Theatre proprietors immediately decided to rebuild, and architect Bullfinch planned a bigger and better showplace. Reconstruction proceeded so rapidly that the playhouse reopened on October 29, 1798, with a new sloped main floor, now called a "parquette," replacing the pit. The stage was raised and lobby changes were made, but otherwise the house was much the same as before.

The Haymarket Theatre, in rear, opened in 1796 (Library of Congress).

Rivalry between the two theatres resumed, but the Haymarket was the loser. On March 3, 1803, a notice appeared in the *Gazette*:

PUBLIC AUCTION

Superstructure of the building and all materials
Appurtenant to the same as it now stands called the
Haymarket Theatre

N.B. All persons desirous to purchase the ground including a most excellent cellar to the whole extent thereof are requested to deliver written proposals for the same.

Other establishments offered theatrical entertainment. Museums, in addition to their curios and exhibits, offered live performances, or "divertissements," by singers, dancers, magicians, ventriloquists, acrobats, and dramatic "lecturers"; the variety (later vaudeville) stage was nurtured in taverns, circuses, and museums. As early as October 10, 1799, the Columbian Museum announced in the *Gazette* a program of "Medley Entertainments"; in 1800 the Concert Hall advertised "Fashionable Variety." In 1802, *Russell's Gazette* and *Boston Gazette* announced that the Columbian Museum was displaying the Prince of Wales' pianoforte.

Daniel Bowen had opened Boston's first museum, containing mostly waxworks, in 1791 at the American Coffee House on State Street, opposite the Bunch of Grapes Tavern. The exhibition was popular and soon shifted to a hall over the new Hollis

Street School. In 1795, the operation, then known as the Columbian Museum, moved to a large and elegant hall at the head of the Mall (Tremont Street) at the corner of Broomfield's Lane (today's Bromfield Street). Dramatic olios and variety acts were added. Unfortunately, on January 15, 1803, the museum was destroyed by fire.

A museum was opened on Ann Street on February 28, 1804, by a Mr. Ph. Woods, in the large building opposite Faneuil Hall, and a considerable number of curiosities were displayed. It did not become a fashionable place for resort, and was sold at auction in 1822, when the best parts were purchased as additions to the New England Museum.

The Columbian Museum reopened in May 1803 in a second-floor hall on Milk Street, opposite the Old South Church. Bowen obtained sufficient capital to erect a five-story brick building immediately north of Kings Chapel burying ground near Common (Tremont) Street. This structure was 108 feet long by 34 feet wide, and on its top was an observatory, surmounted by a statue of Minerva, 86 feet from the ground. Bowen opened this new museum on November 27, 1806, in partnership with William M.S. Doyle, a portrait painter.

On January 16, 1807, that building was destroyed by fire that erupted from equipment used to product *The Phantasmagoria*, a show of "Spectreology and Dancing Witches." Undaunted, Bowen rebuilt on the same site to a height of two stories. This building measured 32 by 85 feet, with the upper hall having a 22-foot ceiling. It opened June 2, 1807. Bowen soon afterward left Boston, and Doyle continued the management until the museum was transferred to the New England Museum, kept by E.A. Greenwood, on January 1, 1825.

Variety[2] was presented in a public room of the Exchange Coffee House, on the square at the head of Congress Street, in the rear of the U.S. Bank. Following a fire in 1822, the house was enlarged, boasting a 28- by 75-foot assembly room. In the 1820s shows were also given at Merchants Hall, 23 Hanover Street, and at Green Dragon Hall on Union Street.

From 1800 through 1835, Concert Hall hosted such variety attractions as "East Indians giving optical illusions and Herculean feats of strength," magic shows, Professor Harrington the ventriloquist, and in September 1835, "Joice Heth, the 161-year-old nurse to George Washington."

About 1811, Boylston Hall opened above the market on Newbury (Washington) Street at Boylston, offering concerts, museum exhibits, and occasional plays. A New York Museum was noted as opening there in 1812 in *Boston Notions* by Nathaniel Dearborn. The November 30, 1815, *Gazette* enthused that "the gas lights which are to be exhibited at the Boylston Museum this evening ... will be burnt upwards of 100 feet from the reservoir which contains the gas, without the aid of tallow, oil, or wick. We understand the streets of London are lighted with this gas in various directions for upwards of fifteen miles."

The New York Museum was the beginning of the New England Museum, which Greenwood premiered on July 4, 1818, in five or six stores at 76 Court Street. This location was in the northern end of Scollay's Block, which separated Court Street from Tremont Row (when this block was demolished in 1870, the enlarged area became Scollay Square). The New England Museum presented curio collections, paintings, wax figures, androids (mechanical figures playing music) and entertainments "in the largest hall in town."

Washington Gardens, at Common (Tremont) and West streets, was a popular summer resort. Its tree-shaded park had advertised concerts as early as 1815. In 1817 "Vauxhall" was added to its name, and the gardens offered entertainment under the illumination of the new gaslights. In March 1821 a notice appeared in the _Boston Advertiser_: "For Sale, shares in the Washington Garden Amphitheatre." On July 2, 1819, this brick structure opened, presenting "songs, addresses, recitations, and short vaudevilles." Boston became a city in 1822; soon this edifice was renamed the City Theatre and presented dramatic and equestrian performances. In 1827 efforts were made to establish the building as a playhouse, the Washington.

In 1826, the _Boston Advertiser_ touted the gallery at Milk and Congress streets presenting Mr. Hubbard with the "Panharmonican" and "Papyrotomia." The newspaper also noted the Concert Hall offered a ventriloquist and brought back "A Brush to Sweep Away Care, a medley to please," and Julian Hall at Milk Street advertised a concert and "Cutting Likenesses," a performer cutting silhouettes of attendees.

Mary Caroline Crawford relates an amusing anecdote concerning the tour of the actor Edmund Kean and his quarrel with the people of Boston in May 1821.

> Upon a previous visit to the New England city, where he opened February 12, 1821 as Richard III, he was received by a huge and highly enthusiastic audience. His acting was the all-engrossing topic of fashionable discussion, and he became the lion of the day. Great pressure was brought to bear upon him to prolong his engagement, which had been for a strictly limited number of performances, but inasmuch as he was booked elsewhere, he had to leave, though regretfully, what he styled in his curtain speech on the last night as "The Literary Emporium of the New World." When he next found it convenient to tuck a few Boston performances into his schedule, it was approaching June, and many Boston folks were out of town. The manager of the theatre told him this and tried to dissuade him from coming, but Kean replied that he could draw at any time, and it seemed that he was right, for on the first night of his second visit, _King Lear_ being the offering, a very fair house was out. On the second night the audience was slim, however; and on the third, when he was billed as Richard III, he could count only twenty people in front upon looking through the curtain at seven o'clock. Whereupon, he refused to prepare for the performance and left in a rage for his hotel.
>
> Scarcely had he gone when the boxes filled up and a messenger was dispatched to bring him back. But he declined to come, and the manager was obliged to explain that his star's refusal to appear was for want of patronage. Of course those present were not pleased and the newspapers had a great deal to say, next day, about the scornful way the tragedian had treated his public. Accounts of the affair spread to New York, and Kean feared a riot.... He published in the _New York National Advocate_ "My advisors never intimated to me," he caustically observed, "that the theatres were only visited during certain months of the year; that when curiosity had subsided, dramatic talent was not in estimation."

As might have been expected, this second tour added nothing to Kean's American reputation. In Boston, where his previous slighting of his audience had been neither forgotten nor forgiven, he was received with hisses and a fusillade of missiles both hard and soft. This, too, after he had apologized for his previous conduct as follows:

"To the editor, Sir, I take the liberty of informing the citizens of Boston (through the medium of your journal) of my arrival, in confidence that liberality and forbearance will gain the ascendancy over prejudice and cruelty. That I have suffered for my errors, my loss of fame and fortune is too melancholy an illustration. Acting from the impulse of irritation, I certainly was disrespectful to the Boston public; calm deliberation convinces me I was wrong. The first step towards the throne of mercy is confession—the hope we are taught, forgiveness. Man must not expect more than those attributes which we offer to God.—Edmund Kean, Exchange Coffee House, December 21, 1825."

None of these museums, halls, or amphitheatres was serious competition to the Boston Theatre, but in 1827 there was talk again of building a new playhouse. Once more a disgruntled popular actor, William Pelby, whetted the appetites of investors and theatregoers. This thespian also had had trouble with the management of the old theatre; admirers rallied around him and proposed erection of a playhouse that he would manage. Yet again, Concert Hall was the setting of a meeting to secure shareholders for the venture; Pelby guaranteed them a percentage of receipts as rental.

Land, formerly used for stables, was purchased on Tremont, near School Street; foundations were laid in May 1827 as the Commonwealth Legislature incorporated "Proprietors of the Tremont Theatre." Its cornerstone was laid on the Fourth of July, and under supervision of architect Isaiah Rogers, construction bustled along, and soon a heavy granite churchlike façade began to grow on Tremont Street. As the roof went on, an opening date was announced, and on September 24, 1827, an unfinished Tremont Theatre opened. Premature premieres have continued to plague audiences to this day.

The house had the standard three tiers of boxes and a gallery, circling around a pit. Box fronts were painted blue with gold moldings, crystal chandeliers hung from the second and third tiers, the ceiling was a light straw color decorated with gold wreaths. The proscenium was topped with a bust of Shakespeare, together with traditional comic and tragic masks, and its stage was the first in Boston to be illuminated by gas. Prices were $1 for boxes, 75 cents for third tier, and 50 cents for pit and gallery.

As with the Haymarket, rivalry between the old and new houses became intense and bitter, and William Pelby was unable to show a profit for the Tremont. He was forced out of his leasehold by a group that hired Junius Brutus Booth to be acting manager. The unfortunate Pelby vowed that he would take his vengeance.

Booth appeared on the Tremont stage before a crowded house, and Clapp Jr. described the performance:

> He was careless and hesitating in his delivery.... He would falter in his discourse, jumble scraps of other plays into his dialogue, run to the prompter's side of the stage and lean against a side scene, while the prompter endeavored to help him forward in the play, by speaking out his part of the dialogue loud enough to be heard in the galleries. In this manner, he made a shift to get through the first

The first Tremont Theatre (Library of Congress).

two acts of the tragedy.... In the early part of the third act, while engaged in parlance with the king of Naples, the audience was surprised by his suddenly breaking off from the measured, heroic dignity of his stage tone, and with a comical simper, falling at once into a colloquial gossiping sort of chatter with his majesty. The audience was thrown into as much astonishment as did the king of the two Sicilys.... Mr. Booth turning around and facing the spectators began to address them in this manner: "Ladies and gentlemen; I really don't know this part. I studied it only once before, much against my inclination. I will read the part and the play shall go on. By your leave the play shall go on, and Mr. Wilson will read the part for me." Here an overpowering burst of hissing and exclamations arose from all parts of this house, while Mr. Booth continued to face the audience with a grinning look, which at length broke out into an open laugh.

Mr. Smith then rushed from behind the scenes upon the stage and led him off, Mr. Booth exclaiming, "I can't read, I am a charity boy; I can't read. Take me to the Lunatic Hospital!" Here the drop curtain fell amid the murmurs and hisses of the house.

Apparently Booth had been drinking heavily before his performance. After a temporary retirement, he returned to the Boston stage.

In the spring of 1832, Pelby returned from the South, cherishing the most hostile feeling against the Tremont, its proprietors, and lessee, by whom, from causes already recorded, he deemed himself injured.

The new theatre did well under various managers, but was never able to produce a decent profit to its investors because the capacity was too small. Boston was still unable to support two playhouses. After two unhappy years the stockholders of both theatres met at Concert Hall to make a deal: the Tremont owners leased the Boston and kept it closed.

However, budding showmen would not let be the status quo. On February 1, 1832, an amphitheatre opened at the rear of the Bite Tavern in Flagg Alley. It was named the Washington Theatre and offered dramatic and equestrian performances. This house debuted with the Indian tragedy *Carabasset*, which was accompanied by tumblers, slack-wire walkers, and a clown. Boxes cost 25 cents, the pit 12½ cents. Although the policy switched to variety shows, the house was never successful. Flagg Alley became Pierce, then Change Alley, running from State Street to the Faneuil market area.

On February 22, 1832, the State Museum opened at Court and Howard streets. However, the greatest event of 1832 was the opening five days later of the American Amphitheatre, at Portland and Traverse streets. The newest newcomer presented dramatic and equestrian performances, had two tiers of boxes, a pit, and a small stage. William Pelby, still unhappy with the Tremont proprietors, secured a lease for this new showplace, changed its name to the Warren Theatre, and converted it for stage productions, opening on July 3, 1832. The *Boston Post* advised that "arrangements have been made for the preservation of order within and without the walls of the theatre."

One can imagine the consternation of the Tremont owners at this turn of events, and they determined to get Pelby. On November 12 they reopened the old theatre under its Federal Street name, using the same stock company performing at both playhouses. The *Boston Post* commented: "It is an old saying that too much of a good thing, etc."

In 1834 the Federal Street Theatre, "Old Drury," presented a one-night performance of "Doctor Divine, the Fire King," an act in which "the good physician" survived being in a hot oven and other fiery acts.

On June 6, 1834, Julian Hall became Mr. Saubert's Theatre, at Milk and Congress streets. The house was fitted up and arranged for a variety performance.

Early in the nineteenth century two taverns existed side by side on Newbury Street (Washington Street) near Hog Alley (Avery Street). One was the Lion, on the site of the Grand Turk Tavern; the other was the Lamb, forerunner of the Adams House hostelry. In January 1832 the *Boston Intelligencer* advertised a reopening of the Lion Tavern "with a good cellar, wild game, and livery."

In late 1835 James Raymond and associates purchased the Lion property, which had dimensions of roughly 55 feet by 176 feet, and construction commenced almost immediately for an amphitheatre designed to hold equestrian and dramatic performances. In November an advertisement appeared in the *Boston Post* seeking "actors for the amphitheater now under construction, manager Mr. Barrymore." A reporter for the *Morning Post* recalled that while visiting the site he had been pressed into ser-

The Warren Theatre in 1832, top, and below, rebuilt as the National Theatre in 1836 (author's collection).

vice painting the theatre's boxes. The Lion Theatre opened Monday, January 11, 1836, in an unfinished state. The *Daily Transcript* wrote that the house "has been built so rapidly that it may be said literally to have sprung into existence."

The theatre had a semicircular, almost U-shaped interior, its stage within the open end. Three tiers of crimson and gilded boxes rose on three sides; gallery seating above them formed the auditorium. An equestrian circle, or ring, was in front of the stage and the pit was in the rear and sides, extending under the boxes.

The stage was not large but had the necessary scenery and machinery. Robert Jones painted its front drop curtain, "Passage of the Alps by Bonaparte." Three companies, dramatic, ballet, and equestrian, appeared in the first program; 40 Hanoverian and Arabian horses performed in the ring accompanied by a 16-piece orchestra. In the spectacle "The Jewess," a procession of elephants, horses, and camels appeared. Décor was by Mr. Reinagle, and William Barrymore was the stage manager. Admission for boxes was 75 cents, pit 37½ cents, and gallery 25 cents. Newspapers assured that "A good and efficient police will be in constant attendance to preserve order."

Later that year a substantial multistory brick building was erected in front of the theatre. Stores occupied the first floor, while an entrance in the middle connected with the Lion auditorium. Upper floors housed offices and apartments. At this time the stage was enlarged.

After two lackluster years, the house became a concert hall, its pit and ring floored over, making it a second-floor theatre, still connected through the front building to the street, while over its entrance "Mechanics Institute" was carved in stone. The house had some theatrical performances and was for a time home of the congregation of the Reverend Theodore Parker.

In 1839 the hall was renamed the Melodeon, presenting concerts, exhibitions, and theatricals, and also was used by the Handel and Hayden Society. In 1850 an enlarged house, 57 feet by 113 feet, 33 feet from parterre to dome, seating 1,500 patrons, held a farewell performance of the Swedish Nightingale, Jenny Lind.

Pelby also took advantage of that slack period to substantially rebuild his Warren Theatre. It reopened August 15, 1836, as the National Theatre, bragging of its gas lighting. This was Boston's first of several like-named houses.

In 1839, Moses Kimball, who had worked in the museum business, bought the contents of the New England Museum, and with these curios and exhibits started an operation in Lowell, Massachusetts, that was not successful. He returned to Boston and in June 1841 opened the Boston Museum and Gallery of Fine Arts, on the site of the old Columbian Museum at Tremont and Bromfield streets. Moses and David P. Kimball emphasized the theatrical aspect of the business and were extremely successful. The *Bostonian*[3] recalls: "The first Boston Museum building was a small but imposing structure, with a portico and handsome pillars in front, above the first story. The music saloon was capable of seating twelve hundred persons. This edifice served the purpose of the proprietors as long as the business was confined to light entertainments."

The professor from Concert Hall days, Jonathon Harrington, took over the premises of the New England Museum at 78 Court Street in 1840, renaming it Harrington's Museum. This entrepreneur-actor was well known, having appeared as ventriloquist and magician in various halls since the late 1820s, and had leased the Boston Theatre in 1834 for a season of variety, with scant success. His New England Museum lasted only two years because the new Boston Museum was proving too much competition. His curio collection was sold at auction; Harrington's Museum was renamed Washington Hall. The plucky professor continued to perform as ventriloquist and magician in various variety engagements as late as 1871.

Another amphitheatre was constructed in 1841 on Haverhill, near Traverse Street, intended for circus performances. Actor and manager Wyzeman Marshall leased the structure for theatricals in 1842 and named it the Eagle (he had previously operated Boylston Hall for a season as a vaudeville saloon). Unfortunately, his new project became direct competition to the National Theatre and its incensed manager Pelby. Marshall had been an actor under his direction, so Pelby took him under his wing "to help the fledgling manager" and bought a one-quarter interest in his friend's theatre.

Late one night Pelby crept into the dark and empty Eagle with lantern and hatchet, climbed into the attic, and commenced to chop away at the roof supports. The structure became so weakened that the new theatre was forced to close, and the National's competition was eliminated. Charges were never brought against William Pelby; Marshall, a wiser man, continued his acting career and in later years played Othello to Edwin Booth's Iago and also managed two of Boston's famous playhouses, the second Boston Theatre and the Howard Athenaeum. He played at the Boston during the season of 1855-1856 as Hamlet, Pizarro, Macbeth, and Julius Caesar.

Chapter 4

Exit Tremont Theatre,
Enter Tremont Temple
The Rise of the Boston Museum
1841–1843

In 1841 the *Post* carried an announcement for concerts in Lee's Saloon at 253 Washington Street, and in March 1842 the *Transcript* ran ads for this enterprise as the Olympic Saloon, announcing "a new entrance from Washington Street."[1] Its parquet floor offered cane bottom chairs, each row being elevated four inches above that in front, and it had box seats, a rural stage drop, and an orchestra perched over its entrance doors. Marble-topped tables were added in July to provide ice cream and refreshments. This house was most likely also named the Apollo Saloon briefly in 1842, when advertisements bragged of a 700-seat "parquet." By 1844 Lee's Grand Saloon became the Boston Gymnasium, and the site's last notices were as the Washington Theatre, which was gone in 1846.

In May 1843 the proprietors of the Tremont realized that they could no longer sustain the heavy losses which that undersized playhouse was continuing to produce, and once again they met in Concert Hall. The property was offered for $12,500. Terms were reached with a Baptist Society, and the last performance was June 23, 1843.

Clapp Jr. recorded the closing scenes:

> On 17th June, President Tyler visited Boston to attend the completion of the Bunker Hill Monument, Webster delivered the oration, the Tremont gave a farewell performance for the hundreds of spectators in town. A benefit for the house's manager, J.S. Jones, was given on June 23, 1843; at its conclusion the entire "dramatis personae" of nearly twenty advanced to the footlights arranged in crescent form and sang a charming Scotch air of farewell.
>
> On the evening of June 26, "The Learned Blacksmith," Elihu Burritt, delivered a lecture in the theatre, the net proceeds of which went towards defraying the cost of the alteration of the theatre into a church, which was done at an expense of about $25,000.

The theatre was then converted into a quasi-church named the Tremont Temple. Its lower portions became stores and offices, and a large hall remained above, used for religious services or rented for lectures, concerts, and meetings.

In the early part of the twentieth century, the *Boston Post* reminisced about that purchase:

> One of the Baptist group was Timothy Gilbert, who was reputed to have been a member of Boston's "Underground Railroad" which aided slaves who were escaping from their southern owners. One Sunday, Gilbert, accompanied by a few black refugees, attended services in his pew at the Charles Street Baptist Church. The rude reception that his guests received from his fellow parishioners so embittered him that he was determined to found his own place of worship ... Timothy Gilbert helped arrange the purchase of the Tremont Theatre in order to provide "a church with free seats where rich and poor, black and white, could worship God according to their own dictates." To bring in the necessary revenue to support the Temple, its halls and spaces would be rented out, when not needed for religious purposes. Early rentals were miscellaneous meetings, political caucuses, concerts, lectures by Webster, Choate, and Everett, an appearance by Jenny Lind, etc. It was here that Gliddon discovered the sex of Anch-pa-mach, to the astonishment of those who witnessed the unrolling of the mummy. The Tremont Temple, through several fires and re-constructions, maintained that policy into the mid-twentieth century.[2]

Following the demise of the Tremont, Boston had only two playhouses, the Boston Museum and the National Theatre; the old Boston Theatre was only operated for occasional rentals. In 1836 the Boston was renamed the Odeon, becoming a concert hall and home of the Boston Academy of Music.

Variety continued to play in the Concert Hall, Amory Hall at Washington and West streets, Washington Hall at 221 Washington Street opposite Franklin, and Washingtonian Hall at 76 Court Street. Concerts and lectures played the Melodeon, Odeon, and the Tremont.

Clapp Jr. commented on June 14, 1841, concerning Moses Kimball's Boston Museum and Gallery of Fine Arts, "The walls of the saloon hung with pictures, and the stage was sufficiently capacious for the performances of vaudevilles, etc. The drop scene was very neat and appropriate, the place was quote comfortable and cosey. The hall was dedicated on the 14th by a grand concert.... These entertainments proved very acceptable to the public."

Clapp Jr. later wrote that

> In February 1843 Mr. Kimball engaged John Sefton and Mrs. Maeder to bring out "operettas," and the 6th inst., the "Masque Ball" was brought out. This was the commencement of dramatic representations at the museum.
>
> The museum attracted all classes, but, of the more wealthy residents. For the pieces were well put on the stage and the actors above mediocrity. The museum was then and is now patronized by a large class who do not frequent theatres, but who have a nice perception of the difference between tweedle-dum and tweedle-dee. We have noticed, however, that many that make a first attempt at coun-

tenancing theatricals at the museum may shortly after be found at the regular theatres, and the museum has done much toward increasing the lovers of drama.

The production of the moral play called "The Drunkard," written by W.H. Smith, decided the fate of the museum, for it attracted to the house an unprecedented number of visitors, and established permanently the popularity of the Boston Museum.

In late 1842 Washingtonian Hall moved across Court Street to number 75; in April 1845 that second-floor house was refurbished and renamed the Boston Olympic Theatre, having a capacity of 300 patrons in parquette settees, box settees, and private boxes.

Chapter 5

The End of the World
Enter the Howard Athenaeum
The Boston Museum Moves
up Tremont Street
1843–1846

In 1841, a religious sect known as the Millerites leased a lot on Howard Street, taking a three-year lease that would revert back to the lessor at expiration. This group believed that the world would end by April 23, 1843; they erected a strange-looking wooden tabernacle on this site.

Clapp Jr. adds:

> The Millerite excitement of 1843-1844 reached its climax in the following year. The venerable Father Miller, finding that the day set apart by him for the closing up of all earthly affairs did not result as he anticipated, entered into another calculation, and discovered a slight mistake of a few hundred or a few thousand years, we forget which. This announcement saddened the hearts of those whom had given up all, and made preparations for immediate departure. Their place of worship in Howard Street, called the Tabernacle, was soon afterwards deserted and remained for a short time a miserable wooden monument, one story high, to the folly of Millerism.
>
> The want of a leading theatre, in a city where strangers were thrown upon their resources in the evening was severely felt, for in the spring of 1845, the Boston Museum and the National Theatre were the only prominent places of public amusement.... The Tabernacle from its central position seemed to offer a very excellent site for a theatre, and W.F. Johnson, W.L. Ayling, Thos. Ford, and Leonard Brayley thought that it might with profit be converted into a temporary residence for Thespis and Melpomene.
>
> The Millerites were not particularly partial to theatrical representations, and that it was evident that some shrewdness must be exhibited in procuring the lease, lest they might think that De Foe's couplet, "Wherever God erects a house of prayer, The Devil always builds a chapel there," was about to have a perma-

31

nent realization. They were at first opposed to leasing it, on any account, but finally concluded a bargain and signed the lease.

On October 13, 1845, the one-story wooden tabernacle on Howard Street became a theatre known as the Howard Athenaeum, having a perfect sight line slope from lobby to stage. A false stone front was erected, a first-class attraction was obtained, and the house was instantly popular. Unfortunately it was destroyed by fire in February 1846.

The old Federal Street playhouse, dropping its Odeon name, made a comeback as the Boston Theatre on August 24, 1846, "enlarged and refurbished." The venerable site advertised a pit, parquet, "proscenium private boxes," and a gallery.

The tabernacle lot on Howard Street lay fallow, except for a spring circus visit, as managers tried to put together funds to build a new theatre on the site. Negotiations were unsuccessful until beer and ale merchants, needing a new location, joined with them. The beverage business would occupy the first floor; a theatre would be constructed above.

On October 5, 1846, the second Howard Athenaeum, unfinished, as were most theatres upon their debuts, opened its doors to 2,000 spectators. As with his Tremont Theatre, architect Isaiah Rogers created a massive granite façade, resembling a church rather than a playhouse. Merchants occupied the first floor, except for a center lobby entrance and stairways to an auditorium that held 1,600 spring-cushioned seats. Around the main floor, running from one side of the stage to the other, was the dress circle. Five dress boxes were its center rear, having private entrances from the foyer, and two tiers of boxes circled above. Seats were covered in crimson and blue damask, and box fronts were warmly frescoed. The stage was 43 feet deep, and the proscenium was 36 feet wide by 32 feet high.

The Bostonian magazine recalled that "the closing of the Tremont Theatre had rather an important effect upon the destinies of the Museum. A vacancy was created in the number of theatres in the city, which was filled by the organization of a small but effective stock company at the Museum, with Mr. William H. Sedley-Smith as its stage-manager. The Museum continued to prosper under the new arrangement in its old quarters until 1846, when its increasing attractions, both in the way of curiosities and dramatic performances, enabled it to outgrow its old home and warranted a change to a larger and more spacious edifice."

Moses Kimball decided to construct a larger and more competitive theatre farther up Tremont Street, just past King's Chapel and its burial ground, the site being partly that of the 1806 Columbian Museum. His new Boston Museum opened on November 2, 1846. *Boston Sights and Stranger's Guides* (1856) reported:

> Perhaps of all the places of public amusement in the good city of Boston, not one is so generally popular as this. Nor is its great success undeserved; for it has ever been the aim of its enterprising proprietor, Hon. Moses Kimball, while providing every possible novelty for the gratification of the masses, to carefully exclude everything that be in the slightest degree objectionable. Hence the museum has become the great family resort, as well as the visitors choicest treat.
>
> First, for its locality, on Tremont Street, between Court and School Streets, it

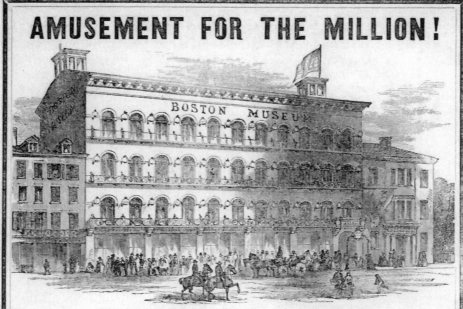

An 1857 ad for the Boston Museum (courtesy of Boston Public Library, Print Department).

stands a spacious and superb building, its front adorned by elegant balconies and rows of ground glass globes, like enormous pearls, which at night are luminous with gas. Three tiers of elegantly arched windows admit light into the building and we reach the interior by a bold flight of stairs.[1]

At the summit of these stairs is an elegant ticket and treasurer's office, and adjoining the entrance to the Grand Hall of Cabinets, which is surround by noble Corinthian pillars. Around the gallery front are arranged portraits of celebrated Americans. On the floor of the hall are statuary and superb works of art, and arranged in glass cases, curiosities from all parts of the world. The galleries, reached by a grand staircase, are filled with the rich and rare products of many a clime; not an inch of space is thrown away. Ascending still higher, we find a superb collection of wax figures, singly and in groups; surmounting all is an observatory, whence splendid panoramic views of the city, the harbor, and its islands may be obtained.

The Museum Theatre is one of the most beautifully decorated, best constructed, and well managed theatres in the United States. The visitor has no rowdyism to fear, and nothing ever occurs, either in the audience portion or on the stage, to offend the most fastidious. As good order is obtained in Mr. Kimball's theatre, as in any drawing room in the land. The company too is always first rate. Some of our best actors have been trained on the Museum boards. But, besides having a stock company which cannot be surpassed, "stars" of the first theatrical magnitude are often engaged, and brilliant spectacles, with all the accessories of superb scenery, delicious music, gorgeous costumes, banners, and other appropriate appointments, are produced several times in each season, in all the magnificence that money and skill can accomplish, and are a marked feature of the place, than cannot easily be surpassed. Few persons who visit Boston ever think of quitting it without paying the Museum a visit, for it contains amusements and information for all.

The Museum building alone cost nearly a quarter of a million of dollars, and covers twenty thousand feet of land, the whole of which, with its numerous cabinets, is crowded with every variety of birds, quadrupeds, fish, reptiles, insects, shells, minerals, fossils, etc. Then there is the Fee-Jee Mermaid, alluded to by Barnum in his autobiography, together with more than one thousand costly paintings, among which is Sully's great picture of Washington Crossing the Delaware, portraits by Copley, West, Stewart, etc. In short, there are to be seen nearly five thousand articles of every conceivable rare and curious thing of nature and art in the Museum, and all for the marvelously small sum of twenty-five cents!

The *Boston Post* described the museum more simply:

The first floor consisted of shops and a museum entrance on one end of the Tremont Street façade. A twelve-foot wide entrance rose from street level to a twelve-foot square landing. To one's right was a box office; to one's left was the Great Hall of natural curiosities, paintings, and sculptures. This vast room ran 103 feet along the second floor street frontage, and was fifty feet wide and 60 feet in height. The museum roof was supported by 20 massive columns of the Corinthian order; above was an arched ceiling most elegantly wrought. At the extreme end of this hall was a 25 foot wide staircase which branched right and left into two of 12 foot width. Over the resultant landing hung Sully's "Washington Crossing the Delaware." Two galleries ran around the hall behind the columns, on these as well as on the main floor beneath, were "58 cabinets of curiosities."

Up those staircases, and the end of the hall, one arrives (to one's right) at the dramatic portion of the establishment by a passage 16 feet in width. This same passage is continued downward by a staircase 9 feet wide to a second entrance on Court Square (useful in case of fire), and upward by a staircase of equal width to the gallery of the "Exhibition Room" (Lecture Hall), holding almost as many people as the lower floor.

There were 1,500 seats in that auditorium, which ran parallel to the great hall, ten iron columns held up the gallery, three chandeliers hung from the French gray and white ceiling. Proscenium boxes were ornamented in white and gold on a ground of light green. The Museum stage was 50 feet deep, 90 feet wide with a proscenium width of 30 feet. Scenery was supported by iron grooves set in the floor; a room under the stage contained dressing rooms and storage. H. and J.E. Billings designed the building; Anthony Hanson superintended construction.

Actor Otis Skinner, in his book *Footlights and Spotlights*, remembered a visit to the Boston Museum at the age of five:

> This dignified place of amusement was exempt from Puritan prejudice; its very name gave it a propriety denied to other theatres. A visit there was most instructive. In orderly alcoves, shelves of minerals, cases of stuffed birds, fossil remains, and curiosities from various parts of the world formed a collection that was presided over by busts and portraits of gentlemen whose respectability no one could doubt. A large painting called "The Roman Daughter" hung over the entrance into the hall of curiosities, representing a beautiful matron who visited her starving father in prison and nurtured him by suckling his old parched lips at her breast.
>
> But, the place of dread in this enchanted palace was the gallery of wax works on the upper floor. Here, I drank horrors by the bucketful. The recollection of this horror chamber lies far deeper than the plays I saw. These were given in what, for politic reasons, was first termed "The Lecture Hall" of the museum, and which gradually assumed the proportions of a stage and auditorium. Ministers of the Gospel could freely patronize such a place of entertainment; their attendance was even sought on a complimentary basis.

The Bostonian continues:

> Another important stellar attraction in the Museum's early history was the elder Junius Brutus Booth, father of the late Edwin Booth, who played most if not all of his Boston engagements during the last two years of his life from 1849 to 1852, at this house. Mr. Booth always drew crowded houses at the Museum by his wonderful power as a tragedian.... He came to this country about the year 1821, became the second manager of the first Tremont Theatre in 1828, traveled through all parts of the country meeting with great success, and died on his passage up the Mississippi River from New Orleans to Louisville in 1852, aged fifty-six years. Mr. Booth's distinguished son Edwin, made his first appearance on any stage at the Museum in 1849, when but sixteen years of age.

Actress Kate Reingold's book, *Yesterdays with Actors*, is quoted by the *The Bostonian*, giving us a look at stage arrangements of the day:

> We entered by a narrow door, from one of the galleries, which gave at a touch, but fell back as quickly with the force of a ponderous spring. A door keeper, seated at the narrow end of a narrow aisle some three feet wide between enormous piles of dusty canvas, permitted none to pass except the actual employees of the theatre. About the same space between the inner edge of the scenery standing in its grooves and the masses stacked along its walls, allowed a scant passage down the side of the stage. At one corner, where the private box is now, was a "property room," behind that the manager's office; on the opposite side, a small space of perhaps six feet wide at one end tapering down to four at the other, was the green room (waiting and meeting space for performers), its furniture a bench about the wall, a cast case, a dictionary and a mirror, over which was inscribed "Trifles make perfection." To move about, except warily, on business, was at any time difficult; at night when carpenters and scene shifters were active, a veritable running the gauntlet. Two dressing rooms in place of the two upper boxes were approached by staircases as steep as ladders, and these were assigned the "leading" man and woman. The others had little bins under the stage and crowded as closely by the machinery of the "traps" and other subterranean contrivances as the space above. I think all that saved me from many a severe fall was the caution inspired by the fear of spoiling fine clothes. I remember, with painful distinctness, my injured feelings when, squeezing through a tight space, I heard my satin "fray" as it brushed through the rough edges of scenes, or in a hurried entrance felt the obnoxious nail that caught my lace flounce, while I had to go straight on, whatever stayed behind; for the stage must not wait!

The Bostonian continues: "In the early days of the Museum there were no reserved seats, the admission being twenty-five cents to all parts of the house. In the more notable engagements, such as those of the elder Booth, the writer has seen the visitors commence to assemble as early as five o'clock in the afternoon and crowd the area in front of the auditorium doors extending down the upper stairs ... and fill a considerable space in the exhibition room, patiently waiting for hours for the opening of the doors, when they would rush in and secure the best seats. Gradually however, a system of secured seats at advanced rates (fifty cents at first) was adopted, and the primitive plan of rushing for places was finally abolished, greatly to the comfort of the patrons."

Chapter 6

Exit the First Boston Theatre
The Adelphi and
New National Theatres
1847–1852

On April 5, 1847, the Boston Olympic, on the second floor of 75 Court Street, became Brougham and Bland's Boston Adelphi Theatre. John Brougham and Humphrey Bland were actors and playwrights; their tiny playhouse advertised a parquette, dress circle, and boxes. The *Evening Transcript* said, "This elegant little place of amusement is now thoroughly established in public favor; full and fashionable audiences visit it nightly. There is not a vestige of the ancient rowdyism apparent."

A later Boston newspaper asked:

> Who of the readers of Notes and Queries, remembers that veritable "Temple of Momus," the little Boston Adelphi Theatre opened in 1847 by John Brougham and Humphrey Bland at the corner of Court Street and Cornerhill, over Waterman's house-furnishing store? The Adelphi was a famous resort for the lovers of pure fun, and there it was that John Brougham, then in his prime both as an actor and an author, produced some of the wittiest plays and most uproarious burlesques that ever came from his ready pen. The company was especially adapted to their proper production, and consisted of Miss Hattie Mace, Mrs. Bland, ... Mrs. Brougham, ... Miss Wagstaff, ... Mrs. Benson, Miss Anna Cruise, ... Mrs. W.H. Smith, Messrs. John Brougham, Humphrey Bland, George Graham, E.B. Williams, Sam D. Johnson, Richard Stephens and others.
>
> John Brougham was the life of the place, and his acting and facetious "Addresses to the Pubic" were inimitable; the most inveterate hypochondriac, had he been present at some of the "wild and untamed" performances, served nightly to the patrons, could not have controlled his risibilities. It was a small place, and even when full, as it generally was, did not greatly enrich the proprietors....
>
> Probably Mr. Brougham never worked harder in his life than during the short career of this little box of a place, every night appearing in two or more pieces (nearly all of them his own) abounding in local hits and witticisms, many pro-

duced on the spur of the moment, and all relished to the utmost to audiences who knew what to expect and never were disappointed.

BOSTON ADELPHI

BENEFIT OF MR. BROUGHAM
Tuesday Evening, June 15th, 1847,
Will be presented the admirable vaudeville of
THE WEATHERCOOK,

Tristram Fickle	Mr. Bland
Old Fickle	Mr. Williams
Briapuit	Mr. Whiting
Sneer	Mr. Johnson
Gardener	Mr. Parker
Footman	Mr. Adams
Variella, with songs	Mrs. Bland
Ready	Miss Mace
Dance	Miss Louisa Pray

To be followed by an entirely new and original and melodramatic
and hippodramatic Burlesque Extraordinary,
to be called
OUR TOM THUMB

Being a humble though ambitious attempt to follow in the footsteps of the illustrious Fielding by John Brougham.

Prices of admission, Dress circle, 50 cents; Parquet and Boxes, 25 cents; Private boxes $4.00

In 1848 the house was renamed Brougham and Bland's Lyceum; later, as one partner defected, it was called simply Bland's Boston Adelphi. John Brougham needed more space for his talents, and by October he had leased the Howard Athenaeum, while Humphrey Bland moved his Lyceum into new quarters just off Court, onto Sudbury, opposite Hawkins Street. William Clapp, Jr., suggested that this site was probably a remodeling of an 1847 amphitheatre constructed to house H. Rockwell's New York Circus. The Lyceum advertised a parquette, dress circle, and upper circle; the Boston Post called it "a beautiful theatre."

In 1848 the Dramatic Museum opened on Beach Street near the United States Hotel; it held a parquette, gallery and private boxes. The house struggled until 1849 as the Beach Street Theatre, then Thorne's American Theatre, but it was closed more than it was open. In late 1850 the house reopened briefly as the Olympic, and then closed forever.

In January 1849 an advertisement appeared in newspapers:

BOSTON THEATRE TO LET

Including scenery, wardrobe, and properties

In June 1850 the old house became the Federal Street Theatre once more, but by September the "to let" sign was rehung.

The second Boston Theatre (top left, tallest building) and the second Tremont Temple (top right, tallest building in middle) (both Library of Congress).

On March 18, 1850, the Lyceum Theatre became the Odeon, advertising a new street level entrance. On its roof flashed a Drummond Light, used in lighthouses, anticipating Broadway and Hollywood premieres 75 years in the future.

In 1850, minstrel shows captivated Boston. "Cooper's Minstrels" appeared at Central Hall, 19 Milk Street, one of the Columbian Museum's many sites; in 1851 the place was "fitted up with 600 seats." In January 1852, Harmony Hall, at Washington and Summer streets, housed "Ordway's Aeolian Vocalists as Whites and Ethiopians," with J.P. Ordway, manager.

In February 1852, a rear portion of the Province House hostelry at 169–171 Washington Street, nearly opposite Old South Church, was converted into Ordway Hall. The *Boston Post* approved of "proper ventilation and good seats." Further remodeling took place in August; other variety shows appeared in this hall from time to time in addition to Ordway's Aeolians.

The Tremont Temple, once the Tremont Theatre, burned on March 30, 1852; its congregation started to rebuild almost immediately, and it reopened December 1853. Fires were quite common in theatres and churches in the nineteenth century with the wooden interiors, seats and wood-fired stoves; three new Tremont Temples would be rebuilt on this site.

In April 1852, the Boston Theatre was sold and scheduled to be demolished, but before any moves could be made, a fire destroyed the National Theatre. The National's lessees appealed to the owners of the old playhouse for its temporary use, and "Old Drury" won a reprieve and continued to operate using the National's bookings until May 8. Its fixtures were then sold and the Boston–Federal Street Theatre was no more.

On May 4, 1852, a notice appeared in the *Post*: "NEW THEATRE, a company is now being formed for the purpose of building a large and first class theatre and Opera House ... to comprise 150 shares of $1000.... Subscription lists are now ready." Immediately after the destruction of the National Theatre by fire, Joseph Leonard, the well-known auctioneer, had published these notices. However, there was a delay in choice of a site, and Leonard directed his attention to the new National Theatre proposition.

On May 10, 1852, a decision was made to rebuild the National Theatre. Contracts were made for the building of a theatre worth $45,000, excluding the land, which was taken on a lease with the right of purchase at an agreed price within a certain number of years. Work commenced almost immediately, and on July 6 the cor-

CONFLAGRATION OF THE NATIONAL THEATRE, CORNER OF PORTLAND AND TRAVERSE STREETS. BOSTON

An April 1852 fire consumes the National Theatre, as shown in a wood engraving from the time (courtesy of Boston Public Library, Print Department).

nerstone was laid along with a metal box containing rare coins, a specimen of California gold, theatre bills, a piece of the foundation of the Federal Street Theatre, copies of newspapers, and a parchment containing a record of its architects, builders, Leonard, and staff.

The playhouse opened November 1, 1852. It was not complete, nor would it be for six more weeks. Architects Joseph F. Billings and Fred C. Sleeper maintained the old style of theatre construction, as a newspaper reported:

> It is about 150 feet long on Traverse Street, by 84 feet front on Portland Street, the rear is on Friend Street. The building has a pleasing architectural front, covered with dark brown mastic. It is well situated on the junction of several great thoroughfares, and in the immediate vicinity of Charlestown, from which it probably derives a large portion of its patronage.
>
> The theatre has convenience of ingress and egress. The principal entrance on Portland Street is from three arched doors to the ticket office. Stairs to the right lead to the first floor, on the left to the family circle or second tier, and from a door on the left of the front to the upper tier or gallery. The lobbies are large, the audience portion of the theater is circular and about 80 feet in diameter. The whole lower floor was used as a parquette, or, as formerly called, pit; there is a

The second National Theatre, in an 1860 photograph (courtesy of Boston Public Library, Print Department).

division between what is commonly called the parquette and the boxes, or dress circle, making the parquette itself about 50 foot diameter. The parquette had seats for a few over 400, dress circle the same number. The family or second circle has seats for between 500 and 600, but has held 700 persons; the gallery seats a few over 1,000 persons; making a total comfortable seated of about 2,500 persons. The stage was 60 feet deep by 76 wide, and is well adapted to the class of performances usually played at this theatre, chiefly "Melo-drama."

Another article gave a more detailed comment: "The National auditorium had a parquette floor with the first tier of boxes level with its rear. There was a second tier above called the dress circle, a gallery and six private boxes. Capacity was about 2,430 seats, a good sized stage measured 76 feet wide and 66 deep, fronted by a 40-foot wide, 38 feet high proscenium. The entire building was a massive 151 feet long by 80 wide; a second 50 by 17-foot building held the green room and dressing rooms."

Chapter 7

Ancestors of the Movie Palaces
The Boston Music Hall
and the Second Boston Theatre
1852–1857

The Boston Music Hall opened in November 1852. This huge building, 130 feet by 78 feet by 65 feet high, sat in the center of a block that sloped downward from Tremont to Washington Street and was between Winter Street on the south and Bromfield on the north. From alleys off Bromfield, the sharp slope of the hill made the hall's massive block granite foundation appear to be holding up some great medieval fortress, with only the moat missing.

Within the hall, two tiers of galleries on each side held three rows each, and two more on the north end were more commodious. An orchestra and organ platform was at the southern extremity facing a flat main floor. (A $60,000 organ, installed in 1863, was one of the largest and finest in existence, built by Walcker, in Ludwigsburg, near Stuttgart, Germany, and contained 5,474 pipes.) Blue and white moreen upholstered chairs, with white ivory numbered tabs at their tops, held an audience of about 2,500 patrons.

The Boston Music Hall had three spacious entrances: Bumstead Place and Hamilton Place were off Tremont Street, while Central or Winter Place (later Music Hall Place) was off Winter Street. Wide connecting corridors ran around the auditorium. All lighting came from above; gaslights were installed at ceiling height on windowed cornices, affording indirect illumination.

The year 1853 was a quiet one on the theatrical scene. Amory Hall offered a bearded lady and later a "Kinetoscope of Cuba"; Edison's motion picture projector of the like name was some three decades in the future. This entertainment was a panoramic canvas painting, which was unreeled from one tag roll across the stage to another—the "moving" pictures of 1853. Horticultural Hall presented "Chang and Eng, Siamese Twins."

At a meeting in the Revere House on April 28, 1852, called by auctioneer Joseph Leonard, participants discussed the building of a new theatre. The meeting was called

The Boston Music Hall, photographed July 4, 1876 (courtesy of Boston Public Library, Print Department).

to order by Joseph N. Howe. E.C. Bates was chosen chairman and B.F. Stevens secretary, and a committee consisting of John E. Bates, Gardner Brewer, Otis Rich, and John E. Thayer was appointed to select a site and solicit subscriptions. On May 15, the Boston Theatre Company was incorporated, with a capital stock of $200,000, which was afterward increased to $250,000, with the price of shares $1000 each. The Melodeon estate on Washington Street was purchased with rear land, which had been owned by the Boston Gaslight Company, for $163,348.80.

The Bostonian noted that "In the fall of 1853 there was produced at the Boston Museum a piece that met with a most extraordinary success.... This was a dramatization of Mrs. Harriet Beecher Stowe's remarkable story of 'Uncle Tom's Cabin.'" Probably the story and the play did more to create a powerful public sentiment in favor of the abolition of the nefarious institution of slavery than any other single influence that went forth in those days, inasmuch as they were an accurate, unexaggerated picture of the methods of the 'peculiar institution.'"

In 1854, crowds of people gathered on Mason Street, which ran between Washington and Tremont streets for one block. They were watching an immense pile of brick rising from a huge and very deep hole, north of Bradford Place. The latter was a small street of Colonial houses and a stable, which ran east to the rear of the Melodeon. Doors and arches that soon appeared at sidewalk level obscured the labyrinth below; numerous iron-shuttered windows were inset along the massive masonry towering above. What marvels were being constructed behind those formidable walls? Bostonians were not to be kept waiting very long: The new and second Boston Theatre opened on September 11, 1854.

Unlike similar houses (Philadelphia and New York's Academies of Music), very little of the Boston Theatre's exterior was visible except for its enormous stage rear on Mason Street. The Lion-Melodeon had been purchased to enable construction of a fitting granite or marble façade on Washington Street, in keeping with the grandeur of the new showplace. Instead, an unpretentious entrance was built just north of the Melodeon. It was a 24-foot-wide, three-story building with its front covered in mastic designed to resemble stonework, and its rear was joined by a one-story ell to the main structure.

There was a serious engineering problem with the construction of the massive auditorium dome. Since such an expanse of ceiling plaster on wooden lathing, without help from below, was practically impossible, wire lathing was used for the first time on record.

From Washington Street, spectators entered a long, elegant inclined vestibule whose walls supported a finely arched ceiling. Midway were two ticket offices set into the wall on the right. Next one entered the inner vestibule and turning to the right, spectators passed under arched doorways and into the spacious parquette lobby. At its far end was a saloon and retiring room for ladies. Arches at one's left led to a "parquette corridor," walled on both sides, which ran around the outside of the auditorium. Narrow doors opened to each aisle, and one could only see into the theatre through small windows in each door.

Directly opposite was a solid oak grand staircase, with heavy railings resting on open panel work, which rose, between Scaglioli columns 16 feet apart, a few steps to a broad landing. There the staircase split into two nine-foot-wide branches winding gracefully back and upward to the dress circle lobby. A magnificent bronze chandelier was suspended from the decorated canopied ceiling over the landing, where a large mirror reflected the ascending patrons.

Directly behind the heads of the staircases were arches affording entrance to the dress circle corridor, along which narrow doors opened to the various aisles, as in the level below. At either side of the dress circle lobby were handsome drawing rooms, and at the dress circle's north end was a grand promenade saloon 46 feet long, 26 feet wide, and 26 feet high.

The second balcony and the gallery or amphitheatre were reached from the great spiral staircase. Each level had its own lobby and restrooms; the uppermost also had a refreshment saloon.

The parquette and each circle tier featured a corridor that extended around the auditorium, allowing numerous entrances and exits to the seats and their ends held small stairs to the proscenium boxes and fire exits to Mason Street. Foot-thick outer walls were painted to resemble stonework.[1] A 12-foot side passage from the parquette corridor connected with an entrance off Mason Street.

The auditorium was 90 feet in diameter, circular yet slightly flattening toward the stage. The distance from the main curtain to the rear of the parquette was 80

The second Boston Theatre's Washington Street entrance had a wood front designed to look like stone (The Harvard Theatre Collection, The Houghton Library).

feet; ceiling height was 54 feet. A space of 10 to 12 feet on the edge of the parquette, nearly parallel with the front curve of the first tier, was separated from the main seating and slightly raised. The entire parquette floor was constructed in a dishing form varying several feet.

First and second balconies rose in horseshoe shape and were topped by the gallery. Hanging in front and a little below the first or dress circle was a light balcony containing two rows of seats. Each tier had 11 boxes in its center, separate from the remainder of its circle. The gallery floor extended back over the corridors below, affording a greater number of seats.

STAGE AND AUDITORIUM OF THE BOSTON THEATRE.

A view of the second Boston Theatre's auditorium before the chandelier. Note the "digital clock" over the proscenium (The Harvard Theatre Collection, The Houghton Library).

In the parquette and the light balcony were iron-framed chairs cushioned on the back, seat, and arms; the seat rose automatically when not in use. The first and second tiers had oak-framed sofas covered with crimson plush while the gallery seats were iron framed and cushioned.

Auditorium walls were done in deep red shades, the frescoed ceiling embraced in its design an allegorical representation of the 12 months, and decorative ornaments were richly gilded. Lighting was from wall brackets and a circular gas "Sunburner" in the dome. On January 2, 1860, a replacement great chandelier was hung. A large "digital-like" clock was part of the upper proscenium arch and consisted of two square openings through which were seen the faces of two vertical white cylinders, bearing the hour and minute figures. These cylinders revolved with a noticeable click, and showed a change of time, one of them hourly, the other every five minutes.

The stage area was below Mason Street level and was 67 feet in depth from main curtain, and from the footlights was 85 feet as its stage thrust 18 feet into the auditorium. The proscenium opening was 48 feet wide by 41 feet high; depth below stage

More views of the second Boston Theatre, this time including the chandelier (The Harvard Theatre Collection, The Houghton Library).

was 30 feet and above was 66 feet to the fly level. Heavy brick walls and a fireproof safety curtain of iron network, balanced by weights and operable from either side of the stage, separated this vast space from the auditorium. At stage left was a green room 18 feet by 34 feet, a star dressing room, the manager's apartments, and a small property room. Above were the actors' dressing rooms with water, heat and necessary conveniences. The next level was the wardrobe room.

On the other side of the stage were additional dressing rooms and a property storeroom above. Across the back of the stage were the paint-works, under front stage were the orchestra's rooms, behind them were quarters for the supernumeraries, below were two or three stories of cellars. Boilers and steamworks were in an outside building; double stage doors for horses and scenery, big enough for carriages, opened from the Mason Street wall. Private doors for actors and an audience entrance were at the corner of the stage building nearest West Street (to the north); a 23-foot-wide passage led to the parquette corridor. The entire structure, from Mason to Washington streets, was built on pillars over a cellar ten feet deep, which furnished a storeroom of great capacity for scenery, properties, etc.

The architects were E.C. and J.E. Cabot, with Jonathan Preston, working from a prize-winning design by H. Noury. The theatre covered 26,149 square feet of land and enjoyed a seating capacity of 3,140 as late as 1901.

Alexander Corbett, Jr., writing in *Bostonian Magazine*, explains more about theatres of the period:

> The pit had but recently been abolished in local playhouses, and there still existed much of the ancient prejudice against the occupants of the lower floor, whom Hamlet so contemptuously refers to as "groundlings, caring only for inexplicable dumb show and noise...." Admission to the parquet, as the orchestra of today was then called, was only fifty cents; the balcony seats, at one dollar, being esteemed more highly, and being the highest priced seats in the house, with the exception of the stage boxes which were six dollars.... It was not until about 1868 that the lower floor became known as the orchestra, and the seats were sold for one dollar.
>
> For many years colored people did not have the same privileges as white folks, as the following announcement from an old program of the house indicates: "A box in the second tier (family circle) has been assigned to colored persons, who can only be admitted that part of the house."
>
> At the time the Boston Theatre was built it was the custom of the local playhouses to have a bar-room on the third tier, corresponding with the family circle of today [1894], and one of the abuses cited by opponents of the drama was the presence, on this tier, of women with more finery than modesty, who frequently exercised a sufficiently fascinating influence upon men in other parts of the house to draw them up to that floor between the acts. Showing a coupon for a seat on the lower floor was sufficient to admit a man to the bar-room floor, and it was said that male escorts often excused themselves to their fair charges, on the plea of wanting to see a man outside, just as they do today, but that they spent the intermission chatting with the women upstairs.
>
> This abuse was not allowed in the new [Boston] theatre, but a harmless substitute for the old bar-room was adopted in the shape of a refreshment bar in the ladies' saloon.... Here ice cream, temperance drinks, and such refreshments were served. A similar affair, though on a more modest scale, occupied a large room on the family circle floor, for many years, peanuts being the commodity most called for.

Corbett Jr. described the grand chandelier:

> The magnificent structure ... cost something like $5,000, although it was suggested by, if not copied from, the only theatre chandelier then in this country, and which was in some Philadelphia house. It was made in that city and was placed in the Boston Theatre in 1856 [replacing the original, a simple circle of gas pipe punctured with small holes]. It had the shape of an inverted cone, was about thirty-five feet in length, and presented to the eye almost a solid mass of glittering prisms. It had nearly a thousand porcelain burners, in imitation of candles, and weighed at least a ton.
>
> It required half an hour to light it, which operation was performed with a forty-foot pole having a bunch of yarn moistened with alcohol attached to the end. The top row of burners, which could not be reached from below, was lit from above, through a hole in the ceiling. An enormous ventilator, directly above this aperture in the ceiling, carried off some of the gas and the intense heat.

As it was necessary to turn on the gas through the whole chandelier before
starting to light it, the martyrdom of the assistant, above, with his head thrust
down through the hole in the ceiling, must have been severe. In 1866, the system
of igniting gas by electricity was applied to that chandelier.[2]

The great chandelier was removed in 1890 and replaced by eight smaller clusters
of electric lights. The great glowing jewel could not find a buyer and was stored in
the attic, where it remained until the demolition of the old house.

After the grand opening, the Reverend Edward Kirk said in a sermon: "One manager recently promised his audience, in opening a new playhouse, that those beautiful walls should be polluted by no vulgarity or profaneness; and yet I find one of the
plays enacted that very evening sprinkled with many genteel oaths; beside one
sufficiently vulgar. You would think from the prize essay then read that we were going
to have a Puritan theatre here to which Cotton Mather and Elder Brewster might
consistently go. But alas! What an entertainment to begin our improving theatricals
with, "The Loan of a Lover" [and] "The Rivals," two silly coarse exhibitions.... No,
Bostonians, this kind of entertainment becomes neither you, your origin, your history, your position, nor the age of the world.... Shame, sons of Pilgrims, heirs of
American institutions, formers of America's destiny."

Thomas Barry was the first manager of the theatre. Beginning with the 1864-65
season, the real managers were Benjamin W. Thayer and Orlando Tompkins, although
it was not until 1973 that their company name was placed on the playbills. Tompkins
died November 29, 1884, after 20 years of management; Eugene Tompkins took over
his father's interest in the company. On May 31, 1901, he retired from the management of the theatre; in 1908 he completed a book, *The History of the Boston Theatre
1854-1901*.

Chapter 8

The Great Financial Panic of 1857
The Prince of Wales
Comes to Boston
1857–1861

On Monday, September 28, 1857, a great financial panic began in the country, with business failures coming daily. By October 5 there was an unprecedented crisis and banks suspended business; on October 6 a great panic occurred in New York City. The 1857-1858 season found the Boston Theatre in bad shape. Bad business continued through the 1858-1859 season and the corporation succumbed to the inevitable and was wiped out.

A new corporation was formed October 9, 1858, as the Proprietors of the Boston Theatre, with capital stocks of $125,000. On January 4, 1859, the portion of the property that included Melodeon Hall next door, was sold at auction, and there was a restriction that no theatrical entertainment could be given in the Melodeon.

Charles Francis Adams, owner of the Adams House next door, was the highest bidder, and he never built on the property. The restriction had little force because the Melodeon continued with minstrel shows[1] and other entertainments.

In 1860 the Melodeon had a churchlike flat floor auditorium, and its balcony, which ran around three sides of the auditorium, was squared. At the back of its stage, which was more like a platform, was a large organ whose pipes surround it.

In 1858 minstrel fever peaked with Pell, Huntley, and the Morris Brothers opening their own Opera House in Horticultural Hall, on School Street, "opposite the Franklin monument, next door to Parker's House." Broadway Minstrels played the Melodeon, and Ordway's Minstrels continued to perform in his hall; Christie's Minstrels played there in 1859. In August 1859 Johnny Pell, J.C. Trowbridge, and brothers Lon and Billy Morris, minstrel men all, leased Ordway Hall for their shows. December 12 newspaper ads announced "The new 1,500 seat Melodeon next door to the Boston Theatre"; J.P. Ordway was musical director, minus his "Aeolians."

In 1860 Horticultural Hall briefly became the School Street Opera House, and in November 1861 it was renamed The Boudoir, a name that was soon discarded.

In October 1860 an exhibition hall called the Aquarial Gardens moved from 21 Bromfield Street to Central Court, just off Washington Street between Avon and Central places, where it was renamed The Boston Aquarial and Zoological Gardens.

The truly spectacular event of 1860 was the October 18 visit of the Prince of Wales, Queen Victoria's eldest son, also known as H.R.H. Albert Edward, later to be King Edward VII. The Boston Theatre (at this time named the Academy of Music) was the scene of a grand ball in his honor. *Bostonian Magazine* commented about the affair:

> The alterations and decorations in the theatre, alone, represented an outlay of $10,000, the whole interior being so transformed as to lose its identity completely. The walls which had for years been criticized as being of too glaring a red, were repainted ashes of roses and pale green, a temporary floor was laid over the tops of the parquet seats, extending clear to the Mason Street wall, on a level with the stage. This floor was in sections, laid on heavy timber supports, and joined as smoothly and tightly as the best dancing-floor in the country. It could be placed in position in about twenty-four hours, and was for many years stored in the cellar, whence it was removed several times during the succeeding twenty years for use upon special occasions.
>
> An imperial tent, such as was used in olden times by monarchs upon the battle-field, covered the entire stage. It was of crimson velvet, the British royal color, the side toward the auditorium, of course was open, and through an opening in the back appeared a representation of Windsor Castle, with a fountain playing in the foreground. Three elaborate chandeliers hung from the top of the tent, and numerous smaller ones were ranged around the sides, alternating between pedestals surmounted with flowers. The sides of the proscenium arch were masked out by long mirrors.
>
> The front of the balcony was shrouded in rich, crimson velvet, having a heavy border of gold; the family circle was gay in decorations, the groundwork of which was orange velvet, and upon which festoons of flowers, and stands of American and British flags, intertwined, and shields alternately bearing three white ostrich feathers on a blue ground, the badge of the Prince. The gallery was dressed in crimson velvet dotted with golden stars, the folds caught up with bunches of flowers and pendants of blue velvet. Crimson velvet was also festooned from ceiling to cornice, in various places, with magnificent effect.
>
> The Prince's box had been especially constructed in the centre of the balcony, exactly opposite the stage. It was dome-shaped, richly hung with crimson velvet, and carpeted with the finest Wilton. Upon the top of the dome, and at each side, was placed an eagle clutching the British coat of arms. Inside were pedestals of potted plants, one of which was knocked over by Lord Lyons, the British Ambassador, during the evening, to the great merriment of the Prince, as well as the whole assemblage. The Prince's personal arms and crest were at the front of the box making the whole picture one of magnificently regal splendor. The passageways and lobbies were all carpeted with dark green, which intensified the brilliance within by contrast....
>
> There was a tremendous crush in which several women fainted, and one fell into a fit. It was said most of the women present betrayed the excitement under which they labored by flushed faces, wild eyes, and more or less disarranged

The Aquarial Gardens

THE LEARNED SEALS.

☞ This intensely interesting Exhibition has lately received very important additions, namely,

A LIVING PELICAN, from the Gulf of Mexico.

That rare and interesting animal, the AGOUTI, from Para.

A pair of live OPOSSUMS, from Georgia.

A Magnificent living specimen of the AMERICAN GOLDEN EAGLE.

A pair of splendid AMERICAN HORNED OWLS, &c. &c.

The MARBLED SEALS astonish and delight every one by their wonderful intelligence ; they readily shake hands and bow to their friends, take a bath at the suggestion of their keeper, go through the manual exercise as seen in the cut above, and one is now taking lessons on the hand organ and exhibits remarkable proficiency.

The LIVING ALLIGATOR and all the great variety of Fish in the Glass Tanks entrance the lover of Natural History.

Also to be seen, the DEN OF SERPENTS, which contains within its transparent walls a large family of Serpents, some of which are over twelve feet in length.

Aquarial Gardens, 21 Bromfield Street.

CUTTING & BUTLER, Proprietors.

ADMITTANCE 25 CTS.   CHILDREN UNDER 10 YEARS, 15 CTS.

An 1860 broadside for the Aquarial Gardens (courtesy of Boston Public Library, Print Department).

dresses. At one time the line of carriages waiting to discharge their contents
extended from the theatre entrance nearly to Cornhill.

At half-past ten, the Prince ... entered by the main lobby and was escorted to
his box, whence, after a few minutes, he proceeded to the floor and joined the
dance, first with Mrs. Lincoln, then the Mayor's wife, and then with Mrs. Governor Banks. At midnight he was conducted to supper, which was served in the old
Melodeon ... access to which was gained by a door ... which was cut through the
wall for the occasion....[2] Before leaving America the Prince remarked that he had
a finer time in Boston than in any other place he visited.

The Boston Theatre's lore of interest for Corbett Jr. continues: "Edwin Booth
was fulfilling a star engagement at the Boston Theatre and was upon the stage at the
hour when his brother shot President Lincoln. Edwin was stopping at the residence
of Orlando Tompkins, one of the proprietors of the theatre, then living in Franklin
Square. It was at Mr. Tompkins' house that Booth received the terrible news of his
brother's insane act, and an hour or two later a kindly worded and sympathetic letter from Mr. Jarrett, the manager of the theatre, informing him of the necessity for
terminating the engagement at once."

Eugene Tompkins, in his *History of the Boston Theatre*, wrote: "Edwin Booth
returned to the Boston stage on Monday, September 3, 1866, making his first appearance after his retirement on account of the assassination of President Lincoln, in the
tragedy 'Othello,' in which he played the title role. He was received by a crowded
house, who greeted him with a spontaneous and long-continued burst of applause
which affected him almost to the point of breaking down."

The Boston Theatre name had been changed in 1859 to the Boston Academy of
Music; grand opera was a featured attraction of the 1859-1860 season. Under the management of Wyzeman Marshall in 1862 the name Boston Theatre was restored for all
time.

Chapter 9

Minstrels, Aquariums and a New Boston Museum
The Second Tremont Theatre and the Selwyn
1861–1873

In 1861, Ordway Hall became Morris Brothers, Pell and Trowbridge's Opera House. The Boston Aquarial and Zoological Gardens offered a theatrical season in which our old trouper, Professor Harrington, appeared. The Massachusetts Horticultural Society moved from its home on School Street into Amory Hall on Washington Street at the corner of West Street.

An interesting transformation took place in June 1862. Boston Aquarial and Zoological Gardens became P.T. Barnum's Aquarial Gardens replete with a museum, a professor, and a lecture hall. The old management packed up its finny attractions and moved to Summer and Chauncy streets, where in December it opened a New Boston Aquarial and Zoological Gardens. (Both of these gardens will become theatres in due course.)

P.T. Barnum's Museum and Aquarial Gardens, with dramas and "Fairy Spectacles," was defunct by summer 1863, and the owners of the site renamed it Andrews Hall and offered it for rent. By July 1863 the New Boston Aquarial and Zoological Gardens (at Summer and Chauncy streets) had become the New Minstrel Hall or Buckley's New Minstrel Hall. "Aquarial Gardens" was tacked onto the name from time to time.

The most interesting occasion of 1863 was the opening of the second Tremont Theatre. About 1860, the Studio Building had been constructed at No. 110 Tremont Street at Bromfield. Allston Hall was one of several within the structure; most likely it was in the leg created by the absorption of Bumstead Place. It was also known as old Bumstead Hall, whose space had been used for minstrel and other shows in 1861 and 1862. In 1863 it was taken over by producer Jane English and renamed the New Tremont Theatre, advertising a parquette, family circle, and private boxes. This short-lived playhouse reverted back to Allston Hall in 1865.

In October 1864 the Morris Brothers were burned out of the Opera House, and a benefit was held for them at the Boston Theatre. They were able to rebuild their house and open again in 1866.

In 1865 Horticultural Hall moved again to the building at Tremont and Bromfield streets, the site of the first Boston Museum, opposite the Studio Building.

Andrews Hall came to life that year with minstrel shows. On October 28 it was renamed the Theatre Comique, advertising its entrance at 240 Washington Street, although it was still in Central Court, just off that main thoroughfare.

In 1866 the Morris Brothers built a new theatre, the Continental, at Washington and Bennett streets. This out-of-the-way house had a parquet, balcony, and gallery. It went through several name changes in 1868, Willard's Theatre and Olympic Theatre, in 1871 Saint James Theatre, and after 1873 the Continental Clothing Factory.

The Melodeon had drifted along with sporadic minstrel shows and exhibitions until its closing in 1863 for repairs. From 1867 to 1878 it was the Melodeon Billiard Hall.[1]

The big news of 1867 was the premiere of Selwyn's Theatre, which opened during a drenching rainstorm on October 29 in the rear of buildings at Washington and Essex streets. Manager John H. Selwyn, a scenic artist and actor with the Boston Theatre, later of the Howard Athenaeum, gave his name to this showplace. From its entrance at 364 Washington Street, a lobby ran 93 feet back to a 68-foot-wide auditorium rear. To the left was the parquet floor, with its circle slightly raised, and six boxes in the rear. Above were stacked two balconies called dress and family circle, while six boxes fronted the proscenium. Walls were blue-paneled on an amber background. Parquet seats were covered in crimson satin, while upper seats were done in Bismarck damask.

Some 50 feet above was a dome beautifully frescoed with panels of amber, blue and scrollwork of the Muses, and in its center blazed a gas burning Frink's reflector chandelier, producing light and ventilation. The heat from these huge gas chandeliers was vented by a shaft to the roof, pulling fresh air into the auditorium from various outside vents, doors and windows.

Selwyn's proscenium arch was 36 feet square, its stage 65 feet deep and 63 feet wide. The new theatre boasted 118 sunken footlights, having three color reflectors of white, red, and green; 196 border lights hung above the stage. All of these gas lamps were controlled from the prompter's desk. Architect B.F. Dwight provided an iron roof, brick division walls, and ample ingress and egress; a second entrance from Essex Street to parquet rear was 12 feet wide by 60 feet long.

In February 1868, the Boston Theatre installed a new stage to house a production of *The White Fawn*, described by the *Bostonian* as one of the greatest spectacular productions of that house's history. The show used 25 trap doors and a dozen sinks—elongated and very narrow sorts of traps, extending clear across the stage, and through which the scenes of a whole setting were made to disappear beneath the stage. It was said that $100,000 was spent on the production, which had a run of 13 weeks, an enormous success for those days.

On August 10, 1868, the Howard Athenaeum became a variety theatre, and Isaac B. Rich and J.C. Trowbridge were managers and lessees. Starting January 1, 1870, Rich

Horticultural Hall moved to the site of the first Boston Museum in 1865 (photograph from the 1870s). Stores were on the ground floor, and the auditorium was on the second floor. In 1882, the new Dime Museum took over the first floor (courtesy of Boston Public Library, Print Department).

and John Stetson became partners and managers; at the end of the 1875-76 season Stetson became sole manager for two more years. Under his management the Howard became one of the country's finest and well-known variety theatres. Many future vaudeville headliners played that gothic house.

In 1869, the Theatre Comique in Central Court (off Washington Street) was renamed the Adelphi, and that old aquarium-zoo building had been rebuilt yet again to compete with Selwyn's new playhouse nearby. Porches were erected over its two main entrances, and passages to the parquet and balcony were enlarged, while its main floor was reconstructed to provide better sight lines. Auditorium décor was done in blue, gray, and buff, rear balcony walls were in the Pompeii style, while the dome treatment was in modern French fretwork of blue and gold with emblems of tragedy and comedy in relief, and the "sun chandelier" had 20 gas burners. The stage was wide at 68 feet, but its depth was only 32 feet; the proscenium, with boxes, was 31 feet wide and 26 feet high. The theatre's 500 red enameled leather chairs were not enough to make this house competitive; it could not survive and was destroyed by fire. The spot became the site of the Jordan and Marsh department store.

September 1869 ads asserted that the Howard Athenaeum was now "all new from pit to dome."[2]

The year 1870 was another year of name changes; Selwyn's was sold to Arthur Cheney and became the Globe Theatre, while the Morris Brothers Opera House was renamed the Lyceum Theatre.

About 1870 the Boston Theatre remodeled the double-walled circular corridor around its auditorium. Most modern theatres had standing room behind the seating area, allowing arriving patrons to view the auditorium. A large section of the Boston Theatre's first-floor dead wall was replaced by a row of heavy arches and pillars, resulting in a great improvement in appearance and convenience, permitting standing areas for more patrons.

Also in the 1870s, a new parquet floor was built about a foot above the old, new folding chairs were put in the lower part of the auditorium and new decorations furnished. ("Folding" meant that the seat could rise as the patrons stood.)

The Boston Museum was a little over 26 years old, and its owners felt the need to modernize to compete with newer and larger theatres. On September 21, 1872, the new house was unveiled to the public. Its façade had been cleaned, painted, and regilded where needed, and a handsome appearance was produced, especially at night, with its multitude of gas-illumined globes lined in rows across the front. The entrance was moved from the right to the left end, closest to Scollay Square. On the right was the ticket office, and just beyond rose a broad stairway giving access to the museum and the theatre. The hall of curiosities remained substantially unchanged, although one of the grand two-story columns was removed to admit construction of the new entrance. Interiors of the museum and theatre were redecorated in a most charming fashion; its exhibit hall was brilliantly re-lamped, and impressive pedestal lights were used at the floor of the grand staircase.

Most important, the auditorium had been lowered one floor and the old stair-

Opposite: The Great Boston Fire of 1872 (Library of Congress).

ways abolished. Patrons entered the theatre portion directly from the grand exhibit hall level. *Bostonian Magazine* called this "a most important and useful change.... Visitors on climbing the steep stairs from the street to the exhibition room did not have their cheerfulness materially increased by this second ascent."

The old flat-floored, shelflike gallery was replaced with a horseshoe-curved stepped balcony, with a new gallery above it. The parquet and parquet circle were revamped to improve sight lines, and the improved ventilation was heartily praised by patrons. The museum's stage had a new wide proscenium; three new private boxes were at each side. Old grooves for holding scenery on stage were gone and the museum now had a fly loft. Seating capacity was 643 for the orchestra, 404 for the balcony, 365 for the gallery, for a total of 1,462 with side boxes. The proscenium was 34 feet wide by 28 feet high. Footlights to the rear stage wall was 44 feet, with the height to gridiron or loft rigging 49 feet. John A. Fox was architect of the remodeling.

A Boston newspaper commented: "There is hardly a recognizable feature of the old establishment left, and the new chairs are a decided improvement over the usual mode.... The decorations are strikingly handsome and appropriate, the idea of a blue sky with fleecy clouds floating across being admirably executed, and scarcely less worthy of commendation is the work on the upper part of the proscenium. The colors employed in the decorations are rich and harmonious, and the private boxes are models of elegance both inside and out. A novel improvement is the sinking of the orchestra under the stage, and the music was distinctly heard as though the performers were in their old position. A thorough inspection and complete observation confirms our opinion that the acoustic properties of the new auditorium are well nigh perfect. Three curtains were displayed, the first of green, the second new act drop by Mr. Phil W. Goatcher, and a fire-proof curtain of iron gauze."

On May 30, 1873, the Globe Theatre (Selwyn's) was destroyed by the old enemy of fire, and plans were immediately drawn for a larger and finer replacement.[3] The destruction of this playhouse inspired the creation of a new venture almost directly across Washington Street.

In the rear of buildings fronting on the west side of that thoroughfare was a large space once used as a riding school, now vacant. One gained access from Washington Street by way of a narrow passage along the north side to this open area, which was some 60 feet wide and 100 feet long. Buildings on both sides of the lot, plus those on Washington Street, practically enclosed the area and became the walls of the new Beethoven Hall. A brick back stage was constructed along the alley open space, Bumstead Court, while a small building was built over the latter, supported by iron trusswork, to become a waiting room for performers and quarters for the janitor. An amply windowed wall was erected behind the Washington Street buildings to complete Beethoven Hall, which opened in 1873.

Patrons approached it along the old carriage passage. The last 30 feet leading to the entrance doors were open to the sky. Once inside Beethoven Hall, ticket office and cloakrooms were on the first floor. Two staircases leading to the second level hall were handsomely finished with black walnut railings and continued to the gallery.

The house was flat-floored, about 60 feet wide by 94 feet long. The 19-foot-deep stage was at the west end (whose rear wall ran at an angle), and décor was in the Gre-

The remodeled Boston Museum in 1872. The entrance was moved to the left (Library of Congress).

cian style of brown, light blue, and red tints. It was advertised the Beethoven Hall could accommodate 1,550 patrons. Early attractions were minstrel shows, variety shows, and French drama, along with an appearance by Buffalo Bill; in October the Howard's John Stetson presented a vaudeville troupe.

Daniel Frohman, in his autobiography, *Daniel Frohman Presents*, described his early years as an advance agent for the Georgia Minstrels' engagement at Beethoven Hall:

> We opened the new Beethoven Hall. I did not have a cent of cash for advertising the minstrels. It had to be done on credit. But I gambled on taking plenty of newspaper space; in fact about five times as much as road companies were in the habit of taking. When the big business began to begin, we could meet this obligation easily. Another idea we used was to hire space for billboards in front of new

Top: The renovated Boston Museum's Tremont Street entrance hall, in a photograph circa 1890. *Left:* The Boston Museum, facing stage and boxes (both courtesy of Boston Public Library, Print Department).

buildings being put up on Washington and Tremont streets, a novelty at that time.

Also I set out to induce some public figures to come and see the show and tell me what they thought about it. As a result, I got testimonials from such a miscellany of the famous as Oliver Wendell Holmes, William Lloyd Garrison, P.T. Barnum, and Clara Louise Kellogg.

Chapter 10

Abbey and Schoeffel Meet John Stetson Head-On

The Park Theatre Is Built in Fifty Days

1874–1879

The new Globe Theatre opened on December 4, 1874. Highlights started with Washington Street front doors of black walnut encasing large plates of glass cut to represent terrestrial globes. The auditorium was decorated in a salmon tint; walls had stenciled figures in brown and gold, hanging above was an immense chandelier of crystal prisms and pendants. The new Globe was larger than its predecessor: Its parquet was 74 feet long by 72½ feet wide, and height to the dome was 65 feet. The house used an innovation in seating arrangements: a row of boxes separated the first balcony from the second, and a family circle was above the latter. Capacity was 825 in the parquet, 475 in the balcony, 650 in the second balcony and family circle for a total seating of 2,180. A 48-foot by 50-foot proscenium fronted a stage 84 feet wide, 55 feet deep, and 75 feet high, with a 25-foot depth.

The year 1875 was uneventful, but 1876 saw the New Boylston Museum open at 667 Washington Street* opposite Beach, an upstairs house not to be confused with Boylston Hall, which had been next door to the north, over the market. The *Boston Post* called it "a cozy little theatre." Star Novelty Theatre was added to its name in 1877.

An amusing incident occurred in April 1877 at the Boston Theatre. During a performance of *Medea*, a young Theodore Roosevelt was ejected from the gallery for creating a disturbance. He was a student at Harvard and was running for one of the secret societies and had been ordered, as part of his initiation, to go into the upper gallery in evening dress and applaud vociferously in all quiet scenes, which he did faithfully. The beginning of his "bully pulpit"?

*Street numbers changed on Washington and the other streets after the Great Boston Fire of 1872, so they may differ from previously mentioned addresses.

The Boylston Hall and Market, at 657–667 Boylston Street (photograph by Baldwin Coolidge, courtesy of Boston Public Library, Print Department).

In November 1877, John Stetson left the Howard Athenaeum to manage the Globe Theatre, and that event would inspire creation of another new theatre.

In 1878, the lower floor, under the auditorium of Beethoven Hall, was leased to G.B. Bunnell for a 15-cent admission museum advertising "a tattooed Greek, a living skeleton, a 635 pound fat boy, dwarfs, albinos, 'The Man of Many Faces,' and 'London Ghosts.'"

The old Melodeon had left show business after 1866, becoming a billiard hall and barbershop. However, on October 15, 1878, it was resurrected as the Gaiety Theatre. *King's Handbook of Boston* described the new house: "It is an attractive and comfortable little theatre, and by reason of its small size is admirably adapted for comedy; the performers being easily seen and heard from every part of the house. It will seat about 800 persons, 500 on the floor, and 300 in the balcony, and has standing room for an additional 200. The auditorium has a bright, cheerful appearance, and the decoration is tasteful. The walls and ceiling are paneled in pink, with buff, gold and purple borders; and the balcony fronts are in bronze, gray, and pink. The stage is 60 feet wide and 30 deep, and the proscenium opening as a width of 32, a height of 38, and a clear opening of 28 feet. The prices range from $1 to 35 cents."

The Gaiety opened with an operatic extravaganza and Salisbury's Troubadours.

J. Wentworth was lessee and manager. The Gaiety operated through 1882, at 545 Washington Street.

Early in 1879, New York theatrical managers Henry E. Abbey and John B. Schoeffel came to Boston with the intent to negotiate a lease for the Globe Theatre, whose owner had died. The impresarios were dismayed to find that manager Stetson was in full control of the theatre, having purchased land on Hayward Place, which ran directly through the Globe's auditorium.

Stetson was a tough but well-liked showman, seasoned by his variety years at the Howard Athenaeum. Actor Otis Skinner wrote that Stetson "was the male Mrs. Malaprop of the theatrical world.: This big, bass, blustering individual had sprung from street life in Boston to the position of prosperous manager. His usual manner was that of a war tank."

A newspaper of the time, commenting on his new Globe Theatre, gives us an idea of Stetson's ploy to

Actor-playwright Otis Skinner, in costume as Hajj in the play *Kismet* (courtesy of Boston Public Library, Print Department).

gain control of the house: "A scene room has long been needed, and, to obtain this, Mr. Stetson has leased the estate on Hayward Place adjoining the stage, and cut through the partition wall a lofty doorway (supplied with an iron door), through which flats can easily be run. The new room thus obtained is 100 feet long, 25 feet wide, and 21 feet high (one foot higher than the flats), and through its center a broad pathway will always be kept clear to afford firemen direct entrance from Hayward Place to the stage, in case of fire. The apartments over the scene room are to be used for wardrobes and storage purposes."[1]

Undaunted by Stetson's ploy, Abbey and Schoeffel went across the street and leased Beethoven Hall, also renting a storefront on Washington Street to provide a new lobby and entrance. Within 50 days they had constructed the Park Theatre within the walls and roof of the hall. The playhouse opened on April 14, 1879, advertising parquet, parquet circle, two balconies and four proscenium boxes.

Moses King, writing in *King's Handbook of Boston*, describes the house:

> The auditorium is 60 feet wide, 63 feet from the stage to the doors, and 50 feet high. On the lower floor are the orchestra stalls and parquet (which comprise the

whole section of the lower floor inside the circle rail), and the orchestra circle (the seats outside the iron columns supporting the dress circle). The first balcony is the dress circle and the "balcony" so called (the first two rows being thus designated), and the second balcony the family circle and gallery. The house seats 1,184. Its interior decorations are tasteful and elegant; and its seats are richly upholstered, roomy, and comfortable, and are so arranged as to afford an unobstructed view of the stage from each. There are four attractive proscenium boxes. The performances are furnished chiefly by "stars" and leading dramatic companies. Henry E. Abbey and John B. Schoeffel are the managers, who also managed the Park Theatre and the Casino in New York. The Park is amply provided with exits, and can be cleared of a large audience in a few minutes. Prices of admission from 50 cents to $1.50.

Chapter 11

The First "Movies" and Summer Theatres
The Boston Bijou and Thomas Alva Edison
1879–1882

On August 11, 1879, the Tremont Temple burned for the second time, and reconstruction commenced almost immediately.

Also in 1879, Institute Hall in the Roxbury district of Boston, at Washington and Dudley streets, became the Dudley Street Opera House. The interior had been altered to conform to the requirements of a theatre. The Dudley had an inclined floor, with opera chairs to seat 700 patrons, and its walls were tinted in a fine salmon color with light brown trim. The ceiling was done in light blue, finely frescoed, and there were three crystal chandeliers. A gilt medallion was at each side of the proscenium, one of music and the other of drama, and its stage was small but sufficient.

In March 1880 a hall over Williams Market, at Washington and Dover streets, became known as Hooley's Theatre (it had briefly been known as the Novelty Theatre).

Horticultural Hall, with its small proscenium stage, offered 40 artists in *The Magic Slipper*, an operatic burlesque. The new owner, like the previous ones, presented theatricals from time to time.

October 17, 1880, saw the opening of the third Tremont Temple, greater and grander.

On April 11, 1881, the Novelty Theatre, formerly Hooley's Theatre or Williams Hall, offered operettas and plays, and shortly afterward was renamed the Windsor Theatre.

In 1881, *King's Handbook of Boston* listed several summer theatres. Halleck's Alhambra at South Boston Point, on East 6th Street, near P, was built by Thomas E. Halleck in the spring of 1880. It was a wooden structure, originally used as a skating-rink; in altering it for employment as a theatre, an inclining floor was adopted. It seated 1,600 and was chiefly a summer theatre, presenting novelty and variety performances.

67

Summer-garden theatres were established in 1879 and 1880. The principal ones were Forest Garden, on the Egleston Square line of the Metropolitan Street Railway, and Oakland Garden, on the Highland Street Railway, both in the Roxbury district. These were lightly built for summer only. The performances were of the variety order or light English opera.

An undated newspaper clipping details one summer's openings:

> The first of the summer theatres to throw open its gates to the public is that at Forest Garden. A description of the improvements made at this popular resort has already been published, and it is only necessary to say that, beside the numerous changes for the better in the grounds, the stage has been greatly enlarged and fitted with all modern appliances, and the natural amphitheatre in front has been provided with new and better seats, and covered with an awning. In the evening at 8 o'clock, the first regular stage performance will occur, the piece being a new, spectacular and musical extravaganza, entitled "Jewels." In this will appear Miss Daisy Ramsden's English extravaganza combination and Saville's English ballet troupe of 24 "coryphecs," and 50 "figurantes" led by Mme. Adele Cornalba. New scenery, gorgeous costumes and accessories are promised and the vocal music will be rendered by selected artists and a chorus of 50. At the close of the performance there will be a grand display of fireworks.
>
> The opening of Halleck's Alhambra at City Point has been postponed ... in order to afford time for the completion of the extensive improvements in progress. These include a reconstruction and enlargement of the stage, the building of a new balcony, the inclining of the floor, and the redecoration of the entire auditorium. The season will be inaugurated by a large pantomime, specialty, and a comedy company.
>
> At Oakland Garden, the improvements are progressing rapidly, and everything will be in order for the opening on May 30. The floor of the pavilion has been inclined and provided with new seats, the stage much enlarged and rebuilt.... The opening attraction will be Haverly's colored minstrels, 100 strong, who will give a performance every afternoon and evening during their engagement. The new arrangement whereby round-trip and admission tickets will be sold on the New York and New England [railway], at the same rates as the horse cars, promises to be a great advantage to the garden. A new entrance has been constructed directly opposite the Mt. Bowdoin station of this road. The Highland Street railway will shortly put on 10 new open cars to run to the garden.
>
> Mr. Frank P. Stone, lessee of the Webster Garden, Washington Street, Dorchester district, has nearly completed arrangements for opening for the season. A high fence has been built around the entire grounds, and inside everything has been done to add to the pleasure and convenience of visitors. A menagerie, consisting of 40 cages of animals, will be presented as an opening attraction.
>
> The Forest Hill Garden in Fall River will be opened on Wednesday, June 15. Excursions, speeches, fireworks, etc., will make the occasion a gala day for the city.
>
> The "Cyclopedia of Boston and Vicinity, 1886" provides us with a unique playhouse, "The Germania Theatre or 'Turn Halle'" is at 27 Middlesex Street between Castle and Dover Street. A pretty little theatre, where performances, in the German Language, are frequently given during the season, largely by ama-

teurs, although tickets are offered for sale to the general public. Prices are usually 50 and 25 cents.

Gray's National Theatre opened on Chardon Street, opposite the Revere House. This hall offered variety shows and should not be confused with the old National Theatre, which burned down about 1865. This new house lasted only a few years.

Four events of 1882 are worthy of notice. Horticultural Hall leased space to a Dime Museum under its second-floor auditorium.

In October, Union Hall, on Boylston Street, presented "The Zoopraxiscope," invented by photographer Eadweard Muybridge. This was a series of timed photographs, made into transparencies. The device projected moving creatures on a screen "by electric light" and was the immediate ancestor of the motion picture.

Terry Ramsaye described it in his 1926 book, *A Million and One Nights*: "The machine consisted of a revolving glass disc on which transparencies were mounted, with an opaque shutter disc with slots corresponding to the pictures revolving in the opposite direction. With a light source behind the disc and a projecting lens in front of the shutter, the controlled coincidence of picture and shutter opening on the line of illumination permitted a glimpse of a phase of motion to be cast on the screen, only to be supplanted at once by another. The optical results were wonderful then, but distressing to consider in the light of today's screen."

In September 1882, George E. Lothrop took over the New Boylston Museum on Washington Street; in October he assumed management of the Windsor Theatre in the South End at Dover and Washington streets; he had big plans. A newspaper ad for the upstairs Windsor proclaimed: "The Equine Paradox! Prof. Bartholomew's 16 educated horses, 16, all appearing at one time on the stage, during more than two hours delightful performance, entirely untrammeled by harness... ALL OF THE HORSES WILL WALK UPSTAIRS!"[1] Famous actress Kate Claxton appeared on October 16 in her famous *Two Orphans* melodrama.

In 1882, Fred Vokes, of the popular Vokes family of performers, initiated the remodeling of the old Melodeon structure, last known as the Gaiety Theatre, into a modern playhouse, in association with George W. Tyler. Vokes dropped out after the opening, then the theatre was named the Bijou and Tyler became manager.

The big news of 1882 was the opening of the Boston Bijou Theatre on December 11, as it premiered the D'Oyly Carte–Savoy Theatre of London production of *Iolanthe*. Premiere seats had been sold at auction. The old Lion–Mechanics Hall–Melodeon-Gaiety had been gutted. Nothing remained of the former theatre except the four walls, and those had been extensively raised to accommodate the height required for the new playhouse.

The Bijou auditorium was eight-sided, with two long parallel sides, one against the Adams House wall, the other against the Boston Theatre. A connection with the front building was by way of three well-concealed iron bridges, stretching 15 to 20 feet between the two structures.

One entered from 545 Washington Street. The former single entrance was made to appear wider by recessing, at an angle, part of the store adjoining it on the north side, and thus another set of doors could be added, with the box office on the left.

DEDICATED DEC. 11TH 1882.   BOSTON BIJOU THEATRE   GEO. H. TYLER, MANAGER.

The Bijou was the first theatre in the United States with electric lights. Thomas Edison supervised the installation (The Harvard Theatre Collection, The Houghton Library).

A new six-foot-side stairway was added on the north side of the original ten-foot stairway, thus two easy staircases rose from a small vestibule to the foyer. At the head of the staircases, to the left, was access to the ladies' parlor, a handsome apartment that fronted on Washington Street, and to the right were offices, the men's room, and a passage from the rear balcony exit stairway. One passed from the upwardly sloped foyer through heavy drapes into another world.

To right and left were stairways to the single balcony, but the patron's eyes were riveted to the beauty of the Moorish style auditorium where fine Arabesque designs graced the walls.[2] Above an almost circular proscenium arch was a painted frieze of

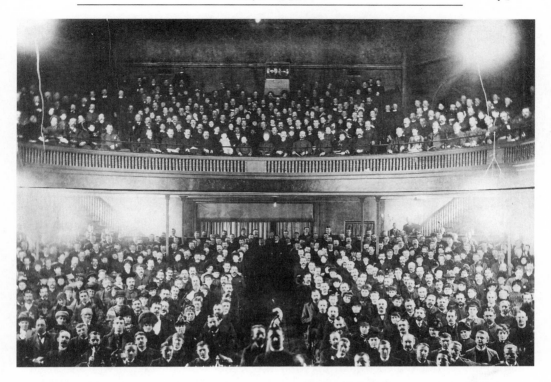

An 1885 photo of the audience, taken from the Bijou stage (The Harvard Theatre Collection, The Houghton Library).

the Fairy Queen, Titania. The warm bronze-tinted glow of both walls and dome was created by a "metalized" stucco of gold, silver, and copper. From the ceiling hung metallic chandeliers left over from an order manufactured by Verity Brothers for the Khedive of Egypt. The pearl-shell sweep of the balcony to the unusual proscenium arch blended with the rich harmony of ornamentation.

The Bijou was the first theatre in the united States to use electric lighting on its stage, personally installed and supervised by Thomas Alva Edison.

In an interview with the *Boston Post* in 1882, Edison admitted that he had hardly slept during the difficult task of fitting up his first theatre: "Well, this theatre business is a new one to us. Now if it was a cotton factory, I would feel at home; but I acknowledge I have been somewhat anxious as to this experiment."

The Bijou boasted 644 electric lights, each equivalent to a 25-watt bulb today and 190 were located in the unusual horseshoe proscenium. That arch had an inner concave trough lined with tin which held a series of three independent light sets of 64 instruments each. Similar reflector lined concave troughs held 144 more lamps on moveable battens above the stage. Bunch lights which were floor mounted boxes, held nine or more lamps.

The Bijou had the help of a Gilbert and Sullivan hit to attract audiences, and while the production received a mixed critical response, the electric lighting was a universal success. The *Boston Globe* was typical in proclaiming: "Never have we seen a steadier and softer light in a theatre than that given by Edison's incandescent burners." The *Boston Advertiser* noted: "It was a remarkably pleasant light, and the noticeable thing about it was the absence of the ordinary bluish tint."

A later press review commented: "The freedom from impure air gained by the use of the electric light will confer incalculable benefits upon the audiences, and the perfect safety insured by its use will give an added sense of security to all patrons."

However, not everyone was content with the removal of stage footlights. One backstage account suggests that "the Bijou's experiment with the elimination of footlights came to at least a temporary halt early in the run of 'Iolanthe.' The suffering caused by the arc of brilliant lights to those on the stage can hardly be realized. The effect was like that of a dozen "calciums" [lights] shining directly into one's eyes. For weeks after my first experience of them, I saw that gleaming little wire constantly before me. The new theatre, the new opera and the electric lighting were all successful, but at the end of the first week the footlights were restored. This was not done for our comfort, but because better stage effects were obtained with them. They seem to be a necessary dividing line between audience and player, in order to put the latter fully at his ease, and their absence on the first night of 'Iolanthe' was most confusing.

Otis Skinner, in *Footlights and Spotlights*, commented: "The scene today, lighted in chiaroscuro worthy of a Rembrandt, would have seemed an incredible attainment in my beginnings when gas footlights and borders, together with the illumination of the blended calcium gas from iron cylinders placed in the wings, changed scenes from daylight to sunset and to moonlight. But now the soft mellow beauty of stage lighting has evolved so gradually from those hot wiggly little wires of the first incandescent lights that it is not a matter of wonder to an audience how these things have come about."

Olive green upholstered seats accommodated 550 patrons in the orchestra (no longer called parquet or parquette) and 400 in the balcony. A single highly ornamented Moorish box was at each side of the stage, almost at floor level.

The Bijou was much praised for its safety features. All plaster was laid on wire, layers of cement separated orchestra and stage floors from the ground floor. The 36-foot-wide proscenium arch was coated with magneso calcite, the stage was protected by a sprinkler system and its walls were lined with fireblocks. At the top of the 65-foot-high stage house were ten large skylights, which could be thrown open from the prompter's box; in case of fire, the draught thus created would draw the flames and smoke upward, away from the audience. The stage roof was 35 feet higher than the dome of the auditorium. The Bijou had 13 exits, including two from the stage and one leading to Mason Street via Bradford Place. The Bijou never had a fire.

The stage was an ample 29½ feet deep by 55 feet wide. There were no fly levels above it, and wing space was limited. Three dressing rooms were on stage, and others were below. New counterbalanced wire rope rigging was used. The architect was George H. Wetherell, interior decoration was by E.P. Treadwell, and N.J. Bradlee and Company did reconstruction work.

BOSTON THEATRE,
539 Washington St.

LAST WEEK OF

Miss Margaret Mather

In the following selections from
her repertoire:

THE HUNCHBACK
[*JULIA*],

Monday and Wednesday Evenings, Feb. 18 and 20.

Romeo and Juliet
[*JULIET*],

Tuesday and Saturday Evenings,
Feb. 19 and 23.

The Lady of Lyons
[*PAULINE*],

Thursday Evening, Feb. 21.

Leah, the Forsaken,
· [*LEAH*],

Friday Evening, Feb. 22.

MATINEES. — Friday Feb. 22,
As You Like It, Saturday Feb.
23, *The Hunchback*.

Every Evening at 7.45. Friday
and Saturday Matinees at 2.

Left: A winter week's shows at the Boston Theatre
from 1884. *Below:* An engraving of the Boston Theatre (both author's collection).

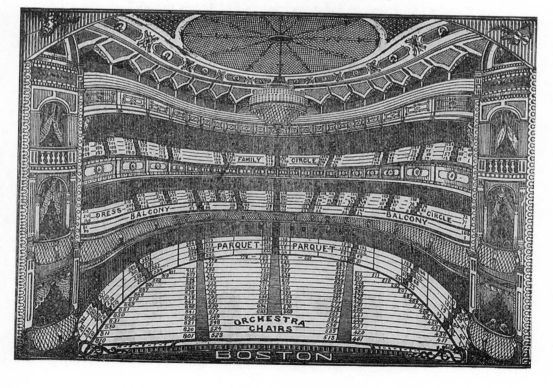

GLOBE THEATRE
598 Washington St.

Commencing Monday, Feb. 18, '84.

Mr. EDWIN BOOTH

Monday Evening, Feb. 18,
HAMLET.

Tuesday Evening, Feb. 19,
KING LEAR.

Wednesday Evening, Feb. 20,
IAGO.

Thursday Evening, Feb. 21,
The Fool's Revenge

Friday Matinee, Feb. 22,
D. H. HARKIN'S
DAMON & PYTHIAS.
At 2.

Friday Evening, Feb. 22,
MACBETH.

Saturday, Matinee, Feb. 23,
HAMLET.

Saturday Evening, Feb. 23,

D. H. HARKIN'S
RICHARD THE III.

Evenings at 7.45.   Matinees at 2.

Above: A winter week's shows at the Globe Theatre from 1884. *Opposite:* An engraving of the Globe Theatre (both author's collection).

PARK ❋ THEATRE

619 Washington St.

COMMENCING

Monday, February 18, 1884.

MR. & MRS.

McKEE RANKIN

Will appear in their

NEW PLAY,

GABRIEL

CONROY,

A dramatization of Bret Harte's charming story of the same name.

Every Evening at 7.45.

FRIDAY AND

Saturday Matinees at 2.

Above: A winter week's shows at the Park Theatre from 1884. *Opposite:* An engraving of the Park Theatre (both author's collection).

BIJOU ✸ THEATRE

545 Washington St.

Monday, Feb. 18,
Tuesday, Feb. 19,
Wednesday and
Wed. Matinee, Feb. 20,

The Beggar
Student.

Thursday, Feb. 21,
Friday, Feb. 22,
Saturday, Feb. 23,
Friday Matinee at 1.45.

Suppi's Latest

OPERA COMIQUE,

A TRIP TO AFRICA.

EVERY EVENING 7.45,

MATINEES AT 1.45

Left: A winter week's shows at the Bijou Theatre from 1884. *Below:* An engraving of the Bijou Theatre (both author's collection).

BIJOU THEATRE BOSTON

BOSTON MUSEUM

Tremont Street.

Second Week, commencing
Feb. 18.

PRINCESS
IDA;

Or, Castle Adamant.

Charming Scenery!

Elaborate

and Unique Costumes,

AND AN

ADMIRABLE CAST!

MATINEES,

Wednesday Friday and Saturday
at 2.

Every Evening at 7.45.

Right: A winter week's shows at the Boston Museum from 1884. *Below:* An engraving of the Boston Museum (both author's collection).

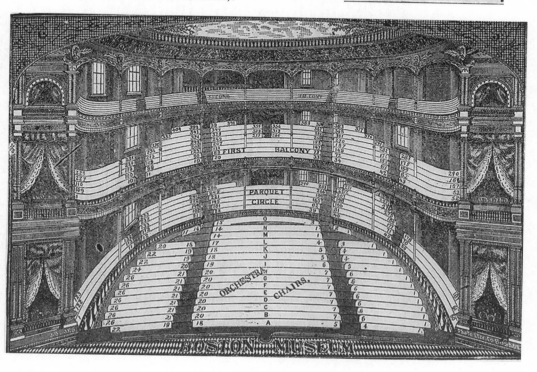

HOWARD ATHENÆUM.

34 Howard St.

ONE WEEK

Commencing Feb. 18th.

Harry G. Richmond

"Up To The Times"

COMBINATION.

Matinee Feb. 22d,

Washington's Birthday,

At 2 o'clock, P. M.

Evenings at 7.45.
Wednesday and Saturday
Matinees at 2.

Sunday Ev'g, Feb. 24th,

A GRAND TESTIMONIAL BENEFIT

Concert tendered to

WILLIAM O'BRIEN.

Above: A winter week's shows at the Howard Athenaeum from 1884. *Opposite:* An engraving of the Howard Athenaeum (both author's collection).

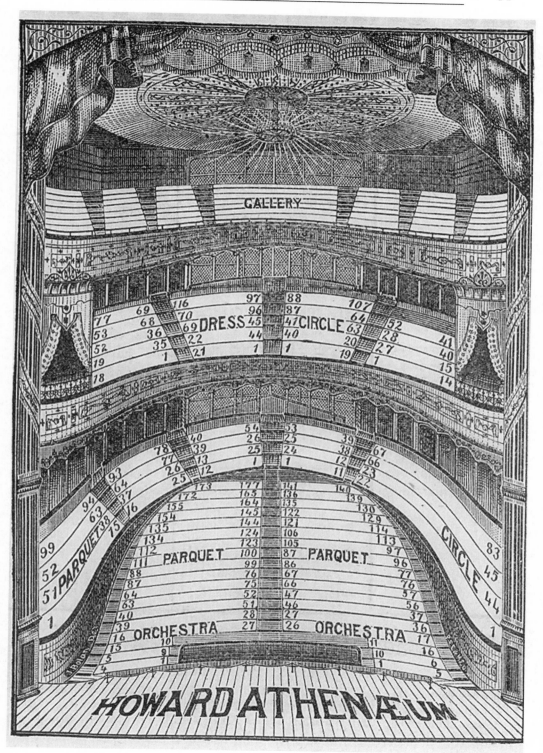

TREMONT TEMPLE.
80 Tremont St.

Tuesday Feb. 19,

8 P.M.

MUSICAL

RECITAL

— BY —

MR. and MRS.

Georg Henschel.

Above: A winter week's shows at the Tremont Temple from 1884. *Opposite:* An engraving of the Tremont Temple (both author's collection).

MUSIC ✛ HALL,

17 Winter St.

SYMPHONY REHEARSALS.

Thursday, Feb. 21st,
Afternoon at 2.30.

—

STODDARD MATINEES.

Saturday, Feb. 23, at 2.30

SUBJECT,

PASSION ✛ PLAY.

—

MR. GEO. HENSCHEL'S

TWENTIETH SYMPHONY CONCERT,

Saturday Eve, Feb. 23,
at 8 P. M.

—

Single Seats for sale at Cashin's Theatre Ticket Office, Young's Hotel.

Above: A winter week's shows at the Boston Music Hall from 1884. *Opposite:* An engraving of the Boston Music Hall (both author's collection).

Chapter 12

Benjamin Franklin Keith
Comes to Boston
Battle of the Museums
The Hollis Street Theatre
1883–1885

In 1883, Horticultural Hall presented Hermann the Magician among other attractions, while below in its auditorium, the New Dime Museum still thrived. Two more museums appeared in 1883. The Boston Dime Museum opened at 4 Tremont Row in Scollay Square, run by proprietors Messrs. Austin and Stone. On January 14, in a store at 565 Washington Street, Baby Alice, the Queen of Midgets reigned with a ten-cent admission fee. Encouraged by that royal success, the tiny store's lessees rented the entire premises and Messrs. Keith and Gardiner opened their New York Museum at 565 and 567 Washington Street on February 18, 1883. Their star attraction was the Three Headed Songstress; Benjamin Franklin Keith was a graduate of Forepaugh's Circus and its sideshow freaks.

By April 1, manager B.F. Keith advertised a "theatorium," or theatre room, on the second floor. The museum was open from 10 A.M. to 10 P.M., "conducted properly and devoid of all objectionable features ... by all means bring the children!" In September, Austin and Stone's Boston Dime Museum also advertised a "theatorium" and embarked on a heavy newspaper advertising campaign.

Austin and Stone's enterprise meandered through several buildings on the Howard Street edge of Tremont Row. Upon entering its lobby patrons noticed a realistic wax figure of a policeman standing by a ticket office, who was affectionately known as "Old Jerry." Next, visitors passed into the Grand Curio Hall, a spacious enclosure illuminated by a large skylight. Platforms lined three sides of the room; on them stood, sat, or laid the attractions, freaks, strongmen, magicians, and other wonders. The fourth side held cages of wild animals, monkeys and snakes. A lecturer led his flock of customers around the hall, pausing in front of each attraction to deliver his spiel. After one go-round patrons were guided into the theatrical portion of the museum, and the "Professor" started another group circling about the Curio Hall.

The vaudeville hall (note the increasing use of that word instead of "variety") was in the rear. Its stage had three boxes, one atop the other, at each side. This tiny auditorium contained a small parquet and two puny balcony circles. All museums featured similar layouts and style of operation, and Austin and Stone had the largest and best-known operation in Boston.

In 1883, the old Providence Railroad Station became the Park Square Garden, an arena, for large events. On June 2, 1884, Austin and Stone produced grand opera there.

In April 1884, the New York Dime Museum "adjoining the Adams House, two doors south of the Boston Theatre, owned and controlled by B. F. Keith," increased its advertising budget. By November 2 the establishment was named Keith and Batcheller's Mammoth Museum, operating continuously from 10 A.M. to 10 P.M. Its theatorium had become the Auditory, and special seats cost five cents extra. (For a brief period in 1885, this operation flirted with the name Gaiety Hall.) Its original space was 35 feet by 15 feet tapering to six feet in the rear. An upstairs lecture hall with 123 seats was added, and the museum offered a curio hall plus a one-hour performance in the hall above. An 1884 program read.

CURIOSITY HALL
BOZ, THE DOG WITH A HUMAN BRAIN
THE ELASTIC SKIN MAN
BURNHAM'S COLOSSAL TABLEAUX OF THE AMERICAN REBELLION
THE THREE HEADED SONGSTRESS
THE BURNING SHIP, marvel of mechanical ingenuity
THE HERODIAN MYSTERY, a living head without a body
ALBERT THE TALKING PARROT
MAN EATING LION SLAYERS, a Darwinian race of Samsons
JIM THE BAD MONKEY
Professor S.K. Hodgdon will at short intervals deliver an interesting lecture
Checks for reserved seats for the stage entertainment are 5 cents
Procure them on either floor

STAGE PROGRAM
CHARLIE SCHILLING, musical comedian
CHARLIE JOHNSON, Buffalo Midget
TOM BRANFORD, Dutch eccentricities, songs, dances
THE MEMPHIS SUTDENTS, Jubilee Singers
COMING SEPTEMBER 29
THE MICHIGAN COLORLESS FAMILY
Like bats and owls, these people have the use of their eyes at night only!

In 1884, Haynes and Jackson's Star Museum was advertised as showing variety at 289 Hanover Street.

On November 9, 1885, the New Boylston Museum became the World's Museum, announcing a greatly enlarged location at 661–663–665–667 Washington Street. The first floor had an aquarium, the second level held a foyer and auditorium seating 1,000

The Hollis Street Church, circa 1880, which was turned into a theatre (Library of Congress).

The Hollis Street Theatre in 1935 (Library of Congress).

patrons, the third story consisted of the balcony and two curio halls, and above all of this activity reigned a menagerie.

On November 9, 1885, top news was the opening of the 1,684-seat Hollis Street Theatre, with the American premiere of Gilbert and Sullivan's *Mikado*. Architect John R. Hall had retained the 1810 Hollis Street Church's walls that were parallel to the street, on each side of the playhouse. Additional solid brick construction, approx-

imately 20 feet at the stage and 43 feet at the entrance, lengthened the structure. Its façade retained a churchlike appearance, but the lofty arched windows were bricked up and covered with shutters.

The Hollis entrance was at the east end, closest to Washington Street. The lobby façade was of brownstone with a highly ornamental design. Numerous round columns were placed at each side of the vestibule, and fanciful scrollwork was above. Spectators passed into a lobby 44 feet deep by 18 wide, with a ticket office at the far end. Doors along the right wall gave entry to the orchestra foyer, where staircases rose to balcony and gallery. Three tiers of gilded boxes were at each side of an almost square proscenium, and an additional two boxes were at both ends of the gallery front. A gold ceiling dome had painted arabesques with eight groups of cupids.

The Hollis Street Theatre had a fine stage separated from its auditorium by 20 inches of brick wall. A 38-foot-wide arch fronted a 51-foot-deep by 73-foot-wide stage, with its gridiron 63 feet above. Dressing, green, and property rooms were in a large separate building at stage right that ran through the Common Street.

Opposite, top: The Hollis Street Theatre orchestra seating and balconies in 1885. *Bottom:* The Hollis Street Theatre boxes and stage in 1885 (both Library of Congress).

Chapter 13

The Year of the "Mikados" and the Grand Opera House

George E. Lothrop's Lady Natators

Colonel Austin and Alexander Graham Bell

1885–1889

During 1885 Keith and Batcheller observed the failures of the various Bijou managers and commenced negotiations to lease that adjacent property. Their continuous variety and curio shows were bursting out of their confined quarters, presently called the Gaiety Museum. The duo had announced that "we must either increase seating capacity or lessen attractiveness of our stage entertainment.... [W]e positive renounce ... the latter course. George E. Lothrop, a partner in the competitive World's Museum, sat in his office at the refurbished yet tiny Windsor Theatre, nursing a similar contemplation.

In turns out that 1886 was *The Mikado* year. Incredibly, its British composer/ authors had neglected to obtain a U.S. copyright on their work, so it was open season for "Mikado" and things Japanese. While still playing its first run at the Hollis Street Theatre, the operetta was also staged at the Globe and Bijou theatres. The Gaiety Museum ran continuous performances of two "Mikado" companies, presented by "Messrs. Albee and Gerould, our Japanese connoisseurs, under direct supervision of Mr. E.F. Albee, assistant manager ... Japanese art in the inner lobby." The World's Museum offered a Japanese village, and Horticultural Hall had "The Original Only Genuine Japanese Village."

At 11 A.M. on August 14, 1886, a momentous transaction took place in the offices of Messrs. Morse and Stern, as Keith and Batcheller obtained control of the Bijou Theatre for six years. The partners hurried the opening of their new home on August 23 with a play, *The Creole*. Their Gaiety Museum continued to operate with stock and variety shows, plus an ever-dwindling supply of curios.

George E. Lothrop had always held controlling interest in the World's Museum. By the end of 1886 he had secured all of its stock and announced that more emphasis would be placed on its stage performances. He and Keith were of the same mind.

A popular post–Civil War attraction was the Cyclorama at 541 Tremont Street, between Berkely and Clarendon streets (on the site formerly occupied by the Moody and Sankey Tabernacle), presenting an exhibition of "The Battle of Gettysburg," day and evening, for 50 cents. Its circular interior walls presented a complete reproduction of that famous battle; spectators were led around an unending floor-to-ceiling mural as a lecturer described the battle on the field pictured before them.

In April 1887 the *Boston Globe* reported that "The Boylston Market Association has notified all of its tenants to vacate by June first, a grand opera house may take place. Armory regiments [tenants] may move to Columbia Rink on Washington Street near Dover." But no opera house ever occupied the Boylston Market space.

However, in May, the *Globe* announced that "a new playhouse, the Casino, will be built on the site of the Columbia Rink ... near the Metropolitan Hotel.... 1,400 seats all on one floor ... lobby 80 × 100 feet ... stage 80 by 42 feet." It, too, never came to be.

In the hot July the Bijou bragged that each of its seats had a ventilator that its occupants could control, "keeping the temperature at 60 degrees."

In August 1887, Keith and Batcheller's Gaiety moved up Washington Street and into the stores on either side of the Bijou entrance. General admission to the curio hall and theatre was still ten cents, but reserved seats cost an extra 5, 10, or 15 cents. That summer the almost circular proscenium of the house was altered to the traditional square shape to provide better viewing. Newspaper ads proclaimed "Gaiety Musee and Bijou Theatre merged into one, B.F. Keith, sole proprietor."

At the close of the year, another new cyclorama building was under construction on Tremont near Chandler Street. "The Battle of Lookout Mountain" would be competition to the show nearby at 541 Washington Street, but through various transitions, this building would instead become a famous playhouse.[1]

In 1888 a new theatre did rise out of the Columbia Skating Rink at 1172–1194 Washington Street, close to Dover, in the then-fashionable South End. January 9 was the opening date of the Grand Opera House. Architects Snell and Gregerson had transformed the 100-foot by 170-foot rink into a massive brick, stone, and iron structure. Its old walls were strengthened and raised from 35 to 70 feet, and a lobby 29 feet deep by 40 feet high ran across the 80-foot front of the building. In its center was a 7-foot by 18-foot ticket office with white and gold painted woodwork. Walls and ceiling were frescoed in carmine glaze. Twenty-five broad lobby doors opened onto the sidewalk, and at each end of the lobby seven-foot-wide staircases, painted white and gold, climbed up and across the back of the room connecting with the first balcony.

The auditorium was 80 feet wide by 87 feet long, and its orchestra floor pitched an excellent 16 inches in 10 feet. There were 12 private boxes, a balcony, and a gallery; and the gallery had separate entrances from Washington Street. The capacity was orchestra 1,200; balcony, 900; and gallery, 800; the total with boxes was about 3,000 seats. A 16-inch-thick proscenium wall opening was 36 feet wide and 40 feet high and held an asbestos fire curtain and border. The stage was a fine 50 feet deep, 80 feet wide, and 65 feet to the gridiron (rigging loft). The auditorium's 70-foot-high dome had a chandelier of 85 gas jets. The house also was wired for electricity.[2]

George E. Lothrop was not about to let his new South End neighbor smother his operation. On August 20, 1888, his Windsor Theatre became the New Grand Museum. His playhouse was above a market building, some 80 feet wide by 280 feet long. This upstairs house never enjoyed anything close to that amount of space, but the museum below was considerably larger. The New Grand's auditorium was decorated in red, gold, and buff tints, its proscenium was done in rich carmine with gold leaf ornamentation, walls were painted to resemble Tennessee marble blocks with leaves, branches, and vines worked in. The orchestra seated 800, and the balcony held 500 patrons. The reader should note that upstairs theatres were quite common in this period.

The size of the museum portion on the ground level may be gauged by the November installation of the "Natatorium," a heated swimming pool that was 80 feet by 16 feet where lady "natators" appeared in contests.

Another impresario, Col. William Austin, formerly of Austin and Stone's Museum, was also busy in 1888, transforming the 111–113–115 Court Street building into Austin's Nickel Museum. A curio hall occupied the first floor; below were bowling alleys and a 130-foot rifle range. The upper floor was a "musee" and auditorium. Austin's showplace opened October 1, and a white and gold sign dominated by two seven-foot nickels covered the 60-foot façade. Great gothic windows of cathedral glass rose above. This second floor had been the site, in 1875, of Alexander Graham Bell's laboratory. The first permanent telephone line came from there.

Chapter 14

Improvements at the Boston Theatre
The Third Tremont Theatre
1889

The Bostonian reported that "In 1889 the Boston Theatre's 'apron,' as the wide expanse of stage which projected into the auditorium was called, was cut down from eighteen to eight feet deep, making room for three additional rows of seats on the orchestra floor; which brought the actors and the audience closer together. For some time actors on the stage had seldom advanced below the first entrance, and the barren waste of stage in front of them always had a chilling effect on both spectator and actor.

"In the early days of the house this apron was considered a valuable adjunct, for in case of necessity, one hundred people could enact a scene upon it. Old-fashioned plays were not so freely chopped up into separate acts and tableaux as modern ones [1894] are, and it was very convenient to have stage room for free action in a front scene while an elaborate and complicated stage picture was in preparation."

Early in 1889, Park Theatre builders and lessees Abbey and Schoeffel learned that they would not be able to renew their leases because landlord Lotta Crabtree had plans. Once again faced with a search for an alternative home for their stage productions, they decided to build their own playhouse. The *Boston Globe* announced in August that the roof of their new Tremont Theatre (No. 3) had topped its granite piers at Avery Street and Haymarket Place. The building was supported elsewhere by pressed brick columns and iron beams rising from concrete foundations. Architects J.B. McElfatrick and Sons designed this house, which stood upon a portion of the site of the city's second theatre, the Haymarket.

The Tremont auditorium was 75 feet wide by 80 feet deep and 75 feet tall. The proscenium width was 33 feet in front of a stage 73 feet wide, 45 feet deep, and 69 feet to the gridiron. Dressing rooms were in a separate building at stage left. Its Avery Street entrance was 15 feet wide and 18 feet tall, but the main entrance was from Tremont Street—being on the main street was a must for theatres. A long lobby through the Codman Building led from there to a spacious room some two stories tall. A stairway ran up its right wall and proceeded left via a railed balcony against the outer wall of the auditorium, and connected with the first circle. Patrons could look down from it to the 28-foot by 63-foot foyer. Another lobby stairway, just outside of the standing-room area entrance, sank to restroom areas and rose to the two balconies.

Walls of the gallery and main auditorium were decorated in an Alhambra mosaic effect, the balcony was in a darker tapestry design, and the main ceiling was a modernized Renaissance Gobelin pattern. Woodwork and papier-mâché of the proscenium arch, boxes, and columns were painted in antique ivory.

Orchestra seats were upholstered in gold plush and set 32 inches back to back, an unusually spacious distance for the period. The main floor was of hard pine over concrete laid on corrugated iron. The theatre opened on October 14, 1889, and capacity was 1,700 seats.

During the summer the Lotta Crabtree family made extensive renovations to their Park Theatre, being necessary to catch up with its hurried 1879 50-day conversion from Beethoven Hall. A new 16-inch wall from foundation to roof separated auditorium from stage. The main floor and stage were fireproofed, being wire-lathed and plastered underneath. A new lobby was constructed of tile, supported by iron beams and brick arches. Wider spacing of seats was executed, and the old-fashioned stage apron was cut back to the proscenium line. A new front structure was erected, named the Crabtree Building, and its lobby contained exits from the rear of the auditorium.

On Thanksgiving Day, a great fire consuming several buildings near Kingston and Essex streets caused gas to be cut off in the area containing the Boston Theatre. Fortunately, the house was being fitted for electricity. Its wiring was so far advanced that footlights could be used, and with the help of calcium lights plus locomotive (train engine) headlights, the stage was sufficiently brilliant to allow the performance to go on. Patrons could not enter from Washington Street, so the stage door on Mason Street became an entrance.[1]

Contemplating all of this activity going on around him, B.F. Keith updated his Bijou Theatre that summer. Starting with the Washington Street vestibule, the woodwork was painted in white and gold, and walls were done in handsome panels of liquoma and lincrusta. Halfway up the staircase the walls were ornamented with designs of the German school, representing Music and Painting. The foyer at the head of the stairway was redone in buff and gold with a flowered ceiling design. On the left, the ladies reception room was separated by a stained glass partition set into a cherry and gold frame, the room tinted in buff and gold with a blue-shaded ceiling. Statues of bronze and alabaster plus bric-a-brac completed the arrangements. The auditorium's Moorish design was refurbished and a new carpet was laid.

Chapter 15

B.F. Keith Invents Vaudeville
Enter Edward Franklin Albee
1889–1891

In September 1889, the Bijou began to advertise variety acts "On the Vaudeville Stage." Batcheller had disappeared from the scene, and a new associate appeared, B.F. Keith's friend from circus days, Edward F. Albee. The Keith family resided on the upper floors of the front building, and it is said Mrs. Keith dusted the theatre while her husband did repairs as vaudeville became big business. The success of Keith's Bijou enabled him, with general manager Albee, to branch out, operating vaudeville theatres in Providence, Rhode Island, and Philadelphia.

Richard M. Ketchum, Will Rogers' biographer, wrote: "So vaudeville had many antecedents, but if any one particular establishment may be said to have put this form of entertainment on the tracks, it was the Gaiety Museum, which opened for business in a deserted candy store in Boston, Massachusetts, in 1883. Operated by a richly mustachioed former circus performer named Benjamin Franklin Keith, who had tired of bouncing around the countryside in wagons loaded with freaks ... in 1885, Keith and a mild-appearing, ruthless chap named Edward F. Albee, who was occasionally described by members of the trade as Keith's 'Richelieu,' were presenting sensationally popular operettas by William Gilbert and Arthur Sullivan, and their success in this venture enabled them to acquire the real estate which soon became the largest chain of theatres in the world."

Benjamin Franklin Keith was born in 1846 at the lower village of Hillsborough Bridge, New Hampshire, and left home at the age of seven, working on a farm in western Massachusetts until he was 18. He was captivated by Amburgh's Circus and left town with it, worked in Bunnell's Museum in New York for two seasons, and was with Barnum's and Forepaugh's circuses. He wound up broke in Boston, seeking a partner to open a museum.

Edwin Franklin Albee was born in 1857 at Machiasport, on Machias Bay, Maine. A 19-year-old Albee left school to join up with P.T. Barnum's Circus in 1876 and became a ticket seller and "fixer," a sort of advance man, trouble-solver, and general con artist. He met Keith through their circus connections and they became steady friends; one legend has it that Albee used his circus' payroll as Keith's investment in the first museum. Albee helped Keith with a "Japanese Garden" for the *Mikado* showings and stayed on.

In January 1891, Keith advertised that, because of enormous attendance at certain hours in his Bijou Theatre and Gaiety Museum, the lengthy bill would be divided. One show would play on the Bijou stage and one in the Museum or "annex hall," and seats were sold subject to delay. Vaudeville was becoming so popular that Keith was pressed for space.

On April 11, 1891, Keith closed a deal to control the Bijou property, together with buildings in its rear, for a long term of years. This deal provided the showman with a roughly 75-foot-wide tract running from Washington through to Mason Street. His news release bragged that the Gaiety and Bijou "made the largest and grandest theatre in America."

After Keith's news release in April, Austin's Nickelodeon closed, and it reopened on Memorial Day as Austin's Palace Theatre, seating 1,100 patrons. Nothing was left of the old operation. The entrance was now as wide as the house itself. There was a commodious foyer with three doors leading to the orchestra and iron stairways rising to the balconies. Auditorium walls were done in buff and lavender and woodwork in white and gold, while the vaulted dome was as azure as the sky with floral wreaths tucked into its corners. The Palace had two balconies and four boxes in two tiers at each side of the stage, and an immense brass chandelier hung from the dome 53 feet above the main floor. The stage was only 46 feet wide and 30 feet deep with a proscenium 25 feet wide and 32 high—adequate but not overwhelming. Austin had beaten Keith.

The World's Museum, after several managements, closed in 1891. It would be remodeled and reopened as the World Theatre. Museums were departing from the theatrical scene that they had helped to create.

On October 5, 1891, the Columbia Theatre opened at 978–986 Washington Street, on the fringe of the South End. A newspaper reported after a pre-opening visit:

> The new house was built by Mr. J.J. Grace and of which Messrs. William Harris and Charles F. Atkinson are the managers and lessees, will shortly be opened to the public. It is situated on Washington Street and comprises the entire block, numbered from 978 to 986 inclusive, located on a sweeping curve of this main thoroughfare. Its commanding front can be seen for blocks in either direction, and a few people have passed the edifice of late without pausing to admire its novel design and rare architectural beauty, so entirely different is it from any other building in this city.
>
> In design it follows the Moorish style. Its towers, grand in their proportions, rise far above the surrounding buildings. The front is composed of pressed brick and terracotta supported by cast iron columns and arches, while the cornices and turrets of the towers are pure copper. A graceful arch extends two stories in height from the street level, while a second circle on the fourth floor level is surmounted with the name of the theatre in bas-relief letters. The upper portions of the lower arch are so constructed as to form a magnificent window of cathedral and stained glass.
>
> The architect has taken "The Alhambra," the perfection of Moorish art, as his

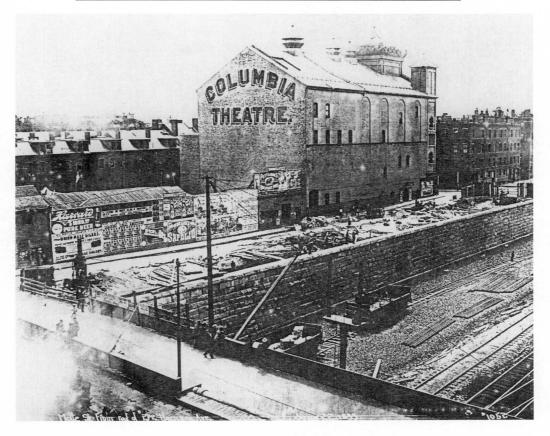

The side (and rear) of the Columbia Theatre was on Mott Street, next to the Boston and Albany Railroad, seen in this 1899 view (author's collection).

ideal for the construction of the Columbia, and both exterior and interior have been worked out to the minutest detail.

One first enters the immense lobby, which extends entirely across the Washington Street front, and is at once impressed with its grandeur and the natural grace of its arrangement. A broad staircase leads to the balcony, carrying a massive bronze railing. At either side two beautiful carved "Newell" posts are surmounted by Arabian figures, holding handsomely designed gas fixtures and great bunches of incandescent lights. To the left of the main entrance is the box office. Adjoining it is the working room of the executive staff of the theatre, with the private office of the management connecting. The walls and ceiling of the lobby are completely covered with stereo-relief work of exquisite design. The floor is a mass of mosaic tiling.

Passing from the lobby to the interior of the house the first innovation to strike the eye is the new and novel arrangement of the boxes and loges. Constructed in groups, every seat in them carries a perfect view of the stage. The line of sight throughout the house is perfect. In fact the auditorium is built upon an entirely new idea known as the Lempert principal of building auditoriums. The result is—not a poor seat.

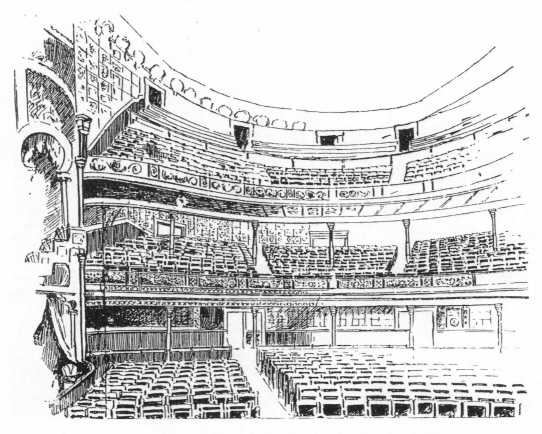

The Columbia Theatre's interior (author's collection).

Everywhere harmony and beauty prevails. Everything contrasts and balances admirably. All the ornamentation has been executed with a view of being seen at proper distance. The main line strikes the eye and as one approaches nearer, the detail of the work grows in beauty. Look where one will, it is a mass of ornamentation beautifully executed in stereo-relief work.

In color all is subdued. Buffs, cream and salmon are the prevailing tints throughout, and considerable gold bronze is used to give relief to the coloring. While everything is rich, the tone is subdued, and the whole is treated more like the parlor of a private house. Thus nothing will detract from the stage effects.

The floor of the auditorium descends with a graceful pitch, seating 750 people comfortably.

Returning to the front of the house, an easy staircase extends to the second floor lobby. The sight is magnificent. The floor is inlaid with fantastic tiling, the decorations harmonize in every detail and the immense cathedral window of variegated colors extends across the entire front of the apartment. The lobby is large enough to accommodate all who may be in the balcony circle. Magnificent furniture with costly rugs are scattered about in lavish profusion. To the right and left are large doors leading to the gallery stairways.

Passing through one of these doors, the balcony is entered. It will seat 400 persons, and every chair commands a view of the entire stage. Again returning to the front of the house, the gallery stairs are taken to the upper floor, the mammoth second balcony. Seats are provided for 800, and while the incline is sharp, the front row is reached without difficulty, owning to the careful arrangement of the aisle steps.

The orchestra floor and first balcony are seated with handsome opera chairs, specially designed for the Columbia. They are richly upholstered in plush, the color harmonizing with the prevailing tone of decoration. In the second balcony the first six rows are opera chairs; the balance being finished in settees.

On the left, facing the lobby on the first floor, is the ladies parlor. The same elegant treatment of stereo-relief on ceiling and walls prevails. Elegant furniture and the richest of carpeting are none too good for the Columbia's lady guests. Leading from the parlor is the ladies retiring room. It is furnished with hot and cold running water, and every convenience that experience can suggest. Under this room and extending beneath the lobby are the gentlemen's smoking and toilet rooms. The decorations are in stereo-relief. The floor is tiled and the furniture is upholstered in leather. Smoking tables, rugs, etc. give it an air of refined comfort.

The manager's business office, on the first floor, at the Washington Street corner, is a little gem in itself. Adjoining it is his private office. It contains a fireplace and all conveniences. Both rooms are richly carpeted, and the furniture is in keeping with the general effect. The box office and cloak rooms are en suite. The former is fitted with patent ticket racks, extra windows, etc., for the gallery entrance. The latter is on Mott Street, about 40 feet from Washington Street. While this is the principal mode of access to the upper floor, it can also be reached by a staircase opening off Washington Street, at the south front of the theatre.

The gas and electric fixtures are in keeping with the character of the house, and were made from special designs by the architect. They are polished rolled brass, and are so arranged that should the electric current at any time fail, the gas can be turned on at once and lighted from an electric spark from an independent source.

The carpets were made for the Columbia. They are soft in color and tone, blending admirably with the prevailing decorations. The furniture and drapery hangings are of the richest material. In the ladies reception room is a mahogany and gold set, upholstered in French tapestry. The lobby has English oak sofas, covered with russet morocco and studded with large antique nails. A massive sofa occupies the center of the room. The smoking room is furnished with oak settees, covered with russet leather. The private boxes are supplied with white and gold chairs, upholstered in ivory, peach and blue brocatelies, while the loges contain mahogany divans and odd chairs, covered with tapestries.

The heating has had special attention. It is the indirect system, therefore ventilating as well as heating. The plumbing and drainage is the best.

A visit and inspection behind the curtain reveals one of the largest, best arranged, and most perfectly appointed stages in the United States, measuring 75 feet from the floor of the stage to the gridiron. On either side, far above the stage, are two fly galleries, used for working all the overhead rigging, such as border lights, grooves, borders, drop scenes, etc. To the left are the prompter's quarters, which are indeed worthy of more than a casual mention. The gas table for all of the gas lighting in the house controls about 800 burners. The gas table is supplied with all the necessary valves and by-passes and contains the most modern and approved appliances. Close at hand is the electric switch board, with its elaborate and handsomely finished switches and appurtenances for working the 1378 electric lights to illuminate the theatre.

The curtain or proscenium arch is 36 feet in height by 38 feet in width. The depth of the stage is 50 feet; width from wall to wall is 71 feet. The first fly gallery is 36 feet; the second fly gallery 45 feet.... In fact the stage is large enough to set any production that may be desired. The trap cellar is of unusual size, with an extra pit for trick scenes. A full set of working traps, bridges, etc. are available when required.

Outside the massive brick wall to the south is the annex building, 23 feet wide and 90 feet long, used as a scene room and for the dressing rooms of the theatrical company. All are completely fireproof, and large, comfortable and extremely cheerful. Every room is separated from the stage by fireproof doors, is handsomely furnished and contains hot and cold water. There are 19 dressing rooms all told, beside the green room, in fact, everybody's comfort and convenience are considered behind as well as in front of the curtain.

The curtains, drops, scenes, etc. are of the most complete character. First there is the asbestos fire curtain, an absolute preventive of fire communicating with the auditorium from the stage, notably so in this theatre, as either side of the curtain runs through a slot in the brick wall, and is held in place by a strong cable. The act drop, as well as the drop curtain, is a marvel of beauty. A full set of borders and one of the largest scene lists ever put into a new theatre, are to be placed in this house as fast as they can be prepared. This important work has been entrusted to the hands of Mr. H.L. Reid, one of the most noted scenic artists of the country. Fire buckets, axes, stand pipes with hose and play pipes are found at all points on or about the stage and auditorium. In fact, the whole house is fireproof. Steel beams and brick arches, cement covered, are reinforced with stereo-relief, which being mainly asbestos is indestructible.

Numerous complete sets of stage furniture, embracing white and gold, gothic, rug, pattern, mohairs and brocatelles, have been provided.

The entire designing and construction of the Columbia is by Leon H. Lempert and Son of Rochester, N.Y., who are also the architects of theatres and opera houses at Rochester, Auburn, Rome, Watertown and other places. The firm has five other theatres building at present, but Mr. Lempert, Sr., has spent fully two-thirds of his time at the Columbia. He has been ably assisted by his son, Leon H. Jr., and Mr. Fred McCormick. Mr. J.J. Grace, the owner of the house, has not stinted the architect in any branch of the work, having on different occasions directed him to make the Columbia the model theatre of the country, and to spare no expense to bring about that result. The exact cost of the Columbia was $325,000.

The *Boston Globe* commented that the Columbia Theatre architecture introduced a new concept, "the Lempert Principle of Building Auditoriums."

Chapter 16

The Bowdoin Square Theatre
B.F. Keith Builds a Palace
1892–1894

On January 10, 1892, B.F. Keith completed the necessary papers permitting him to join his two theatres into a new showplace. The site ran from Washington Street to Mason Street (its western end), and contained Bradford Place, a short lane of early nineteenth century dwellings. Behind these homes were the towering walls of the Boston Theatre, which was the north side of the lot. The Adams House Hotel ran along the south side to Washington Street. The Bijou Theatre's two buildings were the front or east part of the parcel. It added up to roughly 90 by 350 feet, being irregular in shape. All of the Bradford Place buildings, including a stable and several wells, were to be eliminated because of the deep excavation required on the Mason Street end. It was considerably higher than the Washington Street elevation. The Bijou was quickly shuttered.

The Bowdoin Square Theatre opened on February 15, 1892, located close to Scollay Square. C.H. Blackall was the architect, assisted by Leon H. Lempert, architect of the Columbia. Patrons walked through a widely arched 25-foot-high entrance on Bowdoin Square. Its pavement, under Sienna marble walls, was a mosaic depicting two large Florentine lions outlined in black and yellow at the sides of the house's name. Bowdoin Square Theatre was also cut into the finish over the mahogany and beveled plate glass doors. Next, patrons entered a 65-foot-long by 16-foot-wide vestibule, also with a mosaic floor and richly wainscoted walls. A grand lobby ran across the back of the auditorium under an arched ceiling, and staircases led up at each end of this opulent room.

The Bowdoin Square's 70-foot-deep auditorium did resemble that of Lempert's Columbia Theatre. Five boxes descended from the balcony front on each side, and two more were at orchestra level. The Italian Renaissance proscenium, 36 feet wide by 32 feet high, opened onto a stage 66 feet wide, 38 feet deep, and 65 feet to the gridiron.

A newspaper commented:

The decoration in the house has been applied very sparingly with a view to emphasize the proscenium and the boxes. The walls are mottled in shades of pink, red and yellow, giving a quiet subdued effect, which lights up very agreeably at night, and serves to rest the eye, while the finish of the proscenium, gallery fronts, and boxes is in imitation of old ivory, giving a very harmonious effect and bringing into relief every detail of the ornamentation. The orchestra seats altogether 623. The chairs have tilting backs, foot rests, hat racks, and all modern conveniences, and are upholstered in a delicate salmon plush. A notable feature is the large space between the rows of chairs.

The gas and electric features are carried out in harmony with the Renaissance spirit of design. The central chandelier is arranged like a huge expanding flower, kept quite close to the ceiling, and masking the large opening left for purposes of ventilation. There are 120 incandescent lamps arranged in this chandelier, and about 700 distributed through the house.

The stage is one of the largest in the city, being only second to the Boston Theatre, and it is fitted with every modern appliance necessary for working the scenes, including nine traps and six sets of bridges. The entrance from the stage to the house is on the left. The prompter's table and appliances for controlling gas and electric works are on this side of the stage also and are carried out with an elaboration, which is almost a necessary feature of a modern theatre. The width of the stage is 71 feet, the total height over the curtain to gridiron or rigging loft is 67 feet in the clear, the height of the roof being 76 feet.

The three dwelling houses, which occupied a portion of Cames Place at the rear of the theatre, have been so transformed that they would hardly be recognized. One of them has been completely torn out inside from cellar to roof. In the basement, the boilers for the theatre have been located, and the rest of the building is occupied as a scene room, being connected directly with the rear of the stage by large red tin doors. The other two buildings have been remodeled and divided into dressing rooms, there being in all 21 large, well lighted and perfectly ventilated rooms for the artists, affording very unusual accommodations in this respect....

There will be three curtains, the outer, which is made of woven asbestos, will be used only in case of fire. The drop curtain is a drapery design with a landscape accessory, combining and contrasting the beauties of two entirely distinct fields in scenic art.... Provisions against damage by fire are quite ample, including standpipes, with abundance of hose everywhere, with automatic sprinklers running up on each side of the stage and under the rigging loft, as well as perforated pipes which completely enclose the curtain opening. The fly-men who operate the scenes have a special fire escape directly from the gallery, so that in case of fire they can remain at their post until the very last moment without any risk of being cut off by the flames; in fact, the construction of the entire theatre has been of the very best. The walls were built with an air space to insure against dampness, and also with a view to increasing the acoustic properties of the house. No wooded construction is anywhere placed that fire could possibly get at it. In fact, if a large fire were actually built in the middle of the theatre it could burn itself out without any degree damaging the construction. The plastering is applied directly to brick walls upon wire lathing. The floor of the auditorium is laid directly on concrete so there is no chance for the flames to spread underneath. All of the constructive woodwork is treated with fireproof paint so as to be practically indestructible. The archways are all of iron, enclosed by brick-nogged walls, and the windows and doorways opening toward the front building on Court Street are fitted with fireproof shutters, so that if the adjoining premises should catch fire, the flames could not communicate with the theatre. Capacity was approximately 1,500 in orchestra, balcony and gallery; a separate entrance to the latter was of Bowdoin Square.[1]

In summer the unfinished Cyclorama site at Tremont and Chandler streets finally opened as the Arena Garden, with 1,500 opera chairs for patrons watching burlesque, vaudeville and operettas. Unfortunately, the place still looked like a vast unfinished domed building and was not a success.

That summer, various methods of cooling theatres were employed. The Lyceum had a six-foot exhaust fan in its dome, the Columbia used an immense steel fan to draw air over a mix of ice, salt, and ether, to be released up through auditorium vents. Other theatres used similar systems.

On September 19, 1892, the World's Museum reopened as the Lyceum Theatre, and all that remained of the old establishment was the outer wall on Washington Street. Extensive fireproof construction of brick and iron was added to that façade, and its entrance was encased in brick. Wide stairs of easy grade rose to the second-floor theatre. Another entrance with wide stairs climbed to the top gallery from a wide Boylston Street alley, which also connected with the stage and scenery doors. The house boasted a balcony and gallery, and two boxes at orchestra level were at each side of the stage. A color scheme of white and gold was relieved in blue and buff. The Lyceum stage was 35 feet deep and 45 feet high. The capacity was 1,500, and the first floor was let for stores (the museum was no more).

The Tremont Temple burned yet again in March 1893, and once more it was rebuilt, by May 1896. The new structure was the grandest and most fireproof of them all.

On April 9, 1893, newspapers advertised "The Great and Only Casino, Tremont near Dover Street," on April 23, "Arena, Corner Tremont and Chandler, Amateur Circus, and April 30, "Casino, Shannon's Great London Circus" in the old cyclorama building. Two cycloramas would fit this description. One was on Tremont Street near Dover, and it eventually became a wholesale florist market. The National Theatre would be built next door to it a decade later. The Chandler Street location was in operation as the Arena Garden, and would soon become a famous theatre.[2]

In May, George Lothrop leased the Howard Athenaeum and introduced continuous performances of spectacles and dramas at popular prices. He had big plans and admitted that his Grand Museum was not the proper flagship for his enterprises. That deficiency would be remedied.

In August, B.F. Keith's New Theatre was nearing completion. Excavation had started from Washington Street for a lobby to run under the Bijou buildings, connecting with the new structure in the rear. This passage was 177 feet long by 30 feet wide.

To get an idea of the electric power needed to run these modern showplaces, the *Boston Globe* listed the equipment being installed in the sub-cellar below the theatre:

2—200 h.p. Ball and Wood engines used for electric lighting (arc and incandescent)

1—150 h.p. auxiliary engine for same

1—20 h.p. engine for driving big automatic ventilating fan

1—5 h.p. engine for operating automatic stoker for boiler

1—6 h.p. fire pump for supplying automatic sprinklers

1—9½ h.p. fire pump for roof hydrant

2—600 light dynamos

2—1,800 light dynamos

1—30 light arc machine

The year 1894 came in a most spectacular fashion. On January 2, the Globe Theatre was consumed for the second time by one of the greatest fires in Boston history. Faulty electric wiring was the culprit. John Stetson was without a home for his remaining half season of bookings. Stetson leased the Park Theatre across the street and did not rebuild the Globe. In 1896 he opened his Hotel Savoy on the Globe site. It was fireproof, having solid cement floors 20 inches thick.

On March 24, B.F. Keith stood in the lobby of his new theatre, greeting invited guests at a preview (the public opening was two days later). His audience was the cream of Boston society, plus politicos, newspapermen from distant cities, famous

The orchestra reception room at B.F. Keith's New Theatre, with the stairway to the balcony and ladies' parlor, 1894 (author's collection).

The entrance of B.F. Keith's New Theatre, 1894 (author's collection).

The stage setting at B.F. Keith's New Theatre, 1894. The musical accompaniment was a piano and probably a drum. Competition later caused Keith to install a complete orchestra (author's collection).

actors and showmen. Ushers were dressed in emerald green livery suits, knee britches, red vests, lace shirt fronts and gold braided cuffs.

The *Boston Globe* praised the blending of rich warm mellow tones, white, gold, silver, pink and pale blue. "The view of the front lobby is like an opening rosebud.... Rich delicate pink tone of the walls ... scores of incandescent lamps shining through globes like glittering opals ... delicate paintings of cherubs ... glimpses of pale blue skies ... great French mirrors 15 feet high."

A stained glass transom 17½ by 7 feet proclaimed "B.F. Keith's New Theatre," and underneath was the main entrance surrounded by elaborate and symmetrical scrollwork and carvings of various designs. Above and to each side were large winged mythological monsters holding in their mouths long chains, from which were suspended brilliantly glowing lights.

On each side of the loggia, or outside entrance, was a circular ticket office of Sienna marble, plate glass, and ornate designs in silver, and their domes were decorated in stereo relief of ivory and gold. The floor was of mosaic tile, wainscoting was Sienna marble, walls were done in old rose with relief work of ivory and gold leaf, and the ceiling was a typical Keith sky of floating cherubs and floral designs.

The electric generating room below the stage of B.F. Keith's New Theatre had an elevated marble walkway with rails for patrons' visits (author's collection).

Large doors, with stained-glass transoms of green, rose, and opal tints, swung open to the lobby foyer. To the left was a marble fireplace topped with a huge mirror, the ceiling was bordered with more cherubs holding musical instruments, and a second set of glass doors opened into the main lobby. To one's left ran a series of four offices; concealed over these rooms was a passage to the gallery from the front entrance. The lobby floor was covered with white marble, and its walls were paneled with paintings and mirrors. Lunettes over doorways offered more cupids, holding rose garlands, and 82 lanterns hung from the ceiling.

One passed under a broad arch of ivory and gold at the far end of the lobby, where a marble staircase on the left ascended to the balcony. To the right was a recessed room containing a staircase that connected with the Bijou Theatre overhead.

A third set of swinging doors opened to the orchestra reception room. On the right was another stairway to the balcony; beside it was the ladies' parlor. To the left was a fireplace in blue and mottled white tiles, its massive carved cherry mantel topped by a large mirror. Farther left a stairway connected with the men's room below. A deep carmine Wilton carpet covered the floors of the reception area. The ladies' parlor had a gem domed ceiling with Keith's sky-cum-cupids, and another ornate fireplace; toilet rooms were in white marble with silver fittings.

The switchboard room, adjacent to the generating room at B.F. Keith's New Theatre, had marble walls (author's collection).

From the reception area three arches gave entry to the auditorium; its standing-room rail and wainscoting were of cherry wood. The under balcony ceiling offered tints of yellow, green, ivory, and rose; walls were covered with brocade silk of green and rose. Six boxes, similarly draped, were on each side of the stage in three tiers. Above the scrollwork proscenium arch were three paintings depicting Music, Dance, and Comedy.

In the balcony foyer were four arches leading to the seating portion. A flight of stairs rose from this area to a mezzanine floor, under the gallery, which contained lounges, ladies' and men's rooms. Also, from this hall a long descending passage and stairs led, under the Bijou Theatre, to the Washington Street entrance of B.F. Keith's New Theatre. A broad staircase led upward from this mezzanine to the rear of the gallery, where four more arches opened to that seating area. From this uppermost level one could admire the grand chandelier at close range; it was wrought in the shape of a vine in ivory and gold, was 42 feet long, and contained 180 lights.

At the extreme front of the first balcony, behind its right side boxes, was another entrance from Mason Street. That small lobby was treated in Louis XV style with its woodwork in white and gold. Doors and transoms were set with leaded glass in chaste designs. This entry was a scaled-down counterpart of that on Washington Street, also having an opalescent stained glass overhead enclosing the name "B.F. Keith's New Theatre." Thus, Tremont Street patrons could use Mason for entering the theatre.

The new theatre was approximately 163 feet long by 90 feet wide and 82 feet high. The orchestra floor was almost 80 feet square, and the balcony and gallery were 80 feet wide.

Keith's stage was 60 feet wide, 42 feet deep, and 70 feet to its gridiron. It was illuminated by five sets of border lights of 103 each and 108 footlights in white, red, and green. Fifteen dressing rooms with marble floors and running water sinks, plus two bathrooms, were at stage right.

William Birkmire, a theatre planner, wrote in his 1896 volume, *The Planning and Construction of American Theatres*:

> The people realize the improvements which have been made in the last few years in the manner of seating theatres. From the plain, hard, wooden benches which were used in places of this kind we have come to the luxuriously upholstered opera and assembly chairs and folding seats. For example, the automatic assembly chair, a chair having the following distinct features. The retreating or self-folding seat is operated at the will of the occupant; it folds into a minimum of space by slightly pressing the edge of the seat with the limbs in the natural act of arising, it is noiseless and does not require the strength of a Samson to fold the seat. Chairs are made 18, 19, 20, and 21 inches wide; that is, an 18-inch chair refers to the distance from the center of one arm to the centre of the next.
>
> To prevent the irregularities in the aisles, different widths of chairs are used, which difference is not noticeable when the chairs are set up in a row.... One of the newest improvements in chairs is a double-seat sofa or divan, made in lengths of from 36 to 42 inches.

B.F. Keith's New Theatre had 761 orchestra seats upholstered in pale green tapestry and 429 rattan chairs with cushions in the balcony. The gallery had six rows of stationary seats and 12 rows of benches covered with linoleum edged in brass "for sitting or standing." Counting its boxes, seating 66, Keith's could hold close to 1,800 patrons.

Birkmire continues:

> Every appliance for extinguishing fire was available, there were three emergency exits six feet wide, each leading to Gaiety Place [between the Adams House rear and Mason Street]. Wide wrought iron fire escapes ran down the side of the building; there was a large exit to Mason Street at auditorium right. The stage was fronted by an asbestos curtain, and, in ten seconds could be "drenched with a perfect torrent of water." There were five dressing rooms, a chorus and a property room on the stage floor, and ten other dressing rooms arranged on the fly level, each one having outside ventilation and being provided with marble wash bowls, hot and cold water, and other conveniences necessary to the players. There were toilet-rooms fitted with all of the latest improvements, and a feature, which is a decided novelty, is an elegantly appointed bathroom for the exclusive use of the performers.
>
> The handsomest and most expensive engine-room in the way of appointments in this country today will be found in this theatre. It is a veritable marble palace,

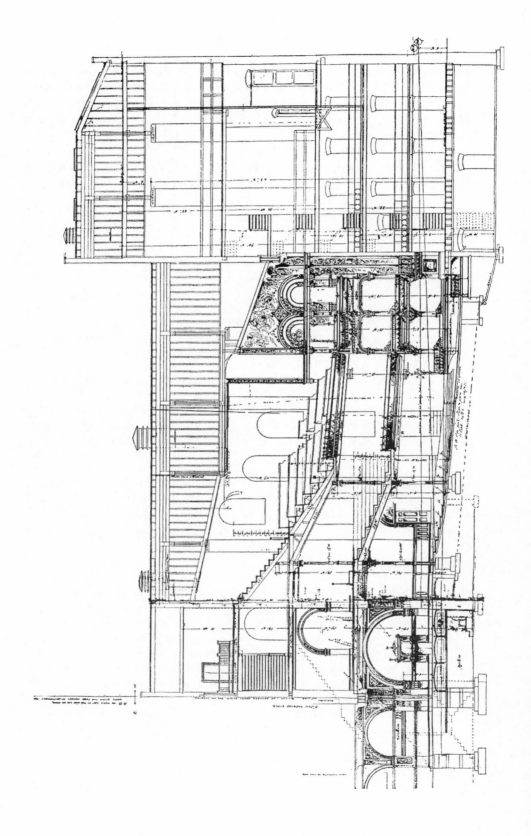

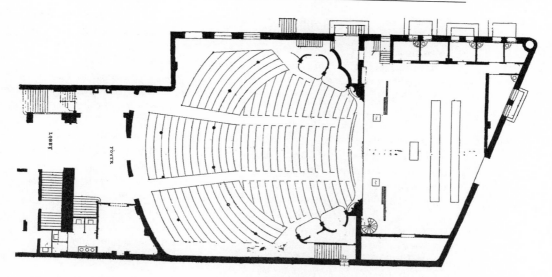

Above: An 1894 floor plan of B.F. Keith's New Theatre, showing the stage and the stairway behind the boxes rising to another entrance on Mason Street (author's collection). *Below right:* Vaudeville genius Benjamin Franklin Keith, photographed in 1902 (photograph from the *Boston-Herald Traveler* Photo Morgue, courtesy of Boston Public Library, Print Department).

fitted up with luxury, elegance, and artistic taste. Its beauty excites expressions of delight and wonder from the thousands who weekly visit the rooms and linger to enjoy them, regardless of the other attractions of the theatre. In fact the highest compliment that can be paid to it is that it contains the best work of E.W. Maynard, who has a national reputation as a theatre architect, having designed, among other noted theatres of Boston, the Castle Superior and the Tremont.

Starting from the main theatre entrance, we pass down a marble staircase and through a long corridor, for the engine-room is 32 feet below the street level. The corridor has a marble floor and a panelled wainscoting of white,

Opposite: An 1894 longitudinal plan of B.F. Keith's New Theatre. The Bijou Theatre was at the upper left, behind Keith's balconies. A long entrance lobby ran under the Bijou (author's collection).

above which the walls are tinted in rose, shading from a deep color at the base to a very light, in fact almost cream, shade at the frieze which surmounts it.

Passing along this corridor we enter the reception-room, which is formed by an alcove 20 feet square, opening into the engine room proper. The floor is of white marble, as also is the wainscoting to a height of 4 feet. Above the wainscoting the walls are shaded from mild green to a light pink. The furnishings of this room are costly and elegant. Electroliers, covered by opalescent globes, throw a soft light about the room, heightening its beauty.

The whole of one side of the reception-room is taken up by a white marble switchboard, consisting of three white marble slabs 10 by 4 feet each. Upon the board are mounted three 1,000-ampere double-pole switches. These main switches feed the current from the large generators to large buss bars in the back of the board. These buss bars further connect, by smaller ones, to sixty-six 100-ampere single-throw double-pole switches. These are connected in the rear of the board to the same number of cutouts, which are mounted on slate. These switches are all quick-break, and are constructed of copper and phosphor bronze, nickel plated and highly polished. The handles are made of highly polished hard rubber, having the appearance of ebony.

At the top of the board are mounted sixty-six so-called pilot lamps. These are so arranged as to form a double scroll, giving a most artistic appearance. There are also three Weston illuminated-dial ampere-meters, having a capacity of 1,000 amperes each, a three-way switch, and an illuminated-dial volt-meter, by which the potential of either dynamo can be measured.

The stage switchboard is 6 by 7 feet, mounted on the wall. On this board are thirty-four 50-ampere double-pole switches, and also twenty-seven regulators to control the stage and auditorium lights. The construction and combination of the switches is such that, by main levers and couplings connecting indicator-switches, all switches can be thrown at one operation, and also closed, thereby producing instantaneous darkness in the house, or gradual changes from red illumination to blue or white on the stage.

Passing from the alcove reception-room, we enter the engine-room proper on a gallery extending entirely around it, on the same level as the room we have left. The floors, like the reception-room, are of white marble and tinted in the same manner. Surrounding the engines is a large nickel-plated railing, along which are placed at intervals newels supporting hammered brass electroliers.

There are three engines and generators, direct-connected; that is, without any belting, the cylinders of engines being 15½ inches in diameter, 14 inches stroke, and the generator of 100 K.W. capacity. The engines without the dynamos, weigh 10 tons each; the floor-space for each being over 80 square feet.

The mechanical work throughout this entire plant for the building is perfect. There is nothing unsightly or painful to the mechanical eye—no nickel plated work except the lubricators and trimmings, but everything is metal finish and shows not only the amount of labor but also care and attention. In fact, for elegance, utility, beauty, and artistic worth, the two rooms, with their furnishings, surpass any of their kind known.

Shorn of the technicalities which would be confusing to the average reader, the above is a description of the machinery and the interesting spot in which it is located. It is a wonderful shop of marble and swiftly moving steel 32 feet underground, as heretofore mentioned, and in proximity to a battery of boilers, but so well ventilated that presence in it is a pleasure. The absolute cleanliness, which pervades every nook and corner of the building, is a matter of comment, and, although thousands of people cross the threshold daily, that same bright, fresh, and wholesome appearance so noticeable at the opening is still apparent.[3]

One interesting feature was the house's ventilating system. A ten-foot blower drew air in from its roof, passed it over heating coils, and forced it down, then up through perforations in the chair legs. This air was eventually drawn out through the gallery ceiling; temperature was controlled through thermostats.

Construction was by J.B. McElfatrick & Sons. B.F. Keith's New Theatre was headed by Edward F. Albee, general manager; bookings were in charge of A. Paul Keith, B.F. Keith's 19-year-old son. The new theatre opened with a comic opera, *Ship Ahoy*, plus vaudeville.

Chapter 17

Cyclorama to
Castle Square Theatre
The End of an Era
1894–1896

A prominent Boston real estate developer, Henry V. Savage, with others, had taken control of the unfinished cyclorama structure on Tremont near Chandler and Arlington streets, which was being used as the Arena Garden. Work commenced in early January 1894 to convert the building into the Alcazar Theatre; However, the project grew along the way and by autumn it opened as the Castle Square Theatre and Hotel.

The playhouse portion opened November 12, 1894, on the spacious square formed by the meeting of Tremont, Chandler and Ferdinand streets. The auditorium retained the circular wall and roof of the old Cyclorama, reinforced by an additional 20 inches of brick; this portion was separate from the rest of the theatre and the hotel, and the stage itself was in still another building.

One entered through a magnificent arch, six stories tall, of imported white brick and terra cotta. Corinthian columns were at either side, and between each set were elaborate iron lanterns under drama masks. Within the arch was a 323-square-foot stained glass window representing a castle amid flowery festoons of olive green, and below were white enameled doors, a mosaic floor, and marble wainscoting.

Quite a distance back, a second set of doors led to the grand foyer, and two Italian marble staircases led to the balcony. Three Gustavino domes, 18 feet in diameter, were in the ceiling, and nine large doorways opened into the auditorium. Inside were walls done in a delicate pink tapestry effect. The drapes were of old rose velour, and the ceiling was robin's egg blue. Nine boxes in three tiers were on each side of the stage, and the ceiling dome was 71 feet above the floor. Capacity was 752 in the orchestra, 450 in the balcony, and 585 in the gallery. With its boxes the Castle Square Theatre could accommodate more than 1,800 patrons.

The proscenium was 40 feet wide by 32 feet high, the stage was 70 feet wide and 52 feet deep, and stage to grid was 72 feet. A sectional part of its floor, 40 feet by 23

The Castle Square Theatre's mezzanine balcony with Gustavino dome in 1894 (author's collection).

feet, was cut into nine traps of 12-foot depth, and six great bridges, which could be raised ten feet.

The theatre used three electric dynamos, which were heavily enclosed and could not be heard in the auditorium. Two produced a 2,000-light capacity, the other lit 500. As in B.F. Keith's New Theatre, heated or cooled air was brought into the house through hollow chair legs and exhausted by fans in the dome.

William H. Birkmire, author of *The Planning and Construction of American Theatres*, wrote in 1896 about this new house.

> Thespis has not a more beautiful temple in this country than Boston's new and most magnificent home of the drama, the Castle Square Theatre, one of the finest, safest, best equipped, most comfortable and most elaborately furnished buildings devoted to theatrical purposes.... Passing through the main doors from the vestibule we enter the "grand foyer." Turning to the right or left we reach the mezzanine balcony by the grand staircases with their handsome electro-bronze newels and balusters, the top of the newels being set off by large electric-light globes. The grand foyer, or lobby as it is sometimes called, is circular in form, 19 feet wide, including staircases, and 60 feet in length. The staircases are each 8 feet wide and built of iron and marble.
>
> By glancing at the ceiling of the foyer we are shown the Gustavian domes blazing with light, which shed their brilliance over the most beautiful paintings that

The Castle Square Theatre's foyer, 1894 (author's collection).

have ever decorated the ceilings of a theatre. Scarcely are the beauties of the domes considered when we discover succession after succession of similar domes, with myriad circles of cherubs reaching away into a seemingly end-less distance. The effect is so real and so astonishing, the purity and transparency of the glass so wonderful, that we had not noticed great mirrors set over the entrance-doors at such angles as to reflect in their clear depths almost every part of the theatre.

From the foyer on the right is situated the ladies' parlor, 12 feet wide by 20 feet long, a dainty resting-place furnished as in the day of Louis XV! Its pretty onyx marble fire-place, combined with the silken finish of the walls, its soft car-pet in delicate design and colors, and the gilded furniture, lend to it an inde-scribable charm which is heightened by large mirrors covering two of its walls. In sharp contrast to the ladies' parlor is the masculine appearance of the gentle-men's smoking-room—12 feet wide by 27 feet long—situated upon the opposite side of the building, but the same lavish generosity has made it an ideal place to court. Its leather-covered furnishings are solidly magnificent, commodious, rest-ful and inviting.

The beauty of the foyer is difficult to surpass. Exits from the auditorium, hung with draperies in softest red, are numerous. Cloak-rooms, dressing rooms, and toilet-rooms are situated with a generous regard to comfort and convenience. The floors are of neat designs in mosaic tilings. Great arches, panelled, and beautified with exquisite paintings, are seen on every side. Directly opposite the vestibule doors are dainty Sienna marble fountains, with gold faucets. The walls

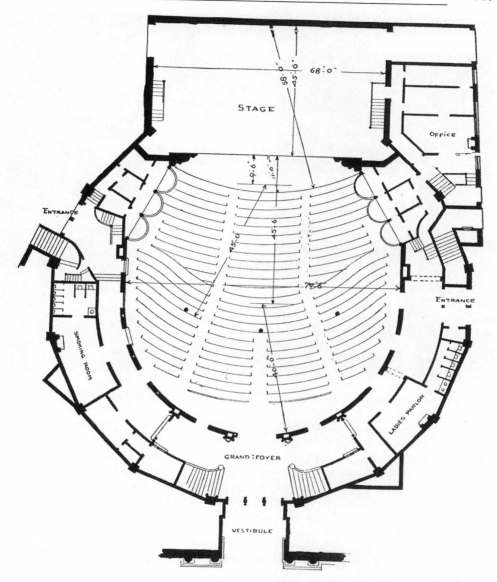

The Castle Square Theatre's parquette plan, 1894. The stage and entrance area were separate structures. The circular auditorium was the former Cyclorama (author's collection).

are finished in satin effect, and the harmony of coloring in this part of the theatre defies description.

As we enter the auditorium ... we see a series of domes supported upon the steel construction of the balcony, and a scheme of decoration after the Italian Renaissance style, the relief work being in cream and gold. Directly over the auditorium an immense circular electrolier, 40 feet in diameter, spreads its twenty arms out from the center of the dome, and its three hundred and eighty

The view from the stage of the Castle Square Theatre, 1894 (author's collection).

incandescent lamps of frosted glass send their rays to every part of the auditorium with a grand illuminating effect. No less attractive are the proscenium arch, and the boxes, twenty in number, furnished with superb designs in stereo-relief. Beautiful beyond all is the sounding board ... with a depth of fifteen feet over the proscenium arch, bearing the most exquisite work in painting about the theatre. Twelve dancing girls, life size in figure, present themselves in artistic abandon. The work is so elaborate that it was first executed on canvas in New York and then brought to the theatre to grace the sounding board.

The Castle Square was a beautiful theatre, as was the Columbia, but a changing neighborhood would do them in. Each was built several blocks away from the downtown theatrical rialto, but both were on a side of the South End whose mansions and homes would be turned into lower-class dwellings.

In July 1894 the Palace Theatre introduced the stage spotlight, the first in the country, using a searchlight like those used on Navy man-of-war ships. The spotlight was fixed to the gallery railing, to illuminate marches and living pictures. In earlier times such lighting was from an electrical current flowing between two sticks of calcium lime, the so-called "lime-light." The power was from jar batteries, which date from about 1800.

On December 23, the Nickelodeon Musee and Parlor Theatre opened on three floors at 51–53 Hanover Street.

The January 1933 razing of the Castle Square Theatre shows the structure of the old Cyclorama dome (photograph by Leslie Jones, courtesy of Boston Public Library, Print Department).

On January 28, 1895, the Bijou Opera House reopened. When Keith had constructed his new theatre, behind and under his old house, he had announced that the Bijou would not be retained. However, the little playhouse was still almost intact, and Keith, not one to waste a dollar, put the Bijou up for lease. Soon newspaper ads announced "Bijou to be reopened! Bijou Opera House, Boston's Parlor Theatre, renovated, stage enlarged! Seat $1.00, 75 and 50 cents. Plays, operettas, minstrels. NOT MANAGED BY KEITH!"

Unfortunately, its few lessees had little success, and the theatre remained closed except for occasional rentals, including a brief run of *Uncle Tom's Cabin* in December 1896. In later years it and the front building floors were used as an extension of a first-floor store called O'Callaghan's. On September 3, 1906, the Bijou came back to life, leased to John Craig's stock company.

On July 20, 1895, the Hanover Theatre announced a magnificently fireproof stage and splendidly constructed auditorium at 187–179 Hanover Street.

In September 1895 Atherton Brownell wrote, for *Bostonian Magazine*, an article titled "Boston Theatres of Today." It is of an era to be remembered, for in the spring of 1896 a new invention would change Boston's theatrical scene forever.

Boston has the reputation of being the best "show town" in the United States, which means that it can be relied upon to put more money into the coffers of theatrical managers than any other city. It also has the reputation of being the most critical city, and certain it is that in its playhouses will be seen gathered audiences which from point of intelligence, will rival any other city, and which are only equaled in London or Paris.

With these things holding true, it is not at all remarkable that Boston's playhouses should represent and reflect this state of affairs, with the result that, not only in point of numbers in proportion to the population, but also in construction and architecture and beauty, the theatres are fully in keeping with the liberality of thought given to the plays themselves.

From the Boston Museum, which is the oldest existing theatre in Boston, to the Castle Square, which is the newest, is a wide step, but so great has been the interest that, while the old cannot keep pace with the new in every point of mechanical construction, there is no theatre that is more thoroughly alive today than the Museum, which keeps pace with the new in things artistic, and which this year returns to a modification of the old stock company system, which was here in vogue for so many years, and which finds so many advocates among what are called "the old-timers."

For many years Mr. R.M. Field has been the sole manager, and he is to be thanked for giving to the world so many of the artists who have found a warm place in the hearts of the people. Who, that ever saw [William] Warren can ever forget him? And he is enshrined along with Mrs. Vincent and the others, whose names are indissoluble, connected with the old house. When Mr. Field abandoned the stock company a few years ago, it was with regret and a secret longing for its return, a thing which has been made possible this year by the combination of forces with Charles Frohman of New York, and Messrs. Rich and Harris of this city, these four now being the controllers of the destinies of the house with Mr. Field as resident manager. The plan for the coming season is a very attractive one and means that by this concentration of effort, there will be presented at this house the most successful plays that are to be obtained on this or any other side of the water; and that the most skillful and noted actors will be located here during the run of any one play. As these runs will undoubtedly be for long periods, it means that the actors will become familiar to our people and that this is one of the cases where familiarity does not breed contempt, the result may be conjectured as most favorable to all concerned.

The Boston Theatre, too, which ranks next to the Museum in point of age, and rivals it in historical interest, seems to have renewed its youth, and opens its season with the promise of those great spectacles which in other days made its name known from one end of the country to the other. Unlike any other theatre in America, probably, its ownership and management has always remained in one family, it having been built by the father of the present manager, Mr. Eugene Tompkins. Mr. Tompkins also enjoys the reputation of being the wealthiest manager in America, and most of this he has gained by his own efforts and shrewdness in theatrical affairs, a trait inherited along with the foundation of his fortune from his father, Orlando Tompkins. The Boston Theatre was a marvel in its day, and it still retains the reputation it then won as a model playhouse. In size it was, and we think still is, the largest in this country, with perhaps one exception, and its acoustic properties are something to make modern architects grieve that they cannot excel them.

Here has been given a spectacle on such a scale of grandeur as has seldom been seen elsewhere, and memories of the days of "Jalma," "The World," "Michael Strogoff" and other spectacular or melodramatic productions are still fond ones to most of us. And in renewing its youth the Boston Theatre has not stopped at new decoration throughout the handsome and great auditorium. With this season Mr. Tompkins returns again to his earlier method, and promises us another grand production, this time of the melodrama "Burmah," with all of the splendor of old, and with the added advantage of the most modern thought and appliances.

From the immensity of the Boston Theatre to the diminutiveness of the Park Theatre is a step indeed, but both are suited to their respective uses. The Park Theatre is more of what may be termed a parlor playhouse and peculiarly adapted to the presentation of light comedy to which it is largely devoted at the present time. It is owned by a woman who is known the country over as "Lotta," but she signs her name in checks as Charlotte Crabtree." And here again it may be noted that there is a coincidence between this house and the Boston Theatre in that its owner is the wealthiest actress in America.

When the Globe Theatre was burned, the house was under the management of Miss Crabtree's brother, but negotiations were at once opened to Mr. John Stetson with the result that he is today its manager. Immediately upon taking control, the house was renovated and redecorated, so that it is now a very handsome place of amusement, and as the limitations of the house were very sharply defined, he has kept it to its legitimate uses as a home of light comedy and of farce, many of Hoyt's most successful farce-comedies first seeing light here.

When the Hollis Street Church was turned into a theatre and opened in 1885, it was generally predicted that it would be a failure. People argued that the theatre-goers would not travel up in that direction but Manager Isaac B. Rich thought he had learned a thing or two in his many years of theatrical management, and subsequent events have shown that he had. It is generally known that a large sum of money was set aside for the purpose of losing at the beginning, in order to draw the people in that direction. Mr. Rich began by building up a clientele for his house, and so successfully that the croakers were soon silenced, and the Hollis Street Theatre stands today as the resort of fashion more distinctly than any other theatre and it has contained many brilliant audiences. Both before and behind the curtain it is noted for the excellence of its management, and its equipment is such that it can stage any play most admirably. The past summer has seen changes and enlargements behind the curtain line which will make it even more roomy and spacious, so that the effects upon its stage may be the more complete. Mr. Rich has established the theatre upon such a firm footing that it now pursues the even tenor of its excellent way, and so valuable is it to the theatrical managers that its time is filled for seasons in advance so far as many be determined. One can always be sure of seeing a certain line of attractions at this house, for it has become the Boston home of many companies from other cities which never think of going anywhere else. Thus, year after year, Augustine Daly's Company, Daniel Frohman's Lyceum Theatre Company, Julian Marlowe Taber, and many others of equal note play from this stage.

Associated with Mr. Rich in the management of this house is his son, Mr. Charles J. Rich, who is following in the paternal footsteps. He is always to be found at the theatre, courteous and solicitous for the welfare of his patrons, and aside from that he has embarked upon management of his own with excellent success.

Even farther up town than the Hollis Street Theatre is the Grand Opera House, which was devoted to its present uses in 1888. It is an exceedingly large theatre, next to the Boston in size, and is now devoted to the popular form of continuous vaudeville performances under the management of Mr. George E. Mansfield, who was one of the managers when the house was first opened. It was for many years devoted to the production largely of melodrama, and for one year it tried the experiment of a stock company; but that not proving successful it came back to its old management, and after a year of the old form, in which the professional matinees on Thursdays were a feature, it is now devoted as above said, to continuous vaudeville.

The Tremont Theatre may fairly be called the first of the modern theatres of Boston, i.e. the first to be built from the ground up for the purpose for which it was designed from modern plans. The result is that it is most complete in every way, not only from an architectural standpoint, but also as decorations and accessories. As it was opened by the British comedian, Mr. Charles Wyndham, that seemed to give it a certain foreign stamp, which later events have carried out and accentuated. Being built and managed by Messrs. Henry E. Abbey and John B. Schoeffel, it is but natural that their attractions from abroad should be seen at this house. Being international managers, they control very largely the American tours of the world's greatest artists; and thus it comes that at the Tremont Theatre has been seen in a short space of time such world-famous players as Henry Irving and Ellen Terry, Coquelin, Sarah Bernhardt, Mounet-Sully, and Rejane. With this class of attractions as a foundation the standing of the theatre is beyond question, especially as the standard is kept up in other lines. The theatre is cosy, and of just the right size to admit of a wide range of productions.

The Columbia Theatre was the next to follow, and in its construction the Moorish style of architecture was used, so that it presents a pleasing change from the more usual forms. It aimed at first to present attractions such as the Museum will this year present, and was under the management of Messrs. Harris and Atkinson, the latter withdrawing later, and his place being taken by Isaac B. Rich and Charles Frohman. With the latter firm withdrawing to the Museum, the Columbia is now under the management of R.M. Gulick, who will present this season a line of melodrama. Mr. Gulick is unknown to Boston as yet, his home being in Pittsburgh, Penn., where has made a distinct success of his Bijou Theatre. With the acquirement of the Columbia Theatre, he now has a circuit of four theatres, in Pittsburgh, Philadelphia, Brooklyn and Boston. He will cater to the middle class of playgoers, with sensational plays at moderate price.... No visitor to Boston feels that his mission has been accomplished until he has seen Keith's New Theatre, which is hardly excelled in the world for lavishness of outlay and the artistic results accomplished. The interior suggests more the interior of the palace at Versailles than a playhouse and in its lobbies and retiring rooms are to be found cabinets of rare china; while the walls are covered with brocades which delight the eye of the connoisseur, and with paintings which are dainty and artistic. Mr. Keith has arrived at the pinnacle in his particular line, and the home of vaudeville is indeed a gem. From the dime museum of other days we have this development, and Mr. Keith is responsible for raising the taste of the public in this line, through continually seeking the best specialties that can be had. And that this is appreciated is shown today by the fact that this house exists. Recently Mr. Keith made a bold and novel stroke in engaging a part of the Boston Symphony Orchestra to play here, and this is just an example of his constant efforts to raise the standard, and it is this which has brought him the wonderful success which has been his.

Following Keith's came the Castle Square Theatre, which is, indeed, a magnificent playhouse, rivaling Keith's in the splendor of its decorations, and almost rivaling the Boston in its size of stage and auditorium.... The Boston Theatre opened its regular season with the promised grand production of the melodrama "Burmah," and this with the new decorations of the house by L. Haberstroh, make both theatre and play a spectacle well worthy of the seeing. While "Burmah" as a play is not the equal of "Michael Strogoff," for instance, its strength as a melodrama is still undoubted, and its great scenic effects, which are made possible by the immensity of the stage, are remarkable in the extreme. It cannot now be said just how long "Burmah" will run, but it will undoubtedly occupy the Boston Theatre for several months to come. When it leaves here for other cities the stage will be occupied with varied attractions of a high class. The melodrama "In Old Kentucky" is one of the attractions to follow, and an engagement which will win critical notice of Boston, is that of Mme. Helena Modjeska, who will present in English, Sardou's Napoleonic comedy, "Mme. Sans-Gene." ... Joseph Jefferson's annual engagement will be played here, an event that always packs the house, for no actor living in America today enjoys the love of the theatre goers as does this last of the representatives of the old school. "Shore Acres," the New England play, by James A. Herne, which made a more decided stir in the dramatic world of America than any other play of recent years, is also to be seen here, and the lovers of the fantastic and wonderful will find their desires met in the Hanlons' new "Superba."

The Museum's season was practically opened with a very funny farce, by John J. McNally, played by a very humorous comedienne, May Irwin, the play being "The Widow Jones," but the regular season proper opens with "The Fatal Card," a melodrama which ran the entire season in New York, and which is expected to attract Bostonians with equal strength. As the length of the run of this play cannot be determined, it is impossible to say just what plays will be seen at the Museum later, for this will be determined by circumstances. William Gillette's comedy "Too Much Johnson," which is said to be funnier even than "The Private Secretary," will probably be produced here, and beyond that will be seen several plays new to this country, which Mr. Charles Frohman has ready to occupy the stage whenever occasion permits.

At the Hollis, the first really important attraction in the line of the drama is Peter F. Dailey in another new farce by Mr. McNally, called "The Night Clerk." The Empire Theatre Company of New York will be seen here in "The Masqueraders," and other successes of the past New York season, as will also the Lyceum Theatre Company in its latest most successful plays. Ada Rehan will appear in her repertoire during the week of October 28, and Olga Nethersole, the English actress, who made such a marked impression last year, will be seen in her old successes, and in a dramatization of "Carmen." Julia Marlene Taber and her husband, Robert Taber, will be seen in Shakespearian plays, and in one or two new ones which have not previously been included in their repertoire. The New York Casino Company will present "The Merry World," which is a burlesque review of the dramatic season, and Palmer Cox's "Brownies" will appeal to the lovers of spectacle. E.H. Southern will be an early comer, and he will this year present "The Prisoner of Zenda," in which he has just won the approval of critical New York. John Drew, likewise, will be seen in one new play and in his earlier successes. From across the water the Hollis will have the latest musical sensation, Humperdinck's opera "Hansel and Gretel," which has set London and the continent by the ears. From London, also, will come the two musical novelties, "The Shop Girl" and "The Artist's Model"—truly a most attractive list.

The Tremont's season opened on September 2, with a magnificent production of DeKoven and Smith's opera "The Tzigane" with Lillian Russell, which will be followed on September 29 by Henry Irving, Ellen Terry, and the London Lyceum Company in "King Arthur, and several other new plays. Their engagement will last four weeks, and will be supplemented by a single week in April. A newcomer from England is the celebrated comedian Mr. John Hare, whose advent is awaited with much interest. Mrs. Langtry will also be seen at the Tremont this season, and such American stars as James O'Neil and Clara Morris, in drama, and Francis Wilson, Della Fox and DeWolf Hopper, in comic opera. The Bostonians always come to the Tremont with their new operas, and this year will be exception, while for the holidays "Little Christopher" will be the attraction. An important engagement is that of Frank Mayo, in his dramatization of Mark Twain's "Pudd'n head Wilson"; also, the Hollands in their new comedy, "A Man with a Past." Gilbert and Sullivan's latest opera, "His Excellency," will be seen here; also, the Cadets in their new extravaganza.

Then later in the season will come Bernhardt, renewing old triumphs, and, doubtless, winning new ones in the plays, which she will bring.

Of the other theatres it is impossible to outline the season in advance.... The Columbia and Park will keep to their announced line, and at the Castle Square we may expect a constantly varying round of opera—change being made each week, except in the case of some new ones, probably, which are not yet announced, but which will be kept on as long as the public demands it. At Keith's and the Grand Opera House vaudeville will remain the rule, the bills being changed constantly. But from this brief outline possibly Boston theatregoers may get some idea of the treat in store for them.

Chapter 18

The Motion Picture Comes to Boston
Keith Builds a Subway
Burlesque at the Palace and Old Howard
1896–1897

On May 18, 1896, Thomas A. Edison's Vitascope motion pictures appeared for the first time in Boston at B.F. Keith's New Theatre, shown at 11 A.M., 3:30 P.M. and 9 P.M., along with vaudeville. The film show consisted of short subjects, none of which ran more than a few minutes, and featured were John C. Rice and May Irwin in a picture of a kiss from the stage comedy *The Widow Jones.* Joseph S. Cifre, in his essay, "Saga of the Movie Industry in Boston," says: "The first motion picture films shown in Boston were projected from a small velour draped booth located in the front of the balcony. The film was 2⅝ inches wide and each frame 2 inches high, it had no sprocket holes and it was run over velvet covered rollers in the projector with a beater intermittent movement."

The *Boston Herald* remarked: "May not small towns see city shows by the Vitascope? May not actresses, who realize how fleeting youth is, preserve themselves in their prime? Indeed to what use may not the Vitascope be put? Lectures of travelers may now be illustrated actively, and take a new lease of life. Victims of seasickness can see life more in the Orient. But all of this is in the future.... Of course, there is not the slightest chance that any universal use of that sort will be made of the invention yet there is a chance that great actors can leave their work behind them. Fancy, if this invention had been made before Edwin Booth died, his business, at least for Hamlet, might have been preserved."

The *Boston Traveler*'s "Stage Whispers" wrote: "Who knows how the new invention and those that are to follow may revolutionize the amusement world. Perhaps our great-grandchildren may know nothing except as historic memories of stage performances as we have them today. Who knows that each country will not have its stage 'foundries,' so to speak, for each of the various forms of dramatic and musical act? Here finely drilled companies could give performances to be perpetuated by the Vitascope and the phonograph or their successors. Duplicates of the records could be sent by flying machines, broadcast all over the world, and London's new play or latest sensational dance could be enjoyed in every quarter of the globe within a few days of the initial presentation."

Motion pictures were a big success and became a regular part of Keith's programming. Even the staid Boston Museum offered a run of films shown by the Eidoloscope on a 20-foot by 40-foot screen.

The Boston Theatre had taken notice of the handsome B.F. Keith's New Theatre next door. After its season ended in 1895, scaffolds were erected and filled the auditorium. An army of painters took possession of the house, the work being in charge of L. Haberstroh and Son, who had been the decorators of the theatre when it was built and had refurbished it once before in 1870. Yet again Max Bachman did the relief and sculptured work. All of the old chairs and benches were removed from the first floor and the two balconies, replaced by modern comfortable seats. The lobbies and foyers were included in the rejuvenation of the old playhouse.

In the summer of 1896, primitive air conditioning efforts continued. The Park Theatre advertised "ice machines"; and Keith's dumped 8,000 pounds of ice into its ventilation system every day.

On August 10, 1896, George Lothrop's Grand Theatre joined the parade of openings. It was still in the same building at Dover and Washington streets, but during the summer the second-floor auditorium had been lowered to the ground floor. Five large wooden doors, with plate glass panels, opened into a 19-foot-by-50-foot lobby, where iron stairs rose to the balcony. The stage was 50 feet wide by 36 feet deep; grid to stage was 64 feet. Capacity was 600 in the orchestra, 375 in the balcony, and 800 in the gallery; and eight boxes, the Grand Theatre could seat 1,835 patrons. Alas, the lady "natators" had departed.

In November 1896 an unusual enterprise opened in the former public library, on Boylston near Tremont Street, as the building was remodeled into the Zoo, a museum offering curio rooms, a menagerie, and "lecture hall." The structure contained two large reading rooms and the second-floor Bates Hall. Charles F. Atkinson was its director.

Frank V. Dunn took over the Palace Theatre in Scollay Square, renaming it the Trocadero, and by 1897 it was the Palace once more, playing Burlesque and vaudeville. By 1898 the Old Howard, formerly the Howard Athenaeum, had begun a new career as a burlesque house, which lasted until a final police raid in 1953.

The year of the motion picture was indeed 1897. Almost every theatre had a go at them under one name or another. At the new Grand, as well as at Austin and Stone's Museum, it was the Bioscope; the Grand Opera House had Lumiere's Cinematographe; Howard Athenaeum rechristened "The Old Howard," presented fight films on the Acmegraph. The Lyceum unveiled the Cinematoscope, and the Palace had the Aumorgraph. Even the Boston Theatre had a four-week run of the Corbett-Fitzsimmons fight, shown, with each reel being round one, by Veriscope. The Zoo used Lumiere's projector in its lecture hall.

In August 1897, George Lothrop took control of the Bowdoin Square Theatre,

This 1906 photograph shows the Tremont Street entrance that led to the Crystal Tunnel to B.F. Keith's New Theatre (Library of Congress).

presenting melodrama at popular prices. The Lothrop Stock Company held forth in that house for many years. He withdrew from his South End Grand Theatre to concentrate on his two downtown operations.

B.F. Keith pulled another rabbit out of his magic hat in September 1897. As the new trolley car subway opened under Tremont Street, Keith opened his Crystal Tun-

This fireplace is a relic from the Crystal Tunnel of B.F. Keith's New Theatre (courtesy of Boston Public Library, Print Department).

nel. Patrons entered from Tremont Street through an archway resting on columns on white marble and wrought iron. The four-story building was topped by a jeweled glass pagoda, beneath, on each floor, were bays and windows of art glass, and 900 electric lights produced a fairyland effect by night. Inside the entrance was green and gold décor over white marble floors, lobby walls were wainscoted with the obligatory

The rear of B.F. Keith's New Theatre on Tremont Street (courtesy of Boston Public Library, Print Department).

Sienna marble, walls were pale green, and there were molded ornaments after Louis XV and a profuse use of rococo. Its dome was indirectly lit and painted by Tojetti to idealize Keith's "Continuous Performances": Twelve nymphs floated in a blue sky, representing the length of the daily show.

This was only the first lobby. The second contained the same marble floors and wainscoting, but there was the Grand Staircase. Patrons entered through one of four heavy swinging doors of French design with stained glass windows featuring Keith's cupids. Walls were in old rose with four French mirrors and two paintings by Tojetti. Patrons could circle around the staircase, which descended in the middle of the lobby. Doors connecting with Mason Street were in the rear of this room.

An arch divided this lobby ceiling; it, too, was indirectly illuminated and painted with draped female figures showering each other with roses. The staircase walls were of Sienna marble; a bronze railing ran around its opening, and at each side were newel posts topped with large French vases lighted from within. Patrons walked down white marble steps to a landing, then proceeded down a few more to the lower foyer.

To one's right was a fireplace of elaborate design; to the left was a pier glass mirror. Straight ahead was the Crystal Tunnel, 12 feet wide and 35 feet long, 25 of which passed under Mason Street. The ceiling was of heavy French plate glass mirrors, which were also used in wall panels. These latter alternated with ones of stereo relief in rococo and Louis XV gray tints; electric lamps were in carved niches. The tunnel was divided into several flights of white marble steps; Keith cupids pranced about the ceiling as it dropped to match each descent. Finally amid more cherubs and marble, one passed through a pair of massive doors, set with art glass, into the theatre, where one entered beside the orchestra level's right side boxes.

Chapter 19

The Last Days of the Boston Museum
European Music Halls in Boston
1898–1899

In January 1898, the motion picture achieved a status of sorts at the Boston Museum: *The Passion Play* was shown and accompanied by a pipe organ. But films never became the theatre's policy; for years the Boston Museum Stock Company had been so popular it kept the house in fashion. The stock policy ended in the 1890s and the theatre had to rely on booking touring shows. Unfortunately, touring companies preferred to play in newer theatres, and this was an upstairs house, with all of those tacky exhibits! The Boston Museum closed in June 1903 and was demolished to make way for the new Kimball Office Building. Despite all of its fame, the old house could not compete with the new theatres.

Charles H. Grandgent wrote an epitaph in *Fifty Years of Boston* in 1932: "Still more tragic was the demolition of the dear old Museum.... Wither have gone the extensive and really valuable ethnological collections that filled the alcoves of the great hall; and whatever can have become of the dusty, dream-haunting waxworks that haunted the top floor?"

In 1898, the Zoo, formerly the old public library building, changed its name to the Sans Souci and added variety acts, operettas, and refreshments. Its Bates Hall lecture room was converted into the First European Music Hall. Book alcoves became tiers of boxes and promenades with tables, sweeping around three sides of the room on two levels. The main floor had an orchestra level and orchestra circle, its chairs had shelves on their backs to hold refreshments, and "polite vaudeville" played every evening, plus Wednesday and Saturday matinees. Alas, the Sans Souci was not heard of after 1898. The building was sold on February 11, 1899, and a new theatre, the Colonial, was to be erected on its site.

The European Music Hall idea lingered a while, as the Columbia Theatre closed for a remodeling into something of that sort. On November 9, 1899, the Columbia Theatre and Promenade Deluxe opened. Smoking was permitted in all seats, boxes, and the promenade, and refreshments were served. The entrance had been removed to the building next door, to its south. There, patrons entered a brilliant and commodious lobby of Corinthian design in pure white and pink or pale red; directly in front rose a massive bronze-railed white marble staircase leading to the balcony. To the right of the new entrance was a ladies' waiting room, to the left, one stepped into the rear of the old orchestra section, now done in shades of red, while pilasters and box underhangs were painted a pale olive green. Walls, ceiling, proscenium, and box fronts had a tracery of white or a pale tint giving a lacelike effect, and orchestra seats were upholstered in cardinal plush. The main curtain was an olive green shade, and every foot of floor space, even in the second balcony, was carpeted in crimson velvet. Former lobbies had become promenades, elevated and opened toward the stage; 11 mezzanine boxes stretched across the front of the second balcony.

Chapter 20

B.F. Keith and the Vaudeville Wars
The United Booking Office
William Morris and
the Boston Music Hall
1900

The year 1900 was a year of competition for domination over high-class vaudeville presented in high-class theatres. B.F. Keith probably had an inkling of what was coming when he conceived the idea of joining the Bijou to his new theatre. In an anteroom, off the north side of the theatre's long lobby from Washington Street, rose a marble staircase leading up to and from the Bijou's right stage side exit. In February 1900, this lobby vestibule became a new and extra entrance to the Bijou; its walls were covered in old gold silk with dados of white marble, chubby Keith cherubs smiled down from the ceiling. At the foot of this new grand staircase, a newel post surmounted by a bronze figure, holding aloft a branch of electric lights, captured the attention of passing patrons. The Bijou was to be used for overflow audiences, greatly enlarging the capacity of B.F. Keith's New Theatre at little cost to him. Together, the two houses could seat close to 3000 patrons.

Keith's initial competitor planned a summer season of cut-rate admission vaudeville, twice a day, at the 3,000-seat Boston Theatre next door. After a brief battle of newspaper advertising, the opposition collapsed, and Keith's continuous performance policy and his great resources of talent prevailed.

Keith had joined with other theatre owners and managers to form the United Booking Office, the U.B.O. This group controlled the most important vaudeville theatres in the United States; to obtain lucrative play dates actors were forced to book their acts through this agency. Keith represented the U.B.O. in Boston, therefore Keith's theatre got the best acts. This cozy arrangement did not sit very well with independent booking agents; one in particular, William Morris, chose to fight Keith and his U.B.O. He was very popular with actors and still booked acts loyal to him. Keith threatened to boycott performers who did not book through the United Booking

Office, while Morris encouraged theatre owners to open houses in opposition to Keith.

Morris found out that a new Symphony Hall was to open in Boston, leaving the 2,500-seat Boston Music Hall without its orchestral offerings. That huge building had been used for wrestling matches, baby contests, and other promotions. It even had a portable proscenium, which could be erected on its shallow stage. But music paid its overhead. Morris convinced real estate developer R.H. Allen to convert the old hall into a vaudeville theatre and guaranteed to book top attractions. Architects Little and Brown, with W.L. Morrison, started remodeling the old Music Hall.

The stage platform, sounding board, and balconies were removed; a new theatrical proscenium stage was erected at the opposite (northern) end of the hall. Starting at the height of the original first balcony, an orchestra floor sloped to a new orchestra pit. The new first balcony was constructed from the level of the old second. Above, and set well back from the balcony front below, was a new gallery. All that remained of the old Music Hall were its walls, ceiling, and those narrow side balconies closest to the new proscenium, which served as boxes. Two elevators connected every floor.

Entrances from Tremont Street's Hamilton Place and Winter Street's Music Hall Place were retained. From Hamilton Place, one entered a paneled vestibule decorated with plaster pendants and garlands in the Greek style. To the left, set in a panel, was the box office. After purchasing tickets, patrons entered the Grand Salon, which ran under the rear of the auditorium. That beautiful room was done in Louis XV period fashion, its vaulted ceiling seemingly supported by dove-gray marble pilasters with gold caps and bottoms, with 16 great mirrors framed in gold in between. A staircase descended to the Winter Street entrance. At the four corners of the Grand Salon were drinking fountains of African marble (water was dispensed from lion heads). The salon's crimson carpeting set off the soft gray and gold coloring of this salon. Artists who had decorated the Castle Square Theatre and New York's Metropolitan Opera House embellished the Music Hall auditorium in Empire Period style. Colors were pale green, salmon pink, shading to a light maroon, and an abundance of gold leaf was added. Three thousand electric lamps were set into the ceiling and cornices; a modern ventilating system similar to that of B.F. Keith's New Theatre was installed.

Morris suggested that a complete orchestra be used to accompany Music Hall's vaudeville (Keith used only a piano and drums). Morris booked a program of headliner acts for the Labor Day 1900 opening. Newspaper advertisements, under the name Boston Music–Musee Hall, announced "Continuous Refined Vaudeville ... *NOT CONTROLLED BY A TRUST*," trust being an unpopular word with the public at the time.

On September 17, the Musee portion opened in the former Bumstead Hall, under the old auditorium level, off the Winter Street entrance. Exhibits, mostly wax figures, were brought directly from the Eden Musee in New York City.

Chapter 21

The Colonial, Majestic, and Globe Theaters
The Brothers Shubert Arrive
1900–1903

The year 1900 ended with the December 19 opening of a magnificent playhouse, the Colonial Theatre. Architect Clarence Blackall drew upon the concepts of the owners, the lessees, and himself. Fortunately, he was given a free hand because the result was sheer beauty. The theatre was in the rear of a new office building on the site of the old public library, last known as the Zoo or Sans Souci, on Boylston near Tremont Street, and facing Boston Common. The *Boston Globe* reported, "It glitters like a jewel box.... It is the best of the old world ideas of decoration of other centuries.... Bits of old galleries and places and theatres ... brought together in a strong mise-en-scene re-gilded and filled out with the necessary harmonizing decorations and modern accessories to make a perfect whole." Two entrances were on Boylston Street. One for the gallery was closest to Tremont Street, and the grand entrance was at the right end of the building, marked by an ornate copper canopy extending slightly over the sidewalk. Doors were of stained mahogany.

A 19-foot-wide vestibule ran straight back for 70 feet. Walls of mottled black and white marble rose nine feet, and above was a border of frescoes of fruit in strong colors, boldly drawn, as in a Pompeian house. An arched ceiling was over all, its panels having wreaths in their center, and below, floors were made of mosaic blocks. A box-office window, finished in mahogany, was set into the left wall.

Patrons entered a wide foyer parallel with Boylston Street and stepped onto a deep scarlet carpet. Walls were adorned with tall plate glass mirrors in gold frames, and the ceiling was covered by a number of rich paintings. The foyer was a combination of earlier French and Italian styles, and woodwork was beautifully carved satinwood. An abundance of gilt appeared on walls and ceiling. This hall was 60 feet long by 18 wide, and at each end were bronze-sided staircases leading to the balcony.

As patrons stepped into the auditorium they were overcome by a feeling of vastness as well as the utter beauty of the elaborate décor. Two balconies, curving from

The Colonial Theatre was opened in 1900 in an office building across from Boston Common (courtesy of Boston Public Library, Print Department).

boxes to boxes, were fronted with belts of embossed gold and cupids sprang forth at intervals. A tall and wide proscenium arch was heavy with gilt and in its top center was a large escutcheon of turquoise blue. On either side of the stage were three tiers of large single boxes between pillars of Sienna marble.

The general tone of the auditorium was Gobelin blue, close to green, in a tapestry effect with stenciled ornaments. Woodwork was "white" mahogany rubbed to a dull finish. Seats were upholstered in dark green leather, bearing the monogram of intertwined C and T on their backs. Below the orchestra floor was a plenum chamber through which air was introduced under the chairs.

On February 8, 1901, the newest Chickering Hall opened on Huntington near Massachusetts Avenue, being the fourth to carry that name, and was designed as a concert or lecture hall. The auditorium was quietly decorated in pale olive green with snow-white pillars and panels, and there was a high ceiling under which was a small 175-seat balcony. Its center orchestra held broad seating curves with two main aisles, and on its sides and back were four to six raised rows of chairs parallel with its walls. Its shallow stage held a big apron, and the auditorium seated 800 patrons. The house was broader than long, and high with a beamed ceiling. Between squares were several hundred feet of thick glass windows for abundant lighting, and it could be raised for ventilation. A long lobby passage with studios led from Huntington Avenue, and a second floor held spaces for offices and schools. This tiny hall would one day become a grand edifice named after a saint.

On February 16, 1903, the new Majestic Theatre opened on Tremont Street, almost around the corner from the new Colonial. Lessees were E.D. Stair and A.L. Wilbur, who had also leased the Boston Music Hall; these men had great plans for Boston's legitimate stage. Architect John Galen Howard designed one of Boston's most charming theatres, its great height dominated that end of Tremont Street, below Boylston. The façade consisted of three tall arched entrances, above which were a frieze and three taller arched windows, nearly three stories, which were pillared and ornamented in a Romanesque style. Over each window was a huge ornamental mask.

Patrons entered into a small but beautiful lobby with mural decorations in panels and lunettes. They were surrounded by fine stained glass windows, mirrored walls, and a heavily gilded frieze in relief. Pillared entrances introduced stairways to the balconies and access to the orchestra. The auditorium was a series of arches proceeding from that of the proscenium, each one swung higher until reaching the gallery ceiling. Every one was handsomely garlanded and interspersed with light globes, with a predominant color scheme of turquoise, blue and gold.

The first balcony had a graceful shallow curve, a welcome departure from nineteenth-century "horse-shoes." The gallery was steep in three step rises, The gallery entrance was on Van Rensselaer Alley, alongside the theatre from Tremont Street.

The rear of the orchestra was paneled in Numidian marble, as was the standing-room rail. On each side of the auditorium were four boxes at the main floor level, and four more above them, slightly below the first balcony level. Tall arches, heavily ornamented, rose above them, and these boxes descended with the slope of the orchestra floor. An ornate proscenium arch was thoroughly gilded; eight light globes were mounted in its top curve.

On August 17, 1903, E.D. Stair and A.L. Wilbur refurbished the old Grand Theatre at Dover and Washington streets and reopened it as the Hub, "Boston's Parlor Theatre."

On September 14, 1903, the new (and third) Globe Theatre opened a few blocks down Washington Street from its predecessors, almost at the corner of Beach Street. Its architect was Arthur H. Vinal. The *Boston Globe* marveled at "an absence of gold, gilt, or glitter, a harmony of architectural lines, a simple beauty of soft neutral coloring.... This is the first impression one receives." The house's prevailing tone was white, and the only other colors used were old rose and green. The interior style was Louis XV. Box, balcony, and gallery fronts were covered in old rose imperial velour, drapes throughout were in the same shade, and orchestra seats were upholstered in old rose leather. Carpets were green.

The Globe's white proscenium arch was studded with electric lights, with a watercolor painting, *Dance of the Muses*, above. There were three boxes—three tiers on each side of two each with an extra one in line with the gallery front, between it and the rest of the boxes. Above their tiers was a fan or flarelike shell, painted white, with a semicircle of incandescent bulbs. The auditorium ceiling was a progression of arches

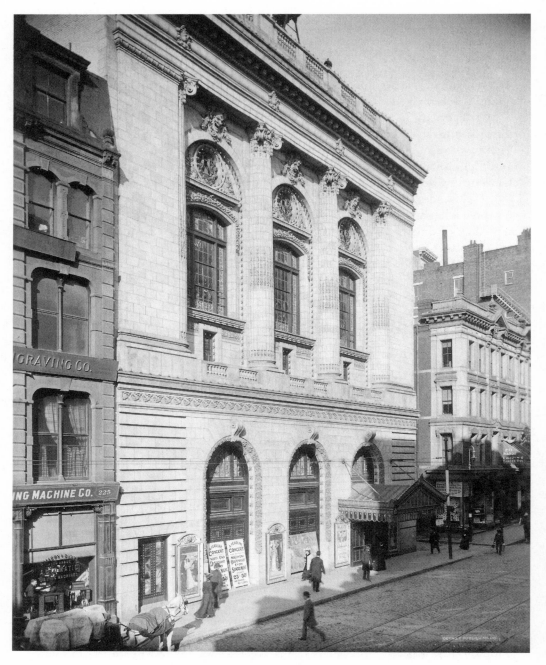

The Majestic Theatre opened in 1903 (Library of Congress).

from the proscenium, and from it hung a chandelier (actually a Verde green bronze skeleton globe), surmounted by a circle of lights.

The auditorium was 75 feet by 74 feet. Seventy-five feet from the stage was considered proper length from stage front in those no-microphone days. Capacity was 637 in the orchestra, 383 in the balcony, 404 in the gallery, and 112 in the boxes, for

The interior of the Majestic Theatre, as shown in a postcard from 1906 or earlier (courtesy of Boston Public Library, Print Department).

The Globe Theatre, which opened in 1903, and on its left, the Premier ten-cent motion picture theatre (courtesy of Boston Public Library, Print Department).

a total of 1,536 seats. Its irregular-shaped back wall stage was 55 feet at its deepest, the gridiron 85 feet high, and the proscenium 34 feet wide by 40 feet high.

The main entrance was 30 feet wide, opening into a lobby 40 feet deep. Beautiful murals topped the doors to the auditorium. Two marble staircases started at each side, rising to the balcony promenade, which had marble pilasters and a mosaic floor, its ceiling arched and illumined by concealed bulbs.

The façade of the theatre was striking: Its two-story entrance arch was four feet deep, cut into panels with centered light bulbs. Facing was light brick and terra-cotta topped with frieze work, cornice, and balustrade (rooftop). On the balustrade were 11 bronze posts five feet high topped with lamps, and clusters of bouquet lights hung between them. On either side of the main arch iron, lamps swung from terra-cotta panels.

Over the doorway the words Globe Theatre were in illuminated letters on a vertical sign which rose to the rooftop. Above the canopied entrance was a large "talking sign" that could be seen by viewers on upper Washington Street, since the Globe was the last playhouse on "Boston's Broadway." The sign had grooves into which individual squares of electric bulbed letters were set, spelling out the current attraction or star. Soon the fronts and roofs of every big city theatre boasted these signs, the ancestor of movie palace marquees.

On September 28, 1903, Sam S., Lee, and Jacob Shubert reopened the Columbia Theatre for legitimate stage productions. These young men had come down from Syracuse, New York, in 1900 to operate a theatre in New York City; there they had run into opposition from "the Syndicate."

In 1896, a group of legitimate stage theatre owners, producers, and booking agents met and agreed to centralize their bookings into one office and to organize their theatres into one chain. Producers would either play through their bookers or not secure key theatres for their shows. Bookers for the Syndicate were able to secure advantageous terms for use of its playhouses. Organizers of the monopoly were Charles Frohman, Marc Klaw, and Abraham Lincoln Erlanger, et al.

The newcomer Shubert brothers fronted an independent movement to do battle with the Syndicate. They produced their own shows and started to build a chain of legitimate theatres. Dissident managers, producers, and actors played along with them, and supporters included E.D. Stair and A.L. Wilbur, who in January 1904 leased the Globe Theatre. That gave them five houses in Boston, the others being the Boston Music Hall, Majestic, Hub, and Shubert's Columbia. In August 1904, they added the Grand Opera House. In competition were the Syndicate's Frohman and Harris, operating the Colonial and Park theatres, plus Isaac B. Rich, who had the Hollis Theatre. For some reason Charles Frohman had leased Chickering Hall, enlarged its stage and presented the morality play *Everyman* along with Shakespeare repertory, a dramatic policy that lasted through 1904.

A king of peace occurred in 1904 when the Shuberts joined forces with Klaw and Erlanger to form the U.S. Amusement Company, whose purpose was to present advanced vaudeville in their theatres, in competition with B.F. Keith. The Music Hall opened its 1904 season with "All Star Vaudeville"; the scheme was to shake down Keith and Albee and get rid of the competition.

Chapter 22

The Music Hall Becomes Loew's Orpheum

A Sleeping Giant Wakes Up

The Poor Man's Amusement

1905–1908

The Boston Music Hall was substantially remodeled yet again. Arthur H. Vinal, the Globe architect, discarded the shelflike boxes and added two tiers of new ones on either side of the proscenium, and the rather Spartan balcony and gallery fronts were redesigned. A new color was created especially for the Music Hall, "Rose Dubarry Red," which was used in redecorating the auditorium. However, the most important development was the addition of a third entrance from 415 Washington Street on Boston's Broadway. On February 12, 1905, the Music Hall was renamed the Empire Theatre.

The Tremont Temple had regularly housed the Burton Holmes travel slide shows, which lately had included motion pictures, and in 1905 the temple presented Lyman H. Howe's *Lifeorama* films as well. Otherwise, the showing of films was at the tail end of vaudeville and burlesque shows. The only subjects lasting more than five or ten minutes were prizefight boxing films, which were shown round by round. The lowering of the picture sheet had become notice to the patrons that the real show was over. Entrepreneurs continued to use the Tremont Temple for higher-class motion picture presentations; in 1906 Holmes, Howe, and a week of "colored motion pictures" appeared.

In November, the Park Square Garden, formerly the Providence railroad station, became a roller skating rink.

Horticultural Hall moved to its new and permanent home at 800 Massachusetts Avenue.

On September 3, 1906, the Empire (Music Hall) Theatre became Percy Williams' Orpheum Theatre, whose operation came about as a result of a feud between B.F. Keith and Williams. Williams vowed to fight Keith in Boston and Philadelphia, while

The Tremont Temple became a movie theatre (author's collection).

William Morris continued to book headliner after headliner into the Orpheum. Keith did likewise. The winners were audiences, who were enjoying this surfeit of entertainment.

On that same date, the Bijou Theatre was reopened and leased to the popular John Craig Stock Company for one year.

Charles H. Grandgent wrote about the movies: "Their ancestors were those none too reputable penny-in-the-slot machines which stood in rows in unused shops and doorways. A real motion picture, though, was exhibited as a curiosity in an office opposite Clark's Hotel about 1902, and a regular show arrived about 1905 on Washington Street.... It took the form of an old [railway] coach in which the public sat, watching the landscape slide by." This was an attraction on Stuart Street called Hale's Tours, operated by William Brady and Adolph Zukor. Customers sat in mockups of train coach interiors, which shook, rattled and rocked as filmed scenery rushed by on a motion picture screen. This was short-lived attraction. The location then became the Unique Theatre, later the Stuart.

Boston's first theatre devoted exclusively to motion pictures debuted September 3, 1906. The Comique was opened by Joe and Max Mark, at 14 Tremont Row in Scollay Square, advertising *The World in Motion*, motion pictures and illustrated songs, for ten cents. The small house operated from 9 A.M. to 11:30 P.M. The program consisted of short films, but soon the management was advertising its best ones by title. A sleeping giant was beginning to stir. It opened one eye in January 1907 as the 250-seat Unique Theatre premiered at 700 Washington Street, at Kneeland, also showing movies and song sides for a dime.

The sleeping giant opened both eyes when a procession of ten-cent nickelodeon openings followed—in March, the Lyric at 734 Washington Street; in April, the Theatre Premier at Beach and Washington Street, next door to the Globe; in June, the Theatre Jolliette near Bowdoin Square; in November, the Star Theatre at 5 Tremont Row and the Scenic Temple in Berkley Hall at Berkley and Warren streets.

Joseph S. Cifre and his family operated a theatre supply business in Boston, and he grew up in the movie business. In his unpublished essay "Saga of the Movie Industry in Boston," he writes that many of the early movie arcades did not provide seating for patrons nor an enclosure around the projector.

The men who operated the projectors came from the theatres: calcium light operators, electricians, stage hands, slot machine repairmen. By 1908, in Massachusetts, all projectionists and assistants (reel boys) had to be licensed.

The Tremont Temple presented the Pathé brothers' *Passion Play* in December 1907, accompanied by a large newspaper advertising campaign similar to those used by regular theatrical productions.

With this sudden interest in films, B.F. Keith discussed with his son Paul ways to enter this lucrative new form of show business. The Bijou was without a tenant again, but both Keiths were occupied with the vaudeville war. Percy Williams was attacking them in Boston and Klaw and Erlanger with the Shuberts were fighting them in other "Keith towns." In late summer, Paul Keith began plans to build movie houses and to convert their Bijou into one of them. (Tenant John Craig and his stock company moved to the Globe Theatre.)

B.F. Keith got Williams out of the Boston Orpheum by giving him a lucrative piece of his United Booking Office. However to Keith's dismay, the Orpheum reopened in September 1907, continuing its vaudeville policy, and being booked by his old foe, William Morris. Moreover, on Labor Day, Klaw and Erlanger put "advanced vaudeville" into their Tremont Theatre in Boston; Keith and his general manager, E.F. Albee, paid them and the Shuberts a small fortune to obtain an agreement that they would stay out of vaudeville for a decade or more. Once more, Keith was in control.

At the end of 1906, the Columbia Theatre had become a burlesque house, the beginning of its slide.

The Boston Theatre underwent a change of management and policy in 1907. Too many new playhouses and too many Syndicate shenanigans were pressuring that grand showplace. A stock company was established on its vast and historic stage.

The Eden Musee moved to 723–727 Washington Street with its waxed figures.

The year 1908 commenced with B.F. Keith's 25th anniversary in show business, and the impresario had two surprises ready for Boston. On February 24, the Bijou Dream Theatre opened, showing continuous motion pictures from 10 A.M. to 10:30 P.M., accompanied by an all-female orchestra, for ten cents. Newspaper ads read "You

B.F. Keith's New Theatre and the Bijou Dream, which played movies from 10 A.M. to 10:30 P.M., circa 1908 (author's collection).

enter by the Crystal Cascade Electric Waterfall, or the 'escalader' from Washington Street. You leave by the Bijou Dream staircase, the Washington Street lobby and Tremont Street Subway of Keith's, or the Crystal Subway of the Boston Theatre to Tremont Street." Paul Keith had remodeled the old Bijou, adding mirrors and marble almost everywhere. The smaller right stairway had new glass steps, and a torrent

When the Bijou closed, it became O'Callaghan's store, circa 1900 (courtesy of Boston Public Library, Print Department).

of water, electrically illuminated, cascaded under them. An escalator, one of the first in Boston, had been cut into the right portion of the main staircase, eliminating the necessity of climbing stairs.

The Boston Theatre had opened a new lobby entry from Tremont Street, adjacent to that of B.F. Keith's entrance. Patrons crossed intervening Mason Street into

Klaw and Erlanger put "advanced vaudeville" in the Tremont Theatre (courtesy of Boston Public Library, Print Department).

one of the old house's former exits, which connected with its Washington Street lobby. It is interesting to note the use of that passage for Bijou patrons. Something was afoot—obviously Keith was dickering for the Boston Theatre lease, or a purchase of the property.

The Bijou, opening as the first "bona-fide deluxe theatre" with a "films only" policy, spurred the competition to place larger advertisements in newspapers. The ads' emphasis was on comfort, coziness, and being "on the ground floor." Theatre Premier offered *The Scarlet Letter*; the Bijou Dream countered with *The Life of Christ*; Premier topped that attraction with films of the then "hot" subject, ruins of neighboring Chelsea's Great Fire. On May 4 the Premier followed that coup with "pictures that talk, the Humanova." Human actors spoke dialogue from behind the screen. And on May 1, the Premier bragged of its 14 electric fans.

Three more dime movie houses opened in 1908. February brought the Pastime Theatre on Avery near Washington Street; March found the Eden Musee at 723–727 Washington Street; and in October the Idle Hour Theatre opened in Castle Square, off Tremont Street.

On July 5, 1908, Keith sprang his second surprise, opening the Boston Theatre with "All Star Vaudeville" plus the Boston Theatre Stock Company. Bijou Dream patrons could also enjoy the show there, paying only the difference in price. The Boston's admission was 75, 50, or 35 cents on the main floor, 25 cents for the first balcony, and ten cents for the top gallery. The Bijou had two exits leading directly into the Boston Theatre's balconies, dating to the 1860 visit of the Prince of Wales, and the wall cuts for entrances to the supper rooms in the old Melodeon, predecessor of the Bijou. All this, and the Kinetograph, too.

The Orpheum dropped vaudeville for the summer. B.F. Keith also shuttered his theatre, although it remained "now open for inspection." Keith knew that his old nemesis would be ready for battle in autumn. On October 5, William Morris reopened the Orpheum with "High Class Vaudeville" and "The Morris-Scope," and he established a branch of his booking agency in that structure as well. Keith had his booking agency in his Tremont Street Building. Keith returned the Boston Theatre to a stock policy—he could not operate two large vaudeville houses side by side and do battle with Morris, too.

Chapter 23

The Gaiety Theatre, the Boston Opera House The Sam S. Shubert Theatre 1908–1910

The year 1908 ended on a high note. November 23 saw the opening of the Gaiety Theatre on Washington Street, partially on the site of the old Lyceum-World Museum, near Boylston.[1] Architect Clarence H. Blackall blended a steel skeleton with reinforced cement to produce a fireproof 1,700-seat showplace with exits on three sides. No posts appeared to be holding up the curved first balcony. Above was a straight-front steep gallery, with 20 brass-railed boxes in three tiers at each side of the old gold proscenium. The auditorium was done in a soft magenta tone.

An office building fronted the Gaiety Theatre, under which ran a long broad vestibule where paneled walls of Pavanazza marble flanked a tessellated floor. Over the main entrance was an iron and glass marquee displaying the head of a "Gaiety Girl," and an ornamental electric device spelled out the theatre name. The policy was burlesque musicals, which was not the near-naked striptease of modern times. The shows were satires of Broadway productions and current events.

By the end of the year the Park Square Coliseum and Winter Garden (the old Providence Railroad Station) was offering movies and a midway for ten cents admission.

The Boston Theatre, under the management of Charles Frohman and William Harris opened on April 16, 1909 (title to the property had passed to Keith interests, in the name of Mary C. Keith). Its new owners found it expedient to lease out the mammoth house as a legitimate stage theatre because the syndicate needed more outlets to counter Shubert acquisitions. Keith had enough problems with his own theatre and the struggle with Morris and the Orpheum. Keith and his son were also watching the progress of motion pictures; they had established the Keith Nickel Circuit in 1908, covering six New England cities: Portland, Bangor, Lewiston, and Biddeford, Maine; Haverhill, Massachusetts; and in Manchester, New Hampshire.

In August, the Tremont Temple hosted the annual return of Lyman H. Howe and his moving pictures; this time he paid for big newspaper ads to announce "Ride on a Runaway Train Through the Tyrolean Alps!

On September 13, the *Boston Globe* told its readers that the "Orpheum will be known as the American Music Hall, thus forming a link in the chain of independent vaudeville theatres ... which William Morris (Inc.) has established from coast to coast."

In October, Potter Hall, at 177 Huntington Avenue, joined the ranks of dime movie and vaudeville houses.

The big event of the year was the November 8 opening of the Boston Opera House on Huntington Avenue. Eben B. Jordan, owner of Jordan and Marsh's Department Store, financed its construction and guaranteed expenses for three years. All seats were sold by subscription before its premiere. Newspapers were so busy describing Boston society stars, their clothes and who owned which box, that very little was written about the theatre itself. One could not help being impressed by accompanying photographs, showing a 12-foot-deep proscenium arch holding the orchestra pit embraced within its vast frame. Two tiers of boxes ran in a semicircle around the main floor. Above these boxes was a first balcony with a few rows of mezzanine seating in the front, and starting at this level were six boxes running to the proscenium at each side, handsomely framed by tall columns. A gallery rose above the balcony.

The *Boston Post* commented, sparingly: "The building is of the Renaissance type, simple in its exterior, but of beautiful lines. The four massive Corinthian pillars, the red brick and terracotta, all harmonize into an effect that is striking and in keeping with the architecture of the neighboring buildings.... The interior is pure Italian of the Renaissance period. There is little floral work and the ornamentation everywhere is in as low relief as possible."

When Jordan's three years of paying Opera House expenses were up, the opera proceeded, not without showing signs of staggering. The next season brought to the vast hall, too big for most purposes, the Jewett Players in Shakespeare's plays. Come 1919, the house was given over, while not closed, to variety performances.

The year 1910 brought two new theatres to Boston. Waldron's Casino bowed on January 3, and the Sam S. Shubert followed on January 24. The Casino was erected behind older buildings that fronted on Hanover Street near Scollay Square. One of the stores, No. 44, became a rather long theatre lobby. The George A. Fuller Company constructed a fireproof steel frame theatre, and its auditorium was pedestrian compared with contemporary showplaces. The two balconies, slightly curved in their fronts, were studded with electric light bulbs. The Casino had nine boxes at each side of the stage on three levels. Its ceiling rose in arches from proscenium to gallery, and the extent of décor, other than color, appears to have been stenciling on box fronts and arches. The theatre was best known as a burlesque house.

The steel, concrete, and brick Sam S. Shubert Theatre, named after the deceased brother, was designed by Boston architect Thomas M. Jones. Its entrance was on Tremont Street about one block from the Majestic. Patrons passed under a marquee of wrought iron and glass, then came into a ticket lobby, whose tessellated floor was slightly inclined. Floors and walls were paneled. Every Shubert-owned theatre now had a photograph of the deceased Sam in its lobby. Next, patrons entered a spacious Grand Lobby. On each side were two ornamented pillars under three arches, which

The Boston Opera House was built on Huntington Avenue (Library of Congress).

supported a heavily gilded domed ceiling. The chandelier was copied from those in the Petit Trianon. Behind the arches were white marble stairs ascending to the balcony. Decorative paintings were done on lunettes over the lobby doors, and drapes were of green plush with gold borders. Walls were tinted in silver, gray, and gold, their bases were Verde antique marble, and a red rug covered most of the mosaic floor.

The Shubert lobby opened into a foyer 15 feet deep by 110 feet running around the entire back of the orchestra and connecting with boxes at each end. This spacious area was decorated in silver and gold Louis XV period style. Florentine doors gave access to a standing-room section eight feet deep in the rear of the orchestra seating.

The auditorium dimensions were 80 feet by 80 feet, and the proscenium arch was 40 feet wide by 33 feet high. Ionic pillars held up a lightly ornamented lintel frieze, and above was a cornice with lunettes rising to a painted ceiling. The interior was decorated in a dull silver gray background with gold ornamental relief work in the spirit of the French Renaissance. On either side of the stage were four orchestra and four balcony boxes draped in red plush. The Shubert main floor seated 650, with 500 in the first balcony and 400 in the second balcony. The stage was 50 feet deep and 68 feet to its gridiron. Scenery doors were on Warrenton Street, and an additional stage door and the second balcony entrances were on Seaver Place.

Boxes and orchestra of the Boston Opera House (courtesy of Boston Public Library, Print Department).

Waldron's Casino, at right, opened in January 1910 (courtesy of Boston Public Library, Print Department).

This theatre gave the Shuberts control of three houses in Boston. The other two were the Majestic and the Globe (they had given up their lease on the Columbia). The syndicate controlled the Tremont, Boston, Hollis Street, and Colonial theatres.

In 1910, after a summer of stock plays, the American Music Hall became the Orpheum once more, playing ten-cent vaudeville with films. Keith was victorious; a vanquished Morris had sold his circuit of theatres to his good friend, Marcus Loew, who owned a chain of small-time, low-priced, vaudeville-plus-picture houses. Small newspaper ads announced the arrival in Boston of "Loew's Orpheum, Pictures and Vaudeville, 10–15–25 cents."

A new motion picture theatre, Jacob Lourie's 800-seat Beacon, opened in February 1910, on Tremont Street almost at Scollay Square. The Beacon was architect Blackall's first film house and joined Boston's thriving multitude of dime movie enterprises. It played films and vaudeville for ten cents.

The Gayety (formerly Gaiety), Globe, and Columbia theatres changed to a policy of 10 and 20 cents admission with vaudeville and pictures.

In 1911, the Tremont Temple showed films of the coronation of England's King

A postcard view of the Shubert Theatre on Tremont Street (courtesy of Boston Public Library, Print Department).

George V, which played for ten weeks. The motion picture was gaining respect as well as attention.

On August 21, 1911, the Columbia Theatre became Loew's South End, featuring his vaudeville and movie combination at low prices. Now Loew had two Boston theatres.

Marcus Loew (photograph by Ameniya, *Boston Herald-Traveler* Photo Morgue, courtesy of Boston Public Library, Print Department).

Chapter 24

The National and the Plymouth
Tremont Temple Becomes
a Movie Palace
Gordon's Olympia and Saint James
The First Feature Length Films
1911–1912

In September 1911, two more new showplaces opened: the National and the Plymouth.

On September 18, the gigantic National Theatre, towering above Tremont Street near Berkeley in the South End, had its grand opening, christened with a near-riot. Eight thousand people surged against its doors, shattering the glass, and police had to call for reinforcements. This was Boston's largest theatre, with 3,500 seats (17,500 square feet of land was under this massive reinforced concrete building).

There was little else remarkable about this structure, other than its size. It had two vast balconies held up by heavy concrete pillars in two rows across the auditorium, one set along the rear of the second balcony that helped to hold up the roof. This gallery was different in that it was probably the first one to have a motion picture projection booth built into its front. This room was at the rear of a wedge-shaped cutback and occupied a tiny space under its floor and over the first balcony ceiling.

The *Boston Post* commented diplomatically: "Construction of the National is plain but very artistic.... Everything possible was done to retain a bright and cheerful atmosphere and to eliminate the cold, bare, gloomy look that is so often found in theatres of great size." The color scheme was yellow with old rose. A blend of red went into carpet, drapes, and orchestra seats. The stage was indeed great, with dressing rooms in a separate rear building.

On September 23, 1911, the Plymouth Theatre opened on Eliot Street near

157

The third National Theatre, awaiting opening in 1911 (courtesy of Boston Public Library, Print Department).

Tremont (later becoming 131 Stuart Street, as that thoroughfare was extended). The house was part of the new theatrical district. The auditorium was constructed along-side Van Rensselaer Alley, in line with the Majestic and across the alley from the stage end of the Colonial Theatre. The Tremont was two blocks distant around the corner, the Shubert one block away. The Hollis Street Theatre was almost directly across the way from the Schubert. The Globe and Park were not that far distant, but would never become part of the new playhouse district. The Boston Theatre, despite its new Tremont Street entrance, was out of bounds for the legitimate stage.

The Plymouth had 1,500 seats in a plain, but not unattractive, setting. The upper boxes were neatly tucked away within the lines of its two balconies gently curving toward a proscenium arch of Numidian marble. Two boxes on each side were at orchestra level, and the prevailing color was brown with touches of gold. Its lobby was a broad vestibule paved with mosaic, and the walls were paneled in Haute Ville marble.

The Shuberts and the Syndicate made peace in 1911, at least for a few more years.

In October, the Washington Theatre opened at Kneeland and Washington streets with movies and vaudeville for ten cents. This house operated until the late 1930s, when it was demolished for a restaurant.

In 1911, the Tremont Temple ran a lengthy Kinemacolor film of the British Coro-

The third National Theatre in 1935, with the old Cyclorama at left (courtesy of Boston Public Library, Print Department).

nation for ten weeks. The temple was not itself a theatrical enterprise, but was merely a lessor of its two halls. The larger second floor contained a good-sized organ and had been rented for travel stereopticon and film shows for several years. It served admirably as a motion picture house with its two balconies and theatre setting.

Clarence H. Blackall was architect of the Tremont Temple; he would later create plans for two Olympias, the Cort, Wilbur, and Metropolitan theatres. He wrote about building the Tremont in a sesquicentennial booklet produced by the Tremont Temple:

> The problems involved in the designing of a building intended for such purposes as Tremont Temple are so far removed from the ordinary run as to require special treatment. Primarily and fundamentally it is a religious structure intended as a home for a church of the Christian religion. Beyond this, however, commercial and financial conditions require that a large portion of the structure hall shall be devoted entirely to business purposes.... The exterior appearance of Tremont Temple is, therefore, necessarily different from any other structure in the country. A large arched entrance extending through two stories occupies the center, flanked on either side by stores, with side entrances forming the extreme of the front of the building in the first and second stories. Above this for a considerable

height there was no occasion for windows of any size, as the large auditorium extends clear out to the front wall, consequently this surface is left with very few openings. The upper part of the building is treated in a measure like a temple with a high colonnade crowned with a flat pediment, the columns being two feet in diameter and carried up through two stories. The open first and second stories mark the commercial element at the bottom, as the colonnade and many windows mark the office divisions; while the plain wall serves to emphasize the extent of the main auditorium.... In designing the exterior of the Temple, color was made a very essential and predominating feature of the design. The unbroken wall surface constituting the principal portion of the façade, through a height of about fifty-two feet and a width of ninety feet, is faced entirely with terra-cotta blocks about five and three-quarters by eleven inches, disposed in a diagonal zigzag pattern, something after the style of the exterior walls of the Doge's Palace at Venice. In the Venetian example these blocks are of hues and yet blended in a delightful manner, so that while the pattern is quite apparent the general effect is not disturbed. Fifteen distinct colors of terra-cotta are used, ranging from almost pure white through buffs, pale browns, deep red, and grays to a medium green. The large lobby occupying the central portion of this diaper work was so placed to relieve the simplicity of the front, but it has a further purpose serving directly to light the gallery lobby. The little narrow slits of windows on the extreme sides likewise give light into small stairways leading to the upper portion of the building. The bull's-eye immediately below the fifth floor are made as they are purposely, serving not to light the interior of the Temple, but rather to afford opportunity in case of fire for hose-lines to be taken into the building. These are the only windows in the street front giving light directly into the Temple proper.

We will now consider the Temple proper which is the main feature of the building. The vestibule at the central entrance in the first story is lined throughout in Sienna marble. On each side of this vestibule are marble stairs, with handsomely carved buttresses, which lead directly to the main floor. Between these is the central corridor, and the ticket office on the right ... beyond which are broad flights of stairs leading up on the right and on the left to the lobby preceding the main auditorium. From the head of these stairs in the main story similar flights continue up to the lobbies of the upper balconies. All of these stairways are of ample width and are thoroughly lighted. There are two separate, independent lines of stairways from each division of the auditorium, the floor, the first balcony and the upper balcony. Besides which, the hall is entirely enclosed by corridors on each side, at the extremes of which on the north and south are lines of stairs leading to the lower floor. There are eight distinct lines of stairways from the upper balcony to the ground.... The provision is such that there ought not to be the slightest difficulty in emptying the entire auditorium of people inside of two minutes. The stairs are constructed entirely of iron, thoroughly fireproof, with marble or slate treads and risers. Each division of the house has its independent lobby of sufficient size to afford standing room for as many people as could be accommodated in the auditorium. Each of these lobbies is connected with the wide corridors which completely encircle the auditorium on each floor level, through which doorways lead directly into the hall, affording means of quick egress.

The main lobby is a room 22 × 58 beautifully decorated with paneled stucco walls and ceiling, with a mosaic flooring and dado of Knoxville marble, and handsome door architraves of Alps green. The ceiling is curved and is designed on a Pompeian motive, with panelled work filled by symbolic designs. At each end of the lobby are handsome drinking fountains of Sienna marble. The lighting of this room is entirely by brackets on the side-walls. The colors are pale green and light shades of cream, picked out with a little strong color of gold.

The lobby of the first balcony is decorated in blues and green, with handsome lamps of an Etruscan pattern hanging from the vaulted ceiling. The lobby of the upper balcony is in the space immediately under the slope of the balcony beams and receives external light from the elaborate bracketed balcony, which appears on the front of the building. At each end of the first balcony lobby are the toilet rooms....

The main Temple auditorium itself is a rectangle 72 × 135 feet with a clear height of 54 feet. It has 834 seats on the floor, 736 in the choir and first balcony, and 1,012 seats in the upper balcony, a total of 2,852. The chairs are as fine as any that have ever been used in this city, they are built of mahogany and upholstered with the finest quality of saddle leather, and are made on the ordinary opera chair plan, with folding seat, hat-racks, etc. They are commodiously arranged so as to give accommodation equal to that of first class theatres. The seats are all numbered and arranged so as to be readily reserved, and ticketed when desired. The interior of the Temple is designed in the style of the Florentine Renaissance.

A large archway, spanning a little over forty feet, marks the center [similar to a proscenium arch]. Underneath the arch resting on bold corbels built out from the wall is the organ, beneath which is the choir gallery with seats for seventy-five singers. The front of the choir galley projects on a slight curve, and drops to within six feet from the top of the speaker's platform. The finish of the front of the choir gallery is of oak with richly carved pilasters and panel work; the whole stained a dark antique color.

The walls of the choir gallery and the recessed arch are lined with handsome Sienna marble carried to the spring of the arch. Above the line of the upper balcony, the side-walls are broken by heavy pilasters marking the lines of the constructive girders, between which are large semi-circular top windows filled with stained glass. The pilasters are of marble the same as Sienna about the choir gallery. The ceiling is unique of its kind. The construction of the building was such as to preclude a ceiling that would have marked transverse or longitudinal lines. Instead, the whole surface is broken up by deep panels eight feet across, with a rich profusion of pendants dropping down at the intersections and elaborately modeled work on the flat surfaces, while the moulded work of the panels themselves is richly ornamented, and the center of each panel is filed with a large elaborate rosette. The electric fixtures, which form so important a feature of the interior, depend from intersections of the lines of the panels. The ceiling is decorated principally in white and gold, with a little dark blue between the rosettes.

The central panel is considerably larger than the others, carried up further and much more elaborate, and is flanked on each side by long, oblong panels decorated in blue and gold. The idea of the electric fixtures was suggested to the architects by the interior mosque of Sultan Mahmood, at Constantinople, which is filled with a profusion of votive lamps, suspended from the high domed ceiling by slender cords reaching the whole height with a large tassel at the bottom. The lights in Tremont Temple drop at irregular intervals from each fixture, and give the effect of the long lines in the Constantinople Mosque. The central chandelier is much larger than the others, and forty-two lights drop from slender pendants. Besides this there are twenty-three chandeliers at regular intervals over the main ceiling, these chandeliers have twelve lights each; and ten chandeliers hanging from beams immediately in front of the organ arch, these having four lights each. Light is also given to the interior by brackets and ceiling lights in the balconies, the total number of lights in this room alone being nearly five hundred.

A great deal of attention has been given to the heating and ventilation of this hall. As has been previously explained fresh air is delivered to the Temple by a large fan, located in the sub-basement, this fan drawing fresh air from out of doors. The air is delivered into the room through openings all along the front of the railing of both balconies and under the large glass windows on the south side as well as through registers in the south wall under the balcony and gallery. There are exhaust registers in the ceilings under the balconies, also the entire main ceiling is hollow, the space around the rosettes in the large octagons being left open so that the air can escape freely into large transverse ducts across the whole width of the ceiling. Between the constructive girders, these ducts are all connected through the north wall to a large passageway built on the outside of the building, and of galvanized iron carried along to the large chimney at the rear, the chimney at this point being enlarged to a size of about one hundred square feet in area. The heat of the smoke pipe and of the steam supply and exhaust pipes which are located in this chimney create a strong drought which in itself is sufficient to exhaust a great deal of air from the hall.

On May 6, 1912, Gordon's Olympia Theatre opened on lower Washington Street, close to Boylston, but near to Beach Street. The theatre offered vaudeville and films. Architect C.H. Blackall started with a vague Greek-styled two-story lobby, open to the sidewalk. Its vaulted ceiling was frescoed with *Orpheus Playing to the Muses* on one side; *The Sun God Driving His Chariot in the Morning with Mercury, the Winged Messenger between Heaven and Earth* on the opposite. As if this were not enough, the *Boston Post* concluded in its appraisal that the centered box office was a "Greek pagoda."

The Olympia auditorium and stage was erected in the rear of its block, and a very long group of vestibules and lobbies ran through a former carpet store building that fronted on Washington Street. These halls included stairways, restrooms, and escalators to all parts of the house. The longish and somewhat narrow theatre held 2,500 patrons in the orchestra, two balconies, and 14 brass-raised boxes in tiers of three and four. Décor was in red, gray, and gold.

On January 22, 1912, the Globe Theatre presented vaudeville and pictures for 10, 15, and 25 cents. In March, the Grand Opera House in the South End became a wrestling arena. The Park Theatre presented its first motion picture in May, at the end of its theatrical season; the house was probably leased by Universal Film Manufacturing Company to shows its *Rainey's African Hunt*.

The Tremont Temple continued to run motion pictures throughout 1912, and even the color coronation film was revived. The *Boston Globe* wrote that "a motor-driven apparatus has been substituted for the hand driven machine and the pictures resulting are clear, flickerless, much truer in color." In 1906, two Englishmen, Charles

Urban and G. Albert Smith, invented a method of producing moving pictures in their natural colors, which they called Kinemacolor. The camera used two filters, red-orange and blue-green, and in projection color was produced using a double aperture and double shutter arrangement. Each alternate frame on the film was sensitive to red and the next one to green; the proper speed was 16 frames (one foot) per second. Kinemacolor, having double frames, required that it run twice as fast as black and white film and at a continuously steady speed or the color effect would be ruined. The resulting motion picture was in shades not unlike those of a color postcard.

In late summer two new theatres opened. Chickering Hall, on Huntington Avenue at Massachusetts, had been gutted and enlarged by real estate developer, M.H. Gulesian, and opened on August 30 as the Saint James Theatre. Architects Peabody and Stearns retained the two-story avenue frontage with its long lobby of shops, adding a sidewalk café. A light gray and dull gold tinted auditorium with red carpeting accommodated 1,800 patrons. Three double boxes rose at each side of the proscenium. The stage was 39 feet by 80 feet with a height to grid of 82 feet. The basement held ventilation equipment plus an ice-making plant. The Saint James balcony area offered a large tea-room; it was an elegant house in an elegant neighborhood.

On September 23, the Huntington Avenue Theatre opened its doors at No. 175 on that busy highway. Owners of the Century Building had gutted its first two stories. Inside, running parallel to the avenue, was constructed a rather low-ceilinged auditorium with a single balcony; from the latter's front, along each sidewall to the proscenium ran two tiers of boxes. This theatre had a small but well-equipped stage, and seating capacity was announced as 1,800. Architect W.C. Nazro designed the theatre. The *Boston Globe* said that the interior wall décor resembled "old Spanish leather."

The National Theatre in the South End removed its orchestra seats and installed tables for a cabaret. Refreshments were served and smoking was allowed.

Chapter 25

Famous Players in Famous Films, in Famous Theatres: Enter Adolph Zukor

1912–1915

In 1912 Adolph Zukor, a former associate of Marcus Loew, purchased the U.S. Rights to *Queen Elizabeth*, a multireel French motion picture, starring Sarah Bernhardt, a famous international actress. Zukor believed that the time had come for films to establish themselves as a theatrical medium in their own right, as a play on film. A successful opening of this production at New York's legitimate stage theatre, the Lyceum, proved Zukor to be right. He then launched his own Famous Players Corporation to make feature-length motion pictures with famous players in famous plays in famous theatres.

Queen Elizabeth (40 minutes) opened in Boston in November 1912 at the new Gordon's Olympia Theatre. A lecturer accompanied the film, and seven acts of vaudeville completed the program. The Olympia policy became "Photoplays and Vaudeville"—feature films had arrived, and the theatrical scene was to change greatly.

In November the Olympia continued with vaudeville but gave attention to its photoplays, adding a three part, 30-minute feature, *The Money Kings, or Wall Street Outwitted*. In March 1913, it top-billed a four-part film starring James K. Hackett, *The Prisoner of Zenda*, a Famous Players production. In June, the Olympia played *A Tale of Two Cities* along with its vaudeville.

In February 1913, the National and B.F. Keith's theatres offered Edison's Talking Pictures, a phonograph and film device, some 13 years ahead of workable sound pictures. The problem was amplification: a phonograph horn, no matter how big, could not carry sound any farther than a few rows.

In February 1913, Loew leased the Saint James Theatre for his low-priced continuous vaudeville and pictures, and the Tremont Temple's large hall became a full-time feature picture theatre. It and some legitimate theatres were the prestige showplaces for films that could command a higher admission than those released to the dime houses.

Also in February, the Colonial Theatre presented Reinhardt's production of *The Miracle* in Lyricscope, and an Italian *Quo Vadis* enjoyed a ten-week run at the Tremont. Even Symphony Hall was leased for a run of *The Life of Saint Patrick*, a sure thing in Irish Boston. In April, Symphony Hall hosted a five-"act" film, *Cleopatra*. In May, the Tremont Theatre offered Buffalo Jones in *Lassoing Wild Animals in Africa and America*. In June, the Olympia featured *A Tale of Two Cities* in "three twenty minute reels," and in November it played Mary Pickford in *Caprice*.

On November 17, 1913, Gordon and Lord's Scollay Square Olympia opened on the site of Austin and Stone's old museum, its auditorium alongside the Old Howard, at Tremont Row and Howard Street. The auditorium's structure ran at a right angle behind a six-story office building, and its stage backed up to Howard Street. Architect Clarence H. Blackall planned the lobby, which was on the left side of the Tremont Row elevation, to tower over Scollay Square with its two-story arched entrance, topped by four floors of bayed office windows and a two-story clock. Over that were three tall flagpoles holding an electric bulb-lettered sign reading "GORDON AND LORD'S."

The outside lobby was of Indiana limestone, and the entrance portion of the façade was outlined in incandescent bulbs, as was the clock. The Olympia's recessed lobby contained a large center box office, and over the vestibule doors was lettered "PHOTOPLAYS AND VAUDEVILLE."

A wide auditorium had a gold-coffered ceiling, and three brass-railed tiers of four boxes each rose on each side of a Greek Temple proscenium. A tall, deep archway, heavily draped in "Alice blue" and gold monogrammed silk velour, stretched from the orchestra floor to the ceiling behind the boxes; the stage curtain was in matching color. This 3,200-seat Olympia also had "moving stairways," but its biggest boast was the $50,000 organ that accompanied its photoplays.

The year ended with the Globe Theatre premiering the film *Traffic in Souls*, an exposé of white slavery.

On January 19, 1914, New York legitimate stage producer John Cort opened a theatre, bearing his name, in Park Square, partially on the site of the old

Adolph Zukor, who launched Famous Players Corporation (photograph by Apeda, *Boston Herald-Traveler* Photo Morgue, courtesy of Boston Public Library, Print Department).

Providence Railroad Station. The Providence Street entrance had, at its left, a stairway to the second balcony, and at the right three doors led into a ticket vestibule. From there a small lobby opened into the right side of a large and spacious foyer that ran across the rear of the orchestra, and a double staircase to the balcony was centered against its back wall. An entrance from Columbus Avenue was at the far end. The parquet and two balconies held 1,800 patrons.

Auditorium sidewalls were a series of arches between engaged columns with boxes in two tiers; a cornice above their tops was carried across the proscenium. Interior décor was gray and pale gold, drapes and curtains were done in Du Barry rose, and walls were paneled in old rose silk damask. Architect C.H. Blackall produced a "post-less" auditorium—both balconies were cantilevered. This beautiful theatre, so far from the theatre district, did not have a long life, and was replaced by a huge parking garage for automobiles.

Feature-length motion picture exhibition increased rapidly in 1914 as a series of white slavery and drug exposure films whetted the public appetite for longer movies. Owners of antiquated legitimate theatres began to think about changing policy, and plans for straight moving picture houses were on architects' drawing boards.

A feature film's average length became 50 to 60 minutes. These films played initially in vaudeville houses, where seven acts could run up to one a half hours. The following film program was typical for a local neighborhood run of 1914:

Paramount Travel Picture	7:50 to 8:05 P.M.
Still Waters, a Paramount feature	8:20 to 9:35
Pippa Passes, a Biograph Drama	9:50 to 10:05
The Belle of Barnegat, a Lubin drama	10:20 to 10:35
A Prince in Disguise, a Vitagraph comedy	10:35 to 10:50

In between films, an organ recital, a singer, and a classic dance entertained the audience.

"Boston Film Notes," a March 28, 1914, column from the show business periodical *Billboard*, read:

> Arch McGovern, the New England manager for George Kleine's features, reports good business throughout the East. "Anthony and Cleopatra" is booked solid until the early summer. He is now busily engaged with the booking of the six-reel feature (60 minutes) "For Napoleon and France," which he anticipates will set a new mark in New England filmdom. Archie has not been in Boston for twelve years and is now busily engaged renewing acquaintances made when he was here with "Sky Farm," at the Music Hall, now Loew's Orpheum.
>
> Many exchange men are making strenuous efforts to place their feature productions in summer parks throughout New England. It is extremely profitable to show good, strong features in preference to musical comedy or vaudeville, and the subsequent lower cost would be a great inducement.... "David Copperfield," in seven reels, opens at Tremont Temple on March 16 for a long stay. The picture was produced in England by the Hepworth Co.; the feature should be well received by literary Boston.
>
> Al Lichtman, sales manager for the Famous Players Co. of New York, was a

visitor at their local office on Wednesday. In an interview he stated that the Boston office of the Famous Players was the finest and best equipped sales office in the United States. He promised that "Tess of the Storm Country," a new five-reel feature, would clean up big in New England. Harry Asher, the local manager, stated that the newspaper publicity in running stories of films was a boon to the public and everyone connected with the film business.

Mr. Eslow, of the Universal Co., reports that "Samson," a new feature, is one of the best his company ever put out.

On April 20, 1914, A.L. Wilbur opened a playhouse bearing his name, on Tremont Street, in the theatre district. Boston's favorite theatre architect, Blackall, created a colonial façade of burned Harvard brick, laid up in old-fashioned bond, trimmed in white marble. Its three main doorways were copied from that of a historic Beacon Hill mansion, neatly executed with white marble columns, pilasters, and a low pediment; above was a fine iron balcony in front of three arched windows framed in marble. The front vestibule had a dado of Pavonazia marble under a vaulted ceiling; ticket offices were at each end. Next came the foyer, stairways at each end rose to the balcony or descended to a 30-foot-by-40-foot lounge, complete with fireplace. The Wilbur auditorium was almost rectangular, being wider than deep. There were only 16 rows in the orchestra. Walls were wainscoted in the English manner; a crystal chandelier hung from the dome. Five hundred seats were on the main floor, while the balcony and gallery provided 700 more. A single box at each side of the stage were extensions of the balcony. A color tone of slightly aged plaster used throughout the house was accented by wine-colored velour drapes. Wilbur was in the Shubert camp.

On May 4, 1914, an 1850 churchlike stone structure just off Copley Square owned by a religious society became a motion picture theatre, the Exeter. It was a second-floor house. Two stairways at each side of the entrance led to a lobby and its auditorium; from there stairs led to the balcony. The main floor seated 830 patrons; its balcony held 436. The house originally played second-run films with three acts of vaudeville, but eventually became a straight picture house.

On June 25, 1914, Jacob Lourie, owner of the Beacon Theatre near Scollay Square, opened a similar small but deluxe movie house built inside an 1876 office building on Washington Street, almost next door to the Boston Theatre and B.F. Keith's flagship. Its two-story arched and pillared front was clean cut, lacked the honky-tonk garish appearance of previous movie theatres, and had an air of permanence that gave credence to the sign hanging in the front archway, "The Modern Theatre, High Class Photoplays."

From this recessed entrance one entered a small lobby with stairs to the balcony on each side. This area gave way to a tiny foyer and then to the orchestra. The auditorium was narrow and long, and a balcony overhung almost two thirds of the floor. Walkways ran from its first row, along each side wall, to exits behind the proscenium. The screen was deeply recessed inside a permanent wood-paneled drawing room setting. The stage started well within this area, and on its level were large ornate double doors at each side. An Estay organ was played in the small orchestra pit.

On September 28, 1914, Marcus Loew added the Globe Theatre to his circuit of continuous vaudeville and film outlets. On October 19, the Boston Opera House, "Boston's Most Luxurious Theatre" offered a "high class" stage show with the film *For Napoleon and France*. Seats cost 25, 35, and 50 cents, boxes 75 cents and $1. A full orchestra accompanied the film.

Adolph Zukor was becoming concerned that his photoplays were not being shown as he had planned ("Famous Players in Famous Pictures in Famous Theatres"). He was unhappy that his Boston openings were in vaudeville theatres or in small dime movie houses. Also, these films were rented at a customary flat fee that did not give him the return that he felt they had earned. His productions were distributed through Paramount Pictures, a company he controlled.

Zukor's Boston film franchise holders, Hiram Abrams and Walter E. Greene, together with Moe Mark, owner of New York City's Strand motion picture palace, took a long lease on the Park Theatre. A $100,000 renovation commenced on that old playhouse (née Beethoven Hall), as it was gutted, except for its stage and four walls. Out went the old wooden galleries and boxes, replaced by a single balcony of steel and concrete. Additional exits were added, and a new, wider lobby reached out to Washington Street. Boston's first movie palace—and the new home for Paramount Pictures—was born.

Patrons entered between polished marble columns into a vestibule of paneled marble wainscoting. Next they passed into a lobby with sidewalls of plaster pilasters and illuminated leaded glass. From each side of a foyer, stairways connected with a mezzanine lounge running under the balcony, and ramps led up to a crossover aisle separating front loge seating from the rest of the balcony. The projection room hung from the ceiling at balcony rear.

The 1,200-seat auditorium was decorated in the style of the Italian Renaissance, with large fluted columns on either side of proscenium boxes hung with red and gold canopies and drapes. Walls were paneled in red satin. A circular dome was surrounded by a coffered ceiling, and over the proscenium was a painting representing "Strength, Music, and Art." An Austin organ and piano sat in the orchestra pit, and musicians were placed on the stage in a garden setting, complete with fountain.

The year 1914 came to a close with the opening of the Toy Theatre at 188 Dartmouth Street near Copley Square. This beautiful small playhouse replaced an earlier one of the same name on Lyme Street in the West End, the darling of Boston Society. The three-story, almost semi-circular, brick façade seemed appropriately colonial in design. A center entrance was flanked by two shops, and in its ticket vestibule were 16 wall panels painted by Clifford Pember in fairy tale picture book fashion. Quaint staircases connected with the balcony from the foyer—these along with balcony railings were a gift of Boston society leader, Mrs. John L. Gardner. Doors to the orchestra were at either end of the foyer, and between these entrances to the eight boxes placed along the auditorium's rear wall. A box-less 32-foot-wide proscenium fronted an adequate 29-foot-by-60-foot stage, since this playhouse was planned for amateur and stock productions.

In 1915 motion picture producers not aligned with Paramount and its growing control of theatres through the United States unhappily watched the rebirth of the Park as an exclusive outlet for Paramount products and were alarmed by Zukor's con-

The Toy Theatre, at 188 Dartmouth Street, in a photograph taken between 1914 and 1922 (courtesy of Boston Public Library, Print Department).

tinuing connection with Nathan Gordon's Olympia Theatres, among others. Several independent producers signed exclusive first-run contracts with the 3,000-seat National Theatre and opened their biggest film, *Tillie's Punctured Romance*, starring Marie Dressler "assisted by Charles K. Chaplin," at the equally large but more prestigious Boston Theatre. D.W. Griffith's *Birth of a Nation* played a long run at the Tremont Theatre and then moved to the Majestic. Even Zukor's Paramount Pictures–Famous Players Corp. decided that the Park was not grand enough for its production of *The Eternal City*, which opened at the Boston Theatre, giving that old war horse a new lease on life.

Keith interests had owned the Boston Theatre since 1909, and now knowing what to do with that vast auditorium, they leased the house to legitimate stage producers. B.F. Keith died in 1914, before the feature film boom was under way. It is amazing that his canny partner and general manager, E.F. Albee, let alone Keith's son Paul, did not catch on to the increasing popularity of photoplays. Their biggest theatre was now leased for the presentation of top films, yet these two executives continued to concentrate on the domination of vaudeville.

Loew also had been of the opinion that vaudeville shows, with low admission prices, were his theatres' main attraction, yet by 1915 he was adding photoplays. Loew also had the vision to see that his old-fashioned two-balcony post-filled houses were obsolete for this new medium, so he closed his Boston Orpheum for a reconstruction.

In August 1915, New York's Selwyn Group took over the Cort, renaming it the Park Square Theatre. In October, the National became the Boston Hippodrome, offering its patrons free parking for their automobiles.

Chapter 26

Boston's First Movie Palace

Loew's Braves Field

The Shuberts Build a Subway and the Copley Turns Around

1915–1924

On December 19, 1915, the 1,500-seat Fenway Theatre opened on Massachusetts Avenue at Boylston Street in uptown Boston. Architect Thomas Lamb designed it in early Adam style. This sandstone, brick, and steel skeleton-framed house had an almost square auditorium and was planned as a motion picture theatre. The change in form was immediately recognized: its six boxes were placed in the front of the single balcony as loges, and organ pipes replaced them at each side of the stage. Lobby and foyer were in marble; décor was maroon and gold, with paintings over the proscenium. The Fenway demonstrated to Boston that big, beautiful theatres could be constructed solely for the presentation of motion pictures—yet it had a fully equipped vaudeville stage, just in case.

On January 20, 1916, Marcus Loew opened his new Orpheum Theatre. He had intended it to be a palace, and it was, a 3,320-seat showplace in the middle of the shopping district. Once again, the 1852 Boston Music Hall had been gutted and rebuilt with additional land permitting greater width. With this, architect Thomas W. Lamb designed the prototype of his later movie palaces. The 1,700-seat orchestra floor rose back from the stage to a wide cross aisle nearly midway, which connected via ramps to a foyer underneath.

A 1,500-seat balcony, almost as large as the orchestra section, was cantilevered over the main floor.

Auditorium décor was modified Adam in ivory, white, old rose, and shades of blue-green. Its proscenium arch of golden hued glass, illuminated from behind, dominated the interior. There were six boxes at each side of the stage. Three were at orchestra level, three above stepped upward to meet the balcony, and from them, giant, handsomely draped marble columns rose to the ceiling. The Orpheum's grand foyer

171

Marcus Loew's Orpheum Theatre, seen from Washington Street about 1925 (courtesy of Boston Public Library, Print Department).

ran under the complete width of the orchestra rear, at the east end, just past a rotunda with balcony stairs and a plaque-bust of Marcus Loew. A large long staircase descended to the Washington Street lobby. At the other extremity of the foyer was a small ticket vestibule, which connected with Tremont Street, via Hamilton Place. Flights of stairs from the grand foyer rose to the orchestra standing-room area, the mezzanine promenade, and the rear of the balcony. The old Music Hall Place entrance, shared with Bumstead Hall, was abandoned; eventually these areas became part of an adjacent department store. Loew's Orpheum Theatre opened with continuous vaudeville and pictures, whose titles were not advertised. But soon the programs did include feature-length films. Marcus Loew had created Boston's first authentic movie palace.

Farther down Washington Street, Albee and Paul Keith remembered that they, too, had a movie palace. The 3,000-seat Boston Theatre became a continuous vaudeville and feature film house. B.F. Keith's theatre next door continued with "high class vaudeville," playing to two reserved-seat performances daily. Keith's 900-seat Bijou, nestled upstairs between the two big houses, played last-run continuous film shows.

At the end of 1916, William Morris took over the Toy Theatre, renaming it the Copley Square. Its premiere attraction was Harry Lauder's play *The Night Before*. Morris tried films, then a stock company, but nothing worked.

During the winter of 1916, fire destroyed a large portion of the auditorium of Loew's South End Theatre. He then commissioned Thomas Lamb to create a new theatre out of the ruins. In September 1917, Loew's new Columbia opened, recovering its original name. It had one cantilevered balcony over the new buff and gold auditorium, with olive green leather-covered seats. Lamb retained the original stage as well as the building's very tall Moorish façade. A large pipe organ for Loew's low price photoplay and vaudeville policy was added.

In October 1917, the Castle Square Theatre took on a short-lived motion picture policy, proud that its booth was on the orchestra floor level, "affording perfect projection and preventing eye-strain." At this point the only legitimate stage theatres without a projection room were the Hollis Street, Plymouth, and Copley Square.

On February 17, 1917, a new movie house, the Lancaster, appeared almost directly across Causeway Street from the North Station terminal. The house was operated by E.M. Loew (no relation to Marcus) and for most of its life was a late-run film house, ideal for travelers waiting for trains. The elevated trolley car line to Lechmere, in Cambridge, passed through a portion of its marquee (many theatres had been forced to incorporate the Boston Elevated Railway in their frontages).

In 1918, a tragic national influenza epidemic closed Boston's motion picture theatres for three weeks; among its victims was A. Paul Keith, his death making Edward F. Albee the sole owner and manager of all B.F. Keith's theatres.

On December 22, 1918, Lee and J.J. Shubert opened their private subway. The Little Building, at Boylston and Tremont streets, had an underground connection to the trolley car station, adjacent to its basement. From this level the building created a French Gothic arcade containing a child's restaurant and shops; elevator and stairways rose to the street and floors above. Van Rensselaer Alley ran between the Majestic Theatre and the Little Building, along the right side of the Plymouth Theatre auditorium and the rear of the Colonial. The Shuberts excavated a passage under this alley. At the south end of the Little Building's basement arcade, a marbled box office was constructed to handle tickets for al Shubert theatres. Beyond and down a few steps, patrons could enter a light gray paneled subway, whose terrazzo floor turned to the visitor's right. Along the left side of this passage were entrances to the Majestic lower lobby and the Plymouth auditorium. A possible further Colonial Theatre connection, through the latter's stage entrance, was planned but never constructed.

On March 19, 1919, the National-Hippodrome Theatre was renovated and renamed the Waldorf by Harry Kelcey, founder of the same-name restaurant chain that was known for its one-armed "table-chairs" and baskets of apples on its counters. He established a policy of two-shows-a-day vaudeville and photoplays, and also operated Waldorf theatres in suburban Lynn and Waltham.

Also in March, Nathan H. Gordon opened his 3,000-seat Central Square Theatre in Cambridge, across the Charles River, as part of his growing Olympia Theatre Circuit. This showplace followed the November 1918 debut of his 3,000-capacity house in Uphams Corner, Dorchester. These two neighborhood behemoths, in addition to Boston's existing Loew's Orpheum, Waldorf (National), and Boston Theatre, ran shivers through the owners of Boston's downtown small or obsolete theatres. Heads were scratched, bankers were consulted, and again architects drew up plans for more movie palaces.

Meanwhile, Gordon "personally offered" Mary Pickford's *Daddy Long Legs* on a reserved seat, two-shows-a-day policy at the Tremont Theatre. The film then moved to the Tremont Temple for an extended advanced price run.

Adolph Zukor, Paramount Pictures and Famous Players Lasky Corporation acted. The Park Theatre's new management announced "Photoplays for particular people ... transforming this famous playhouse from a gilded showplace to the drawing room atmosphere of a sumptuous residence ... exclusive first runs of Paramount-Artcraft Super Productions," and "requiring a slight advance in seat prices." Jake Lourie's Modern and Beacon theatres joined to present "The Exclusive First Run in Greater Boston of Paramount-Artcraft Specials." Gordon, a Zukor friend and customer, "personally offered" a steady stream of advanced admission films at the Tremont Temple. A $50,000 Hope Jones organ was installed in his Washington Street Olympia, a new instrument especially designed for motion picture houses.

On January 20, 1920, Famous Players–Lasky Corp. and Alfred S. Black, a Boston-based theatre owner, formed Black New England Theatres Inc. as 50-50 partners. This company was to become N.E.T.C.O. (New England Theatre Company), operating Lourie's Modern and Beacon theatres and motion picture houses in Boston suburbs and throughout New England.

In August 1920, Gordon took control of the Old South Theatre on Washington, opposite Milk Street. The theatre had a colorful past, this operation being within the historic heavy brick walls of the eighteenth-century Province House. Portions of that hotel had housed 1857's Ordway Hall, 1861's Opera House, and the 1870 Lyceum Theatre. Since 1871, through several fires, these old walls had enclosed various other enterprises. About 1907 a final conflagration gutted the building once more, and then the Old South Theatre, a motion picture house, was constructed about 1908. Gordon further remodeled the house into a first-run showcase; a new organ was installed to be played by the Olympia's renowned organist, Arthur J. Martel.

In 1920 Marcus Loew's newspaper advertisements announced that stock was for sale in his Orpheum Theatre, and shares were offered for his State Theatre, under construction "to be 20% larger than the Orpheum!" This financial-page type of pro-

The Province House housed the Old South Theatre, which later was turned into
a first-run movie house (Library of Congress).

motion continued well through 1921, when in May it was advertised that "work has
begun again on the new State Theatre Building."

In 1921, the 1907 agreement that kept the Shuberts from competing with Keith,
Klaw and Erlanger in the vaudeville business expired. They threatened to restart the
Shubert Advanced Vaudeville Circuit, but this time Edwin F. Albee, head of the B.F.
Keith's theatres, told them no. The Shuberts abandoned their vaudeville circuit in 1923.

A special motion picture house venture was advertised on April 11, 1921, as the Suffolk Theatre opened at Temple and Derne streets facing a side of the State House. An organ had been installed in the 1,100-seat auditorium of the Suffolk Law School; all proceeds went to the endowment fund. The project didn't last long.

The seating shortage in downtown theatres, caused by the growing motion picture industry, was seen in the increased use of legitimate stage theatres for premieres of big films which then went into film houses.

The Modern, Beacon, and Park shared the run of Douglas Fairbanks in *The Nut*, while *Passion* played all five of Gordon's theatres at the same time. His Washington Street Olympia and Old South became a double run similar to that of the Modern and Beacon.

The 3,700-seat Loew's State Theatre opened as a picture palace on March 13, 1922, having many features similar to Loew's Orpheum. Here, too, Thomas W. Lamb was the architect; his familiar mezzanine under the balcony circled an oval well overlooking the orchestra rear. The vast auditorium was almost as wide as it was long. The interior was decorated in café au lait, tones of gray and touches of blue. Its ceiling had a gold double dome in which was concealed an Echo Organ about a massive chandelier. Lights under the balcony were behind opalescent glass ornamented with bronze lacework. Three upper boxes and three orchestra boxes graced each side of the 54 foot by 28 foot proscenium arch. Ruby drapes rose behind them. Although the State had a fully equipped stage and a separate rehearsal hall, it opened to a policy of first-run films accompanied by its organ and, at the beginning, a 30-piece symphony orchestra. It was never to become a full time vaudeville theatre.

The Old South Theatre was demolished in May 1922; Olympia Realty Company had leased the site for a period of 50 years from the trustees of Massachusetts General Hospital. It was announced that a new Province Theatre and office building were to be erected, but the colorful and historic chimneys of the old hotel would be retained as décor. Alas, no theatre was ever to be part of that building.

In 1922, as the city extended Stuart Street past the Copley Theatre, that petite 600-seat playhouse closed in June, and the entire structure was moved a few hundred yards around the corner from Dartmouth onto the new Stuart Street. The auditorium was then cut in half and "stretched" sufficiently with the new brickwork to add 400 more seats. For a short time the theatre was unapproachable only by a sort of runway over muck and mire.

The *Evening Transcript* commented on its December 5 reopening night: "Spanning the rude arch which is now Stuart Street, a wooden bridge leads the Copley theatregoer from either Dartmouth Street or Huntington Avenue to the newly decorated theatre.... The balcony has been considerably increased in depth, as has the orchestra. Cold white and pale gold make an almost too colorless auditorium, but the foyer is vivid with vermilion shaded lights."

The *Boston Globe* was kinder: "The Copley remains the same cozy and 'intimate' theatre it always was. There has been no change in the original size of the auditorium except to increase the distance from the stage to the cute little boxes at the back of the house and to extend forward the balcony ... without detracting from the former excellent acoustics ... backstage there have been no changes."

In October 1922, the 656-seat Fine Arts Theatre opened as an upstairs house that was part of the uptown Loew's State Theatre Building with an "around the corner" entrance. It had a small but fully equipped stage, planned as a rehearsal hall. It was Boston's first art film house, opening with a British import.

On the evening of June 25, 1923, Marcus Loew staged a special theatrical venture by leasing Boston's baseball park, Braves Field, for movies and vaudeville. The field's dimensions were 65 feet by 600 feet, seating an audience of 10,000 patrons. Two huge moving picture screens and a stage for a 40-musician jazz band and dancers were erected. To top it all off were fireworks."[1]

In April 1924, *Billboard* magazine announced that a new ruling had been made by Boston's Department of Public Safety. Restrictions on Sunday vaudeville performances were modified to allow the appearance of acrobatic acts, jugglers, black-face comedians, female impersonators and various other classes of entertainers previously barred. Permission, however, had to be obtained by applying to the department. Dancing was still taboo on the Sabbath.

Chapter 27

The Third Boston Theatre
The Mighty Metropolitan
The Mystery House
1925–1927

Nathan Gordon's Olympia Theatre Circuit had opened two more large neighborhood theatres in 1924. These events, plus the opening of Loew's State Theatre, jolted Edward F. Albee into action. His 70-year-old multibalcony Boston Theatre had capacity but was obsolete for the proper presentation of films in competition with modern picture palaces. B.F. Keith's New Theatre was equally impractical. On August 10, 1925, title to the Boston Theatre passed from Keith's Boston Theatre Company to the President and Fellow of Harvard College, which was to fund the construction of a new theatre, a memorial to B.F. Keith, on the site. A replacement was needed for the Boston, and space was obtained in the rear of a huge defunct department store building at Washington and Essex streets.

Meanwhile, Nathan Gordon, Adolph Zukor, and sundry investors agreed to finance the building of Boston's largest theatre. Construction began at Tremont and Hollis streets, next door to the Wilbur Theatre, for the new colossal flagship theatre for Paramount Pictures.

The old Boston Theatre held its last performances on October 4, 1925, and the next day, the almost-4,000-seat Keith-Albee Boston Theatre opened at Essex and Washington streets. On the screen was Reginald Denny in Carl Laemmle's *California Straight Ahead* plus a Charlie Chase comedy, *The Caretaker's Daughter*, accompanied by the $50,000 Wurlitzer organ. The vaudeville portion was:

Julia Arthur
"The Dancing Syncopators"
Ann Francis and Wally "The Sunshine Girl and Boy"
Claude De Carr & his company of comedians and acrobats
Dan Coleman "The Famous Irish Comedian"
Carr Lynn's first American appearance, an English comedian
Helen Jackson and Margaret Shelly, with piano and song

The Keith-Albee Boston Theatre, the third Boston Theatre, was at Washington and Essex streets (The Harvard Theatre Collection, The Houghton Library).

The next to last act was always the star position. The Boston advertised four shows daily, while B.F. Keith's New Theatre maintained its two-shows-a-day, reserved seat, high-class vaudeville policy. Those stage performances ended with a showing of an Aesop's Fable cartoon, a pictorial review, and the Pathé News.

Patrons entered the new Boston Theatre from Washington Street along a marbled and mirrored lobby, hung with elaborate Czechoslovakian crystal chandeliers. The Boston's auditorium occupied the entire rear of the block, parallel with Washington Street. At the end of the entrance lobby patrons could take a stairway to the balcony mezzanine or continue on to a large promenade in the rear of the orchestra. Along the left was a white marble standing-room rail running slightly behind huge white marble pillars rising to the top of the mezzanine under the balcony. On the right side was a second entrance from Essex Street, centered in a two-story wall. At each side of its doors, a staircase rose to the mezzanine, which overlooked the entire standing-room area. The *Boston Globe* said, "You feel somehow as if you were in one of those trans–Atlantic liners."

The auditorium had three descending boxes, from balcony level, on each side of the proscenium. Underneath was one long single box with several rows of seats, slightly raised from the orchestra level, and walls were done in a black and gold brocade. A good-size stage was several stories below street level, and its facilities for actors were superb, offering baths, showers, and a nursery. The theatre was a typical Keith-Albee palace: huge, overpowering, and uninspired.

On October 17, 1925, the nearly 5,000-seat Metropolitan Theatre opened at Tremont and Hollis streets. Its management was a marriage of convenience between Edward F. Albee and Adolph Zukor. Albee controlled vaudeville, and Zukor controlled motion pictures. Zukor was creating a chain of motion picture palaces from coast to coast. His Paramount arm had purchased Nathan Gordon's Olympia Theatre Circuit in May. But vaudeville was still a necessary adjunct to films, and the Keith booking office furnished that.

Even as Albee addressed the audience at the opening of the Metropolitan, his fellow orator, Zukor, was gently pulling the rug out from under his feet. In less than a year that giant showplace of New England would be controlled by Publix Theatres, which was created to operate the more than 200 theatres run by Famous Players–Lasky.

Patrons entered the Metropolitan through bronze doors into a marble ticket lobby with panels and friezes elaborately decorated in relief and gilded.

Next came an inner lobby where two staircases rose to mezzanine corridors. Piers and pilasters were Botticino marble under a ceiling mural by Amarosi. The Grand Lobby was a vast arched and pillared hall, as large as most of Boston's theatres. Three mezzanine balconies looked down on it, between rose and jasper colored marble pillars supporting arches loaded with ornamental relief. At the far end the Grand Staircase, modeled after that of the Paris Opera House, rose to the first mezzanine. To the right were bronze doors opening onto Hollis Street, to the left were entrances to the orchestra level, and below all was a huge oak paneled lounge for 2,000 patrons. In later years the Met added a large ice cream soda fountain and café in its center.

The auditorium was under a vast dome with a sky-blue circular ceiling, and in its center was a gold sunburst. Beneath were music and drama murals proceeding

The Metropolitan Theatre, at Tremont and Hollis streets, had 5,000 seats for moviegoers (Tichnor Bros. postcard circa 1930s, courtesy of Boston Public Library, Print Department).

about the house from the central painting over the proscenium. Arched walls on the sides of the auditorium were of black mirrors bordered by gilt frames and pilasters. Two grand exits at each side of the proscenium were pillared and arched with elaborate carvings and topped by groups of statuary. The orchestra pit sat within the proscenium arch, its symphony size being a show in itself.

Capacity was 2,318 in the orchestra, 284 in a mezzanine under the balcony containing the projection room, and 1,805 in the steep balcony, totaling 4,407 seats. The cost of construction was $3,875,000, financed from first mortgage bonds secured by the office building in front and the Wilbur Theatre next door. In keeping with the size of the showplace was its list of architects: C.H. Blackall, Clapp and Whittemore, C. Howard Crane, Kenneth Franzheim, George Nelson Meserve, and associates.

The Metropolitan presented a first-run film, symphony orchestra overture and ballet, followed by vaudeville. It booked famous stars like Amos and Andy, Kate Smith, and Rudy Vallee, whose acts were not completely absorbed by the house's vastness and grandeur. Such huge auditoriums hastened the demise of vaudeville, whose very intimacy had been its greatest attraction.

On November 10, 1925, the Repertory Theatre of Boston opened at 264 Huntington Avenue, almost directly across from Symphony Hall. This playhouse was executed in the Georgian period of English Renaissance. Its wide façade rose behind a stone terrace and balustrade. The lower portion was of rusticated limestone; above was a wall of dark red toned Harvard water-struck brick. The fluted pilasters, cornice, and balustrade were limestone. At either side were entrances of white segmental bays. On the right was a flagstone floored lobby done in soft browns, orange, and a delicate sunlight (between cream and yellow), a color scheme that was carried throughout the theatre.

Auditorium walls below the single balcony were oak paneled. Soft orange drapes hung above the double box at balcony level on each side of the proscenium; the main curtain was of violet silk velour, and star-shaped light fixtures were used about the auditorium. The building also contained a 450-seat hall paneled in oak. The Henry Jewett Repertory Company opened on the 70-foot-by-23-foot stage.

On December 7, 1925, the Tremont Temple presented talking motion pictures using Dr. Lee De Forest's Phonofilm process, billed as "Vaudeville on the Screen Perfectly Synchronized." Star turns of Weber and Fields, Eddie Cantor, and other Broadway acts were featured. The show played only one week, then silent films returned to the screen.

The year ended with Keith-Albee interests having a go at managing the Saint James Theatre and presenting a stock company on its stage. This branch of entertainment was popular at the time; prosperous stock theatres operated in suburban Somerville and Malden. These players would continue to attract audiences until photoplays began to have sound.

Despite the windy days of early March 1926, crowds of curious people lined Boston's curving Mason Street, little more than an alley. Spectators jostled one another in their eagerness to watch demolition of the 1854 Boston Theatre, which they could not view from any place except at its stage end because the old playhouse was surrounded by buildings on its other sides. On every lip and in every mind was the question "Where is the Mystery House?"

The great brick-and-iron shuttered stage house backing up to Mason Street was almost gone. People could see past the tattered proscenium arch into the almost circular auditorium since the roof was gone. Clouds of plaster dust swirled among its colonnades and three balconies, as lengths of plaster from one of the world's first metal-lathed domes draped vulgarly from the topmost amphitheatre, down to the parquet circle. Crippled cherubim and mutilated decorative work lay in grotesque heaps on the remains of the great orchestra floor.

The previous day newspapers had caught public attention with lurid headlines and *The New York Times* led the way:

"MYSTERY HOUSE FOUND WITHIN THEATRE WALLS

...the walls of the famous old structure had been built around an ancient house ... two and one half-story frame [building] in exceptionally good repair despite its 150 odd years."

The *Boston Globe* reported, "Looks as if it might be the rear wall and roof of a dwelling of 150 years ago."

And why should it not be? In 1894 when B.F. Keith built his new theatre against the Boston Theatre's south wall, some eighteenth-century homes on and along Bradford Place had to be demolished. A colonial well was found during excavations. An adjacent tavern had been torn down in 1835 to build an equestrian theatre, the Lion, named after that hostelry. By 1839 the building became the Melodeon, forerunner of the existing Bijou Theatre. Keith built his theatre behind the latter.

Small wonder that sightseers had thronged Mason Street to view the "mystery house." People had to look along the newly exposed north wall of Keith's, which became that of the Bijou. A curious structure could be seen at the farthest boundary of the demolished building, where the great spiral oak staircase had wound up to the galleries. This apparent house was at a right angle to that of the Bijou Theatre, and slate shingles and windows could be glimpsed.

On March 8, 1926, the *Boston Globe* deflated the growing legend of the mystery house. The so-called colonial dwelling was merely the westerly end of the long lobby from Washington Street. Very little of the Boston Theatre exterior was visible except for its stage wall. The Melodeon (Bijou) was purchased to provide an entrance on Washington Street in keeping with the grandeur of the new showplace.

Instead, an unpretentious entrance was constructed just north of the Melodeon. While the massive auditorium and stage portions were constructed of masonry, the narrow entrance lobby building was a wooden structure. The Washington Street façade was designed to resemble blocks of stone, its height being about 60 feet with two visible stories above a rather tall first floor. The two upper floors ended abruptly about 40 feet from the street, leaving only a one-story connection to the Boston Theatre.

At the western end of this lobby, inside the theatre, a nine-foot-wide freestanding spiral staircase of oak rose from the basement to the second balcony and gallery or amphitheatre. Parquet and first balcony patrons would turn right from the lobby into a handsome foyer with a grand staircase in its rear.

Destruction of the second Boston Theatre, 1926 (photograph by Leslie Jones, courtesy of Boston Public Library, Print Department).

Opposite: The demolished second Boston Theatre, 1926 (The Harvard Theatre Collection, The Houghton Library).

Another scene of destruction of the second Boston Theatre, 1926 (photograph by Leslie Jones, courtesy of Boston Public Library, Print Department).

The space above this one-story western end of the main lobby in fact created a multistory air well, 20 feet wide by 40 feet long. This huge shaft provided light and air to the rear windows of the Boston Theatre, those of the Bijou, and those of the upper two floors of the truncated Washington Street entrance building, whose rear end was slate-sheathed about its windows. That portion had been rented to various businesses and tradesmen and had a separate entrance from the street.

Offices of the Boston Theatre's management looked out over this well, as did the former apartments of B.F. Keith and his family, who at an earlier time lived atop the Bijou's front building. When Keith assumed control of the Boston Theatre in 1909 he discontinued public use of these upper lobby floors, so entry could only be obtained from the west lobby roof or from the Bijou. During the following 17 years those upper floors lay forgotten, as the Bijou became the Bijou Dream, a movie house. The venerable Boston Theatre was showing continuous vaudeville and motion pictures when it was decided to replace it with a new modern palace.

The "mystery house" controversy stirred the memory of a 98-year-old woman, who thought that she remembered the tenants of that dwelling. Wasn't there, she thought, a lady named Dunbrack who sold snuff and refreshments to theatregoers? *Boston Globe* researchers found that a vendor named Marm Dunlap did sell snuff and kept a little restaurant close by the Boston Theatre. Marm had been a household word in Boston and was famous for her gingerbread. Alas, Marm Dunlap's shop was at the first Boston Theatre on Federal Street from 1794 to 1852. The 98-year-old woman had confused memories of the two Boston Theatres—indeed, she had visited them both.

This fictional story of the mystery house continued to be circulated, and despite newspaper retractions, it was even included in a U.S. Department of the Interior Historic American Building Survey published in 1983.

Chapter 28

"Auld Lang Syne" at
B.F. Keith's Theatre
The Voice of the Screen
The B.F. Keith Memorial Theatre
1926–1929

In the summer of 1926 "Ice Plants and Refrigerated Air" cooled the Metropolitan, Loew's State, and Scollay Square Olympia theatres.

Later, on October 27, the Colonial Theatre introduced the Vitaphone, a talking motion picture system in which the sound was recorded on discs similar but larger than phonograph records that were synchronized with the film by means of a common motor. Large electric speakers were placed behind or in front of the screen. The film program consisted of talking, singing, and musical short subjects preceding the featured picture, *Don Juan*, starring John Barrymore. That was accompanied by a recorded orchestral score. Sound has been available since Edison invented the phonograph, but the problem had been to attain enough amplification. Western Electric solved that dilemma with the Vitaphone.

Also in October, it was announced that the Keith Memorial Theatre would rise on the site of the demolished old Boston Theatre. This showplace would commemorate the centennial of vaudeville and its Memorial Hall would contain portraits of B.F. and A. Paul Keith.

On October 29, the Bijou Theatre closed for extensive renovation. Its 44-year-old Arabic-Moorish décor was tired and dated, and auditorium sight lines were inadequate for its motion picture policy. There was no longer need for a stage and the 65-foot-high scenery loft, and elimination of these two theatrical appendages would qualify the theatre for the less expensive "hall" license. The stage was cut back to a mere platform, almost to the rear wall and a new screen was painted onto the latter. A smaller proscenium arch was installed about 20 feet behind the original one. The right half of the new ceiling had a large grille, above which were the new organ's pipes, and the upper stage house was closed off permanently. Thomas Lamb, architect of the new Keith Memorial Theatre, most likely had a hand in this reconstruction, but architects J.E. McLaughlin and James Mulcahy were credited. A small orchestra pit in the extended auditorium floor contained a new organ console and an upright piano, which was played during comedies and cartoons. The Bijou reopened February 25, 1927, and was little changed until its closing in 1943. The Bijou was the last theatre in Boston to switch from silent to talking pictures; installation of a speaker pushed its new perforated screen almost to the edge of its shallow platform.

In May 1927, the Modern and Beacon theatres were equipped with the Vitaphone, and *Don Juan* was presented at popular prices.

On November 20, 1927, the famous hotel next door to B.F. Keith's New Theatre, the Adams House, closed its doors. That popular gathering place stood in the heart of the old theatrical rialto on Washington Street. To its north were B.F. Keith's New Theatre and his Bijou, the site of the second Boston Theatre (soon to be a memorial to Keith), the Modern, and a few blocks farther to Loew's Orpheum Theatre. To the south were the Park, new third Boston Theatre, Washington Street Olympia, Gayety and Globe theatres. Keith had started his first museum in a building adjacent to the Adams House.

On June 25, 1928, B.F. Keith's New Theatre advertised "Auld Lang Syne Week," a farewell bill, as the old house was to close and give way to vaudeville at the new Keith Memorial. The final performance was on June 30, featuring stage-load of vaudeville stars including Ethel Barrymore, Will Cressy, Chick Sale and Fred and Dorothy Stone.

One newspaper commented: "There have been plenty of notable 'first nights' in theatrical history and this will surely go down as the most notable 'last night' of any theatre in the country. It was well staged from beginning to end. In some ways it was a sort of reunion both back stage and front stage, for 'back stage' were more great vaudeville people to take part in the program than probably were ever assembled in this city. Front stage were the patrons who were considered the best judges of vaudeville in this country.... For the old timers brought back the spirit of B.F. Keith and of the old days of vaudeville, and at the same time they were a surprise because of their youth."

This was the year of talking pictures. The first film with vocal sequences, Al Jolson's *The Jazz Singer*, opened its regular run at the Modern and Beacon. The Olympia and Fenway installed the Vitaphone (sound on disc) and Movietone (sound on film). Movietone would prevail, but in the beginning theatres had to use both systems. The *Boston Post* called these systems "Audible Pictures."

By July 28 more film dialogue emanated from Boston theatre screens. The Washington Street Olympia and Fenway offered "The First 100% Talking Motion Picture"— Lionel Barrymore in *The Lion and the Mouse*, with a musical score plus a little dialogue. Other "talkies" included Conrad Nagel in *Tenderloin*, and finally, the first truly 100 percent all-talking picture, *The Lights of New York*. This film started as a 20-minute short subject from Warner Bros. and by adding three reels the studio produced a crude but authentic all-talking picture that did tremendous business wherever it was shown and heard. The *Boston Globe* forecast a future for sound films. Newspaper ads announced Vitaphone, Movietone, Firmaphone, Photophone, Synchrosound, and Metro-Movietone.

This also was the year that Keith-Albee vaudeville theatres merged with those of the western Orpheum circuit, and the new company was named Keith-Albee-Orpheum, or K-A-O Theatres, and covered the entire United States. Joseph P. Kennedy was chairman of the board.

The B.F. Keith Memorial Theatre opened October 29, 1928, occupying the site of the second Boston Theatre. Entrances were on Washington Street and Tremont Street, the latter utilizing the old B.F. Keith's lobby, then crossing Mason Street into an arcade running parallel with the south side of the new auditorium. This shop-lined passage met the Washington Street lobby at its foyer entrance, where one turned left into the theatre or could continue on to the main street.

The old B.F. Keith's theatre was not demolished, but remained shuttered. Keith interests did not own either it or the Bijou Theatre, but were lessees. The Keith family had willed the property to the estate of Cardinal William H. O'Connell, who had financed the original construction to provide a clean family-type vaudeville theatre.

Thomas W. Lamb and Edward F. Albee had turned out a beautiful theatre. From the white stone façade on Washington Street patrons entered an outer lobby and ticket office elaborately done in brass-covered grillwork and carved marble. Next came an inner lobby with beautiful crystal chandeliers, columns, vaulted ceiling and fine stone carvings. Up a few steps was a vestibule or landing. A second box office for reservations was on the left, and to the right were bronze doors leading into the theatre's main lobby, Memorial Hall. Straight ahead ran an arcade of shops to Mason Street and access to the old Tremont Street entrance.

Under the great hall's 40-foot-high vaulted ceiling was a richly "Albee red" paneled room, which boasted 16 huge marble columns weighing seven tons each. They had been quarried in Italy and shaped and polished in Vermont, with the look of richly veined white onyx. They stood on green marble bases under heavily gilded capitals. In corners of the hall, niches contained life-size statues in white Carrara marble. To the left, between pillars on the mezzanine level, were "balconettes" with grilled facings in bronze, where one could gaze down into Memorial Hall.

Over all were three immense crystal chandeliers. The grand staircase rose from the far end, and at its head in a white marble niche sat a great bronze bust of B.F. Keith, atop a green marble base. Many old-time vaudeville folk said that the bust was "counting the house." Bronze doors to the left, under the mezzanine, led to a wide standing-room area. Under all was a large lounge loaded with the usual heavy armchairs, sofas, and antique paintings of Keith's theatres. The mezzanine was equally loaded. As in the Metropolitan and Boston theatres, there was an emergency room and uniformed nurse.

The B.F. Keith Memorial's 2,900-seat auditorium, with its great domed ceiling, was done in ivory and gold, crimson damask panels, red and gold drapes in Albee style. Its stage was 35 feet deep by 55 feet wide and featured an animal elevator that could lift an elephant from below. A special feature of the auditorium was its parquet circle in the rear. Elegant white marble railings separated the elevated levels, beyond the standing-room balustrades. The house had planned two shows a day with reserved seating, and its parquet circle and boxes could command higher admission

The B.F. Keith Memorial Theatre, 1928 (Library of Congress).

prices. Opening policy was "vaudeville at 2:15 and 8:15 P.M., photoplay at 1, 4, 7, and 10 o'clock, continuous shows Saturday, Sunday, and holidays." The *Boston Globe* summed up all this glamour: "Well, it is certainly a splendid memorial to B.F. Keith, but it will also stand as a monument to the genius of E.F. Albee."

Samuel Sayward, writing in a theatre trade magazine, the *Motion Picture Herald*,

The B.F. Keith Memorial Theatre, standing-room area (Library of Congress).

wrote that the B.F. Keith Memorial Theatre "was erected under the personal supervision of Edward F. Albee as a tribute to his lifelong friend and business associate
B.F. Keith, who died 14 years ago. Together they created the Keith-Albee vaudeville
circuit, which, long eminent in the East, is not, through its merger with Orpheum,
the biggest in the nation."

Sayward noted that Keith's primary objective was to elevate vaudeville to a higher
plane. Toward that, he provided elaborate and beautifully decorated quarters for
actors and actresses.

"Stepping off the spacious stage at the rear left, one enters the chorus room, where
provision is made for quick changes for the girls," Sayward wrote. "Opening from
this room is a large, well lighted, beautifully tiled shower room. Passing from the chorus room one reaches a delightful lobby or reception room, beautifully furnished in
pale blue and decorated in gold and ivory. Here a corridor runs parallel with, but
away from the stage, and from this corridor open the private rooms for the artists.
Every one of these rooms is beautifully furnished. Every one has a private bath and
shower adjoining.

"There are similar rooms for the men. But that is not all. There is a nursery for
the children of the artists, fitted with every conceivable kind of toy for the little tots.

Note the parquet circle used around back and sides of the B.F. Keith Memorial Theatre (Library of Congress).

There is a library. There is a billiard room for the men. There is a barbershop and a beauty parlor. There is a gymnasium, handball court. There is a complete electric laundry and an electric kitchen, which would be the envy of every apartment dweller. There are private elevators. And all these are for the performers. At the end of the corridor, where it reaches the stage door, sits an attendant. If one of the artists hurries

Under the balcony at the B.F. Keith Memorial Theatre (Library of Congress).

out leaving a door unlocked, a tell-tale light in this attendant's booth shows it. Everything possible has been done to make the stay of the performers pleasant.

"A trip below stage reveals another unusual section of this theatre.... It is the animal room, provided for the beasts in animal acts. The room is well lighted and well ventilated, and at one side of the room is a huge bathtub, built into the floor,

The rear balcony at the B.F. Keith Memorial Theatre (Library of Congress).

like those one finds in modern bathrooms, except that it is many times as large. This is the bath for the animals and is sufficiently large for the largest polar bear. A private elevator operates from this room to the rear of the stage.... [W]hile elaborate quarters have been provided for the artists, hardly less attractive quarters have been provided for all employees of the theatre. Every employee has his own room, while equipment such as he requires in his daily tasks, and every room and every suite is provided with showers."

Sayward wrote that Albee oversaw details for the lavish decor, including period furni-

E.F. Albee (photograph by Blank & Stoller, *Boston Herald-Traveler* Photo Morgue, courtesy of Boston Public Library, Print Department).

The Crystal Lobby entrance off Washington Street at the B.F. Keith Memorial Theatre (Library of Congress).

ture, tapestries, ceramics and bronze, glass and marble. The theatre was carpeted black with figures in dull gold. The walls, paneling and pillars were in ivory, decorated with gold. The murals in the dome were soft shades of gold and blue.

However, no provision was made for wiring the house for movies with sound. "The new Keith Memorial is built in the hope that it will be known as the Home of Vaudeville in America," Sayward concluded.

Chapter 29

Albee Out, Kennedy In, RKO Is Born
The Shuberts in Receivership
The Great Depression and Proven Pictures
Memories of the Scollay Square Palace
1929–1937

A photograph of Joseph P. Kennedy was almost obscured in the newspaper coverage of the Keith Memorial Theatre grand opening. He had big plans for the future of K-A-O Theatres, and they did not include Albee. By January 1929, Keith-Albee-Orpheum Theatres had been merged into a new corporation called Radio-Keith-Orpheum, or RKO. The new group was a blending of Kennedy's F.B.O. film company with that of Pathé Studios (soon to be Radio Pictures), K-A-O theatres, and the Radio Corporation of America (RCA), which held patents for the Victor, or Photophone, talking picture sound system. E.F. Albee was gently eased out of power.

In the fall of 1928, New England Theatre Operating Corporation (NETOCO) theatres leased the Casino Theatre on Hanover Street, putting in a new Wurlitzer organ and featuring films and vaudeville and in December it took over the Globe as well. Charles Waldron was manager.

On April 1, 1929, the old B.F. Keith theatre reopened as Shubert's Apollo, advertising its entrance as 162 Tremont Street. The vertical sign outside read "Apollo," but Memorial customers still used the Mason Street crossing, where Shubert patrons took the stairway down to the old theatre's Crystal Tunnel entrance. By 1930 even a name change to Lyric Theatre could not help. The old Keith's simply could not make it as a legitimate house because it was too far off from Boston's new theatrical Rialto, at lower Tremont and Boylston streets.

On September 1, 1929, the Saint James Theatre became part of the Publix (Paramount) chain, and was renamed the Uptown. The Park was remodeled yet again and touted as a movie palace.

The stage play *Strange Interlude* was banned and opened in nearby Quincy, where it was advertised as "Not a Movie!" The Puritans were still watching over their city: Sunday performances containing dancing were banned, actors could only walk around the stage as music played, and few theatres had Sunday stage shows, at least until midnight.

The city censor viewed every new motion picture, and cuts were made for Boston showings. There was an additional list, given to exhibitors, of cuts to be made for a Sunday showing. To make certain that these deletions would be made, the city required a special weekly Sabbath license. Each theatre had to submit its list of cuts directly to the censor's office to obtain that Sunday's license, and police monitored movie houses to make sure that it had been obtained. Wrestling scenes had to be cut out of film features for Sunday showings.

To stay in step with the new construction and to create another movie palace, Paramount Pictures' partner, NETOCO, closed its Globe Theatre during the summer of 1929 for extensive remodeling. The house opened in December with its gallery removed and replaced by a mezzanine fronting a new steep balcony reaching back and up under a greatly raised new roof and ceiling. One box and exit from the gallery remained. The theatre's fine stage and boxes were retained along with its famous wrought iron globe chandelier. The Globe façade grew much higher with a plain yellow brick wall, its only ornamentation being one projection room vent near its top.

The Tremont Theatre installed equipment for sound film, and its orchestra floor was rebuilt and enlarged by removing the parquet circle in the rear.

The building at 357 Charles Street became Our Theatre, a small playhouse, and later was renamed the Elizabeth Peabody Theatre.

In May, the B.F. Keith Memorial Theatre shed "Memorial" from its name, becoming "RKO Keith's," presenting two shows of vaudeville a day, with no feature films. The Saint James Theatre was taken over by Publix (Paramount) theatres and was renamed the Uptown, playing the same pictures as the Olympia.

Boston's first 24-hour movie theatre, the Strand, opened in 1930 under the Crawford House in Scollay Square. In a few years that space would become a nightclub, featuring Sally Keith, Queen of the Tassels.

On April 15, 1930, Famous Players–Lasky Corporation became Paramount Publix Corporation, which on April 21 gobbled up NETOCO, a former Paramount partner. Publix became the dominant film house chain in Boston, and RKO and Loew's had only two theatres each. To top off its triumph, on November 10, Paramount Publix signed a contract with the Adams House Realty Corporation to build the Boston Paramount Theatre, with a 25-year lease.

In 1931, the Shubert brothers shocked the theatrical work by going into equity receivership. Lee Shubert and the Irving Trust Company were appointed co-receivers to continue to do business "for the expected benefit of the creditors."

The city's first 24-hour movie theatre was the Strand, under the Crawford House in Scollay Square, seen February 27, 1930 (photograph by Leslie Jones, courtesy of Boston Public Library, Print Department).

In April 1931, *Boston Post* columnist Henry Gillen announced, "The last show is playing the Palace Theatre in Scollay Square this week—*The American Wrecking Company*—and it is bringing down the house, brick by brick and beam by beam, seats, gallery, wings, dressing rooms, orchestra pit, lobby and all....

"The list of those who made the Palace popular is unbelievably starred with names that still persist in entertainment circles and hold their popularity, as well as the many who have long since died, but are remembered by old-timers. Upon its stage performed Al Jolson, Weber and Fields, Montgomery and Stone, Clark and McCullough, Gallagher and Shean, Mack Sennett, Eddie Cantor, Fanny Brice and Will Rogers. And there were Jim Jeffries, John L. Sullivan and a host of others."

Robert Campbell and Peter Vanderwarker wrote about the new City Hall Plaza in their 1992 book, *Cityscapes of Boston:* "They called it the new Boston, and they tore down much of the old one to make room for it. The change happened in the 1960s, the era remembered for urban renewal, or, as many have punned, urban removal. The old photo, showing the same site, reveals a Victorian commercial building from around 1850, to which the New Palace Theatre, a vaudeville and movie house, was added at some point—check out the two top floors. In the years about 1870, they housed a tinker in electronics named Charles Williams. Inventors liked to hang out there. One of them was the 21-year-old Thomas Edison, who invented an electronic vote-counter and stock-ticker before moving on. Another was a Scottish-born genius named Alexander Graham Bell. Here Bell performed the crucial experiments that led to his invention of the telephone."

Bell's laboratory was saved and reproduced in the lobby of Bell Telephone's new office building.

E.M. Loew's new Gayety Theatre offered two feature films and five acts of vaudeville, with admission 25 cents at all times.

The last movie palace, the Paramount Theatre, on the site of the old Adams House, opened to an invitation-only premiere on February 25, 1932. Its tall white granite façade held the largest and brightest marquee and vertical name sign on Washington Street. Architect Arthur H. Bowditch produced an art deco, 1,800-seat theatre in the narrow and tight space available.

The shallow Paramount lobby was paneled in polished oriental walnut and African ebony. Gold leaf was worked into auditorium decor with an effect of platinum in its columns, and metal fixtures were chrome-plated. The ceiling was iridescent in gold leaf, Italian blue, with flambeaux streamers in contrasting corals, old rose, and cobalt blue. Damask panels on the walls, with a green theme color and pastoral scenes, contributed to the forced intimacy of the house. A gold curtain hung in the tall narrow proscenium, and a gold organ rose before it in the new theatre, "specially constructed for talking pictures."

The gloom of the Great Depression hung over Boston, and every theatre advertised "Big Shows! Little Prices! and "1,000 seats for 25 cents!" The proud Tremont Theatre became the home of the "proven pictures." Old films and double features changing every few days were offered at 15 and 25 cents, and the policy caught on. The new proprietor, Frederick E. Lieberman, also leased the Majestic Theatre for "proven pictures." His subsequent elimination of union stagehands and union projectionists brought about bombings of both houses, but fortunately no one was injured and little permanent damage was done.

Burlesque dancer Sally Keith, Queen of the Tassels, performed at the Theatrical Bar, in the 1940s (photograph by Bruno of Hollywood, courtesy of Boston Public Library, Print Department).

Loew's State and Orpheum played first-run double features, and vaudeville

A 1935 winter scene of Washington Street: the Paramount, Normandie Ballroom, Bijou and Keith Memorial theatres (courtesy of The Bostonian Society/Old State House).

was eliminated. Only the Metropolitan and the RKO Boston Theatre still played stage shows with a first-run feature. The Bowdoin Square and Gayety theatres continued a policy of vaudeville and double-feature last-runs at low prices. The Old Howard and Waldron's Casino played burlesque with old films between stage shows.

When movies joined vaudeville and gradually became an equal, the stage show could run about 70 minutes. The feature films had a similar running time, with news and comedy. As vaudeville faded, its time had to be made up, hence one reason for the double-feature film program. Studios turned out these "co-features" with lesser stars and production costs. Series films like *Blondie*, *The Jones Family*, *Charlie Chan*, *Boston Blackie*, *The Saint*, *Maisie*, *Mr. Moto* (starring Peter Lorre) and *Andy Hardy* were popular as second features.

In 1934, Paramount-Publix's reorganization plan was submitted to a judge, and all property was placed in the hands of a new company. Boston's former Publix theatres became the M&P (Mullins and Pinanski) chain, a partner with Paramount Pictures.

With Prohibition ended, and alcohol now legal, the old B.F. Keith's Theatre became the Normandie Ballroom, a nightclub. Its auditorium was turned into a dance floor with tables, and the lobby to Washington Street became Boston's longest bar, and a restaurant was added in 1935.

The roof collapsed and killed several workers during the razing of the Hollis Street Theatre, as seen September 28, 1935 (photograph by Leslie Jones, courtesy of Boston Public Library, Print Department).

A disaster occurred on September 13, 1935, as the old Hollis Street Theatre was being demolished. Its roof collapsed and fell on workers below, killing several, a sad ending for a grand old theatre.

Old showmen always believed that converting churches to theatres brought bad luck. But many theatres were created out of old churches and survived. The Tremont Temple, once a church, was safely used for movies and is still standing.

Stage shows continued at the Metropolitan and Boston, but vaudeville was dropped everywhere else in favor of double-feature films. The Keith Memorial did offer a few stage shows for the 52nd anniversary of Keith's Vaudeville.

The old B.F. Keith theatre became the Normandie Ballroom in 1935 (courtesy of Boston Pubic Library, Print Department).

The Boston area got its first drive-in theatre in 1936 in Weymouth, and the city's first newsreel theatre opened in the South Station. The RKO Boston Theatre began a stage show policy of big bands, popular with youths, plus a feature film. The musicians' union forced the theatre to keep its pit musicians in addition to those on stage.

In January 1933, Paramount-Publix Theatres joined other theatre chains in equity receivership, with Adolph Zukor as receiver. The act included the mighty Boston Metropolitan and the new Paramount Theatre.

The Boston Theatre closed for the summer and by September, the Keith Memorial had dropped vaudeville in favor of first-run double-feature films. The Boston did return to stage shows in the fall.

The Syndicate had a rough year in 1933. They were losing theatres in every city. The Shuberts, however, were able to buy back all of their theatres from receivers, and at reduced prices, too. Many Syndicate houses fell into their hands.

In November 1933, the venerable Park Theatre became Minsky's Burlesque and showcased striptease acts. In 1937, Minsky and his ladies left the Park Theatre and it was remodeled and reopened as the Hub Theatre. Loew gave up the Columbia Theatre as the South End continued its slump into poverty. The Columbia reopened as

The Castle Square Theatre during its razing, January 1, 1933 (photograph by Leslie Jones, courtesy of Boston Public Library, Print Department).

a burlesque house. Across the street were two ten-cent movie houses and several restaurants offering a full meal for 25 cents.

The Shuberts took over the Copley Theatre and refurbished it. The best and biggest motion pictures once more began to premiere at the Shubert, Colonial, or Majestic theatres at a higher-priced reserved seat run before being released to regular lower admission houses.

A 1930s look at Scollay Square: at left, the Scollay Square Olympia and Rialto theatres, and at right, the Crawford House (the Strand had become Sally Keith's Theatrical Bar) (courtesy of Boston Public Library, Print Department).

The Tremont Theatre was so successful with its cheap admission price revival film policy of "proven pictures" that its operators leased the Repertory Theatre on Huntington Avenue as well. The Repertory's lower hall became Boston's second newsreel theatre, a growing fad in those pre-television days.

In February 1938, the Metropolitan Theatre dropped its stage shows. The RKO Boston followed suit, playing first-run double-feature films for 15 cents. But the RKO Boston returned to vaudeville in March. Patrons preferred old successes at the Tremont to brand-new "ho-hum" films.

In July, the Bijou became part of Lierberman's "proven pictures" circuit, but a name change to Intown Theatre did not catch on, so the Bijou it remained.

The Park underwent three months of reconstruction to emerge as the Trans-Lux, the "Modernistic Theatre," on September 10, 1938. Its stage and boxes had been removed, and indirectly lit sports murals were cut into new acoustically plastered auditorium walls. New greater back-to-back distanced seats were installed so one did not have to stand up to admit a fellow patron to his row. The theatre entrance was modernized and featured Boston's first turnstile box office. In other theatres of the Trans-Lux chain, films were projected from behind their screens, allowing auditori-

Plenty of signs for one theatre in this circa 1938 photo: RKO Keith's, the B.F. Keith Memorial Theatre, and atop the upright, the triangular insignia of KAO (Keith-Albee-Orpheum).

ums to use brighter lighting so patrons could come and go easily. In Boston there was not enough space to use rear projection, so the screen was recessed as far back from the proscenium line as possible so that the traditional Trans-Lux brighter auditorium could be used. A union stagehand sat in the first row to operate the curtains. The policy for Trans-Lux was a selective combination of newsreels changed twice weekly, plus short subjects. By February 26, 1939, Trans-Lux had added a feature film to the short subjects.

The Copley Theatre became host to productions by the federal government's Works Progress Administration's Federal Theatre project for unemployed theatre workers.

On December 16, the old B.F. Keith theatre began a new career as a movie house. All vestiges of bar and ballroom were removed and new seats were installed. Sporting a bright streamlined entrance, it opened as the Normandie Theatre, named after the famous ocean liner. After a premiere run of *I Was a Captive of Nazi Germany* and *The Fight for Peace*, owner Fred E. Lieberman introduced his "proven picture" policy. Thanks to his success with old movies at cheap admissions, four of Boston's historic theatres had received a new lease on life: the Tremont, B.F. Keith's, the Bijou, and the Repertory.

To continue doing such business, it was necessary that plenty of seats be available at all times. In the late 1930s Lieberman performed drastic surgery on the Tremont, removing its stage. The house remained open during construction, and its moving pictures continued to be shown on a small screen painted on the front of a tall, wide barricade. Beams, which had supported the boxes, proscenium and the roof trusses, were left in place at each side of the auditorium. The stage had been removed, and new orchestra flooring sloped down to its back wall under a new ceiling. The screen was hung on the back stage wall inside a tiny proscenium. There were no curtains.

Chapter 30

U.S. Sues Paramount Pictures Over Monopoly

Walt Disney's Fantasia Saves the Majestic

The Coconut Grove Tragedy, Bye Bye Bijou

1938–1949

In 1938, the federal government filed suit against Paramount Pictures Inc., Loew's Inc. (MGM), Radio-Keith-Orpheum (RKO), Warner Bros. Pictures Inc., 20th Century–Fox Corp., Columbia Pictures Corp., and Universal Pictures Corp., alleging monopolistic practices were being used to drive independent theatres out of business.

In April 1939, the tiny Telepix, yet another newsreel theatre, opened in a Park Square office building's lobby. In August, the Gayety returned to a burlesque policy. On September 3, 1939, Britain and France declared war against Germany, but the biggest entertainment news event in Boston was the premiere of *Gone with the Wind*, which settled in for an exclusive long run at Loew's Orpheum.

In September 1940, the Repertory Theatre shook off its mantle of "proven pictures" to return to legitimate theatre once more, enjoying a long run of the play *Life with Father*.

Also in 1940, the Old South Newsreel Theatre opened. It had no connection with the earlier house of the same name, despite having nearly the same location. It was part of a new office building and appeared to be a portion of the first and second floors scooped out as an auditorium. Heavy posts were obvious at four sides of an almost square space.

The year 1941 opened with some excitement in Boston as a team of experts from RCA and Walt Disney's film studios arrived to select a theatre to house *Fantasia*, a symphonic cartoon feature film which used stereophonic sound for the first time. The winning theatre had to have sufficient space to accommodate the great quantity of equipment required.

Three soundtracks were carried on three reels for three lampless projectors, synchronized with a fourth one that showed the motion picture. The three dummy projectors connected with their own speakers behind the screen, creating stereophonic sound. One can imagine the size of the projection room that was needed. (The film itself carried a regular soundtrack in case of emergency.)

Supporters of the Boston Opera House, which had become something of a white elephant, campaigned desperately for the film, to "Save Our Opera House." But the film opened January 28, 1941, at the refurbished Majestic Theatre, whose façade carried a huge marquee advertising *Fantasia* in attention-grabbing neon and bulbs, a show in itself. Disney's trailblazing production enjoyed a long run in Boston because there were no other showings in New England.

After the attack on Pearl Harbor on December 7, 1941, Boston became crowded with servicemen from many countries, who, along with defense workers, brought business back to theatres, restaurants and nightclubs. The Old Howard, Waldron's Casino, and the Globe Theatre were running burlesque shows including daily midnight shows, except Saturday. Only movies were shown on Sunday—its midnight stage show started at 12:01 A.M. Monday.

November 28, 1942, was a night of horror as flames raced through the Latin Quarter Nightclub, in the film district near lower Tremont Street. Few customers were able to escape through its locked exits and its one-way revolving door entrance. Many celebrities, including cowboy movie star Buck Jones, perished; the death toll was 491 customers and employees.

Ben Rosenburg, managing director of the Metropolitan Theatre, and a friend of the club owner, Barney Welansky, gave this author an account of the tragedy.

"I walked over to the Coconut Grove Night Club which was located in the Film District, a stone's throw from the Metropolitan, to see Barney. The only entrance to the nightclub was via a revolving door. The normal capacity for the club was approximately 500. I pushed on the door and actually had to fight my way in. There was a sea of humanity on the inside. There had to be 1,000 to 1,100 in the club, many in uniform. I pushed my way to the bar and asked Jimmy, one of the bartenders, where Barney was. He replied 'back in the kitchen helping out.' Some of the help did not show up; maybe got drunk or something.... At any rate I told Jimmy I would wait outside and asked him to tell that to Barney when he came up from the kitchen. Again, I literally fought my way out through the revolving door.... To make a long story short I did not go to the Grove on Saturday night. I worked. About 9 or 9:30 P.M. I heard sirens outside the theatre. I went out front, saw one of the policemen on my beat, and asked why all the sirens were blaring away. He replied, 'There is a terrible fire at the Grove.' I told my assistant that I was going over to the Grove.... Why weren't the patrons able to use the exit doors to escape? The exit doors had a breakable tape [rope] on each one. A breakable tape, so-called because when hit in the center, it parts and allows one to push down on the exit door bar, thus opening the door. The tapes were usually red velvet or green and mainly were used for decorative purposes. I would never allow them in my theatres. Why didn't they part when struck at the Grove?

Barney had the center pieces soldered because many patrons often skipped out with-out paying their bills. People died because they were piled up like rats in a trap, at the exit doors, and died from suffocation not from fire. Barney was indicted, went to jail, and died in two years. Why weren't the premises inspected? Good question. No politicians or the fire commission served time."

Little of the club's décor was fireproof; public outrage at this ghastly result of sheer negligence of safety standards and enforcement doomed many of Boston's older theatres.

In January 1943, Governor Leverett Saltonstall asked the legislature to enact laws for the public safety. As the Suffolk County Grand Jury handed down ten indictments for negligence leading to the Coconut Grove tragedy, Boston Mayor Maurice Tobin asked for creation of a safety department, and inspection of halls and theatres was intensified. Theatres were stripped of their drapers in boxes, doorways, and hallways; a second nightclub fire in the "Grove area" added to public concern.

One night in 1943, the projectionist at the National Theatre, an old friend of the author, invited him and a former usher to tour the old B.F. Keith theatre (now Normandie) and the Bijou after closing. We met with the projectionist at the Washington Street lobby at midnight to begin a flashlight and nightlight tour (the night lights were tall iron stands holding a single encaged heavy-duty bulb). The floor-based lights were more commonly used, easy to move around, and appreciated by the clean-ers. Sometimes these were hung on balcony fronts, and at the Normandie they were used as house lights as well. All other lighting, except for exit signs, had been dis-connected; the old chandelier was high up above us somewhere in the dark, dust, and cobwebs. Motion pictures ran continuously, never stopping until the last show ended, and the elegance of intermissions was long gone.

The Keith stage was bare except for its tilted screen, surrounded by black drapes (curtains were never used because such operation would require the hiring of union stagehands). We passed an old bell in the wings, which I remembered from my first appearance on this stage, at a Christmas children's show, and the motion picture screen was where Saint Nicholas and I had met, some 20 years earlier. The speaker system behind was most unusual: Three horns, side by side, each about six to eight feet long, were stretched out almost to the rear stage wall. Up-to-date speakers were coiled to conserve space. These were installed during national defense preparedness time, and new speakers were not being made. The house had managed to secure new seats, but the sound system dated to 1928 and the first talkies.

Tiers of dressing rooms rose up into dark shadows, but the darkness was too scary for us to explore with only our flashlights.

A surprise awaited us in the basement. There was a large white room, whose walls appeared to have been ravaged, as if some kind of equipment had been wrenched out of them. Only later did I learn that this room and an adjacent furnace room were part of a group housing B.F. Keith's electric generating system. The plant had given up its dynamos, copper and scrap metal for the war preparedness effort.

Our guide took us back through a passage under the auditorium ending in the men's lounge, just below the standing-room area. After admiring the hand-some marble fireplace still remaining in the lobby above—all of Keith's other treasures were gone—we climbed the staircases to the projection room in the second balcony.

Coming back down our group stopped in a lobby just below, from which we stepped into an exit passage leading away from the theatre toward the Washington Street entrance. At the first flight down there was a landing, and to the left were doors leading into the Bijou, its stage right exit. We entered that venerable site, which dated to the Lion Theatre of 1836. On the few feet left of the original stage sat a motion picture screen with one compact coiled horn behind it, and an older silent "picture sheet" was plastered on the wall behind.

The old Bijou was the birthplace of Keith vaudeville and the first U.S. theatre to use electric lighting. Its auditorium, lit by a sole work light, was heavily shadowed. New red velour seats were visible beneath the horseshoe balcony, but its small but elegant dome was lost in darkness, as were the organ grilles set in the proscenium plaster. I noted that we had used one of the Bijou's stage-side exits to enter. The exit on the other side of the stage went down into the Normandie Theatre lobby. In an emergency, the only other way out was down the Bijou entrance stairs to Washington Street. One balcony rear exit had gone through the front building, doubling back to the upstairs lobby of the Bijou. The two exits that had gone through the B.F. Keith Memorial Theatre were now bricked up.

Our group returned to the exit passage and trotted down several flights of stairs to find ourselves in the front lobby of the Normandie Theatre, from which we had started. A single box-office was there.

The RKO Boston continued its film and stage shows. Many theatres ran all-night shows for the benefit of defense workers.

Downtown houses reminded patrons concerned with oil rationing that "these theatres do not use oil heating." Indeed, they did not. Their houses were heated by steam from Boston power plants, piped to them and metered exactly as if it had been fuel.

On January 1, 1944, a new safety code went into effect for halls and theatres, and rigid restrictions were imposed on new licenses and renewals. Second balconies and galleries were closed in the Old Howard, Gayety, and Normandie theatres, and cross aisles to exits were required in all auditoriums. The Boston Garden's capacity was cut by 6,000 seats, but the greatest casualty of these new regulations was the Bijou Theatre. Other than its lobby stairway down to Washington Street, its only other exits were through the Normandie Theatre, because additional exits through the B.F. Keith Memorial Theatre had been bricked up in 1938. The site was landlocked by the Paramount, Normandie, and Keith Memorial buildings. This historic 107-year-old theatre closed its doors on December 31, 1943. Its entrance became a carry-out restaurant, and the auditorium above was quiet until demolition of the old B.F. Keith's theatre in 1951.

By 1944 motion picture distributors had realized the tremendous amount of business generated by revivals of old films. The obvious example was Lieberman's "proven pictures" chain, which screened old prints in combinations at rentals as cheap as $15 per title. Secret checking of these theatres by film distributors proved that they were out-grossing first-run houses. Owners of revival houses suddenly found that these lucrative prints had been junked as "unserviceable." Henceforth, motion picture distribution companies would release their own reissues at the rental of a percentage of the gross receipts.

In Boston, the "proven pictures" circuit was the hardest hit. Without a steady supply of cheap films it could not survive, so the Normandie Theatre was leased to James J. Mage's "V" Newsreel Corporation. The old house (B.F. Keith's) was refurbished and fronted by a marquee with flashing neon and bulbs, adjacent to that of the Paramount next door.

This situation brings to mind the equally awkward arrangement of the Scollay Square Olympia and the next-door Rialto Theatre. Both marquees were side by side, with no separation. On the south side one could only read what was playing at the Rialto, while on the north side people only saw what was being shown at the Olympia. Since the Rialto was there first, it had the right to maintain its marquee. It was open all night, showed last-run movies, was cheap and was a smelly "crap can," as the industry called such houses. The marquees maintained their Siamese twin relationship until both were demolished to make way for the new Government Center.

The Shuberts' Majestic Theatre began showing exceptional first-run films twice a day, with reserved seats at higher prices.

By 1945, the Tremont, Old South, and Majestic houses were operating as first-run outlets for lesser quality films. Many independent (not aligned with the studios) exhibitors were encouraged by the ongoing 1938 suit by the federal government to break up studio-theatre owner monopolies. To many of these theatre owners it was obvious that the government would prevail, and some first-run United Artists, Columbia, and imported films were being rented to their theatres. Major distributors were also experimenting with first-run reissue combinations, like those of Lieberman's proven pictures. The films played in independent houses using new advertising campaigns.

Theatres playing these first runs were the New Normandie and Tremont, playing a United Artists film; the Tremont and Old South Newsreel with a Columbia release; and Disney's *Pinocchio* at the Tremont, Majestic, and Old South Newsreel theatres. The Old South experimented with first-run foreign language films.

In September 1946, the Gayety was given a new name, the Victory. It played second-run double features at low prices and was fully refurbished. The owner, E.M. Loew, had great plans for lower Washington Street. In 1947, he purchased the Globe Theatre, renamed it the Center, and ordered his architect to restore and modernize the house for legitimate stage use.

William Risman engineered an extensive renovation of the theatre, from its stage to an impressive front lobby and attention-grabbing marquee. Inside, the original basic white was retained and renewed, making a contrast with new tangerine upholstery for the seating and its main curtain. Art deco light fixtures were designed in heavy white plaster.

The Center Theatre opened on February 18, 1947, with Ben Hecht's *A Flag Is Born*, a play about the new state of Israel. In April it offered *Everything on Ice*, a copy of the "Ice Capades" arena show, and it was a flop. The Center then played a heavily advertised revival of the Korda brothers' British film *The Thief of Bagdad*, which did tremendous business. Loew realized that he would never be able to compete with the Shuberts' growing control of the legitimate stage. So in May the Center became a successful double-feature revival film house. Loew also operated the National Theatre on Tremont Street in the South End, the Strand on Huntington Avenue, and the Lancaster on Causeway Street at the North Station.

On November 11, 1947, the Tremont became the Astor Theatre. The house was remodeled, its gallery shaved back as far as structurally possible, and its projection booth was dropped to the balcony below. New seats were installed, and a new false ceiling was hung to level off Lieberman's earlier surgery. The Astor boasted a "three dimensional screen" and dubbed itself "the theatre of the future." John Ford's controversial *The Fugitive*, a first-run RKO picture was screened for the premiere. For Christmas the Astor landed Goldwyn's *The Bishop's Wife*, starring Cary Grant.

On November 10, 1948, a refurbished Beacon became the Beacon Hill Theatre, subsisting on foreign first runs and films moved over from the Astor.

Benjamin Sack, a millionaire metal dealer, was entering the movie house scene. Elsewhere in the city, television sets were being sold with ten-inch screens.

In February 1949, Paramount Pictures, which owned the largest chain of motion picture theatres in the United States, settled its portion of the government antitrust suit by means of a consent decree, agreeing to divest itself of about 800 houses. Further, the existing Paramount corporation would be dissolved, and a new theatre company would be able to compete equally for Paramount films. In time, other film producers followed the Paramount example.

The effect of the Paramount consent decree became noticeable in Boston even before its signing. Newspapers advertised previous Publix Theatre holdings and partnerships under two new ownerships. One company, New England Theatres Inc., a Paramount partner, operated the Metropolitan, Paramount, Fenway, and Scollay Square Olympia theatres, plus 12 neighborhood houses. A new rival organization, American Theatres Corporation, had the Washington Street Olympia, Modern, and Esquire (Repertory) theatres, along with 29 neighborhood houses.

On January 5, 1949, the Washington Street Olympia was remodeled, got new seats and was renamed the Pilgrim Theatre. On February 19, an equally renovated Modern became the Mayflower Theatre. Along with the Esquire (former Repertory Theatre), they all advertised a "Cycloramic Screen and Multisound."

The year continued with some strange name changes. E.M. Loew renamed his Victory the Publix Theatre, and updated the lobby and added new seats. The Laff-Movie became the Art-Movie briefly and for a time in 1950 was known as the Mirth-Movie.

In 1949, television screens were up to 12 inches.

Chapter 31

U.S. Sues Shubert Over Monopoly
3-D, CinemaScope and Cinerama
Ben Sack Steps In and the
Boston Opera House Steps Out
1950–1958

On February 21, 1950, the U.S. government filed an antitrust suit against Lee Shubert, Jacob J. Shubert, Marcus Heiman, the United Booking Office Inc., Select Theatres Corp., and L.A.B. Amusement Corp., contending that the defendants had discriminated against their competitors to control the legitimate stage business. Producers and managers had been compelled to book their shows through the United Booking Office, which was owned 50/50 by the Shubert brothers and Marcus Heiman, its president. The Shuberts had 40 theatres in eight states, and in New York City they controlled about half the playhouses. If a production played a non–Shubert house outside of New York, it could not play a Shubert theatre there, and vice versa.

The Shubert United Booking Office, formed in 1932, differs from the earlier one designed by B.F. Keith and associates.

The defendants claimed that their operations were not subject to antitrust laws, a contention upheld by a federal court decision on December 30, 1953. The government appealed to the U.S. Supreme Court. Meanwhile, the Shuberts conducted business as usual, maintaining the same kind of monopoly that they had fought against so strongly in 1900. In Boston they controlled the Opera House, Shubert, Plymouth, Colonial, Wilbur, Majestic and Copley theatres, and many of their holdings were being leased as motion pictures houses.

In September 1950, the Copley had been leased to Trans-Lux Corporation, and a new entrance was constructed to connect with 22 Huntington Avenue. The Majestic was in and out of film operations.

Drive-in theatres increased and flourished, Boston had two television stations, and 20-inch screen sets were on the market as well as room air-conditioners. Potential theatregoers could enjoy entertainment in the comfort of their homes or in automobiles at the drive-ins. Plus, in 1951, mediocre films were the bane of the motion picture industry.

RKO Corporation was dissolved in 1951, going along with Paramount's consent decree. The exhibition arm became RKO Theatres Corporation. The new production-distribution outfit, RKO Pictures Corporation, went steadily downhill. Loew's Inc., which owned Metro-Goldwyn-Mayer Pictures and Loew's Theatres, had not yet split up. However, the studio's output of successful films was inadequate to supply its two 3,000-seat first-run movie palaces in Boston, which no longer were allowed to play first-run films together.

The motion picture industry embarked on an elaborate advertising campaign in 1951 called "Movietime U.S.A.," but it had no effect on lackluster business. Most pictures were no better, and some worse, than the fare being offered on TV for free. Theatre owners beseeched producers for assistance, but producers were torn between supplying theatres and the possibly more lucrative operation of feeding television stations. Studios were quietly considering fortunes to be gained with the backlog of features in their vaults.

Response to the exhibitors' plight was a sort of "if you can't beat them, join them" plan. Twentieth Century–Fox Film Corporation's solution was announced in the *Boston Herald* as "Eidophor," a theatre television projector that would bring big events, Broadway, shows, sports, and more to the theatre screen in color. On December 11, 1952, the Pilgrim Theatre used RCA's black-and-white TV projection system to present the opera *Carmen* direct from the stage of the Metropolitan Opera House in New York City.

These were stopgap measures; it was obvious that when theatre patrons had their own television sets that they would not attend motion picture theatres to see televised events. Producers and exhibitors realized that they had to offer the public something that they could not enjoy at home.

In 1951, the old B.F. Keith's Theatre (later Normandie, last known as the Laff-Movie), was demolished, and its long-closed second-floor Bijou was razed to its auditorium floor. The floor became a roof over street-level businesses. The entire front building, which had contained entrances to both theatres remained, but all floors above were vacant.

In late November, the Cine opened at 357 Charles Street (site of the old Peabody Playhouse), but it did not enjoy a long stay.

In 1953, as Magnavox offered a 27-inch television set, motion picture theatre response was to make motion picture screens physically bigger. Boston's movie houses advertised "Giant Screen," "Panoramic Screen," "Wide View Screens," and a "Magic Mirror Screen" (installed in the Keith Memorial).

The second step was the introduction, or reintroduction, of 3-D motion pictures, a process that went all the way back to the stereoscope of the 1800s.

MGM offered the 3-D short by Pete Smith in the 1930s. The audience wore special glasses with one red cellophane lens, the other green. The secret was to make each eye see a different picture. A camera with two lenses shot two films, one through a red lens, the other through green. Both negatives were printed on a single film, one in red, and the other in green. Patrons' special glasses made each eye see a separate image, resulting in the illusion of three dimensions.

Top: In 1951, the old B.F. Keith's New Theatre (later the Normandie and Laff-Movie) was demolished. *Bottom:* A worker amid the rubble of B.F. Keith's New Theatre (both photographs by Leslie Jones, courtesy of Boston Public Library, Print Department).

In 1953, this process had been improved by substituting colorless Polaroid filters to make each eye see separate images, shown by two projectors using matching filters, resulting in stereoscopic motion pictures when shown on a silver-coated screen. Most importantly, the film could not be shown on television.

The Pilgrim Theatre was the first in Boston to present 3-D movies, offering a series of five short subjects. The first feature film, the quickly and cheaply made *Bwana Devil*, opened at the Metropolitan Theatre before 4,300 Polaroid-glasses-wearing customers, and the movie was a smash. Better feature films including *House of Wax* brought customers back to the theatres; however, there were objections in having to wear special glasses to enjoy the films. Many "quickie" films were made in this process, and the novelty quickly wore off. Better 3-D films were made, such as Alfred Hitchcock's *Dial M for Murder* and MGM's musical *Kiss Me Kate*; however, they arrived too late.

In May 1953, *Boston Herald* drama critic Elinor Hughes wrote of a private screening that she had attended at the Metropolitan Theatre. Twentieth Century–Fox Film Corporation had demonstrated its new wide angle screen system, "CinemaScope," a method of filming scenes through a wide angle lens combined with an anamorphic one. The anamorphic lens squeezed the large shot onto standard 35-millimeter film; in projection the process was reversed and the compressed image was stretched over a slightly curved screen, about twice as wide as it was high. Magnetic sound was recorded on the film in four tracks, and three speakers spread out behind the wide screen reproduced three channels. The fourth strip played through speakers installed around the auditorium walls, surrounding the audience with stereophonic sound. Hughes wrote that she felt as if she were viewing a live performance from the first row of a theatre balcony.[1]

Distributors and exhibitors made certain that important films not filmed in CinemaScope were at least shown with stereophonic sound and projected on the largest screen that theatres could fit inside their prosceniums.

On October 7, 1953, the first CinemaScope feature to hit the theatres, *The Robe*, opened on a 51-foot-wide by 20-foot-high screen at the B.F. Keith Memorial Theatre. Newspaper advertisements heralded "The Modern Miracle You See Without Glasses!" In her review, Hughes wrote "CinemaScope has abundant possibilities and should prove a contribution of lasting value toward better quality picture making."

Also in 1953, the Cinerama Corporation took over the Boston Theatre, much to the relief of a distressed RKO Theatres Corp. The house underwent a conversion for the process that CinemaScope had imitated. The Cinerama system required three projectors that simultaneously showed three overlapping pictures on a 180-degree curved screen, giving the impression of one single extremely wide motion picture. Improved stereophonic sound added to the reality of the system. Projection booths had to be constructed at both sides and center of the auditorium. Because of the great height of the screen and a balcony overhang, these rooms had to be under the balcony edge, and all orchestra seats behind them were removed. The enormous screen thrust past the proscenium sides and required removing the boxes and part of the arch. The operation cost $250,000, including a new sign at the Washington Street entrance.

This Is Cinerama bowed on December 30, 1953, with two shows a day, all seats reserved. Marjory Adams, film reviewer for the Boston Globe, pronounced it "the beginning of a new era in motion pictures." That it was. Cinerama and CinemaScope changed the shape of the screen forever—the old square picture became rectangular, and older pictures lost their tops and bottoms when projected on the new screens. Newer "non-scope" films were adjusted to allow for this change by printing a rectangular picture from side to side on each motion picture frame, leaving clear space at top and bottom. Projectionists used a different aperture plate, cut to black out empty portions.

Jack L. Warner of Warner Bros. Pictures cut a deal on August 30, 1953, with Zeiss-Opton lens manufacturers of Germany for special lenses for the Warner Super-Scope wide screen system, avoiding any royalties that Fox's Cinemascope might charge him for using its system. Other companies (Panavision, Superscope, and Metroscope) followed suit. Paramount came out with its system, VistaVision, which was a 65- or 70-millimeter film negative reduced to 35 millimeters for theatre showing. The process debuted in 1956 with The Ten Commandments, and VistaVision produced a remarkable clarity on the screen.

In 1954, the Esquire (formerly the Repertory Theatre) was saved from demolition by the Boston University Theatre Arts Department, under the new College of Music. The theatre became the Gershwin Theatre workshop.

The Old Howard was forced by the city to omit the word "burlesque" from its advertisements. On February 22, 1954, its new policy proclaimed "Boston's Only Variety Stage Show"—Puritanism was apparently still very much alive. But after a few weeks, "lady stars" crept back into its ads and shows. The Old Howard closed by 1955.

More major motion pictures found their way onto the Astor and Beacon Hill screens as producers and distributors began to feel more comfortable with the loss of their own theatres.

In 1956 the second-floor Fine Arts Theatre, in the rear of State Theatre building, renamed itself the "Off Broadway Stage." It originally was a rehearsal hall for vaudeville.

The Tremont Temple offered a film on a "panoramic screen," Billy Graham's Fire on the Heather. Admission was free because the show was sponsored by the Christian Businessmen's Commission. It was the last picture show for that one-time first-run theatre; afterward the Temple cased commercial leasing of its auditorium.

In 1956, the Shubert Organization arranged a consent decree with the federal government, ending six years of antitrust litigation. On February 17, it promised to sell 12 theatres in six cities within two years, and it would dispose of the United Booking Office by June 30, 1957. In Boston the Shuberts had to eliminate their interests in either the Colonial Theatre or in both the Shubert and Wilbur, so they decided to sever themselves from the Colonial. The brothers kept the Shubert, Wilbur, Plymouth, and Majestic theatres plus the Boston Opera House.

On September 13, 1957, the Majestic became the remodeled Saxon Theatre, operated by Benjamin Sack, who also owned the Beacon Hill. The Saxon operated with a 70mm film process called Todd-AO, featuring the screen version of the stage hit musical Oklahoma!, shown two shows a day at reserved seat prices. CinemaScope

The Paramount, left, and RKO Keith's (the old B.F. Keith Memorial Theatre),
circa 1955 (Library of Congress).

used a 35mm film with lenses to give the widescreen effects; the Todd-AO process used an actual wide film, projecting a much sharper image on its wide screen. Sack, having wet his feet with the Beacon Hill, jumped into Boston's theatrical pool. In August he also took over the Plymouth Theatre, and it became the Gary, a first-run movie house.

In November 1957, a second-floor room at 54 Charles Street was converted into a theatre, the Charles Playhouse, which at the outset featured amateur productions, but was so successful that its founders began to search for more professional quarters.

Color television broadcasting started in 1957, and more motion picture films were sold to that medium.

On January 31, 1958, Sack reopened the Copley as his new Capri Theatre, another first-run house. By this time motion picture distributors were renting their films to the highest bidding theatres, and each film was sold separately. Nonrefundable film rental guarantees for the engagement were required, payable in advance. Small theatres with low overheads were able to outbid larger houses. The smaller houses could play long runs of successful films, while the 3,000-seat palaces, with burdensome operating expenses, could not compete. Previously they had overcome their handicap by offering to play a film in two theatres, but now that practice was illegal. New England Theatres Inc. dropped its control of the Fenway, which soon became an art film house; Loew's Theatres sought a buyer for its white elephant, the State Theatre.

In the spring of 1958 the Boston Opera House was demolished.

Chapter 32

The Old Howard's Swan Song

Ben Sack Takes Over the Met and Keith's

Pornography Comes to Washington Street

Sarah Caldwell Gets Her Opera House

1958–1979

In 1958, the Charles Playhouse moved into a former church-turned-nightclub on Warrenton Street behind the Shubert Theatre. The Casino was still running "girl shows" and in June called itself "The Old Howard Casino, always something doing!"

Sarah Caldwell, artistic director of the Boston Opera Group, made good her promise of a new home, moving into the remodeled Fine Arts Theatre, at the rear of Loew's State movie palace. This small former rehearsal hall, with a large stage, reopened as the Little Opera House.

A new opera house was proposed as a part of a metropolitan arts center on the Charles River in Brighton. In July 1959, there was discussion of erecting a $3 million opera house in the new Government Center, which replaced Scollay Square, or in the theatrical district. No opera house was ever constructed at any of these sites.

In late August 1959, Loew's found a buyer for its State Theatre, and the last picture show was on August 24, 1959. That palace was henceforth known as the Donnelly Memorial.

In 1960, the Trans-Lux Theatre, which had been flirting with sex films, moved wholeheartedly into that policy, jolting the company's stockholders into demanding a name change (it soon became the new State Theatre). This house was the first of the many lower Washington Street theatres showing sex films.

221

A glimpse of the Old Howard Theatre, circa 1930. It was razed in 1962 (photo-graph by Leslie Jones, courtesy of Boston Public Library, Print Department).

The Old Howard after the 1961 fire (courtesy of Boston Public Library, Print Department).

In October 1960, the Boston Opera Group moved from the Little Opera House downstairs to the bigger stage of the Donnelly Memorial. Their previous home, the small upstairs rehearsal portion of the building, reopened once again as the Fine Arts Theatre, showing foreign and art films.

By 1961, it was obvious that the big Metropolitan Theatre had fallen onto hard times. Boston's largest showplace could not survive with the mediocre film fare left to it, and its owners sought a way out of their losses.

The Howard National Theatre Museum Committee, made up of dignitaries including burlesque queen Gypsy Rose Lee, had petitioned the Boston Redevelopment Authority, on March 15, 1961, to save the famous Old Howard as part of Boston's theatrical history. It would be restored to its October 1846 appearance, being the old-

Gypsy Rose Lee, who worked to save the Old Howard, was surprised at the changes in Scollay Square (courtesy of Boston Public Library, Print Department).

est existing theatre in America. There had been some debate as to the claim, but the committee reminded the authority that Philadelphia's Walnut Street Theatre had been built as an amphitheatre for circus use and that the Dock Street Theatre in Charleston, South Carolina, was a reproduction of the original.

The shuttered Old Howard Athenaeum suffered a three-alarm fire on June 20, 1961.

In 1962, the New England Medical Center purchased the Metropolitan Theatre, its office building, and the Wilbur Theatre. New England Theatres Inc. gave up its mammoth headache and retreated to the Paramount Theatre, its new flagship, heading only five neighborhood houses.

As the Metropolitan closed, Boston newspapers announced that Benjamin Sack was adding that movie palace to his chain of smaller, but successful, theatres. Sack's Music Hall opened on July 13, 1962. In honor of the newly refurbished theatre, Mayor John F. Collins proclaimed Sack Theatres Week. Sack's entry into the theatre business was as savior, yet it was actually the beginning of the end for Boston's movie palaces.

Sack's Capri Theatre (the former Copley) was taken by the state to provide a Back Bay access for the new Massachusetts Turnpike. Sack then leased E.M. Loew's Strand Theatre, a few blocks distant on Huntington Avenue, which he remodeled and renamed the Capri, opening it July 6, 1962.

On August 1, 1962, the *Boston Herald* reported a $200 million rebuilding of downtown.

In 1963, of all the major picture theatres in downtown, only the Pilgrim, Paramount, Keith Memorial, Mayflower and Loew's Orpheum remained. RKO had relinquished ownership of the Boston Theatre to Cinerama. The remaining legitimate stage houses were the Wilbur, Shubert, and Colonial theatres. The Donnelly Theatre (former Loew's State) and the Music Hall (former Metropolitan) were used for occasional stage performances.

In 1963, E.M. Loew became aware that Boston's West End Rehabilitation Project was bringing residents back into the North Station area, where his Lancaster was the only theatre. Streetcars and subway trains came up from underground facing the North Station, with the Boston Garden above it. Trolleys ascended to the left and passed over the Lancaster entrance, but removal of the elevated railway was planned to take place in two years.

Loew decided that this was the time to bring back a cinema that people could get to on pubic transportation. Architect William Risman was instructed to gut the house for a new life as the West End Cinema. The old front building, through which the lobby ran, was demolished, and a 30-foot-high all glass entrance was constructed in anticipation of the elevated train structure being demolished. It presented a view of a big abstract mural, designed by Norman Ives, which reflected the colors used in the interior's black ceiling, white walls, and scarlet carpet. The cinema seated 600 patrons on one level.

On February 6, 1964, Boston's last new single-screen motion picture theatre, the Paris Cinema, opened at 841 Boylston Street, opposite the Prudential Tower.

In 1964, the first twin movie theatre (two separate auditoriums in one structure), named Cinema 1 and 2, appeared in Peabody, a suburb of Boston. The ability of small independent theatres with lower overheads to snatch first-run films from mighty movie palaces had been shown. Now, two or more theatres operating in one building with one low overhead were about to doom the single-screen motion picture theatre.

In 1965, American Theatres dropped the Pilgrim from its circuit and the former Olympia screened sex films, leaving the small Mayflower as flagship of eight neighborhood theatres. The Donnelly Memorial Theatre became the Back Bay Theatre, continuing its sporadic policy of stage bookings.

In 1965, film distributors dropped downtown's exclusive first-run policy. These films began to play in one downtown theatre simultaneously with several suburban houses. This change was a heavy blow to the first-run palaces, Loew's Orpheum and Paramount theatres along with the Astor and Ben Sack's remodeled houses. The motion picture distributors' reason was that the new larger first-run opening saved the heavy advertising outlay required for two separate runs. Previously, downtown premieres had been followed two weeks later by the first neighborhood release, with another round of advertising.

In June 1965, Sack bought the B.F. Keith Memorial Theatre. The house was closed and refurbished, and big new marquees went up at the Washington and Tremont street entrances. The large bronze bust of B.F. Keith was removed from its marble base and stored in a mezzanine ladies' room closet. Sack's Savoy Theatre opened on August 3, 1965, with the *Boston Herald* reporting that Sack "has restored the elegance and splendor of the theatre."

B.F. Keith's bust was later removed, with Sack's permission, by three theatre historians (one being the author), and is stored in a secure location.

The Cinerama Theatre ran out of its three-film, three-projector productions and began a series of conventional motion pictures, shot in 70mm and shown on the big screen using the Cinerama label.

On February 17, 1966, Sack's 800-seat Cheri Theatre opened as the first floor of a parking garage between Boylston Street and Huntington Avenue, opposite the main entrance of the Sheraton Hotel, in the new Prudential Center.

In April 1967, Walter Reade Theatres, a New York movie chain, opened the Charles Theatre at 195 Cambridge Street. Also in 1967, the Mayflower-Modern Theatre found that it could no longer compete with neighborhood first run theatres and then began an adult film policy.

About 1968 the Uptown–Saint James Theatre property was sold to the Christian Scientist Church (its mother church was nearby).

The year 1969 found the remaining large movie palaces, Sack's Music Hall and the Savoy, having difficulty in obtaining exclusive first-run films because their heavy overheads would not permit them to play pictures along with neighborhood theatres. The Paramount and Loew's Orpheum ventured into multiple first runs but found that only the top-grossing productions gave them enough revenue to keep running, and there were not enough of those.

On December 17, 1969, Sack opened the Pi Alley Cinema, another movie house-cum-garage, at 237 Washington Street; it was soon to be twinned. A four-screen theatre opening in the suburbs offered competition for twin houses, and that was just the beginning of multiscreen cinemas.

The Fenway Theatre enjoyed fresh life again as the Theatre Company of Boston took over its stage.

The Boston Theatre closed in 1971 and in July 1974 reopened as the Essex I and II, starting with an action film policy and then moving into pornography, joining most of lower Washington Street's sex houses.

On Washington Street, General Cinema Corporation leased the Paramount Theatre in October 1968, continuing its first-run picture policy. The Back Bay Theatre-Donnelly-Loew's State was demolished.

Concerned citizens, shaken by the loss of that 3,000-seat theatre, organized an

What remained in the 1970s: the Opera House, the B.F. Keith Memorial and Savoy
had been in the two buildings at left, the Bijou and the Lion had been in part
of the middle building in the center, and the Paramount had been in the building on the right (photograph by Charles M. Ahronhein).

association for the performing arts whose purpose was to raise funds to build an arts
center. Sack's Music Hall and the Savoy presented occasional road stage productions,
opera and ballet, on their stages. But in September 1971, Ben Sack, owner of the
Savoy, turned its stage area into Savoy 2 and its dressing rooms into apartments.

Actually, once again, Ben Sack had preserved a fine showplace. The Savoy 2 was
created only by building a wall within the proscenium arch, and the wall could easily be removed. The original B.F. Keith Memorial Theatre was virtually intact. Even
its stage was not harmed: A drop ceiling covered the new addition, leaving the gridiron and stage housing untouched.

The year 1972 found Sack Theatres operating yet another garage/movie house,
Cinema 57, at 200 Stuart Street. It was a very long and large theatre, which shortly
afterward was twinned.

On January 18, 1972, the Orpheum was abandoned by Loew's Theatres, and the
house reopened as the Aquarius, adding a welcome stage and 3,000-seat home for
Boston's performing arts. Although the house would eventually lose its long marble-

A 1974 look at the Paramount and the Savoy 1 and 2 (the former B.F. Keith Memorial Theatre). The Hardy shoe store was the old entrance to the B.F. Keith theatre, and the Amusement Center was the entrance to the Bijou (author's collection).

stepped Washington Street entrance, the Hamilton Place entry, off Tremont Street, was preserved. Loew's Theatres stayed on in Boston, operating Abbey 1 and 2 in Kenmore Square for a time, but eventually sold its theatres.

In March 1972, General Cinema Corporation, the last big-time tenant of the Paramount Theatre, gave up. New management struggled to keep that beautiful art deco showplace in operation with double-feature films at low prices. In April, the Astor Theatre dropped its exclusive first-run policy.

Down on lower Washington Street, the Center Theatre survived, playing action films, and later made money with Oriental chop-socky pictures. Its neighbors the State (old Park) and Pilgrim were profiting with porn shows. The Pilgrim became nationally famous in the 1970s when a powerful congressman, Wilbur Mills, appeared

A 1982 look at the former B.F. Keith Memorial Theatre and the Modern Theatre (photograph by David Prifti, courtesy of Boston Public Library, Print Department).

on stage with his amour, burlesque queen Fanne Foxe. That entire area had become depressed and dangerous; its nickname was the "Combat Zone."

Despite the shape of things in that neighborhood, E.M. Loew, well-known for his stubbornness, would not make his Gayety-Victory-Publix a porno house and kept it running until 1973 with double features at low prices. He owned the building, and his offices were there. Loew died in 1984 at the age of 86.

On December 5, 1972, *Boston Herald* drama critic Eliot Norton noted "the brightest possibility is that we will have, sooner or later, a new Boston Opera House, largely because Sarah Caldwell and the trustees of the Opera House Company of Boston have been able to solve, at least tentatively, the problem of cost." In May 1974, Caldwell and the Opera Company used the Aquarius, under its old name of Orpheum Theatre. Its vaudeville stage was far from that of an opera house, and the wandering group was still searching for a permanent home.

In 1973, Walter Reade Theatres opened the Charles East and West Cinemas at 105 Cambridge Street in the Charles River Plaza. Ben Sack moved his Beacon Hill theatre into the new Beacon Hill Theatres 1-2-3, in the deep basement of a new office building at No. 1 Beacon Street.

In June 1974, the Paramount Theatre took its only route to survival and became a porno palace. Only the Savoy 1 and 2 remained as a first-run movie house on Washington Street, once Boston's Broadway. Both houses screened action movies and black films, which became popular in big cities during the 1970s.

On October 19, 1978, it was reported that Ben Sack was closing his Savoy Theatre, and as of midnight, the Opera Company owned the theatre, having paid $885,000 for that privilege.

On August 15, 1979, "midst bamboo trees of Madame Butterfly's house" on the Savoy stage, the Opera Company of Boston burned the mortgage of its new Opera House.

Chapter 33

Lose Some, Save Some
Bringing Back Boston's Downtown
Memories of the Bijou
1979–2002

Sack's Music Hall (former Metropolitan Theatre) became the Wang Center for the Performing Arts. Extra land, behind the Wilbur Theatre to Stuart Street, permitted lengthening the depth of the stage to 60 feet to accommodate opera and touring shows such as *The Phantom of the Opera*. The house was restored to its former glory as were the Colonial, Shubert, and Wilbur theatres.

The Opera House (former B.F. Keith Memorial) was refurbished, except for a leaking portion of its ceiling, which was hidden from the audience by a large tarpaulin. Volunteers kept the theatre fresh and beautiful, but its management limited the number of touring stage shows, and opera could not survive. Washington Street was a dangerous place to be at night, attracting a rough crowd. All land south of the boarded-up Paramount Theatre, down to Boylston Street, had become a parking lot.

Rescue came, as the national Clear Channel Communications purchased the Opera House property and negotiated for land adjacent to its stage. It also controlled the Colonial, Wilbur, and Orpheum theatres.

The parking lot to the south along Washington Street became a huge multi-use building with a multiplex cinema, boasting a Tremont Street entrance.

The Mayflower (Modern) still stands. The RKO Boston-Cinerama-Essex lost its Washington Street lobby, which is now a transit subway entrance. Its interior became a warehouse divided into two floors, with a stage and 3,000-patron capacity.

The Orpheum is a highly successful music center. It lost its Washington Street entrance, but the remaining access from Tremont Street via Hamilton Place is more than adequate.

Emerson College purchased the Majestic Theatre, restored it and reopened it as the Cutler Majestic Theatre.

The Center Theatre (Globe) long ago lost its stage to a Chinese market, which inched its way up into, and took over, the orchestra floor. Above is a Chinese restaurant where one may dine amid the remains of the Globe's boxes and the top of its proscenium arch.

The Gayety Theatre, diagonally across Washington Street, became a warehouse, and is closed. In late 2004, Boston's mayor proposed demolishing the building for an apartment building.

The Gayety was the first theatre to be constructed in Boston strictly for burlesque performances—do not confuse this form of entertainment with the strip tease shows of the 1930s. The dictionary defines burlesque as "a witty or derisive literary or dramatic imitative work—broadly humorous theatrical entertainment consisting of several items (as songs, skits, or dances)." Most of the revues were satires of Broadway shows.

The house was taken over by motion picture exhibitor E.M. Loew in 1931, who established a policy of five acts of vaudeville, two feature films, and 15 and 25 cents admission.

All of Ben Sack's multiscreen theatres have been sacked for other uses.

The National Theatre closed in 1977, being in a newly fashionable and restored South End, it became part of the Boston Center for the Arts complex, which had a long-term lease on the facility.

Your author adds his memory of Boston's South End, where he was an usher and later assistant manager of the National Theatre during the late 1930s. It was a 3,000-seat, two-balconied barn. The steep second balcony was not used—we ushers had to carry heavy metal cases of film up countless flights of inside exit stairs to reach that top balcony level. Then one had to haul them down a narrow stepped passage to the tiny projection room, which was cut into the front of this balcony.

Abandoned organ pipes occupied old and dusty wide gallery boxes, which were duplicated at each side of the first balcony and along the front sides of the auditorium. Ushers seated customers in the first-floor boxes for an extra 25 cents each person.

The National's orchestra level seated 1,000 patrons for 20 cents each; above in the balcony another 1,000 chairs cost a dime. The stage was tall, wide, and deep, and dressing rooms were in a separate rear building. With vaudeville long gone, ushers used those star dressing rooms, wondering which great actors had used them. There was also a furnace room with an enormous sump pump (the theatre sat on manmade land, taken from the Back Bay of the Charles River).

The last time I stood on its stage was during a visit of a theatre history group to Boston in 1983; the house had been long closed. The orchestra pit and the first three rows of seating were filled with water seeping from the old Charles River bay; I wondered if its boat-sized boxes would soon be floating.

The stage was used professionally only once while I worked there, for an appearance of movie cowboy Ken Maynard and his horse. Ushers had to roll the heavy sound speakers by hand off into the wings.

The National had Amateur Nights every Sunday, where contestants performed "in one," that is, in front of the curtain. Those nights were wild, drawing a boisterous audience not averse to throwing objects at the performers. Other theatres with amateur nights had to hang a chicken-wire shield on stage to protect the contestants.

The National did not go to that extreme, but the manager, his assistant, and a policeman stood facing the audience while standing in front of its unused orchestra pit and organ remains. An usher was placed in each of the side boxes to keep watch. We never saw much of the would-be actors, since our eyes were focused on the audience. It all reminded me of wardens guarding their prisoners: The South End of Boston was really rough in those days, fallen from the rest of Back Bay elegance.

A neighbor of the National was the 1891 Columbia Theatre, which Marcus Loew had remodeled after a fire, and was, in 1940, still in good condition, playing films ahead of the National, but charging the same low prices. The huge Columbia was fronted by, and practically attached to, the elevated railway—one could still admire the Moorish façade and its three tall towers. Across the street were two one-floor theatres, the Apollo and the Cobb, once nickelodeons but then truly crap-cans, playing the very last runs, admission 10 cents at all times. Several nearby restaurants offered a complete meal for 25 cents, which was salvation for the Depression's unemployed, who slept in those nearby dime movie houses. The Columbia was demolished in 1957.

After being boarded up and partly under water, the National was demolished in 1996 for more arts space. The Columbia, Apollo, and Cobb were long gone.

The Pilgrim–Washington Street Olympia, home to Fanne Foxe and her stripteasers, folded and was demolished for a large parking lot. The Scollay Square Olympia and its neighbor, the all-night Rialto Theatre (originally the Star, one of the last nickelodeons), were swallowed up by Government Center, along with the Old Howard.

The author remembers the Rialto from when he worked at the National Theatre. The el trains shut down at midnight, so he had to keep warm in that old crap can every winter night while waiting for the hourly night car. That trolley car started above ground at Scollay Square and ran under the elevated tracks to North Station, where night buses waited. The Rialto had a stench that was indescribable. It ran the very last run of films, and half or perhaps more of the audience was asleep. I think the theatre only closed in the morning just long enough to clean.

E.M. Loew's West End Cinema (the former Lancaster) wound up as a Pussycat Cinema sex movie theatre. The Boston Garden is gone, along with the elevated trains. The old Stuart Theatre at Washington and Stuart streets had also gone the Pussycat route, and is now a store.

The Paramount Theatre, in 2002, stood out on Washington Street, with its famous white granite front restored, along with its handsome art deco vertical sign rehabilitated so that its flashing sparkle is as new.

The theatre's prospective owners had planned to secure the parking lot next door on the south end of Mason Street, which was the site of B.F. Keith's first palace in 1894.

The author has pounded that famous pavement times beyond count. The Opera House was the B.F. Keith Memorial Theatre, and Tremont Street patrons had to make that crossing across Mason to enter the main auditorium. There has been a theatre on that site since the Boston Theatre in 1854; B.F. Keith's 1894 theatre was next door to the south, where the parking lot is. The subway remains under Mason Street, which once connected that theatre to its Tremont Street lobby. The rear end building of the parking lot shows the connection of Keith's long lobby from Washington Street. Above it remains a roofing covering auditorium floor of the old Lion-Melodeon-Bijou, reminding one of the tremendous amount of theatrical history in that area. Theatres were there long before the condo arrived. The Bijou was the first theatre in America to use electricity and was the birthplace of vaudeville. Where the Paramount Theatre stands was the site of the famous Adams House hostelry, where politicians and the theatrical community gathered.

It all boils down to the distance between the rear end of the Tremont Street condominium and that of the Opera House; the only view from the former was the latter. So, however far the theatre's stage comes out into Mason Street, the view will not change.

On September 26, 2002, The Associated Press announced that after a court ruling, Clear Channel Entertainment would proceed with a $30 million plan to extend the 2,500-seat Opera House onto a street and turn it into a major performance center.

In November, Mayor Thomas M. Menino presented Clear Channel with a building permit to allow work to begin on the restoration of the historic B.F. Keith Memorial Theatre. He commented, "We can breathe new life into the Opera House, Downtown Crossing, and the arts scene in Boston."

The true sorrow is the condition of the adjoining Bijou building, between the Opera House and the Paramount Theatre. Above are the remains of 1836's Lion Theatre, Melodeon, and the Bijou, which was B.F. Keith's first real theatre, the birthplace of vaudeville. The author received permission from the building owners to go through what remained of the structure, which had housed the entrances to both theatres. That of Keith's was at that time a shoe store; that of the Bijou was part of an amusement arcade, whose southern inner side wall had retained the formerly elegant cupid decorated decor of Keith's lobby. An attendant took me to the rear of the arcade, where we climbed up shaky wooden steps, which suddenly became a marble stairway, a part of the Bijou's stage left exit. Then we emerged from a door onto the roof. From that point we crossed what was formerly the orchestra floor of the Bijou. The imprint of the stage was still visible as was that of the slanted auditorium—the wrecking squad had unwittingly created an imprint of the Bijou. I looked about and noticed markings on both side walls—those of the Keith Memorial–Opera House to the north still showed outlines of the Bijou balcony. New brick, covering old doors, indicated where the Prince of Wales had come into the Melodeon for his supper, during a ball given at the Boston Theatre next door. (In later years youthful Bijou patrons used these connections to sneak into the Keith Memorial without paying.) The opposite common wall of the Paramount Theatre retained marks of the Bijou balcony and stage. As we entered the old front building I looked up where the Bijou projection booth had hung; bricked up lobby doors remained below.

This brick structure dated back to about 1836, built as an entrance to the Lion Theatre, which eventually had become the Bijou entrance. Through the years it also was used as an annex to the adjacent Adams House, an exit from the Bijou balcony, a billiard hall and barbershop, the 1878 Gaiety Theatre, and even a small department store.

I roamed slowly through the old building. One could see where beautiful mantels had been wrenched from old fireplaces. A small elevator was at the north side of the building; its cab lay long deceased in the basement, the shaft cobwebbed and silent. In the early days of vaudeville B.F. Keith and his family had lived on the top floors.

I discovered the remains of a single toilet in one room. Its use required ascent of about three steps, because its siphon had to be above floor level since it could not be cut through floor and ceiling below. Many disgruntled vaudevillians called this Keith's throne room.

A tour of the basement was the saddest part of the trip, starting with the slabs of granite that are the original foundation walls, near which was a huge pile of glass, metal, and pump remains, all that was left of the magical waterfall stairway up to the Bijou. Against the south wall were tall, bricked-up windows of Keith offices, which once shared an air well with the Adams House next door. The rear was a jumble of debris. The parking lot had covered all remains of the old Keith theatre, dumping much of it into the Bijou cellar.

Why cannot this circa 1836 building become a monument to the birthplace of vaudeville? The city has restored the Opera House and the Paramount Theatre is currently undergoing renovation. The Lion–Mechanics Hall–Melodeon-Gaiety-Bijou stands between them, waiting to be discovered.

Appendix 1

Boston Theatres in Chronological Order

1775 Faneuil Hall   During the British occupation (1775 to 1783) used as a theatre, under management of Gen. John Burgoyne, actor and playwright. Faneuil Hall was later used for meetings and lectures.

1792 New Exhibition Room   August 10, 1792, on Board Alley, between Milk and Summer streets (present-day Hawley Street). Demolished June 1793.

1792 Concert Hall   Built about 1750, southeast corner of Hanover and Court streets. Demolished in the 1850s.

1794 Boston Theatre   February 3, 1794, Federal and Franklin streets. Also known as The New Theatre, Federal Street Theatre, and Odeon Theatre. Nickname: Old Drury. Demolished 1852.

1795 Columbian Museum, No. 1   At Broomfield's Lane (Bromfield Street) and the Mall (Common). Destroyed by fire January 15, 1803.

1796 Haymarket Theatre   December 26, 1796. On Common (Tremont) Street, close to Boylston Street, near Sheaf's Lane. Demolished 1803.

1803 Columbian Museum, No. 2   At Milk and Oliver streets, opposite Old South Church. Moved 1806.

1806 Columbian Museum, No. 3   On a lot north of Kings Chapel Burying Ground. Destroyed by fire January 16, 1807. Rebuilt June 1807. Closed January 1, 1825. Collection sold to New England Museum.

Circa 1811 Boylston Hall   Over the Boylston market, at Boylston and Newbury (Washington) streets. Also known as New York Museum briefly in 1812.

Circa 1815 Washington Gardens   At Common (Tremont) and West streets. Also known as Vauxhall Gardens (1817), City Theatre (1822), Washington Theatre (circa 1827).

1818 New England Museum   July 4, 1818, 76 Court Street. Also known as Harrington's New Museum, Harrington's Museum (1840), Washington Hall (1842). 1843–51 moved to Court Street; see 1842 Washington Hall.

1827 First Tremont Theatre   September 24, 1827, Common (Tremont) Street near School Street. Sold June 23, 1843. See 1843 Tremont Temple.

1832 Amphitheatre in Flagg Alley   February 1, 1832, Flagg Alley (later Change

Alley), between State Street and Faneuil Hall. Briefly known as the Washington Theatre.

1832 American Amphitheatre (National Theatre No. 1)   February 27, 1832, at Portland and Traverse streets. Also known as Warren Theatre, July 3, 1832; National Theatre, August 15, 1836. Burned April 22, 1852. Rebuilt November 1, 1852. Also known as Willard's National Theatre, People's National Theatre. Burned about 1863.

1833 Washington Hall   Formally Shawmut Hall at 221 Washington Street, next to Marlboro Hotel, opposite head of Franklin Street. Also known as State Museum, 1834–35; Papanti's Hall, 1837; Washington Hall, 1848.

1836 Lion Theatre–Melodeon   January 11, 1836, Washington Street (today, 545). Also known as Mechanic's Institute, 1839; Melodeon, 1840; Melodeon Billiard Hall, about 1867; Gaiety Theatre, 1878; Bijou Theatre, 1882; Bijou Opera House, 1895; and later, Bijou Dream, Keith's Bijou, RKO Bijou, Intown, Bijou. Closed December 31, 1943. Demolished 1951.

1841 Lee's Saloon   253 Washington Street. Also known as Olympic Salon, Apollo Saloon, 1842; Lee's Grand Saloon, 1844; Washington Theatre, 1845.

1841 New York Circus Amphitheatre–Eagle Theatre   Haverhill Street near Traverse Street. Also known as Marshall's Eagle Theatre, 1842–1843. Demolished 1843.

1841 Boston Museum and Gallery of Fine Arts   Site of Columbian Hall, at Tremont and Bromfield streets. Moved up Tremont Street in 1846.

1842 Washingtonian Hall   Moved from Harrington's Museum (New England Museum), 76–78 Court Street, to 75 Court Street. Known as Washington Hall, 1845. In 1846, moved to 221 Washington Street. See 1845 Boston Olympic Theatre.

1843 The Tremont Temple   No. 1 converted from the Tremont Theatre, dedicated December 1843. Burned March 30, 1852.

> No. 2 rebuilt December 1853. Burned August 11, 1879.

> No. 3 rebuilt October 1880. Burned March 1893.

> No. 4 rebuilt May 1896, still in existence 2005.

1845 Howard Athenaeum–Old Howard Theatre   Howard Street, remodeled from church, opened October 13, 1845. Burned February 1846. Rebuilt October 5, 1846, as Howard Atheneum. Closed after police raid during the 1953-1954 season when known as the Old Howard Theatre. Burned June 20, 1961. Demolished 1962.

1845 Boston Olympic Theatre   75 Court Street, former site of Washington Hall (moved from 76–78 Court Street). Also known as Brougham and Bland's Boston Adelphi Theatre, 1847; Brougham and Bland's Lyceum, 1848; Adelphia Saloon, 1850.

1846 New Boston Museum   Tremont Street between School Street and Scollay Square. Opened November 2, 1846. Remodeled in 1872. Closed June 1, 1903. Demolished summer 1903. Kimball Building on site.

1848 New Amphitheatre–Bland's Lyceum Theatre   Sudbury Street, opposite Hawkins, near Court Street. Also known as Blands Lyceum Theatre, September 20, 1848; Lyceum Theatre, January 1850; The Odeon, March 1850; Lyceum Theatre, October 1851; Eagle Theatre, May 1852; Goodall and Olwine's American Theatre, March 1853. Closed in 1854, converted to other use.

1848 Dramatic Museum October 16, 1848, on the north side of Beach Street near the U.S. Hotel. Also known as Thorne's American Theatre (or Museum), 1849; Beach Street Museum, October 1849; Olympic Theatre, closed October 1850 after a short season, was converted to other use.

1852 National Theatre, No. 2 November 1, 1852. Rebuilt on site of old National (see 1832 American Amphitheatre). Burned 1863.

1852 Boston Music Hall Bumstead Place, Hamilton Place, and Central Place (later Music Hall Place, 17 Winter Street). Converted into Empire Theatre, Orpheum Theatre, completely rebuilt as Loew's Orpheum Theatre, and in 1972 Aquarius Theatre. Name reverted to Orpheum, existing.

1852 Ordway Hall Was part of the Province House hostelry. Before the Great Fire, at 165 Washington Street, afterward 315–329 Washington Street (varied numbers). Also known as Morris Bros., Pell and Trowbridge's Opera House, 1861; Opera House and Trowbridge's Opera House, 1869; Lyceum Theatre, 1870. About 1870 converted to hotel use. About 1889 destroyed by fire, rebuilt as craftsman's shops. About 1907 burned to its four walls. About 1908 rebuilt as the Old South Theatre. Demolished May 1922.

Circa 1853 Horticultural Hall, No. 1 13 School Street. Also known as Pell, Huntley and Morris Brothers Opera House, January 1858; School Street Opera House, 1860; The Boudoir, 1861. In 1861 moved to Amory Hall, 501–507 Washington Street.

1854 Boston Theatre, No. 2 September 11, 1854, at 539 Washington Street. Briefly known in 1860 as the Academy of Music. Demolished 1925–26.

Circa 1855 Williams Hall 1138 Washington Street, over Williams Market. Also known as Hooley's Theatre, 1880–1881; Novelty Theatre, 1880–1881; Windsor Theatre, 1881; and later, Grand Museum, Grand Theatre, and Hub Theatre.

1860 Boston Aquarial and Zoological Gardens Moved from 21 Bromfield Street to Central Court, at Summer, Bedford, Washington and Chauncy streets. Also known as Boston Aquarial Gardens, 1862; Barnum's Aquarial Gardens, June 1862; P.T. Barnum's Museum and Aquarial Gardens, 1863; Boston Aquarial and Zoological Gardens, Andrews Hall, October 1863; Theatre Comique, October 1865; Adelphi Theatre, September 1869; Adelphi Theatre Comique, 1870; Adelphi Theatre, 1871. Destroyed by fire. Jordan Marsh department store built on its site.

1861 Horticultural Hall, No. 2 In Amory Hall, 501–507 Washington Street, at Washington and West streets. In 1865 moved to 100–104 Tremont Street.

1861 Allston Hall–Tremont Theatre No. 2 In Studio Building, 104–116 Tremont Street. Also known as Jane English's New Tremont Theatre, Jane English's Theatre at Allston Hall, and Theatre Francais, 1863; New Tremont Theatre, 1864–1865; Allston Hall, 1979; Great European Museum, 1880.

1862 New Boston Aquarial & Zoological Gardens Summer and Chauncy streets, moved from Central Court. Also known as New Minstrel Hall, and

Aquarial Gardens, 1863; and later, Buckley's Serenaders New Music Hall and Buckley's Music Hall.

1865 Horticultural Hall, No. 3   100–104 Tremont Street. Demolished about 1901.

1866 Continental Theatre   744–756 Washington Street, near Bennett Street. Also known as Whitman's Continental Theatre, 1867; Willard's Theatre, September 1868; Olympic Theatre, October 1868; Saint James Theatre, August 1871. After 1873 converted into Continental Clothing Factory.

1867 Selwyn's Theatre   October 29, 1867, at 364 Washington Street. Also known as Globe Theatre, 1870. Burned May 30, 1873. Rebuilt and reopened December 3, 1874. Destroyed by fire January 2, 1894. In 1896, Hotel Savoy built on its site.

The reader should note that after the Great Fire, street numbers changed on Washington and other streets.

1873 Beethoven Hall–Park Theatre   413 Washington Street at opening, after the great fire, 619–621 Washington Street. On April 14, 1879, became the Park Theatre. Also known as Minsky's Burlesque, Hub Theatre, Trans-Lux Theatre, and State Theatre. Closed 1895, demolished 1990 for temporary parking lot, site now redeveloped.

1876 New Boylston Museum   659–667 Washington Street. Also known as New Boylston Museum and Star Novelty Theatre, 1877; New Boylston Museum, September 18, 1882; and then, World's Museum, World's Theatre; Lyceum Theatre, September 19, 1892. Demolished about 1907.

Circa 1877 Union Hall   18, later 48 Boylston Street. In 1890s became part of the Young Men's Christian Union Building.

1878 Gaiety Theatre   Remodeled Melodeon Theatre, October 15, 1978.

1879 Dudley Street Opera House   Remodeled Institute Hall.

1882 New Dime Museum   Under Horticultural Hall, Tremont and Bromfield streets.

1882 Bijou Theatre   Formerly Lion Theatre, Mechanic's Hall, Melodeon, Gaiety, reconstructed as new. Demolished 1951.

1883 Boston Dime Museum–Austin and Stone's Museum   1–4 Tremont Row at Scollay Square. Razed about 1912.

1883 Park Square Garden   Old Providence Railroad Station, Park Square.

1883 New York Dime Museum, Keith and Bacheller's   565–567 Washington Street. Also known as Keith and Batcheller's Mammoth Museum, Keith and Batcheller's Gaiety Hall and Museum, Keith and Batcheller's Museum. Moved into Bijou Building.

1884 Keith and Gardner's New York Museum   565–567 Washington Street. Also known as Keith and Batcheller's Mammoth Museum, Keith and Batcheller's Gaiety Hall and Museum. Moved into Bijou Building, 1887.

1884 World's Museum   661–667 Washington Street. See also 1876 New Boylston Museum.

1885 Hollis Street Theatre   14 Hollis Street, former Hollis Street Church reconstructed into theatre. Opened November 9, 1885. Demolished 1935; building collapsed during demolition, killing several workers.

1888 Grand Opera House   1126–1194 Washington Street. Opened January 9, 1888. Demolished late 1930s. Brass letters spelling out Grand Opera House remained imbedded in the front sidewalk until 1960s.

1888 Nickelodeon, Austin's Nickelodeon Museum   109–113 Court Street. Also known as Palace Theatre, May 30, 1891; Trocadero Theatre. Demolished in 1931. A portion of the attic above the entrance was saved during demolition and displayed in the lobby of the telephone company main office building as a museum of Alexander Graham Bell's 1875 laboratory.

1888 New Grand Museum   August 20, 1888. Was second floor Windsor Theatre at Washington at Dover streets, and its first floor became a large museum.

1889 Tremont Theatre, No. 3   Opened October 14, 1889, at 176 Tremont Street. Later known as Astor Theatre. Demolished July 1983.

1891 Columbia Theatre   October 5, 1891, at 978 Washington Street. Also known as Columbia Music Hall, Theatre and Promenade; Loew's South End Theater, 1911; Loew's Columbia Theatre; Columbia Theatre. Demolished 1957.

1891 Austin's Palace Theatre   April 1891, rebuilt from Austin's Nickelodeon. Briefly known as the Trocadero. Demolished.

1892 Bowdoin Square Theatre   February 15, 1892, at 1 Bowdoin Square. Demolished 1955.

1892 Lyceum Theatre   September 19, 1892, at site of World's Museum, 661–667 Washington Street.

1894 B.F. Keith's New Theatre   March 24, 1894, at 547 Washington Street. Also known as Apollo Theatre, Lyric Theatre, Normandie Ballroom and restaurant, Normandie Theatre, Laff-Movie, Art-Movie, Mirth-Movie, Laff-Movie, Art Movie. Demolished 1951.

1894 Castle Square Theatre   Opened November 12, 1894, at 421 Tremont Street. During construction known as Alcazar Theatre. Incorporated into Cyclorama building. Also known as the Arlington Theatre. Demolished 1932.

1894 Nickelodeon Musee and Parlor Theatre   December 23, 1894, at 51–53 Hanover Street. Also known as Eden Musee, 1896; Nickelodeon.

1896 The Zoo   106 Boylston Street (old public library building). Also known as Sans Souci. Demolished 1899.

1896 Grand Theatre   Was Williams Hall, Windsor Theatre, at Washington and Dover streets.

1900 Boston Music–Musee Hall   Opened Labor Day 1900. Reconstructed Boston Music Hall.

1900 Colonial Theatre   Opened December 19, 1900, at 106 Boylston Street. Existing.

1901 Chickering Hall   239 Huntington Avenue. On August 30, 1912, remodeled into St. James Theatre, later known as Uptown Theatre. Demolished.

1903 Majestic Theatre   Opened February 16, 1903, at 219 Tremont Street. Also known as Saxon Theatre. Existing as the Cutler Majestic Theatre.

1903 Hub Theatre   Opened August 17, 1903, at Dover and Washington streets. Refurbished by E.D. Stair and A.L. Wilbur. Was Grand Theatre.

1903 Globe Theatre   Opened September 14, 1903, at 692 Washington Street. Also known as Center Theatre, Pagoda Theatre. Existing as Oriental market and restaurant.

1904 Horticultural Hall   Moved to 800 Massachusetts Avenue.

1905 Empire Theatre   Renamed February 12, 1905; was Music Hall.

1905 Monaco Theatre   Green Street, corner of Hale.

Circa 1905 Olympic Theatre   No. 3 or 6 Bowdoin Square, in St. James Hotel. May also have been Theatre Jolliette. Motion picture house, probably was Walker's Museum of 1904. Demolished in the 1930s.

Circa 1905 Puritan Theatre   Washington Street, a true nickelodeon, almost under the elevated railroad. Lasted into the late 1960s. Demolished 1970s.

1906 Theatre Comique   Opened September 3, 1906, at 14–16 Tremont Row, Scollay Square. Motion picture theatre. Demolished.

1906 Orpheum Theatre   Renamed Music Hall, Empire. Leased by Percy Williams.

1907 Unique Theatre   Opened January 1907 at 700 Washington Street. Moving picture house, on the site of Hale's Tours, a movie–train ride novelty. Also known as Stuart Theatre, Pussycat Theatre. Part of office building; theatre portion converted to store.

1907 Lyric Theatre   March 1907, 734 Washington Street. Moving picture house. Demolished.

1907 Theatre Premier   Washington and Beach streets. Moving picture house. Converted to store.

1907 Theatre Jolliette   Near Bowdoin Square Theatre, short-lived motion picture house. See circa 1905 Olympic Theatre.

1907 Star Theatre–Rialto Theatre   5–7 Tremont Row, Scollay Square. Moving picture house. Later known as Rialto Theatre. Demolished in mid–1962, for Government Center.

1907 Scenic Temple   December 31, 1907, at Berkely and Warren streets. Motion picture house. Was Berkely Hall.

1908 Gaiety Theatre   November 23, 1908, at Washington Street near Boylston Street. Also known as Gayety Theatre, Victory Theatre, Publix Theatre. Site is that of World Museum, Lyceum Theatre. Existing January 2002 as warehouse. Plans being made for other use of the site after demolition.

1908 Pastime Theatre   Avery Street near Washington Street. Moving picture house. Reverted to store.

1908 Eden Musee   723–727 Washington Street.

1908 Idle Hour Theatre   Tremont Street, near Castle Square Theatre. Short-lived motion picture house.

Circa 1908 Old South Theatre   Part of Province House, rebuilt inside its brick walls after a fire that leveled the original.

1909 Boston Opera House   Opened November 8, 1909, at 343 Huntington Avenue. Demolished 1958.

1909 American Music Hall Was the old Music Hall. Also known as Empire, American Music Hall, Orpheum, and Loew's Orpheum.

1909 Potter Hall 177 Huntington Avenue. Dime movies and vaudeville. Demolished.

1910 Waldron's Casino Opened January 3, 1910, at 44 Hanover Street. Leased to NETOCO (Paramount) briefly in 1940s. Closed in 1962, demolished for Government Center.

1910 Shubert Theatre Opened January 24, 1910. Also known as Sam S. Shubert Theatre. Existing.

1910 Beacon Theatre February, at 47–53 Tremont Street. Also known as the Beacon Hill Theatre. Relocated in 1973 to new theatre of same name, lower level of office building at 1 Beacon Street. Closed.

1910 Loew's Orpheum Boston Music Hall, taken over and renamed by Marcus Loew. Rebuilt 1916.

Circa 1910 Apollo Theatre A 700-seat one-floor motion picture house on Washington Street opposite the Columbia Theatre, next to the Cobb Theatre. Lasted into the 1940s.

Circa 1910 Cobb Theatre A 700-seat one-floor motion picture house on Washington Street, opposite the Columbia Theatre, next to the Apollo Theatre. Lasted into the 1940s.

1911 National Theatre No. 3 Opened September 18, 1911, at 535 Tremont Street. Also known as the Hippodrome, Waldorf Theatre. Demolished about 1996, to expand arts center.

1911 Plymouth Theatre Opened September 23, 1911, at Eliot Street near Tremont Street, later known as 131 Stuart Street. Also known as the Gary Theatre. Demolished about 1980.

1911 Washington Theatre Opened October 2, 1911, at 720 Washington Street. Motion pictures and vaudeville. Demolished in the 1930s.

1911 Loew's South End Theatre Renamed Columbia Theatre.

1912 Gordon's Olympia Theatre Opened May 6, 1912, at 658 Washington Street. Also known as Pilgrim Theatre. Demolished 1996.

1912 Saint James Theatre August 30, 1912. Was Chickering Hall, a new theatre using old entrance. Later renamed Uptown Theatre. About 1968, sold to Christian Science Church and demolished.

1912 Huntington Avenue Theatre, Strand Theatre September 23, 1912, at 175 Huntington Avenue. Possibly was Potter Hall. Also known as Strand and Capri theatres. Demolished about 1968.

1913 Scollay Square Olympia Theatre Opened November 17, 1913, at Tremont Row at Howard Street. Also known as Scollay Theatre. Demolished in 1962 for Government Center.

1914 Cort Theatre Opened January 19, 1914, in Park Square. Also known as Park Square Theatre, Selwyn Theatre. Demolished about 1926 for auto parking garage.

1914 Wilbur Theatre Opened April 20, 1914, at 250–252 Tremont Street. Owner A.L. Wilbur originally named it Ye Wilbur Theatre. Existing.

1914 Exeter Street Theatre Opened May 4, 1914, at 26 Exeter Street. Converted from meeting hall. Mostly motion pictures. Closed in 1984, converted to retail use.

1914 Modern Theatre   Opened June 25, 1914, inside lower stories of older building at 525 Washington Street. Also known as Mayflower Theatre. Last use was as storage space.

1914 Toy Theatre–Copley Theatre   Opened December 1914 at 188 Dartmouth Street near Copley Square. Later the building was turned around, with entrance at 461 Stuart Street. Later, new entrance from 22 Huntington Avenue. This theatre is best known as the Copley. Later renamed Capri Theatre, demolished 1962 for Massachusetts Turnpike entrance. First Toy Theatre was a stable on Lyme Street.

1915 Fenway Theatre   Opened December 19, 1915, at 136 Massachusetts Avenue. Also known as the Berklee Theatre, owned by Berklee School of Music. Existing.

1916 New Loew's Orpheum Theatre   January 20, 1916. New theatre using old Music Hall with added space.

1917 Lancaster Theatre   Opened February 17, 1917, across from North Station and Manger Hotel. Also known as West End Cinema and Pussycat Theatre. Demolished about 1990.

1920 Gordon's Old South Theatre   Washington Street, opposite Milk Street. Was 1908 theatre rebuilt in ruins of Province House and refurbished with new organ. Demolished in May 1922 for a new theatre (never constructed).

1921 Suffolk Theatre   Opened April 11, 1921, at Temple and Derne streets. Auditorium of Suffolk Law School. Short-lived.

1922 Loew's State Theatre   Opened March 13, 1922. Also known as Donnelly Memorial and Back Bay Theatre. Demolished 1968.

1922 Fine Arts Theatre   Opened in October 1922 at 70 Norway Street. Also known as State Theatre, 750-seat rehearsal hall for Loew's State Theatre; the Little Opera House; Off Broadway Stage. Demolished 1968.

1925 Keith-Albee Boston Theatre   Opened October 5, 1925, at 616 Washington Street at Essex Street. Also known as Cinerama Theatre, Essex 1 and 2 theatres. Existing as warehouse.

1925 Metropolitan Theatre   Opened October 17, 1925, at 268 Tremont Street. Also known as the Music Hall, Wang Center for the Performing Arts. Existing.

1925 Repertory Theatre   Opened November 10, 1925. Also known as Civic Repertory Theatre, Esquire Theatre, Boston University Theatre. Existing.

1928 B.F. Keith Memorial Theatre   Opened October 29, 1928, at 539 Washington Street. Also known as RKO Keith's Theatre, Savoy Theatre, Savoy 1 and 2 theatres, Opera House. Existing.

1929 Uptown Theatre   September 1, 1929, name change from Saint James Theatre.

1929 Our Theatre, Elizabeth Peabody Theatre   357 Charles Street. Also known as the Peabody Playhouse; Cine Theatre, 1952. Demolished in the 1950s.

1929 Shubert Apollo and Lyric Theatres   Old B.F. Keith's Theatre, entered from Tremont Street.

1930 Strand Theatre 21 Scollay Square, in and under the Crawford House. Became nightclub in late 1930s. Demolished in 1950s for Government Center.

1932 Paramount Theatre Opened February 25, 1932. Existing, but closed.

1933 Minsky's Burlesque Theatre Was Park Theatre.

1937 Hub Theatre Old Park Theatre, Minsky's Burlesque.

1938 Trans-Lux Theatre September 10, 1938. Was Park Theatre, Minsky's Burlesque, Hub Theatre. Remodeled into newsreel theatre, later added feature films.

1938 Normandie Theatre Was B.F. Keith's Theatre, Shubert and Apollo theatres, Normandie Ballroom.

1939 Telepix Newsreel theatre in Park Square office building.

Circa 1939 Kenmore Square Theatre Motion picture house, street-level entry with 65 seats, lower level 636 seats. Demolished.

1940 Old South Newsreel Theatre Opened September 1940 in new office building. No connection with previous Old South Theatre (Ordway Hall). Converted to stores in 1950.

1940 Joy Street Play House Joy Street, was converted carriage house.

Circa 1944 Laff Movie Theatre December 16, 1938. Was Normandie Theatre (and B.F. Keith Theatre).

Circa 1945 New Normandie Theatre Was B.F. Keith's old theatre, Laff Movie, used briefly for first-runs.

1946 Victory Theatre Was Gayety Theatre (built as Gaiety Theatre); new name in September.

1947 Center Theatre February 18, 1947. Was Globe Theatre, remodeled by E.M. Loew as legitimate playhouse, became motion picture house.

1947 Astor Theatre November 11, 1947. Remodeled Tremont Theatre, first-run movies.

1948 Beacon Hill Theatre No. 1 Beacon Hill Theatre remodeled by Ben Sack. Later, name was transferred to a new office building theatre at Beacon and Tremont streets.

Circa 1949 Pilgrim Theatre Was the Washington Street Olympia Theatre, remodeled and renamed.

Circa 1949 Mayflower Theatre Was the Modern Theatre, remodeled and renamed.

Circa 1949 Publix Theatre Final name of the Gaiety, Gayety, Victory. Still standing, but faces demolition.

Circa 1949 Esquire Theatre Renaming of Repertory Theatre. Sold to Boston University, in use for Huntington Theatre Company.

Circa 1949 Art-Movie Old B.F. Keith's Theatre, Normandie, Laff Movie.

1950 Trans-Lux Copley Theatre Old Copley Theatre leased by Trans-Lux Corporation, new entrance created at 22 Huntington Ave.

Circa 1950 Mirth Movie Theatre B.F. Keith's Theatre, Shubert Apollo, Lyric, Normandie, Laff Movie, Art Movie. Demolished in 1951 for parking lot.

1951 Cine Former Peabody Playhouse, 357 Charles Street. Short-lived.

1953 Cinerama Theatre December 30, 1953. Third Boston Theatre, at Essex and Washington streets.

1956 Off Broadway Theatre   Former rehearsal hall of Loew's State, Fine Arts Theatre.

1957 Saxon Theatre   September 13, 1957, converted from former Majestic Theatre, existing as Cutler Majestic.

1957 Gary Theatre   Former Plymouth Theatre. Demolished.

1957 Charles Playhouse, No. 1   54 Charles Street, second-floor hall. Moved 1958 to Warrenton Street.

1958 Capri Theatre, No. 1   Former Copley Theatre, leased by Ben Sack as movie theatre.

1958 Charles Playhouse No. 2   Former church and nightclub on Warrenton Street, behind Shubert Theatre.

1958 Little Opera House   Loew's State Rehearsal Hall, Fine Arts Theatre, The Off Broadway Stage.

1959 Donnelly Memorial   Was Loew's State Theatre.

1960 State Theatre No. 2   Renamed Park-Trans-Lux Theatre. Demolished for parking lot about 1990.

1962 Sack's Music Hall   Was Metropolitan Theatre. Existing as the Wang Center.

1962 Capri Theatre No. 2   Formerly the Strand Theatre, Huntington Avenue.

1963 West End Cinema   Was Lancaster Theatre. Later known as Pussycat Theatre.

1964 Paris Cinema   1841 Boylston Street, Boston's last new single-screen theatre. Demolished about 2000.

1965 Back Bay Theatre   Was Loew's State and Donnelly Memorial Theatre. Demolished.

1965 Sack's Savoy Theatre   Was B.F. Keith Memorial, RKO Keith's Theatre. Existing as the Opera House.

1965 Sack's Cheri Theatre   Part of new garage building, Boylston Street and Huntington Avenue.

1966 Charles Theatre   195 Cambridge Street.

1968 Sack's Pi Alley Cinema   237 Washington Street, later twinned.

1971 Savoy Theatre No. 2   Stage of Keith Memorial–Savoy Theatre converted to cinema in September.

1972 Aquarius Theatre   January 18, 1972. Was Loew's Orpheum, using only Hamilton Place entrance. Later reverted to Orpheum Theatre name. Existing.

1972 Cinema 57   Office building and parking garage, 200 Stuart Street. Now Stuart Street Playhouse.

1973 Charles East and West Cinemas   105 Cambridge Street.

1973 Beacon Hill Theatres 1-2-3   1 Beacon Street, part of new office building. Theatre not existing.

1974 Essex Theatre 1 and 2   Formerly RKO Boston Theatre, Cinerama. Existing as warehouse.

1979 Opera House   Formerly Keith Memorial, RKO Keith's, Savoy theatres. Existing, to be restored.

1979 Wang Center for the Performing Arts   Former Metropolitan Theatre, Music Hall. Existing.

Miscellaneous Halls, Saloons, and Museums

Circa 1807	PANTHEON HALL. Pond and Newbury (Washington) streets, south of Boylston Market.
1813	ROMAN MUSEUM. 17 Newbury (Washington) Street.
1820–1821	MERCHANT EXHIBITION HALL. 23 Hanover Street. Had boxes and a gallery, 25 and 50 cents.
1822	BOSTON MUSEUM, MARKET MUSEUM. Ann Street near the market. Contents purchased by the New England Museum.
1826	JULIAN OR JULIEN HALL. Congress and Milk streets. In 1834 it became Mr. Saubert's Hall.
1834	CONGRESS HALL. Hanover and Commercial streets, at the Globe Hotel.
1837	NATIONAL GALLERY. 63 Union Street. Wax figures, some variety shows.
1838	WAX MUSEUM. 55 Union Street
1838	TREMONT HALL. Enter from Phillips Court.
1848	MINERVIAN HALL. 329 Washington Street.
1850	CENTRAL HALL. 19 Milk Street.
1850	ATLAS HALL. 417 or 517 Washington Street, "a few doors above Melodeon."
1851	HARMONY HALL. Washington and Summer streets.
1857	NASSAU HALL. Common and Washington streets.
1861	CHICKERING AND SONS HALL. Washington Street, enter at Avon Place.
1866	MERCANTILE HALL. 16 Summer Street (Theatre Francais).
1871	BRACKETT'S HALL. 304 Washington Street.
1874	BURNELL AND PRESCOTT'S MUSEUM. 511 Washington Street (possibly).
1875	MECHANICS HALL. Bedford Street at Chancy Street.
1876	WESLEYAN HALL. 36 Bromfield Street.
1877	NEW ERA HALL. 170 Tremont Street.
1877	LIBERTY TREE MUSEUM. Washington Street at Essex Street.
1879	REVERE HALL. Bowdoin Square, probably part of the Revere House.
1879	BUMSTEAD HALL. 15 Winter Street.
1884	HAYNES AND JACKSON'S STAR MUSEUM. 289 Hanover Street.
1898	AUSTIN'S AQUARIUM. 890 Washington Street, most likely in old armory.
1892	NICKEL MUSEUM. 17 Hanover Street.
1892	GLOBE MUSEUM. 187–189 Hanover Street, at Cross Street.
1892	BOSTON CIRCUS. Same address.
1895	HANOVER THEATRE. Same address.
1896	HUB MUSEUM. Same address
1904–1904	BOWDOIN SQUARE MUSEUM–WALKER'S MUSEUM. 3 Bowdoin Square, in St. James Hotel. Probably became the Olympic Theatre.

Appendix 2

How Patrons Got to Boston Theatres

In the beginning, most customers lived with in the peninsula that was Boston, a giant fist poking out of the towns of Roxbury and Dorchester, aimed at mainland Charlestown. Surrounding waters on the east were of Boston Harbor with a touch of the Mystic River, on the west the Charles River and its pelican-chinned Back Bay. Through the narrow waters above the knuckle, called the Fort Point Channel, Charles Bridge crossed from docks below Copp's Hill at Prince Street, over to Charlestown, where roads led to points north and east. Later, a second connection, the Warren Bridge, was added. At the thumb, the Cambridge and West Boston bridge crossed the Charles River, while on the east side of the fist, ferryboats connected with East Boston and points north on the Atlantic coast. Soon, another bridge crossed from Charlestown's Navy Yard, over the wide Mystic River, to Chelsea, Everett and points north. Stagecoaches, or tallyhos, were the initial transportation to Boston for out-of-town travel.

By 1850, rail lines entered into Boston via Charlestown, and Back Bay became crisscrossed by Providence Railroad and Worcester trains traveling on wooden pile trestles ending in Park Square and Kneeland Street.

The bay was being filled in and would become what was called "made land," keeping the name "Back Bay." It became a very elegant neighborhood with Beacon Street mansions and included the beautiful residential squares of the South End, at Tremont Street. All railroads coming from the North terminated at stations along Causeway Street or nearby.

In 1875, a narrow gauge steam railroad ran from Lynn, a large industrial city on the coast north of Boston, to East Boston, where a ferry connected its riders with the city. This popular line was electrified in 1929 and ran until 1940.

All railroads scheduled their train times to allow theatre patrons to get into Boston for the theatre and to bring them home again after the show. This was a profitable policy for railroads and is still in effect.[1]

The horse and carriage was the local transportation, the family car of its day.

Opposite, top: **The Charles River Bridge from Charlestown to Boston, 1789.** *Bottom:* **The South Boston Bridge, circa 1830 (both Library of Congress).**

View of the BRIDGE over CHARLES RIVER.

tance, he had either to hire a private vehicle at a heavy expense, | railroads are an advance on omnibusses. For some years they | quisite rural beauty, which amply repay an occasional visit.

THE BOSTON AND CAMBRIDGE NEW HORSE RAILROAD.

A horse railroad in front of the Revere House, circa 1853 (Library of Congress).

About 1826, horse-drawn and side-seated omnibuses served theatregoers within the city via regularly scheduled routes. These vehicles, slightly longer than a stagecoach, had one door, in the rear, and offered a rough ride. In 1853, the Metropolitan Railroad Company's horse-drawn streetcars began running on metal rails, and with the cars' front and rear entrances, were the ancestor of the electric trolley car. In 1865 an attempt was made to use steam-powered cars, but the project failed by 1867. By 1900, electric trolley cars were in.[2]

Then came a big transportation problem in the late 1890s, as trolley cars tied up themselves and other street traffic in downtown areas. So, in 1897 Boston got a subway, the first in the United States, and the line initially ran from a Boylston Street entrance to a large underground station at Park Street, beneath the Boston Common Mall.[3] Soon a new subway, from the North Railroad Station on Causeway Street, ran to and through the Park Street terminal. This line was extended north from the terminals onto elevated tracks over the Charles River into a new station, Lechmere, in Cambridge.

Starting in June 1901, elevated electric trains ran from Dudley Street Terminal

Opposite, top: Omnibuses in front of the second Boston Theatre, which opened in 1854. *Bottom:* In 1872, an outbreak of "horse influenza" caused the hiring of men to pull horse-cars in Boston (both Library of Congress).

ENTRANCE TO THE NEW BOSTON THEATRE, WASHINGTON STREET.

CONDUCTORS AND DRIVERS DRAWING THE HORSE-CARS IN THE STREETS OF BOSTON.

A bird's-eye view from the north; Bunker Hill Monument is on the left; note the number of railroad bridges (Library of Congress).

in Roxbury, going underground through downtown Boston, rising at North Station to elevated tracks running to Sullivan Square terminal at Charlestown. Suburban trolley cars discharged passengers at each terminal; riders rode "the El" to various Boston stations. At the time of World War I, the El was extended from Sullivan Square, across the Mystic River to Everett Terminal at ground level.[4]

At first the Boston Elevated Railroad had to use part of the trolley subway, operating its trains from North Station through it to a new exit at lower Tremont Street, where they rejoined the elevated structure running to Dudley Street. Meanwhile, after the El's downtown tunnel was finished, the trolleys got their subway back.

This was all well and good unless you lived in Charlestown or in the South End, where the noise and "daylight dusk" of the elevated trains began to annoy the residents, who moved, leaving neighborhoods to decline. After the new tunnel under downtown Boston was completed, passengers went underground at North Station and popped up again almost in the lap of the Columbia Theatre.

With the introduction of motor cars came motor buses, which gradually reduced the number of trolley cars. Automobile use became so popular that in the 1920s two large new garages were constructed in the theatre district, one on Beach Street just off Washington Street, the other in Park Square near the site of the old Providence Railroad Station and the Cort Theatre. These were self-parking facilities: Drivers received a ticket, drove up spiral ramps, found a parking space, and took the elevator down to street level. After returning from the show the system was reversed and drivers paid the parking fee on the way out, at the street end of the ramp. Other parking systems followed these pioneers, so going to a show in Boston by car has never been a problem.

Chapter Notes

Chapter 1

1. Although Hornblow, writing in 1919, lamented the lack of information of the period, Mary Caroline Crawford added much to this "lack" in 1913. She most likely also quoted Seilhamer in her writings as well.

Chapter 2

1. Salem, Massachusetts, was the site of the famous witch trials and hangings, so appearances there for a few weeks of "theatricals" is questionable.

2. This ruse had the actors standing in line perfectly still, yet reciting their parts exactly as if it were a dramatic performance.

Chapter 3

1. The "contemporary" quoted by Mary C. Crawford in her history was not identified, although it probably was Seilhamer.

2. "Variety" was the ancestor of vaudeville. A show was made up of several acts, with singers, jugglers, dancers, rope-walkers (tightrope performers), ventriloquists and magicians.

3. *The Bostonian* was a magazine published in the late 1890s, it had no connection with today's Bostonian Society.

Chapter 4

1. The word saloon in these times was most likely a salon, which served refreshments. Alcoholic beverages were usually available in the top balcony, over the boxes.

2. All commercial rentals at Tremont Temple ceased in 1957.

Chapter 5

1. The reader should note that this entrance was at the south end of the building; in a later remodeling the entrance was moved to the north end and the former became an exit.

Chapter 7

1. In later years the walls facing the auditorium were opened up as areas for standing-room patrons. A thrust stage was used in most theatres of the time. In the Boston Theatre it aided actors to project their voices, and it also permitted crowd scenes for the theatre's famous spectacles and permitted scene changes behind the proscenium as the play continued.

2. Gas chandeliers were lit before opening and turned off after the show. The heat from these jets helped ventilation, pulling foul air out through vents in the roof. Footlights were usually controlled from the stage manager or prompter's desk.

Chapter 8

1. A minstrel show was an evening's entertainment of singers, comedians and musicians sitting on elevated rows on stage. These were usually white men in black makeup, but sometimes only the comedians were in blackface. There were a few real black minstrel troupes.

2. Part of the wall of the Boston Theatre and that of the Melodeon were back to back; the doors between the two houses remained throughout the demolition of the Boston Theatre and the construction of the Keith Memorial Theatre in 1928. In the Keith, one door of the Bijou standing-room area led to the men's lounge; a balcony exit connected with a Memorial stairway. This arrangement provided exits for the Bijou until bricked up in 1938.

Chapter 9

1. A barbershop was added to the existing billiard space, both on the second floor. The barbershop probably was in the Washington Street frontage, which had light from many windows facing the street. The billiard hall was up a few steps in the flat-floored auditorium. The street level of the building had storefronts and the upper floors were used for rentals. The property was owned by the adjacent Adams House until 1908.

2. A theatrical season ran from autumn until late spring. Theatres closed for summer and actors toured small and rural locations or vacationed. Theatres were usually "refurbished" during off-season.

3. The problem of fire in these theatres and halls was serious. The structures were mostly constructed of brick with wood floors, beams, and roofing. Early lighting was by candles, then oil, and then gas, all flammable. Faulty electric wiring also caused fires in electricity's early days.

Chapter 10

1. Flats were wood-framed scenery painted on canvas, up to 20 feet tall. They were held in stage floor grooves.

Chapter 11

1. It was a custom with animal performers, appearing in upstairs houses, to "walk up" the theatre stairs, as extra advertising.

2. Moorish and Arabic designs were extremely popular and were to decorate many Boston theatres. The Alhambra inspired many architects even into the days of the motion picture palaces.

Chapter 13

1. This cyclorama should not be confused with the nearby one at 541 Tremont Street displaying "The Battle of Gettysburg."

2. Electricity was not completely reliable in its early days, so many new theatres installed gas as a backup. Gas remained as emergency lighting in auditoriums for many years until electric battery emergency lights were used. New residences of the time used fixtures for gas and electric.

Chapter 14

1. In similar emergency situations, the gas company supplier would run tubes down alleys to keep its biggest customers in business.

Chapter 16

1. The emphasis of fireproofing theatres occurred after several tragic fires. In 1876, Conway's Brooklyn Theatre had a disastrous fire when a gas jet and a scenery piece

caused a conflagration on stage, which was then drawn into the auditorium by draft from the dome ventilator. Three hundred people were killed (238 in the gallery), and New York wrote a new code of safety for theatres.

2. These cycloramas were very popular after the Civil War, but when the public interest waned the buildings had no further use nor interest.

3. Theatres needed more electric power than existing local plants could give, so they had to provide their own generators. B.F. Keith made them an attraction in his new house.

Chapter 23

1. In later years, the spelling of its name changed to "Gayety." The Melodeon was renamed the Gaiety before becoming the Bijou. Keith also flirted with the name Gaiety for his dime museum.

Chapter 26

1. Ernest Emerling of Loew's Theatres told the author about this showing, while doing research for a history of S.Z. Poli's theatres. The leasing of a baseball field for a theatre was an obsession of Loew, being a one-time trial and possible publicity stunt. It was far too expensive a project to succeed. There had been outdoor theatres since the time of the ancients; many modern theatres had outdoor movie screens for summer movies on top or behind their houses. The drive-in movie theatres grew out of these projects.

Chapter 27

1. The "mystery house" was a myth, which continued long after the newspapers admitted that it did not exist. The author remembers being told about it in his childhood. In 1983, the U.S. Historic American Buildings Survey (HABS No. Ma-1078) stated that there had been a mystery house discovered during demolition. This book's author called to report the error.

Chapter 31

1. Fox Film Company experimented with wide screen pictures about 1926, using a wide-angle lens called "Magnascope" to blow up certain scenes from the silent film *Old Ironsides*, but only in larger theatres. A 1930 Fox talking motion picture, *The Big Trail*, starring John Wayne, was shot in normal 35mm and also on 70mm film, but the larger version was only shown in large cities.

Appendix 2

1. Thomas J. Humphrey and Norton D. Clark, *Boston's Commuter Rail* (Boston: Boston Street Railway Association, 1986).

2. Frank Cheney and Anthony M. Sammarco, *Boston in Motion* (Mount Pleasant, S.C.: Arcadia Press, 1999).

3. Bradley H. Clarke and O.R. Cummings, *Tremont Street Subway: A Century of Public Service* (Boston: Boston Street Railway Association, 1997).

4. Frank Cheney and Anthony M. Sammarco, *When Boston Rode the El* (Mount Pleasant, S.C.: Arcadia Press, 2000).

Bibliography

Books

Allvine, Glendon. *The Greatest Fox of Them All*. New York: Lyle Stuart, 1969.

Birkmire, William H. *The Planning and Construction of American Theatres*. New York: John Wiley, 1907.

Campbell, Robert, and Peter Vanderwarker. *Cityscapes of Boston*. Boston: Houghton Mifflin, 1892.

Clapp, William W., Jr. *A Record of the Boston Stage*. New York: Benjamin Blom, reprint of 1853 edition.

Crawford, Mary Caroline. *The Romance of the American Theatre*. New York: Halcyon House, 1940 reprint of 1913 and 1925 editions.

Dearborn, Nathaniel. *Boston Notions*. Boston: Nathaniel Dearborn, 1848.

Frohman, Daniel. *Daniel Frohman Presents: An Autobiography*. New York: Claude Kendall and Willoughby Sharp, 1935.

Grandgent, Charles H. *Fifty Years of Boston*. Boston: Boston Tercentenary Committee, 1932.

Green, Abel, Laurie, Joe, Jr. *Show Biz from Vaude to Video*. New York: Henry Holt, 1951.

Hornblow, Arthur. *A History of the Theatre in America: From Its Beginnings to the Present Time*, Vol. 1. Philadelphia: J.B. Lippincott, 1919.

Ketchem, Richard M. *Will Rogers: His Life and Times*. New York: Simon & Schuster, 1973.

Laurie, Joe, Jr. *Vaudeville from the Honky-Tonks to the Palace*. New York: Henry Holt, 1953.

Ramsaye, Terry. *A Million and One Nights: A History of the Motion Picture*. New York: Simon & Shuster, 1964.

Skinner, Otis. *Footlights and Spotlights: Reflections of My Life on the Stage*. Indianapolis: Bobbs Merrill, 1924.

Tompkins, Eugene. *The History of the Boston Theatre 1854–1901*. Boston: Houghton Mifflin, 1908.

Winsor, Justin. *The Memorial History of Boston*. Boston: Ticknor, 1881.

Pamphlets and Cuttings

(From the Rare Book Department of the Boston Public Library)

"The Auditorium," New England News Company, 1895.

"B.F. Keith's New Theatre," George H. Walker, Boston.

"Boston Museum Retrospect and Scrapbook," 1880-1881 season.

"Boston Sights and Stranger's Guide," 1856.

"The Boston Stage," newspaper cuttings.

"Boston Theatricals," newspaper cuttings 1854–1876.

"Historical Review of the Boston Bijou Theatre," Edward O. Skelton, 1884.

"Pictorial Diagrams of Boston's Theatres,"

Chicago, Milwaukee and St. Paul Railway, 1880.

"Programme, Keith and Batcheller's Mammoth Museum," September 27, 1884.

Unpublished Essays

Cifre, Joseph S. *Saga of the Movie Industry in Boston*, undated.

Rosenburg, Ben. *Living on Borrowed Time*, undated.

Historic Building Surveys

Hollis Street Theatre, MASS—157

B.F. Keith Memorial Theatre, MASS—1078

Newspaper and Periodical Clippings

Brownell, Atherton. Untitled articles in *The Bostonian*, September 1894.

Corbett, Alexander, Jr. Untitled articles in *The Bostonian*, October 1894.

"Federal Court Says Theatres Not Subject to Anti-Trust," *The New York Times*, January 3, 1955.

Gilliam, Henry. "When Grandma Was a Girl," *Boston Post*, 1950.

Milanesi, Craig R. "The National Task Force," *South End News*, 1984.

"Mystery House Found Within Theater's Walls," *The New York Times*, March 1926.

Sayward, Samuel. "A $5,000,000 Theatre, No Profits Are Asked," *Motion Picture Herald*, 1928.

"Shuberts' Consent Judgment," *The New York Times*, December 30, 1953.

Stebbins, Oliver B. Untitled articles in *The Bostonian*, November 1894.

"Supreme Court Reversal," *The New York Times*, March 1926.

Library of Congress Newspaper Collection

1799, Russell's Gazette.
1800, Boston Gazette.
1801, Columbian Centinel.
1802, Palladium.
1809, Boston Patriot.
1812, Boston Yankee.
1816, Boston Daily Advertiser.
1816, Boston Commercial Gazette.
1817, Boston Intelligencer.
1818, Independent Chronical.
1819, Evening Gazette.
1824, Eastern Argus (Portland, Maine).
1825, Boston Courier.
1830, Daily Evening Boston Transcript.
1834, Boston Morning Post, Boston Post.
1856, Boston Evening Telegram.
1872, Boston Globe.

Theatre Trade Periodicals

The Cahn-Leighton Official Theatrical Guide
Daily Variety Magazines
The Film Daily
Gus Hill National Directory
Julius Cahn–Gus Hill Theatrical Guide and Moving Picture Directory
Julius Cahn's Official Theatrical Guide
The Motion Picture Herald

Index

Abbey, Henry E. 65, 66, 95, 124
Abbey 1 and 2 228
Abrams, Hiram 168
Acmegraph 128
Adams, Charles Francis 51
Adams, Marjory 218
Adams, Samuel 10, 13, 14
Adams House 51, 234, 235
Adelphi Theatre 59
Albee, Edward F. 97, 98, 143, 146, 170, 173, 178, 180, 190, 195, 197
Alcazar Theatre 116
Allen, R.H. 136
Allston Hall 55
American Amphitheatre 24
American Coffee House 10, 19
American Music Hall 155
American Theatres Corporation 213
Amory Hall 29, 55
Amos and Andy 182
Andrews Hall 55, 56
Andy Hardy 201
Apollo Theatre 197, 233
Aquarial Gardens 52, 53
Aquarius Theatre 227
Arena Garden 105, 116
Astor Theatre 213, 228
Atkinson, Charles F. 98, 128
"Auld Lang Syne Week" 189
Aumorgraph 128
Austin, Col. William 94
Austin and Stone 86, 87
Austin and Stone's Museum 128
Austin's Nickel Museum 94

B.F. Keith Memorial Theatre 188, 189, 190–196, 197, 201, 202, 203, 206, 211, 217, 225, 226, 227, 233, 234
B.F. Keith's New Theatre 105, 106, 107, 108, 109, 110, 111, 113, 115, 117, 124, 127, 128, 135, 136, 148, 178, 180, 189, 210
Bachman, Max 128
Back Bay Theatre 225
Barnum, P.T. 62
Barry, Thomas 50
Barrymore, Ethel 189
Barrymore, John 188
Barrymore, Lionel 189
Batcheller, George R. 92
Bates, E.C. 44
Bates, John E. 44
Beach Street Theatre 38
Beacon Hill Theatre 213
Beacon Hill Theatres 1-2-3 229
Beacon Theatre 155, 167, 189
Beethoven Hall 60, 61, 64, 65, 96, 168
Bell, Alexander Graham 94, 200
The Belle's Stratagem 18
Bernhardt, Sarah 124, 126, 164
Bijou Dream Theatre 146, 147, 150
Bijou Opera House 121
Bijou Theatre 69, 70, 71, 72, 78, 92, 93, 96, 97, 98, 103, 110, 113, 135, 145, 146, 150, 188, 189, 190, 201, 205, 210, 234, 235

Billboard 166
Billings, Joseph F. 40
Bioscope 128
Birkmire, William 111, 117
Birth of a Nation 170
The Bishop's Wife 213
Black, Alfred S. 174
Black New England Theatres Inc. 174
Blackall, Clarence H. 103, 137, 151, 155, 159, 162, 165, 166, 167, 182
Bland, Humphrey 37, 38
The Blockade of Boston 8, 9
Blondie 201
Board Alley 10, 12, 14
Booth, Edwin 27, 35, 54
Booth, Junius Brutus 22, 35
Boston Academy of Music 29, 52, 54
Boston Advertiser 21, 72
Boston Aquarial and Zoological Gardens 52, 55
Boston Blackie 201
Boston Center for the Arts 232
"Boston Film Notes" 166
Boston Garden 211, 233
Boston Gazette 1, 6, 19
Boston Globe 71, 93, 95, 102, 105, 108, 137, 139, 152, 162, 163, 176, 180, 183, 186, 189, 191, 218
Boston Herald 127, 215, 217, 225, 226, 229
Boston Hippodrome 170
Boston Intelligencer 24
Boston Museum 29, 32–36, 44, 57, 59, 61, 62, 79, 122, 128, 133

Boston Museum and Gallery
  of Fine Arts 26, 29
Boston Museum Stock Com-
  pany 133
Boston Music Hall 43, 84,
  136, 139, 143, 144, 171
Boston Olympic Theatre 30
Boston Opera Group 221,
  223
Boston Opera House 152,
  153, 154, 168, 209, 220
Boston Post 24, 28, 29, 34-35,
  38, 39, 63, 71, 152, 157, 162,
  189, 199
Boston Sights and Stranger's
  Guides 32
Boston Theatre (first, 1794–
  1852) 15, 16, 17, 18, 22, 27,
  29, 32, 39
Boston Theatre (second,
  1852–1927) 45, 51, 52, 54,
  56, 59, 63, 69, 73, 96, 103,
  122, 123, 125, 128, 135, 146,
  148, 150, 151, 155, 167, 170,
  178, 184, 185, 186, 202, 203,
  217, 225, 226, 23; demoli-
  tion of 182–183; "mystery
  house" controversy 183,
  186, 187
Boston Theatre (third) see
  Keith-Albee Boston Theatre
Boston Theatre Company 44
Boston Theatre Stock Com-
  pany 150
Boston Transcript 28
Boston Traveler 127
Bostonian Magazine 16, 26, 32,
  35, 36, 44, 49, 52, 56, 60,
  95, 121
Bowditch, Arthur H. 200
Bowdoin Square Theatre 103,
  128, 201
Bowen, Daniel 19, 20
Boylston Hall 20, 27
Boylston Hall and Market 64
Brady, William 145
Braves Field (Boston) 177
Brewer, Gardner 44
Brice, Fanny 199
Brougham, John 37
Brougham and Bland's Boston
  Adelphi Theatre 37
Brownell, Atherton 121
Buckley's New Minstrel Hall
  55
Bulfinch, Charles 15
Bumstead Hall 136
Bunnell, G.B. 64
Burgoyne, General John 7, 8

burlesque, definition of 232
The Busybody 8
Bwana Devil 217

Cabot, E.C. 48
Cabot, J.E. 48
Caldwell, Sarah 221, 229
California Straight Ahead 178
Cantor, Eddie 182, 199
Capri Theatre 220, 225
Caprice 165
Carabasset 24
The Caretaker's Daughter 178
Carmen 215
Casino Theatre 197
Castle Square Theatre 117,
  118, 119, 120, 121, 122, 125,
  136, 173, 204
Castle Square Theatre and
  Hotel 116
Center Theatre 212, 228, 231
Central Square Theatre 174
Chaplin, Charles K. 170
Charles East and West Cine-
  mas 229
Charles Playhouse 220, 221
Charles Theatre 226
Charlie Chan 201
Chase, Charlie 178
Cheney, Arthur 59
Cheri Theatre 226
Chickering Hall 138, 143, 163
Christian Businessmen's Com-
  mission 218
Cifre, Joseph S. 146
Cinema 1 and 2 225
Cinema 57 227
CinemaScope 217, 218
Cinematographe 128
Cinematoscope 128
Cinerama 217, 218
Cinerama Theatre 226
City Theatre 21
Clapp, William W., Jr. 1, 6
Clapp and Whittemore (archi-
  tects) 182
Clark and McCullough 199
Claxton, Kate 69
Clear Channel Communica-
  tions 231
Clear Channel Entertainment
  234
Cleopatra 165
Cobb Theatre 233
Coconut Grove Night Club
  209
Collins, Mayor John F. 225
Colonial Theatre 137, 138,
  143, 155, 165, 204, 225, 231

Columbia Pictures Corp. 208
Columbia Theatre 98, 99,
  100, 103, 120, 124, 133, 143,
  146, 156, 203, 233
Columbia Theatre and Prome-
  nade Deluxe 133
Columbian Museum 19, 20,
  26, 32, 39
Comique Theatre 145
Concert Hall 10, 11, 17, 18, 19,
  20, 21, 22, 24, 26, 28, 29
Continental Clothing Factory
  56
Continental Theatre 56
"Cooper's Minstrels" 39
Copley Square Theatre 173
Copley Theatre 176, 204, 207
Coquelin 124
Corbett, Albert, Jr. 16
Corbett, Alexander, Jr. 49
Cort, John 165
Cox, Palmer 126
Crabtree, Charlotte (Lotta)
  95, 96, 123
Craig, John 121
Crane, C. Howard 182
Crawford, Mary Caroline 3,
  8, 12, 13
Cressy, Will 189
Crystal Cascade Electric
  Waterfall 147
Crystal Tunnel 129–132
Cutler Majestic Theatre 231
Cyclorama 93, 116, 119, 121,
  159

Daddy Long Legs 174
Dailey, Peter F. 125
Daily Transcript 26
Daniel Frohman Presents 3, 61
De Forest, Lee 182
Denny, Reginald 178
Dial M for Murder 217
Dime Museum 57, 86
Don Juan 188, 189
Donnelly Memorial Theatre
  221, 223, 225
Doyle, William M.S. 20
Dramatic Museum 38
Dressler, Marie 170
Drew, John 126
Dudley Street Opera House
  67
Dunlap, Marm 186, 187
Dunn, Frank V. 128
Dwight, B.F. 56

Eagle Theatre 27
Eden Musee 146, 150

Edison, Thomas Alva 70, 71, 72, 127, 200
Edward, H.R.H. Albert (Prince of Wales) 52
Eidoloscope 128
"Eidophor" 215
Elizabeth Peabody Theatre 198
Empire Theatre 144
English, Jane 55
Erlanger, Abraham Lincoln 143, 146
Esquire Theatre 213
Essex I and II 226
The Eternal City 170
Evening Transcript 37, 176
Everything on Ice 212
Exeter Theatre 167

Famous Players Corporation 164
Famous Players–Lasky Corporation 174, 180, 198
Faneuil Hall 3, 7, 8, 9, 14, 20
Fantasia 208, 209
Federal Street Theatre ("Old Drury") 15, 24, 38
Fenway Theatre 171, 226
Field, R.M. 122
The Fight for Peace 207
Fine Arts Theatre 177, 221, 223
Fire on the Heather 218
Firmaphone 189
First European Music Hall 133
A Flag Is Born 212
Footlights and Spotlights 3, 35, 72
For Napoleon and France 168
Ford, John 213
Forest Garden 68
Fox, Della 126
Fox, John A. 60
Foxe, Fanne 229, 233
Franzheim, Kenneth 182
Frohman, Charles 122, 124, 125, 143, 151
Frohman, Daniel 61
The Fugitive 213

Gaiety Museum 92, 93, 97, 98
Gaiety (Gayety) Theatre 64, 65, 69, 151, 200, 201, 211, 212, 232
Gallagher and Shean 199
Gardiner, John 12, 13
Gardner, Mrs. John L. 168
Garrick, David 8

Garrison, William Lloyd 62
General Cinema Corporation 226, 228
General Court of Massachusetts 5, 6
George A. Fuller Company 152
Gilbert and Sullivan 89
Gillen, Henry 199
Gillette, William 125
Globe Theatre 59, 60, 63, 64, 65, 74, 92, 106, 123, 139, 142, 143, 146, 155, 162, 165, 167, 198, 209
Gone with the Wind 208
Gordon, Nathan 170, 174, 178
Gordon's Olympia Theatre 164
Grace, J.J. 98
Graham, Billy 218
Grand Opera House 93, 124, 128, 143, 162
Grand Theatre 128, 129, 139
Grant, Cary 213
Gray's National Theatre 69
The Great Boston Fire of 1872 58
Great Depression 200
Green Dragon Hall 20
Greene, Walter E. 168
Greenwood, E.A. 20
Griffith, D.W. 170
Gulesian, M.H. 163
Gulick, R.M. 124

Hackett, James K. 164
Hall, John R. 89
Halleck, Thomas E. 67
Halleck's Alhambra 67, 68
Hancock, John 14
Handel and Hayden Society 26
Hanover Theatre 121
Hare, John 126
Harper, Joseph 12
Harrington, Jonathon 26
Harrington's Museum 26, 27
Harris, William 98, 151
Haymarket Theatre 18, 19
Hecht, Ben 212
Heiman, Marcus 214
Henry Jewett Repertory Company 182
Herne, James A. 125
The History of the Boston Theatre 1854–1901 50, 54
History of the Theatre in America 1, 5
History of the United States 6

Hitchcock, Alfred 217
Hollis Street Church 88, 123
Hollis Street Theatre 89, 91, 92, 123, 155, 173, 202
Holmes, Burton 144
Holmes, Oliver Wendell 62
Hooley's Theatre 67
Hopper, DeWolf 126
Hornblow, Arthur 1, 5, 6
Horticultural Hall 43, 51, 56, 57, 67, 69, 86, 92, 144
House of Wax 217
Howard, John Galen 139
Howard Athenaeum–Old Howard Theatre 27, 32, 38, 56, 59, 64, 65, 80, 105, 128, 201, 209, 211, 218, 222, 223, 224, 233
Howard National Theatre Museum Committee 223
Howe, Joseph N. 44
Howe, Lyman H. 144, 151
Hub ("Boston's Parlor Theatre") 139, 143
Hub Theatre 203
Hughes, Elinor 217
Humperdinck, Engelbert 126
Huntington Avenue Theatre 163

I Was a Captive of Nazi Germany 207
Idle Hour Theatre 150
Irving, Henry 124, 126
Irving Trust Company 198
Irwin, May 125, 127
Ives, Norman 225

J.B. McElfatrick & Sons 95, 115
The Jazz Singer 189
Jefferson, Joseph 17, 125
Jefferson, Joseph, III 18
Jeffries, Jim 199
Jewett Players 152
John Craig Stock Company 145, 146
Jolson, Al 189, 199
Jones, Buck 209
Jones, J.S. 28
Jones, Robert 26
Jones, Thomas M. 152
The Jones Family 201
Jordan, Eben B. 152
Julian Hall 24

KAO (Keith-Albee-Orpheum) see Keith-Albee-Orpheum (K-A-O Theatres)

Kean, Edmund 21, 22
Keith, A. Paul 115, 173, 188
Keith, Benjamin Franklin 86,
  92, 96, 97, 98, 103, 113, 121,
  129, 135, 143, 144, 145, 146,
  150, 151, 167, 170, 173, 178,
  183, 186, 188, 214, 226, 235
Keith, Mary C. 151
Keith, Paul 146, 147, 170, 173
Keith, Sally 198, 200
Keith-Albee Boston Theatre
  178, 179
Keith-Albee-Orpheum (K-A-O
  Theatres) 190, 197, 206
Keith and Batcheller's Mam-
  moth Museum 87
Keith Memorial Theatre see
  B.F. Keith Memorial The-
  atre
Keith Nickel Circuit 151
Kelcey, Harry 174
Kellogg, Clara Louise 62
Kennedy, Joseph P. 190, 197
Kimball, David P. 26
Kimball, Moses 26, 29, 32
Kinemacolor 158, 163
Kinetograph 150
King's Handbook of Boston 64,
  65, 67
Kirk, the Reverend Edward
  50
Kiss Me Kate 217
Klaw, Marc 143, 146

L. Haberstroh and Son 128
L.A.B. Amusement Corp. 214
Laemmle, Carl 178
Lamb, Thomas W. 171, 173,
  176, 188, 190
Langtry, Lillie 126
Lassoing Wild Animals in Africa
  and America 165
Latin Quarter Nightclub 209
Lauder, Harry 173
Lee, Gypsy Rose 223, 224
Lempert, Leon H. 102, 103
Lempert Principle of Building
  Auditoriums 102
Leonard, Joseph 39, 43
Lieberman, Frederick E. 200,
  207
The Life of Saint Patrick 165
Life with Father 208
The Lights of New York 189
Lind, Jenny 26
The Lion and the Mouse 189
Lion Theatre 26
Little and Brown (architects)
  136

Little Building 173
Little Opera House 221, 223
Loew, E.M. 173, 212, 213,
  225, 229, 232
Loew, Marcus 155, 156, 164,
  167, 170, 171, 172, 173, 174,
  177, 233
Loew's Inc. 208, 215
Loew's South End 156
Loew's Theatres 215
Lorre, Peter 201
Lothrop, George E. 69, 92,
  93, 94, 105, 128
Lothrop Stock Company
  129
Lourie, Jacob 167
Lyceum Theatre 39, 59, 105,
  128, 174
Lyricscope 165

M&P (Mullins and Pinanski)
  chain 201
Mage, James J. 212
The Maid of the Oaks 8
Maisie 201
Majestic Theatre 139, 140, 141,
  143, 155, 170, 200, 204,
  209, 212, 231
Mansfield, George E. 124
Mark, Joe 145
Mark, Max 145
Mark, Moe 168
Marshall, Wyzeman 27, 54
Martel, Arthur J. 174
Massachusetts Horticultural
  Society 55
Mayflower Theatre 213, 225,
  231
Mayflower-Modern Theatre
  226
Maynard, E.W. 113
Maynard, Ken 232
Mayo, Frank 126
McLaughlin, J.E. 189
McNally, John J. 125
Melodeon 26, 29, 44, 45, 56,
  64
Melodeon Billiard Hall 56
Melodeon Hall 51
Menino, Mayor Thomas M.
  234
Merchants Hall 20
Meserve, George Nelson 182
Metro-Goldwyn-Mayer Pictures
  215
Metro-Movietone 189
Metropolitan Opera House
  136, 215
Metropolitan Theatre 180,

  181, 201, 202, 203, 205,
  209, 217, 223, 224
The Mikado 89, 92
Millerites 31
Mills, Wilbur 228
Minsky's Burlesque 203
The Miracle 165
Mirza and Lindor 18
Mr. Moto 201
Mr. Saubert's Theatre 24
Modern Theatre 189
Modjeska, Mme. Helena 125
The Money Kings, or Wall Street
  Outwitted 164
Montgomery and Stone 199
Morning Post 24
Morris, Billy 51
Morris, Clara 126
Morris, Lon 51
Morris, William 135, 136, 145,
  146, 150, 151, 155, 173
Motion Picture Herald 191
Mounet-Sully 124
"Movietime U.S.A." (ad cam-
  paign) 215
Movietone 189
Mulcahy, James 189
Muybridge, Eadweard 69

N.J. Bradlee and Company 72
Nagel, Conrad 189
National Theatre 25, 26, 27,
  29, 39, 40, 41, 105, 157, 158,
  163, 170, 210, 232, 233
National-Hippodrome Theatre
  174
Nethersole, Olga 125
New Boston Aquarial and
  Zoological Gardens 55
New Boylston Museum 63,
  69, 87
New England Museum 20,
  26, 27
New England Theatre Com-
  pany 174
New England Theatre Operat-
  ing Corporation
  (NETOCO) 197, 198
New England Theatres Inc.
  213
New Exhibition Room 10, 12,
  14
New Grand Museum 94
New Minstrel Hall 55
New York Museum 20, 86
Newell, Timothy 9
Nickelodeon Musee and Par-
  lor Theatre 120
The Night Before 173

Normandie Ballroom 201, 203
Normandie Theatre 207, 210, 211, 212
Norton, Eliot 229
Noury, H. 48
Novelty Theatre 67

Oakland Garden 68
O'Connell, Cardinal William H. 190
Odeon 29, 32, 39
Oklahoma! 218
Old Howard *see* Howard Athenaeum–Old Howard Theatre
Old South Newsreel Theatre 208, 212
Old South Theatre 174, 175, 176
Olympia Theatre 162, 233
Olympia Theatre Circuit 174, 178, 180
Olympic Theatre 56
O'Neil, James 126
Opera House (Morris Brothers, Pell and Trowbridge) 51, 55, 56
Opera House (former B.F. Keith Memorial) 230, 231, 233, 234, 235
Opera House Company of Boston 229, 230
Ordway, J.P. 39, 51
Ordway Hall 39, 51, 55, 174
Orpheum Theatre 144, 146, 150, 151, 155, 171, 172, 173, 174, 176, 200, 208, 226, 229, 231
Otis, Harrison Gray 13

P.T. Barnum's Aquarial Gardens 55
Palace Theatre 120, 128, 199
Paramount Pictures Inc. 168, 174, 178, 201, 208, 213
Paramount Pictures–Famous Players Corp. 170
Paramount Publix Corporation 198, 201
Paramount-Publix Theatres 203
Paramount Theatre 198, 200, 201, 203, 224, 225, 226, 228, 229, 231, 233, 234, 235
Paris Cinema 225
Park Square Coliseum 151
Park Square Garden 87, 144

Park Square Theatre 170
Park Theatre 65, 76, 95, 96, 106, 123, 128, 143, 162, 168, 198, 203
Parker, the Reverend Theodore 26
The Passion Play 133, 146
Pastime Theatre 150
Pathé Studios 197
Peabody and Stearns (architects) 163
Pearl Harbor 209
Pelby, William 22, 24, 26, 27
Pell, Johnny 51
Pember, Clifford 168
The Phantom of the Opera 231
Phonofilm 182
Photophone 189
Pi Alley Cinema 226
Pickford, Mary 165, 174
Pilgrim Theatre 213, 215, 217, 225, 228
Pinocchio 212
The Planning and Construction of American Theatres 111, 117
Plymouth Theatre 157, 158, 173
Potter Hall 152
Powell, Charles Stuart 10, 14, 17, 18
Preston, Jonathan 48
The Prisoner of Zenda 164
Proprietors of the Boston Theatre 51
"Proprietors of the Tremont Theatre" 22

Queen Elizabeth 164
Quo Vadis 165

Radio Corporation of America (RCA) 197
Radio Pictures 197
Radio-Keith-Orpheum (RKO) 197, 208, 215
Rainey's African Hunt 162
Raymond, James 24
RCA 215
Rehan, Ada 125
Reingold, Kate 36
Rejane 124
Repertory Theatre 182, 205
Rialto Theatre 212, 233
Rice, John C. 127
Rich, Charles J. 123
Rich, Isaac B. 56, 123, 124
Rich, Otis 44
Risman, William 212, 225

RKO Boston Theatre 201, 203, 205, 211
RKO Keith's Theatre 198, 206
RKO Theatres Corporation 215
The Robe 217
Rogers, Isaiah 22, 32
Rogers, Will 199
Romance of the American Theatre 3, 8
Roosevelt, Theodore 63
Rosenburg, Ben 209
Rowe, John 9
Russell, Lillian 126
Russell's Gazette 19

Sack, Benjamin 213, 218, 220, 225, 226, 227, 229, 230, 232
Sack Theatres Week 225
Sack's Music Hall 225, 226, 227, 231
"Saga of the Movie Industry in Boston" 146
The Saint 201
Saint James Theatre 56, 163, 164, 182, 198
Sale, Chick 189
Saltonstall, Governor Leverett 210
Sans Souci 133, 137
Savage, Henry V. 116
Savoy 1 and 2 227, 228, 230
Savoy Theatre 226, 227
Sayward, Samuel 191
Schoeffel, John B. 65, 66, 95, 124
Scollay Square Olympia Theatre 165, 212, 233
Sedley-Smith, William H. 32
Select Theatres Corp. 214
Selwyn, John H. 56
Selwyn's Theatre 56
Sennett, Mack 199
Sewall, Samuel 6
Shubert, Jacob J. 143, 146, 173, 214
Shubert, Lee 143, 146, 173, 198, 214
Shubert, Sam S. 143, 146
Shubert Theatre 152–153, 204, 225, 231
Skinner, Otis 35, 65, 72
Sleeper, Fred C. 40
Smith, G. Albert 163
Smith, Kate 182
South End Theatre 173
Southern, E.H. 126

stage spotlight, first use of 120
Stair, E.D. 139, 143
Star Museum 87
Star Theatre 146
State Museum 24
State Theatre 174, 176, 178, 200, 221, 228
Stearns (architect) see Peabody and Stearns (architects)
Stetson, John 59, 61, 64, 65, 106, 123
Stevens, B.F. 44
Stone, Dorothy 189
Stone, Frank P. 68
Stone, Fred 189
Strand Theatre 198, 199, 225
Strange Interlude 198
Stuart Theatre 233
Studio Building 55
Suffolk Theatre 176
Sullivan, John L. 199
Symphony Hall 165, 182
Synchrosound 189
the Syndicate 143, 145, 158, 203

Taber, Julia Marlene 125
Taber, Robert 125
A Tale of Two Cities 164, 165
Tamerlane 8, 9
The Ten Commandments 218
Tenderloin 189
Terry, Ellen 124, 126
Thayer, Benjamin W. 50
Thayer, John E. 44
Theatre Comique 56, 59
Theatre Company of Boston 226
Theatre Jolliette 146
Theatre Premier 146, 150
Theatre Royal 17
The Thief of Bagdad 212
This Is Cinerama 218
Thorne's American Theatre 38
3-D motion pictures 215, 217
Tillie's Punctured Romance 170
Tobin, Mayor Maurice 210
Todd-AO 218, 220

Tompkins, Eugene 50, 54, 122
Tompkins, Orlando 50, 54, 122
Toy Theatre 168, 169, 173
Traffic in Souls 165
Tragedy of Zara 8
Trans-Lux Theatre 205, 221
Treadwell, E.P. 72
Tremont Temple 29, 39, 67, 82, 105, 144, 145, 146, 151, 158, 159-161, 162, 164, 182, 202, 218
Tremont Theatre 22, 23, 24, 28, 32, 39, 55, 95, 124, 149, 155, 165, 170, 174, 198, 200, 205, 212
Trocadero 128
Trowbridge, J.C. 51, 56
Twentieth Century–Fox Film Corporation 208, 215
Two Orphans 69
Tyler, George W. 69

U.S. Amusement Company 143
Union Hall 69
Unique Theatre 145, 146
United Booking Office (U.B.O.) 135, 146, 214
Universal Film Manufacturing Company 162
Universal Pictures Corp. 208
Uptown Theatre 198
Urban, Charles 162

"V" Newsreel Corporation 212
Vallee, Rudy 182
Veriscope 128
Victory Theatre 212
Vinal, Arthur H. 139, 144
VistaVision 218
Vitaphone 188, 189
Vitascope 127, 128
Vokes, Fred 69

Walcker, E.B. 43
Waldorf Theatre 174
Waldron, Charles 197

Waldron's Casino 152, 155, 201, 209
Walter Reade Theatres 226, 229
Wang Center for the Performing Arts 231
Warner, Jack L. 218
Warner Bros. Pictures Inc. 208
Warren Theatre 24, 25, 26
Washington Gardens 21
Washington Hall 27, 29
Washington Theatre 24, 158
Washingtonian Hall 29, 30
Weber and Fields 182, 199
Welansky, Barney 209
Wentworth, J. 65
West End Cinema 233
West End Rehabilitation Project 225
Western Electric 188
Wetherell, George H. 72
The White Fawn 56
The Widow Jones 127
Wilbur, A.L. 139, 143, 167
Wilbur Theatre 182, 224, 225, 231
Willard's Theatre 56
Williams, Charles 200
Williams, Percy 144, 146
Wilson, Francis 126
Windsor Theatre 67, 69, 92, 94
Winter Garden 151
Woods, Ph. 20
Works Progress Administration's Federal Theatre 207
The World in Motion 145
World Theatre 98
World's Museum 87, 92, 93, 105
Wyndham, Charles 124

Yesterdays with Actors 36

Zeiss-Opton 218
Zoo 137
"The Zoopraxiscope" 69
Zukor, Adolph 145, 164, 165, 168, 174, 178, 180, 203